Inspector Faro's Casebook

The Second Omnibus

Alanna Knight is a novelist, biographer and playwright. *A Quiet Death*, *To Kill A Queen* and *The Evil That Men Do* continue her novels in the popular series featuring Inspector Faro. Alanna Knight is a member of the Crime Writers' Association and Secretary of the Society of Authors in Scotland. She lectures in the Scottish Arts Council's Writers in Public scheme and is an authority on Robert Louis Stevenson. Married with two sons and two granddaughters, she lives in Edinburgh.

The Inspector Faro series

Alanna Knight

Inspector Faro's Casebook

The Second Omnibus

A Quiet Death
To Kill A Queen
The Evil That Men Do

PAN BOOKS

A Quiet Death first published 1991 by Macmillan
First published by Pan Books in this edition

To Kill A Queen first published 1992 by Macmillan
First published by Pan Books in this edition

The Evil That Men Do first published 1993 by Macmillan
First published by Pan Books in this edition

This omnibus edition published 1996 by Pan Books
an imprint of Macmillan Publishers Ltd
25 Eccleston Place, London, SW1W 9NF
and Basingstoke

Associated companies throughout the world

ISBN 0 330 34855 8

1 3 5 7 9 8 6 4 2

A CIP catalogue for this book is available from
the British Library

Phototypeset by Intype London Ltd
Printed and bound in Great Britain

Inspector Faro's Casebook

A Quiet Death

For all my family
and many friends in Dundee

'Better a quiet death than a public misfortune'
Old Proverb

Detective Inspector Jeremy Faro had not the least idea that a funeral, melancholy enough but entirely innocent of crime, would lead to a startling confession from his stepson and that a suicide from the unfinished Tay Bridge would open up a sinister trail of seemingly unconnected events.

Events which were to culminate in one of the most baffling and personal dilemmas of his career, and a series of crimes which had tragic and far-reaching repercussions several years later.

Faro was to represent the Edinburgh City Police at the funeral in Angus of a former colleague. Will Gray had died in retirement at the ripe old age of ninety and although funerals were sober, sad occasions, he was almost looking forward to this one. In addition to the unique chance of renewing auld acquaintance over nostalgic drams with old chums, it also provided an excuse to visit his stepson.

9 Sheridan Place, Edinburgh, seemed strangely silent without Vince. Faro had ample opportunity to consider the future of the home they had shared until recently. He was increasingly aware of how his footsteps echoed on stairs and through empty rooms meant for a family of children and servants, mocked and reproached one solitary widower.

The truth was undeniable but less than pleasant. The handsome villa in the expanding suburb of Newington was far too big for him since Dr Vincent Beaumarcher Laurie was now resident doctor to the ever expanding firm of Deane Enterprises in Dundee. And Deane's had triumphantly netted, against fierce competition, the building materials contract for the bridge over the River Tay.

In the two months since his stepson's departure, Faro realised how much he had come to depend on the arrival of the postman and Mrs Brook's delivery of the morning mail to his study. In fact, he prided himself that he could deduce from her footsteps, brisk or tardy, whether or not she carried that eagerly awaited letter.

His hopes were mostly shattered. Vince was an indifferent correspondent at the best of times, but Faro tempered disappointment with a ready excuse. Of course, the lad's present hectic employment allowed him no idle time for letter-writing.

Faro sighed. Vince might well be far too busy, but not so himself. That spring had been remarkable for a particularly dull patch in the Edinburgh City Police's annals of crime.

There were no really 'interesting' cases on which to flex his powers of deduction. Recent investigations had been limited to petty frauds and the wearisomely repetitive activities of Edinburgh's habitual minor criminals.

Faro's famed and dramatic appearances in the Sheriff Court were required merely to identify witnesses while he secretly longed for action, for the chase and duel to the death with dangerous opponents worthy of his skill. A little ashamed to admit that he was ill-adapted to the tranquil life he had so often longed for in times of danger, Faro discovered that peace for him spelt only monotony and boredom.

Was he growing old? he thought nervously. Were these the normal reactions of a man not much past forty? Failing completely to suppress a wistful longing for the faces of his old adversaries, he wondered where they were now. Had they been converted to good deeds and growing flowers in peaceful tranquillity?

And Faro was uneasily aware that unless eyes and ears were constantly alert and watchful for clues and suspects, that extra sense developed by more than twenty years with the City Police would atrophy. Detective Inspector Jeremy Faro would then be of no more use than a newly recruited junior constable.

Preparing to leave Edinburgh for the funeral in the Angus village of Errol, Faro requested a few extra days' leave, partly for the arduous train journey involved and also to visit Dundee. There he hoped to surprise Vince with his unexpected appearance.

His arrangements almost complete, he encountered a breathless Mrs Brook panting upstairs and dramatically flourishing a letter.

'It's from him, sir. It's from the dear lad – at last.'

Thanking her, Faro eagerly tore open the letter. The handwriting was familiar but almost completely illegible. Vince, it appeared, had succumbed to the doctor's pride and privilege of writing that not a soul could read. With a sigh, however, not altogether unpleasurable, Faro sat down to decipher the contents.

'My dear Stepfather,' he read, 'prepare yourself for a surprise, perhaps even a shock.' And in bold capitals heavily underlined: 'I AM ALMOST A MARRIED MAN.' The words leaped out at Faro and he read them twice over before proceeding.

There now, Stepfather, just as you predicted, I have met the girl of my dreams. I love and am loved and we are to marry as soon as her grandfather (and Guardian) gives permission as she is still but twenty.

Most revered and devoted Stepfather, I beg of you to prepare to receive a stepdaughter-in-law who will in every conceivable way measure up to your desire for my happiness. And one who having heard much about you, longs above all things to make your acquaintance at the very earliest.

I would most earnestly wish this to be before our wedding and would bring her to you but, alas, we can ill afford the time with many arrangements on hand. May we therefore

beg that you pay us a visit as soon as is convenient and
give us a father's blessing. I am, as ever, Your obedient
and affectionate Stepson,

Vincent B. Laurie.

Having carefully reread the letter several times, Faro discovered
that his first feelings of delight were now mingled with faint
irritation that in a matter of such concern and importance, Vince
had imparted so little information.

Why, he had not even remembered to include his fiancée's
name. Typical of the lad, of course.

With a fond smile, Faro laid the letter aside. This news, so
totally unexpected, was good indeed, the very best in all the
world. He had always believed that Vince (the invincible where
matrimony was concerned) would sooner or later fall in love.

He sighed. His dearest wish for the lad had been granted but
there was an obverse side to this good fortune which affected
him personally. The camaraderie of their bachelor estate, the
companionship of father and son must henceforth take a minor
rôle in this new scheme of things.

He closed his mind to such unworthy thoughts, and looking
around, nodded vigorously. How strange the coincidence of his
decision that the house was no longer suitable. Almost as if that
keen extra sense which was at once the plague and blessing of
his life had been preparing him for the inevitable changes which
must come about with Vince's marriage.

'Time to move on, old chap. A new wife, however charming
and well-disposed, is not going to want a policeman stepfather
living in the house with them.'

At least this house he had grown to love so well would be
saved from a sale to strangers. Indeed he hoped it would now
revert to the original purpose the builder had in mind. No doubt
in due time Vince and his bride would fill these empty rooms
with laughter of children and the bustle of servants.

'And about time. That's what houses are for,' said Mrs Brook, jubilantly echoing his own thoughts when he rushed downstairs to the kitchen to share this joyful news over a glass of her favourite port.

Even as they talked, he could see she was making her own plans, extending her duties as the efficient housekeeper she had proved to be by engaging extra servants. At this stage he would not spoil her innocent pleasure with the information that although she might well continue to reign over 9 Sheridan Place, he would no longer be her employer.

Knowing that Vince would hotly disapprove, Faro decided to keep an eye open for a small apartment nearer the Central Office. If he looked sharp about it, then he might be able to present the newly-weds with a *fait accompli* when they returned from their honeymoon, thus saving Vince any protest or his bride any embarrassment.

Leaving the house, he closed the front door and looked sadly at the place which until recently bore the brass plate: 'Dr Vincent Beaumarcher Laurie, General Practitioner in Family Medicine'.

They had hung it together on Vince's twenty-first birthday when after a term with the police surgeon he had hoped to set up his surgery in the ground floor rooms. Alas, he had tried but with so little success that without his stepfather's support, the spectacle of starvation would have loomed large.

The suburbs of Newington and Grange on the sunny southern slopes of the city had become increasingly popular with a new and prosperous merchant and professional class. In such a community, well supplied with physicians, Dr Laurie suffered from two drawbacks. He looked uncommonly young for his age with his head of blond curls and light build. Time would take care of that, of course, but the main trouble was that he was unmarried.

The area attracted large well-off families, modest matrons who required cosy middle-aged doctors in whom to confide their medical problems and to look after them in childbirth. It was now *de rigueur* in this new middle class to have one's own physician in attendance at the accouchement instead of the friendly neighbour who in the poorer areas acted as midwife.

Vince's own mother had died of childbed fever taking with her the newborn son Faro had craved. He never ceased to mourn her and the fatal risks and frequent deaths of women in childbirth had been one of the main reasons for Vince's choice of a medical career.

He adored his two little stepsisters, Faro's daughters Rose and Emily, who lived in Orkney with their grandmother and Faro had long ago decided that his stepson's natural ability to gain the trust of children, allied with a sharp insight into how their minds worked, might prove invaluable for an unmarried family physician.

Vince's boast since undergraduate days had been 'he who travels fastest travels alone'. With his sights long set on becoming 'Queen's physician' perhaps that love of children would be his sole purpose in eventually marrying at all.

Heads of houses, however, gentlemen if not by birth then by achievement, considered it indelicate, hardly respectable, to have their daughters intimately examined, those pains peculiar to young unmarried ladies discussed and investigated by doctors who looked no older or more reliable than their own young bachelor sons.

Vince was also painfully aware that his background as assistant to the police surgeon was not perhaps the happiest recommendation for dealing with genteel families. The cutting up of corpses, as the general public saw his activities, suggested a lacklustre approach to family medicine.

'Since all his previous patients have been dead ones,' as one of his well-meaning patients somewhat tactlessly put it.

Sobered and dismayed by the failure of his practice, Vince had taken the appointment at Deane's Dundee factory with cheerful courage.

Now his unexpected and exciting news seemed in keeping

with the warm sunshine and the awakening of lifeless branches in a positive bridal display of blossom. Faro's spirits were again lifted by that joy of renewal in the earth's yearly resurrection which even the prospects of the daunting journey ahead did not immediately quell.

As the crow flies, only forty-six miles separated Edinburgh from Dundee, a journey that should have been a mere bagatelle for a Britain whose web of railroads made accessible distant towns and opened up new opportunities for the labouring classes. Now men could seek employment further afield than the restrictions imposed by walking distances from their own tiny villages.

In the case of Edinburgh and Dundee, however, the deceptively short distance was hampered by the two wide estuaries of Forth and Tay. And their as yet unspanned waters, to be crossed by ferry, turned what should have been a delightful and invigorating prospect of travelling by train at a thrilling thirty miles an hour into the vast proportions of a nightmare.

This was no journey to be undertaken frequently or by busy men thought Faro as he left Sheridan Place at dawn and walked briskly down the Pleasance towards Waverley Station.

With what seemed to intending passengers uncommonly like adding insult to injury, the North British Railway Company ran their best train of the day at 6.25 a.m. According to the timetable it took three hours and twelve minutes.

But that was in only the most favourable weather conditions. In point of fact, the journey could and almost always did take considerably longer. In winter, or in summer storms, the uneasy waters of Forth and Tay stirred angrily, thereby causing delays, additional misery and acute discomfort to passengers.

As a stiff wind buffeted him over Waverley Bridge, Faro considered with some apprehension the wild clouds screening a reluctant sunrise. No doubt a gloomy prophecy for a journey even less agreeable than previous experiences which, like painful toothache, he preferred not to dwell upon.

Taking his place in the fireless buffet room of the station

among the shivering group of passengers, all valiantly grasping steaming hot cups of coffee which warmed icy hands but had little in the way of taste as commendation, he was told that the train was late.

Frustration and impatience at this stage of the journey boded ill and Faro bitterly regretted his lack of time and forewarning to take the ship overnight from Leith. This was his normal method of travel when occasion led him to the north-east coast of Scotland. Even with his abominable tendency to seasickness, it still remained the happier alternative.

The train arrived at last. 'Engine trouble,' grumbled the porter.

Now mauve in countenance, chilled to the bone, the passengers struggled aboard with their luggage only to find themselves considerably worse off than before. The carriage lacked any internal heating and the train trailed two odorous fish trucks.

Travelling through the suburbs of Edinburgh, occasionally alerting the sleeping occupants with a shrill hoot, the train arrived at Granton-on-Forth, where everyone disembarked and boarded the ferry.

Its appearance was at first sight consoling, low in the hull with beating paddles on either side, high slender smoke-stacks and raking masts. A graceful boat indeed, resting lightly on the water, but as the stiff gale, white-lacing the waves, set upon them amidships, the passengers, Faro included, were soon taking refuge against the bulkheads where they wrestled with the urgent demands of heaving stomachs.

Faro was in difficulties. The din of paddles made his head ache and the presence close at hand of fish 'fresh that morning' but already succumbing to speedy decay was extremely offensive.

The short journey across the Firth of Forth seemed abominably long; his discomfort acute, he was grateful to see dry land at Burntisland. There he joined the general pandemonium to seize a seat on the train which would carry them the further thirty-six miles to the south side of the Tay estuary. Taking careful note of how the wind was blowing, he wisely chose a seat facing away from the billowing clouds of smoke and cinder.

Fascinated as he usually was by guessing the character and occupation of his fellow-passengers, the four who shared his compartment were readily dismissed as a young wife with a snivelling child and her volatile mother, plus an elderly clergyman. Their characters and conversation left little room for speculation or the scent of mystery.

An inveterate gazer-out-of-windows, he was further frustrated as the Kingdom of Fife was blanketed by heavy mist, rendering visibility negligible. Disappointed that spring had chosen this moment for a bleak return to desolation, he prepared to pass the time as agreeably as possible. With the help of one of his favourite travelling companions, Mr Charles Dickens, he applied himself once again to his current reading: *The Mystery of Edwin Drood*.

The tedium at last over, he greeted with relief the station at Newport where another ferry-boat now waited to carry them across the Tay. Relieved that the weather had improved enough to make their destination visible, he observed the ancient castle at Broughty Ferry bathed in a flicker of sunlight.

Soon he would be meeting Vince and his bride-to-be. But before that, here was what the newspapers called 'one of the marvels of the modern world, the Bridge across the River Tay'.

It was, he decided, something of a disappointment. Marked by half-finished piers on either side of the estuary, it resembled nothing more than a gigantic loosely knitted iron ribbon with ends trailing into the water.

Boarding the ferry, the air was clouded by the glow and smoke belch of nearby foundries. As they drifted into the water, their ears were assaulted by the thunderous beat of the pile-drivers while their eyes smarted from the furnaces' acrid fumes.

Observing this scene of high activity, Faro thought it odd that there had been so little progress to show on the bridge for two years' work. Even making allowances for marvels of engineering well beyond his comprehension, he could not visualise that frail structure supporting anything as robust and substantial as a railway bridge.

And he remembered that when the bridge was being planned, an old man, an apple-grower famous for his true prophecies as the Seer of Gourdiehill, had seen its completion and downfall.

'This rainbow bridge', Patrick Matthews had called it, and on his deathbed he had had a final terrible vision: 'A great wind will wrench at the high girders, crushing the bridge, and a heavy passenger train with the whole of the passengers will be killed.'

A black cloud blotted out the sunlight, shrouding the half-finished bridge in sudden gloom.

Faro shivered, remembering the last words of the Seer's prophecy: 'The eels will come to gloat in delight over the horrible wreckage and banquet.'

At Faro's side on the ferry, the minister who had spent most of the train journey sleeping heavily had regained animation:

'Ah, sir, we are now witnessing the famed Thomas Bouch's creation. He has travelled a long way from aqueducts to the longest bridge in the world.'

As he gazed at the massive iron structures, Faro shrugged aside his misgivings. 'There is a saying that children and fools should never see things half completed.'

'O ye of little faith,' quoted the minister with a smile and a reproachful nod. 'Think what a difference it will make to our travel and to our prosperity. God be praised that man's achievement will mean an end to all that wearisome changing of trains and ferries,' he added fervently.

'Amen to that, sir.'

The minister waved a hand in the direction of one of the high girders. 'Astonishing, is it not? Why, the novel concept of weaving iron and masonry through two miles of air and water has delighted the whole of Scotland. They can talk of nothing else.'

'Not only in Scotland, sir. The popular press would have us believe that the idea of bridging the Tay has set fire to the nation's imagination. In London, I understand, folks believe that all that is new and good and noble in this century of scientific endeavour must be done by Englishmen.'

The minister gave him a hard look. 'Indeed, sir, we are living in an age of new gods and although our people sneer at the ignorant superstitions of poor African savages and those other races we are bringing to civilisation by God's word, they see no cause for dismay in the blind trust they are placing in their own industrial witch-doctors.'

Awaiting Faro's nod of approval, he added proudly, 'I am glad you agree, sir, for that was the subject of my sermon in Edinburgh from which I am newly returned.'

It seemed that having detected a sympathetic ear and a captive audience, the minister was eager to deliver that sermon once again. However, before he could utter more than a philosophical sentence or two, he was forestalled by the rapid approach of the quayside at Broughty Ferry where a band of raggedy children shrilly assailed them with demands for ha'pennies and sweeties.

'Get along with you,' said the minister indignantly. Turning to Faro he added by way of apology, 'They mean no harm, but they so enjoy tormenting strangers.'

'Then let us make this a memorable day for them,' said Faro good-humouredly. Digging into his pockets he threw a handful of coins which were pounced upon with noisy delight and even some thanks in his direction.

'You spoil them with such generosity,' said the minister reproachfully. 'You have children of your own?'

'Yes, sir. Two wee daughters, a little better behaved but with every child's weakness for ha'pennies and sweeties.'

'You are bound for Dundee?' said the minister. 'Ah, then our ways part here. I wish you well, for the worst is over.'

Bidding him good day, Faro boarded the train and ten minutes later he alighted in Dundee Station where the platform soon emptied of passengers.

But of Vince there was no sign.

Now chilled to the bone, Faro paced briskly up and down in a vain attempt to restore his circulation. He was accompanied in this activity by a middle-aged man who walked back and forth with the impatient angry look of one who had just missed his train.

Raising his hat politely, Faro asked, 'Are you awaiting the Perth train, sir?'

The man merely scowled and, biting his lips, continued his perambulation fast enough to discourage further conversation. His occasional pauses were merely to glare across at the unfinished piers of what would some day be the Tay Bridge.

Faro, who considered such behaviour extremely boorish, again consulted the timetable outside the station-master's office. He had hoped to spend an hour with Vince before the arrival of his train for Errol, but as the minutes ticked away, he was seized by a sudden foreboding.

The lad should have had his telegraph. So where in the world was he?

Then a sudden diversion swept all other thoughts from his mind. A train had arrived from Aberdeen and as it emptied, the pacing man came leaping forward to grapple with a youngish fellow who had descended from first class.

Holding him in a fierce grip, he forced him to the very edge of the platform, so that he tottered unsteadily above the rails.

'Murderer,' shouted the older man. 'Vile murderer. I ought to push you under the next train and let it decapitate you. For that is all you deserve, after what you did to my lad.'

The youngish man had been taken by surprise. He could do nothing but gasp, struggle feebly and call for help.

Faro and the porter dashed to his assistance but the older man was strong and for several dizzy seconds the four trembled above the rails, surging back and forth in a wild dance. At last they succeeded in separating the two men.

'Thank you, sir, for your intervention.'

The younger man would have been handsome but for a tight closed-in look about the eyes and mouth. It added considerably to his thirty-odd years. 'This madman means my death.'

'Aye, that I do. And never forget it. This is our second encounter, Wilfred Deane, and next time I swear to God I will kill you, as you killed my poor laddie.'

'What's happening? What's going on here?' The station-master emerged to see what all the noise was about. 'Oh, it's you again, is it, McGowan? I've warned you before.'

A uniformed coachman appeared through the barrier and rushed to Deane murmuring apologies and concern.

'Yes, damn you, you should have been here to meet me on time. I might have been killed.'

'That one was threatening to murder your master,' said the porter.

'Murder, is it?' said the station-master. 'Hold him fast, Jim. It's the police for you, my man. Upsetting my passengers.' And to Deane, 'My apologies, sir. You have my assurances – it won't happen again, sir.'

'I sincerely hope not. It will cost you your job next time, Station-master. Pray bear that in mind. You are responsible for the conduct and safety of fare-paying passengers and for keeping madmen away from your platform.'

The station-master, nonplussed, grew red in the face with anger and embarrassment. 'If this gentleman – you, sir,' he said indicating Faro, 'will kindly assist me in restraining McGowan, I will send Jim for the police.'

Mollified, the youngish man bowed stiffly. 'See to it, Station-master.' And dusting down his sleeves as if to remove all traces of the incident he hurried the coachman towards the exit.

Watching them leave, the station-master said: 'Off you go, Jim.'

McGowan, held captive, suddenly began to weep in a helpless broken way, a weakness so out of keeping with his former belligerence that Faro called to the departing porter: 'Wait,' and to the station-master: 'It so happens that I am a policeman.'

'Are you indeed?' The station-master stared at him doubtfully.

'You don't look like one, if you'll forgive me saying so,' he added in tones of ill-concealed sarcasm.

Faro drew out his wallet. 'My card, sir.'

The man's eyes bulged as he read. 'Oh, sir, my apologies. Of course I've heard of Detective Inspector Faro. You're quite famous.'

Faro smiled. 'Then perhaps you will trust me to take care of your prisoner.'

'Indeed I will. He won't escape from you.'

McGowan was still weeping abjectly as Faro took his arm gently and led him to the only shelter, a somewhat inhospitable waiting-room. Its only furnishings besides a couple of slatted wooden benches were a few faded posters urging travel by railway. But the alluring sylvan scenes they depicted were not to be found, he suspected, anywhere outside the artist's vivid imagination.

Suddenly McGowan gripped Faro's arm. 'How can I ever thank you, sir. The scandal – after losing our lad – my wife's been in a poor way ever since, and I fear it would have finished her.'

Faro consulted his watch. It seemed unlikely that Vince would appear now. He had some time before his train and he was curious.

'Would you care to tell me about it?'

'You won't let them put me inside, will you, Inspector?'

The man before him seemed less like a potential murderer than anyone he had ever met. 'I don't think that will be necessary.'

'Wilfred Deane murdered my laddie.'

'Is he of the Deane Enterprises family?'

'He is that. He runs the show now that his old grandfather Sir Arnold is past it.'

'I see. Begin at the beginning, if you please, Mr McGowan.'

'We are from the Highlands, Inverness way. I was dominie there and Charlie was our only lad. Twelve years married, we had given up all hope of a family when he was born, the bairn of our old age you might call him. From when he was a wee boy he was clever. We scrimped and saved to put him through the University at St Andrews. He graduated with flying colours a couple of years ago and went to Deane's. He was in their finance department.

'This was right at the beginning of their contract for the Tay Bridge and he seemed to be happy at first, enjoying his work. He married Mary, his childhood sweetheart, and they seemed like two turtle doves.

'Then the last time they came to visit us, he was different. Silent, worried-looking, like he had something on his mind and was about to tell us. A week later, Charlie came alone. The manager of his office, an elderly bachelor called Simms who had been with the firm for years and had been very kind to Charlie and Mary, had been dismissed. Deane's said he was dishonest, but Charlie didn't believe that for a moment. Simms had told him that he had been suspicious of the finances for some time and was carrying on a private investigation into the firm's dealings.'

McGowan paused. 'Those were his exact words. Almost the last words he ever spoke to me and I shall remember them to my dying day.'

As he listened, Faro wondered what on earth had led him to befriend this stranger. The scent of a mystery – or was it instinct, combined with an odd compassion for the bereaved father and a spontaneous dislike of Wilfred Deane?

With a painful sigh, McGowan continued. 'Two days later, we read in the papers that Simms had been visiting the bridge and had been hit by a falling girder. He had died instantly.'

He was silent for a moment before continuing, his eyes welling with tears as he spoke. 'We expected Charlie and Mary for supper that night and when they didn't appear, my wife was alarmed and sent me to the office next morning. I was informed that Charlie had failed to show up. I went to their home, but they weren't there. Everything put away neat and tidy, but no papers, nothing personal, not even their wedding photograph.'

He shook his head. 'I didn't want to alarm the wife, she's in poor health as I told you. It was just as if they had gone off on holiday and hadn't told us. I wish to God that had been the way of it. Three days later, the police came and said my laddie's body had been washed up at the Ferry.'

'What about his wife, Mary?'

McGowan looked at him slowly, shook his head. 'She's never been seen again. We've been in touch with her folks, we've notified the police, but it's as if she's vanished from the face of the earth.'

He paused. 'I fear the worst. She's been done away with too.'

'Come now, Mr McGowan, let's not be too hasty in jumping to conclusions.' The policeman in Faro hinted that if murder was involved then it was more likely that young McGowan had done away with his wife and committed suicide, the familiar pattern of the *crime passionnel.*

As if he read Faro's thoughts, McGowan leaped to his feet. 'Hasty, is it? My son was a good Catholic, human life was sacred to him. His own and anyone else's. As for Simms, the way I look at it, his accident was arranged too, like my laddie's. They both died because of what Simms had found out. And Wilfred Deane murdered them.'

It was a shocking story. Though exaggerated by McGowan's despair, Faro wondered if there might be some grain of truth in it.

'You can easily find out if I'm speaking the truth, Inspector, the police at Dundee have all the details.'

Faro nodded vigorously. 'I will certainly do that. You have my word, Mr McGowan.' And as a shrill whistle indicated the arrival of the Perth train, 'Not that I don't believe you,' he added hastily, 'rather that I do and I want to help you if I possibly can. Let me have your address.' Watching McGowan scribble it on a piece of paper, Faro said: 'I will do this on one condition only.'

'And what is that, Inspector? I have very little money.'

'I don't want your money. Only your solemn promise that you will refrain from molesting Wilfred Deane any further. For if you are arrested and charged, it will be a serious offence and I cannot guarantee to help you. Do you understand?'

McGowan smiled and held out his hand. 'I give you my word, the solemn oath of a Highland gentleman. I swear to God that I will never again take the law into my own hands regarding Wilfred Deane. I leave it to the Almighty – and you, sir, to deliver him to justice.'

As Faro emerged on to the platform, McGowan saluted him; 'I will take my leave by the side gate,' he whispered. 'I would rather not encounter the station-master alone.' And as the Perth train steamed in: 'I can never thank you enough, Inspector. You have given me new hope.'

Searching the platform with one last despairing glance for Vince, Faro nodded briefly and boarded the train. Settling back in his seat, he realised that McGowan's fearful story had put him in the right state of mind to conjure up a whole volume of sinister reasons for his stepson's non-arrival.

Vince was always so reliable. Why then had he failed to meet the train?

The guard had already waved his flag when a young lad came panting along the platform yelling: 'Mr Faro? Mr Faro?'

Faro leaned out of the carriage. 'Over here.'

The train was gathering steam. 'I have a message for you, from Dundee,' he shouted breathlessly, thrusting a piece of paper into Faro's hand. 'There's been an accident.'

There was no possibility of leaving the train now.

Faro sank back into his seat and thanked God that the note was scribbled in Vince's familiar hand.

'I am urgently needed at the Infirmary. Will meet you for luncheon tomorrow at the Glamis Hotel (opposite the railway station).'

As the countryside chugged past the windows, Faro felt he had plenty to keep his mind occupied after his conversation with McGowan. He had given his word to the boy's father. Without stirring any troubled waters with the Dundee City Police, he could make a few discreet enquiries into the death of Charlie McGowan, and his young wife's disappearance. He could verify that Simms' death had been accidental.

A strange ugly business, with some decidedly sinister undertones. As the unfinished bridge retreated into the distance, Faro decided that if there was indeed corruption and fraud within Deane Enterprises and they were supplying the building materials, then a lot more lives of innocent unsuspecting people might be at hazard.

The journey to Errol was mercifully short. He was met by Tom Elgin, limping across the platform. A former constable with the Edinburgh City Police, Tom had been injured in a riot in the Grassmarket and no longer fit for active service had returned to Angus to become gamekeeper to the aristocratic family his forebears had served for generations.

To a man whose daily dealings were with violent death, the passing of a ninety-year-old who slips peacefully away in his bed at the end of a long and happy life was an occasion for gladness rather than bleak despair.

The wake included a great deal of food and a considerable number of drams to speed Will Gray on his way. Truth to tell, Faro was in no fit condition to return to Dundee or anywhere else for that matter, even if a late train had existed. He was readily persuaded to stay the night with Tom.

'The funeral? More like a reunion with old friends,' he told Vince when they met next day at the Glamis Hotel.

'So it would appear,' said Vince whose amused glance took in his stepfather's somewhat shattered appearance. 'Well, I take it that you received my letter,' he added shyly.

'I did indeed. My heartiest congratulations, lad. This is great news.'

'I thought you would be pleased.'

'And when am I to have the pleasure of meeting your fiancée?'

'Even at this moment, she is waiting to receive us. Come along, Stepfather. The hall porter will get us a cab.'

As they waited in the foyer, Vince asked: 'How was your journey from Edinburgh?'

'A nightmare, as usual,' said Faro huffily. 'The sooner they get that bridge finished the better.'

'Oh, we're coming on,' said Vince cheerfully as the cab arrived and from its windows they surveyed the skeleton of the bridge with its still wide central gap.

'Any fool can see that the joining of those two piers from Wormit to Dundee is nowhere in sight,' said Faro. 'They're certainly taking their time about it.'

'Oh, I gather there have been plenty of complications – and still are.'

'Such as?' demanded Faro eagerly.

Vince shrugged. 'Too long to go into at the moment.'

'Hmphh,' said Faro, and peering out he added: 'Doesn't look very substantial to me.'

Rumours had reached the Central Office and filtered through the popular press of terrible accidents and of the wild war waged between the Caledonian and the North British Railways over monopoly rights.

Tom Elgin had told him that the city of Perth had been far from pleased, jealous that the bridge might diminish their own river trade. And now he had also received, at first hand, hints of sinister goings-on from McGowan.

'Will it ever be strong or safe enough to carry a train, I wonder?'

'Safe as houses or, as they advertise, sound as Deane's,' was Vince's reply. 'The fact that they secured the contract puts a rather different complexion on the matter. Deane's stand for respectability and honest dealings.'

'Sound as Deane's' had been a familiar phrase in Dundee for the past fifty years, ever since Sir Arnold Deane had set a new fashion of combining expertise in finance with compassion for his employees. His boast was: 'We are all brothers here, all one big family.'

'Incidentally, Stepfather, Sir Arnold is a patient of mine,' Vince added casually.

'Congratulations, lad.' And in view of that information, Faro had second thoughts. He would keep McGowan's story to himself meanwhile. Indeed it had become more extraordinary and unbelievable over the last twenty-four hours. Was he wasting his sympathies on a madman?

As if in confirmation of his thoughts Vince said: 'Deane's are into everything these days, Stepfather. Sometimes one would think they had invented the word progress. And the good thing is that in their case, everyone benefits by their prosperity.'

Faro looked out of the window and discovered they were now following the Monifieth Road, alongside the river east of Dundee.

On the steep hills rising to the left perched the elegant handsome mansions built by the jute lords.

'Where are we heading, lad?' he demanded curiously.

Vince smiled. 'Deane Hall.'

'*The* Deane Hall?'

'The same,' said Vince with a grin.

Glancing sideways at Vince he noted his air of suppressed excitement. 'Home of the Sir Arnold, Baron of Broughty Ferry, who is a patient of yours?'

'Excellent, Stepfather, excellent,' said Vince.

'Vince, is there something you have forgotten to tell me?'

'Not forgotten, just hadn't time to go into it. Didn't know whether you would approve. Rachel is the Deane heiress—'

'Rachel – the young lady you are to marry?'

'Of course.' Observing his stepfather's expression he added, 'Oh Lord, did I not even tell you her name?'

'You omitted that vital clue. But please proceed . . .'

'Rachel inherits next month when she comes of age. She is Sir Arnold's only grandchild.'

'Well, well, you have done well for yourself, lad. First the resident doctor and then the heiress's husband,' said Faro with a smile.

'It's a family tradition. After all, Sir Arnold's father was a poor Yorkshire lad who came to Scotland and ended up by marrying his boss's daughter, who was also an heiress.'

Faro said nothing and, alarmed by his silence, Vince said hotly: 'If you're thinking it is her money—'

'Of course I'm not, lad—' Observing Vince's dark frown, he added hastily, 'A figure of speech and in my usual bad taste, I'm afraid. The policeman in me sometimes forgets. Do forgive me.'

Vince did so readily. 'Let me tell you, even if Rachel had been the poorest of the workers I have to attend in the factory, I still would want to marry her. She is so beautiful, the loveliest raven black hair, eyes like violets—'

He paused, suddenly embarrassed. 'But you will see for yourself in a few moments. We met one day quite by accident, when I was attending her grandfather . . .'

Faro listened, smiling, delighted by his stepson's happiness but at the same time wondering how on earth the lad was to support an heiress. Certainly not on his salary as resident doctor.

But Vince was no longer aware of reality or indeed of his stepfather's presence. And with compassion Faro recognised that Vince had happily surrendered his grasp of the practicalities of life. Gazing fondly at the lad, he observed him in the throes of that state of temporary insanity which Faro considered, from his own bitter experience, as being 'in love'.

Deane Hall was a mansion with a setting worthy of the Baron of Broughty's rôle in society and commerce. Battlemented, turreted as any castle of old, it overlooked the unfinished piers of the Tay Bridge.

One day, Sir Arnold expected that a fine monument gazing down upon the river would be the city fathers' acknowledgement of his rôle in Dundee's progress and Deane's contribution to the longest bridge in the world. A bridge that would stand for ever, carrying the railway linking the northernmost towns and cities of Scotland with those of the rest of Britain. Most gratifying of all was that this vital link had acquired royal approval, giving Her Majesty and the royal families of Europe easy access to Balmoral Castle.

Vince was arguing with the cab driver who was unwilling to tackle the last hundred yards of almost vertical climb from the ornate gates to the front door. Receiving his fare he dismissed his passengers brusquely and drove off leaving them to puff up the steep drive.

Faro sighed. 'Times have indeed changed. One would imagine he was doing us a great favour, bringing us here at all.'

'It's going down rather than up they really fear, Stepfather. They reckon that wealthy folk like the Baron who choose to live on inaccessible hilltops can afford their own sturdy carriages to bring up their affluent guests. Besides the exercise will do us good,' he added with a cheerful grin.

'Don't you think I get enough of that every day in Edinburgh?' grumbled Faro.

The driveway emerged on to a terrace which again afforded a panoramic view of the hills of Fife. The university town of St Andrews with its spires was minutely visible and to the west the faint undulating slopes of the Grampian Mountains.

Faro whistled. 'Well, that makes it almost worth the climb. What a magnificent landscape.'

'And one which is even better from the drawing room and the upstairs windows.'

Narrowing his eyes, Faro said: 'The bridge will certainly look most impressive when it's finished.'

'Sir Arnold is banking on it. He has, I understand, sunk a considerable part of his fortune into the construction. His engineering works supply the nuts and bolts, his weavers supply the cloth for sacking, overalls—'

'Overalls? That is progress indeed.'

'He firmly believes in attending to the needs and comfort as well as the safety of his workers. They eat a good nourishing meal once a day too, compliments of the firm. A splendid canteen, I can assure you, and one I am often very grateful to patronise.'

'Less fortunate workers must envy them. Sounds quite idyllic.'

Vince frowned. 'It does – but alas, progress has a knack, which I'm sure you've noticed, of crushing the helpless who cannot keep up with it.'

'How so?' asked Faro as they climbed an imposing set of stone steps guarded by two ferocious heraldic lions.

'The working conditions give me cause for concern. Small wonder they need a resident doctor,' whispered Vince as he rang the doorbell. 'I am constantly dealing with terrible – and, I feel, quite unnecessary – accidents and maimings. The men blame shoddy materials and unsafe conditions of work. Some have even

tried, poor beggars, or their dependants have tried, to bring
Deane's to court.' He laughed grimly. 'But Wilfred is too smart
for them.'

'Wilfred?'

'Sir Arnold's second cousin. He's a lot younger, of course.'

So that was the Wilfred Deane who had been set upon by
McGowan.

The door was opened by a butler. 'Dr Laurie to see Miss
Deane, if you please.'

'Are you expected, sir?'

'No, I am not. But here is my card – and my stepfather's.'

Faro produced his card which the butler consulted gravely
before transferring it to the silver tray. 'If you will be seated,
gentlemen, I will see if Miss Deane is at home to receive you.'

As they waited, Faro marvelled at this replica of a vast medieval
hall. Ghostly suits of armour, ancient flags and every degree of
opulence surrounded them. A huge log fire burned in a stone
fireplace, wastefully consuming what looked like whole trees to
keep warm no one in particular.

Occasionally he glanced at his stepson's excited face, flushed
and smiling, a lover's face of anticipation and longing as he
tapped his foot impatiently.

Faro meanwhile tried to suppress his own anxieties. A veritable
parade of dismal practical questions surged through his mind,
concerning Vince's ability to support a wife accustomed to such
a life-style as that in evidence.

The butler returned, carrying his silver tray which still bore
their cards. 'I regret, gentlemen, that Miss Deane is not at home.'

'You mean she is out?' said Vince in tones of surprise.

'I mean, sir, that she is not at home,' the butler replied
carefully.

'Look, you know me. I am Sir Arnold's physician,' said Vince.

The butler's face was impassive. 'Is it then Sir Arnold you wish
to see, sir?'

'No,' said Vince desperately. 'Look, would you please tell

Rach— Miss Deane, Dr Laurie is here to see her. And that I have brought my stepfather to meet her.'

The butler's face was impassive as he ushered them politely but firmly towards the front door. 'Perhaps you would be so good as to leave a message, sir. I will see that it is delivered to Miss Deane at the very earliest.'

'Tell her I will call again. Tomorrow afternoon at three thirty.'

'Very well, sir. Good day.'

As they walked down the drive Vince, bewildered and mutinous, wore an expression Faro recalled from his difficult early years, when deprived of a particularly toothsome treat, or dragged unwillingly from a child's tea-party.

'Never mind, lad. She probably forgot all about it.'

Vince seized on his words eagerly. 'That's it exactly, Stepfather. Such a commitment of social engagements. The mind positively reels. I did tell her when you were arriving, but you know what girls are like, with milliners and dressmakers, and friends for ever calling and leaving cards . . .'

Faro listened patiently, but he wasn't particularly impressed or convinced. He had seen something that his stepson in his preoccupation had mercifully missed.

As they walked across the gravel towards the drive, he had turned to look back at the house. At one of the grand windows upstairs a girl with raven black hair, most elegantly attired in afternoon dress, was watching them leave. As she caught his curious gaze, she stepped back hastily, but Faro had not the least doubt from Vince's description that the watcher was Miss Rachel Deane.

And that sight disturbed him exceedingly.

As they walked back down the hill Vince continued to provide perfectly valid reasons, which even Faro could not fault, for Rachel Deane's non-appearance.

At last they reached Paton's Lane, a mean street of high and gloomy tenements. On the very edge of Magdalen Green its prospects were made marginally more dismal by the shadow and noisy sounds of activity drifting from the direction of the unfinished bridge.

'Here we are, Stepfather.'

Faro followed Vince into a narrow close, up a dark and dank stone stair to the third floor where the odorous smells became unmistakably boiled cabbage. At the end of a chilly dark passage Vince opened a door and for a moment Faro toyed with the notion that his stepson was visiting a sick patient and had absent-mindedly forgotten to inform him.

Until he announced: 'Home at last.'

If this was home, then Faro was aghast. An iron bedstead, a chair and table which by the amount of papers and writing materials also served as a desk, a crude shelf above containing medical books. A press stood on a sadly uneven floor whose bare boards were visible through an inadequate strip of cracked and faded linoleum.

Totally unable to conceal his feelings, Faro asked: 'Lad, are you so short of cash? You had but to ask—'

Vince drew himself up proudly. 'Never, Stepfather. Never again. I intend to make my way in the world alone. It is about time and I cannot sponge on you for ever. You have done more than enough for me.'

'There's no talk of sponging among kin – you know better than that, you're my lad – whatever I own is yours, or will be some day.' He made a weary gesture round the room 'To think of you living in such squalor. Surely you could have found yourself some respectable private lodging? In a better part of the town,' he added indignantly.

'I could indeed, but by my reckoning, a doctor if he is to be any good at all, should be on hand when his patients need him and I couldn't be closer to mine. A workers' doctor must understand the needs of the men – and women – he has chosen to serve. I have a proper fully equipped surgery and consulting room in the factory of course.'

At his stepfather's dour expression, he smiled wryly: 'I assure you that you need have no fears on the score of respectability. The McGonagalls are paragons. Besides,' he went on reassuringly, moving the lace curtain aside, 'look out there. Is that not the most exciting prospect?'

Before them stretched the impressive but distinctly unbeautiful panorama of the bridge. The height of skeletal iron piers threatened to dwarf everything in the immediate vicinity, but it too had become a pale ghost, almost obliterated by a monstrous cloud of fine dust from foundry chimneys.

On ground level far below, all footpaths had ceased to exist, vanishing under the mud stirred everywhere by bands of navvies striving to connect roads with the landfalls, an activity accompanied by an ear-splitting din. The blast of explosives shook the room in which they stood, vying with the incessant rhythm of rivets driven home against steel girders while the creak of cranes elevating materials skyward added their unlovely screech to the scene.

'Behold,' said Vince proudly, 'history in the making. And that is the important thing, Stepfather.'

'That's all very well. But I don't think I'd wish to have the bridge's presence outside my window, so to speak, a constant companion night and day.'

His weary glance took in the contents of the room. 'At least it looks clean enough,' he conceded. For the shabby wood gleamed, the oilcloth sparkled, and the room smelt distinctly of polish.

'Of course it is. That bed is spotless. Mrs Mac is very particular, changes the sheets every week.'

Faro found little consolation in such an assurance as the pleasant Edinburgh house Vince had left loomed in his mind, a modest paradise in comparison.

Knowing that argument was useless, he said weakly, 'I'd just like to see you with more comfortable lodgings. You gave me to understand that Deane's were paying a good salary.'

'Moderately good, Stepfather, considering what my earnings were in Sheridan Place,' Vince added bitterly. 'But I have another reason for living frugally at present. Don't you see, by staying here I can put by a little every week, which I will need of course, once Rachel and I are married.'

Faro was appalled. Shock at finding his stepson living in this wretched room had momentarily put out of his head that Vince was to marry Deane's heiress. God in heaven, how could the lad be so blind, remembering the splendour they had glimpsed, the mock-medieval hall, every sign of wealth and comfort.

Any comparison between Rachel Deane's home and this squalid lodging was not only unimaginable but obscene.

'Has Miss Deane visited you here?' he asked idly.

'Please call her Rachel, Stepfather. There has been no occasion for her to do so. And until the engagement is formally announced it would not be proper—'

Faro was spared any further comment as an infant wailed somewhere nearby. Vince went over and opened the door. The cries grew louder.

'That's the McGonagall baby.' Vince listened and was reassured by rapid footsteps. 'Mrs McGonagall isn't far away.'

Smiling at Faro, he continued, 'That was my other reason for choosing this lodging. The McGonagalls have six children, steps of stairs you might say, as well as an orphaned cousin from Ireland. William, the husband, is a weaver with Deane's but he has aspirations to being an actor – a tragedian, he prefers to call himself. I attended him – just a minor accident with one of the machines – and he asked me to look at Jean, Mrs Mac, who had bronchitis.

'Well, when I came along I saw what a struggle they had. She's from Edinburgh, does some cleaning to make ends meet. Funny, in a way she reminded me of our dear Mrs Brook – same voice, you know, and an absolutely splendid cook.'

Vince paused awaiting his stepfather's approval. When Faro remained silent, he added: 'I do think I was a little homesick and when she told me she had a spare room, I said yes, I would take it. She was so grateful, said I was offering far more than it was worth. But I feel better about it, helping a family with my little rent.'

Faro suppressed any adverse comment. There was no dealing with a philanthropic Vince. Once his thoughts of chivalry were aroused, no knight of old in shining armour could have fought more vigorously for a lost cause.

And this particular lost cause, thought Faro, was one without any real solution, with Deane's good works just one drop in an ocean of grim poverty. Poverty so deep-rooted he did not see the much-vaunted building of the Tay Bridge bringing any substantial relief, lining as it would only the pockets of its wealthy share-holders.

As for the common man, he would find other bridges, other roads to build, his life of grime and hardship remaining virtually unchanged.

'There is a room for you, Stepfather, next door. Would you like to see it? Of course, if it isn't good enough and you don't like it, you can go to a hotel.'

Faro followed him reluctantly. As he expected, the room was

almost identical except for touches here and there of a feminine presence.

'This belongs to Kathleen, the cousin from Ireland. Came over when her mother died. Thought the streets of Dundee were paved with gold. Willie adores her and had aspirations for her to be an actress, too. Apparently she isn't quite ready for Shakespeare, so he got her a job in the factory.'

'Is she not needing this room?'

Vince frowned. 'You'll like this, Stepfather. Sounds exactly like one of your baffling mysteries. Seems she went out to work one day with her friend Polly – they shared this room. That's weeks ago and no one's seen them since.'

Sounds outside the door, a man's voice calculated to carry a great distance and enthral an audience, announced the arrival of William McGonagall, even before Vince's smile confirmed that his landlord had returned home.

'You'll like McGonagall, he's a grand old chap, very colourful – shares your passion for the Bard,' he whispered opening the door.

The figure who appeared was slightly unreal. Below middle height, sturdily build, melancholy dark eyes gazing from a pale face, framed by black shoulder-length curls under a wide-brimmed hat, the kind worn by priests. His frock-coat, once black but still impressive despite its green tinged antiquity, was an unlikely choice for a worker in the weaving factory.

Seeing Vince, he rushed forward hand outstretched: 'Dear lad, dear lad. How goes it with you?' And turning to Faro, he took off his hat in a sweeping gesture which matched the theatrical bow.

'And you, sir, must be Dr Laurie's famous stepfather, the Chief Inspector.' As they shook hands he regarded Faro shrewdly. 'Your activities in the realms of criminology are well known to me. My sister-in-law who inhabits your fair city of Edinburgh has mentioned your name.' Another bow: 'Allow me to present my card and credentials, sir.' Faro glanced in some surprise at the small package. 'If you would care to attend this evening's performance of *Macbeth*, there are two free tickets. The noble Inspector's presence would add lustre to your humble servant's performance.'

Faro suppressed a smile, for there was nothing at all humble in this extraordinary man with the booming voice and eccentric garb.

Leaning forward confidentially, McGonagall placed a hand on his arm and his face now serious, he continued: 'Indeed, I am delighted to make your acquaintance. Fate must have sent you to Dundee at this time,' he added gloomily and looking over his shoulder, he gestured towards the room at the end of the corridor.

'But let us be comfortable, for I have a melancholy tale to unfold. If you will be so good as to follow me into our humble kitchen, Mrs M will provide us with refreshment.'

Jean McGonagall hastily buttoned up her gown as the men entered and laid the now sleepy baby in a somewhat battered cradle. After quickly introducing her to Faro, McGonagall said in a lordly manner:

'And now, be so good as to provide sustenance for these gentlemen.'

Faro took the proffered seat in one of the rickety chairs by the side of a blackleaded and highly polished steel range with ashpan and fender. The room was humble indeed, shabby but again well cared for within its limits. Four wooden kitchen chairs and a large scrubbed wooden table occupied the centre floor, while a recess held a double bed. Lace curtains adorned the one solitary window above a sink with well-polished brass tap.

Dominating the mantelpiece, a pendulum clock with ferocious tick, a brass tea caddy, and a pair of china dogs. Opposite, a dresser displayed a variety of unmatching china teacups and plates, interspersed with photographs. Mostly of McGonagall, presumably in costume from his leading Shakespearean rôles.

Faro was suddenly aware that McGonagall was addressing him.

'As I remarked earlier, sir, it is fortuitous indeed that you should be visiting Dundee at this time. Dr Laurie may have told you that my niece and her young friend disappeared—'

'Willie,' said Jean chidingly. 'They didn't disappear. You are too dramatic, dear. We had a postcard that they had found employment with a milliner's in Regent Street. They only went to London to improve their prospects,' she added apologetically.

'Poor Polly certainly did not improve hers,' said William heavily. When his wife gave a startled 'Oh!' he withdrew a piece of newspaper from his pocket and spread it on the table.

'You remember reading in the newspaper two days ago that the body of an unknown young woman had been recovered from the Tay – a suspected suicide—'

'Oh dear God, not our Kathleen—'

'No, woman, not Kathleen,' McGonagall replied impatiently, turning to Faro. 'If I had not been a tragedian I think I would have made an excellent detective—'

'For God's sake get on with it, Willie,' cried his wife, nervously twisting the ends of her apron. 'If it isn't Kathleen, who is it?'

'Hear me out, woman, for pity's sake. Where was I? Oh yes, I have already indicated that I have a naturally curious nature and ever since the two girls disappeared, I have been keeping a watchful eye on the newspapers and have made it my business to keep the police informed for their missing persons files—'

'You never told me,' was the reproachful cry from his wife.

'I did not want to alarm you unnecessarily, especially when you seemed quite content to believe they were bettering themselves in London.'

He sighed and winked at the two men. 'I am a little more worldly-wise than Mrs McGonagall, gentlemen, and when I read of this apparent suicide I decided to give the matter my personal attention.'

Another dramatic pause while he drank deep. Jean McGonagall had set before the company enamel cups of bitter black tea, thereby providing Faro with some difficulties. This he guessed was Irish tea, beloved of the navvies, for even the tough Edinburgh constables didn't make it this strong in the Central Office.

McGonagall looked at each of his small audience in turn before proceeding. 'I have newly returned from the police station—'

'It is Polly, isn't it?' said Jean with a sob.

He nodded. 'Sadly, my dear, it is Polly. I was able to identify her body in the mortuary. There is no doubt about it.'

With a glance at his wife who was now weeping noisily, he drew them aside. 'And now do you get my drift, gentlemen? The two girls were inseparable, so where in dear God's name is our Kathleen?'

Stretching over to the mantelpiece, he took down a picture post-card of Trafalgar Square and studied it carefully. 'The question remains, sirs, is she still in this milliner's shop in Regent Street?'

'May I see?' Faro was more interested in the postmark than the cramped ill-written message. But as was so often the case when such matters were of crucial importance, the date was completely illegible.

Jean McGonagall, drying her eyes, snatched up a rather blurred photograph from the dresser. The girl smiling coyly through a cloud of blonde curls was little more than a child. 'This is our Kathleen.'

'Bonny lass, she is,' said McGonagall proudly.

'She is indeed,' said Faro.

McGonagall nodded. 'Hasn't changed very much since that was taken either, three-four years ago.'

'Willie insisted on it,' said Jean bitterly. 'More than we ever did for our own bairns and cost us a fortune, it did.'

'Hush, woman.' And apologetically to the men: 'Photographs are an absolute essential for a potential thespian.'

'Thespian, indeed,' muttered Jean. 'She didn't take much of your advice, did she?'

Before this domestic argument swamped McGonagall's revelations, Faro interrupted: 'What about the unfortunate girl Polly's
family?'

'She didn't talk much about them,' said Jean. 'They were tinker
folk, attached to a travelling circus.'

'So you would find it very difficult to inform them.'

'Almost impossible, sir.' McGonagall sighed deeply. 'There are
bands of these folk roaming the country, making camps outside
towns. Sometimes they come to Magdalen Green, set up a penny
gaff, a show under canvas, and by next morning they have
vanished into thin air.'

'And mostly not empty-handed, either. They even steal clothes
drying on the lines,' Jean put in. 'Kathleen always said Polly was
ashamed of her background and wanted to better herself. You
remember, Willie. She didn't like performing in a circus with
wild animals, neither. Thought it wasn't ladylike. Said she smelt
of lions all the time. Poor lass, oh, the poor lass.'

She began to cry again and this wakened the baby who added
its dismal wail to the melancholy scene. As Jean rushed to the
cradle, McGonagall jerked his head towards the door, a finger to
his lips.

As they followed him into the corridor, Vince said comfort-
ingly: 'No doubt Kathleen is still in London, but Polly changed
her mind and came home.'

'Let us hope that was the way of it. I am feeling quite desperate,
gentlemen.' He bit his underlip. 'I have a feeling that there is
something more than suicide in this.'

'What gave you that idea?' demanded Faro sharply.

'I detected a certain reluctance in the police officers to show
me the body. And when at last they did, I was invited to sit
down and answer a number of questions I would have considered
quite unnecessary for the mere identification of a dead body.'

Pausing dramatically he surveyed his audience. 'Indeed I began
to feel certain that – that, well, they suspected I had something to
do with poor Polly's death. I became very indignant at such an

idea.' And hanging his head, 'I am ashamed, quite ashamed, gentleman, to admit to you that I vented my wrath on the unfortunate police constable who was questioning me before storming out in an attitude of high dudgeon.'

He leaned forward, put a finger to his lips and whispered: 'I am quite certain, gentleman, that I was followed home.'

And springing forward, he twitched aside the curtain on the landing window. 'To be sure, I was right, gentlemen. Look for yourselves. He is still there. That is the very man standing at the corner.'

Faro looked down into the street and sighed. 'I'm afraid you're right.'

'So you do believe me, sir.' McGonagall seemed surprised.

'I believe you.'

Faro was in no danger of mistaking a police constable out of uniform, trying with difficulty and in extreme discomfort to look nonchalant and blend into the background.

McGonagall stared into Faro's face. 'You surely do not think they believe I have had something to do with that poor child's death?' There was unconcealed terror in his voice.

'Let us say I think they are just doing their duty. If you are the only person who has turned up to identify the body, then they are being ultra-cautious and getting as much information as they can.'

'But if I had committed this terrible crime, surely I wouldn't have gone near the police station? Surely my action proves my innocence,' McGonagall protested.

Faro shook his head. 'Not necessarily. There are those murderers who get their ultimate satisfaction in a final contemplation of their gruesome handiwork.'

McGonagall had paled visibly. 'Dear God, what am I to do?'

'Nothing. They'll give up after they get more evidence.'

'Evidence? You mean the invasion of my home, the terrifying of Mrs McGonagall? This is dreadful, sir, dreadful. It is bad enough having the worry of Kathleen without being involved in her friend's suicide.'

Faro was aware of a familiar prickling sensation in the region of his spine. The presence of the constable outside McGonagall's home confirmed that the police had reason to believe there was more to the girl's death than suicide.

Suicide was already the wrong word. Murder was more like it.

And there was only one way to find out.

5 As they left Vince's lodging, Faro was unable to resist walking past the plain-clothes constable. 'Well done, lad. Keep it up,' he whispered.

The young man, recognising the voice of authority, saluted smartly thereby giving the whole game away. Faro raised an admonishing finger and with a sad shake of his head, still chuckling, caught up with Vince.

As they approached the town centre he asked idly where the police station was located.

'You are not going there, Stepfather? I thought you were on holiday?' There was no reply from Faro. 'You cannot resist a mystery, can you?'

'There is something wrong, Vince. Take my word for it.'

'Oh, for heaven's sake. That constable could have been watching the tenement. There's plenty of petty crime in Paton's Lane, believe me.'

When his stepfather remained silent, he said: 'Regarding the girl Polly, there is a perfectly logical explanation which I am sure must have occurred to you almost immediately, as the reason for her suicide.'

'One you considered too indelicate to mention to McGonagall?'

Vince nodded grimly. 'Exactly. I suspect that neither of them went to London nor had they any intention of so doing. As you well know, in every big city, here and in Edinburgh, there are what are known in polite society as gentlemen's secret clubs, patronised by the wealthy.

And a positive refuge for young women whose ambitions are stronger than their morals.'

'Would Polly not have been more use to them alive than dead?'

'I think you'll get your answer from the police surgeon at the mortuary. I presume that is your destination,' he added in disgust.

When Faro mumbled: 'Something like that,' Vince continued: 'The answer is easy. The wretched girl probably found herself pregnant. In eight cases out of ten, that is the reason for suicides among young unmarried girls. Either betrayed and abandoned by a lover they cannot face the future or disowned by parents unwilling to endure a daughter's disgrace.'

Not either, sometimes both, thought Faro grimly, remembering how his dead wife Lizzie had been made to suffer, a fifteen-year-old servant girl, for bringing Vince into the world.

'Polly must have been pretty sharp about it,' he said, 'seeing that she had only gone missing for a few weeks.'

'Come, Stepfather, you can do better than that. I imagine that girls, the pretty ones with potential, are discovered and recruited on the weaving factory floor. Not literally, of course,' he added with a grin. 'They probably work part time in the select clubs until they soon find that working hours in both establishments and keeping up a pretence of home life are too exhausting and opt for the more lucrative nightwork. I would presume that Kathleen Neil wanted to spare McGonagall's feelings, hence the postcard from wherever it was posted.'

Faro was not convinced nor was he to be diverted from his purpose by Vince's argument.

He had no difficulty in identifying himself in the police station. They were fortunate, he was told, that the police surgeon had been called in to deal with a fatal accident enquiry. He was to be found in his temporary office.

'Is this an official enquiry?' asked Dr Ramsey nervously. He was young and clearly impressed to learn that Dr Laurie had been assistant to the Edinburgh City police surgeon.

Vince quickly explained that this visit was on behalf of his landlady, Mrs McGonagall, quite distraught about a missing female relative. Ramsey listened with an expressionless face.

Then abruptly he led them to the mortuary and raised the sheet on a girl who had been pretty and voluptuous too. Surprisingly, however, the medical exchanges between Ramsey and Vince, including the fact that Polly Briggs had been a virgin, made nonsense of an unwanted pregnancy or indeed of prostitution.

Vince was also puzzled. 'I wonder why she committed suicide, then. An unhappy love affair, do you think?'

'Perhaps,' said Dr Ramsey.

'Have you any theories?' Faro asked.

'No. None at all. Now if you will excuse me, gentlemen . . .'

Faro looked sharply at the young doctor. His negative was a fraction too emphatic, his first eagerness to be helpful had faded rather suddenly. It indicated a refusal to discuss the subject any further, unusual between two doctors with a common background.

As they left that sad icy room of death they almost cannoned into a constable ushering a wild and distraught-looking man towards the door.

'Another poor soul come to identify a victim. God, how I used to hate those moments,' said Vince, 'when there is nothing you can say or do to give any comfort.'

At the front door, Faro paused. 'I think I will just pay my respects to Superintendent Johnston before I leave.'

Vince looked at the clock. 'And I have a surgery in half an hour. See you later, Stepfather. Enjoy the play.'

'Are you not coming too?'

'Not tonight. I have an engagement.' With a gentle smile, 'Besides I've seen McGonagall's Macbeth twice already.'

'Oh. Is it worth my while?'

Vince laughed. 'Knowing your sensitivities, I wouldn't recommend it if I had any doubts. But this is a performance not to be missed. You have my word,' he added as they parted.

Faro was warmly welcomed by Superintendent Johnston, who had called upon his assistance on several occasions to investigate murder or fraud cases where there was involvement with an Edinburgh area.

'What brings you here?'

'My stepson, Dr Laurie, had business with Dr Ramsey. Concerning the girl who was found drowned. The suicide.'

The Superintendent nodded sympathetically. 'That was Briggs, her father, just gone along to make the formal identification. Poor man, he'd just heard about it. Someone read it in the paper and told him. Apparently the lass has been missing for weeks now. Tinkers they are, left their travelling circus in Fife. He's been searching for her everywhere.'

Faro looked up with new interest. 'I wonder, could I have a word with him before he leaves?'

At the Superintendent's puzzled glance, he said: 'My stepson lodges with the man McGonagall who came in earlier today. A young relative, a girl, was friendly with the dead lass. She is also missing.' His enquiring glance brought no response. Obviously the Superintendent knew nothing of any misfortune to Kathleen Neil.

'McGonagall, eh? We thought he might have done her in. Gave orders to have him watched. Looks weird and wild enough. But you can't go on appearances,' he added in what sounded like regret.

Promising to dine with the Superintendent and his wife on some future visit, Faro excused himself quickly and walked towards the mortuary where Polly's father was just emerging.

Overcome with grief, the tears sprouting from his eyes, Briggs sobbed noisily into a large red handkerchief. To question him at such a time seemed a terrible intrusion into his agony.

'My condolences, sir,' said Faro. 'Come, let me help you to a seat – over here.'

'She's dead, my bonny bairn,' was the savage reply. 'What can you do to help?'

'I am a detective inspector, sir. We have knowledge that her friend Kathleen Neil with whom she lodged at the McGonagalls' was with her a few weeks ago. She is still missing. I am trying to trace her and any information you have might be of considerable assistance.'

'Kathleen Neil, that one. What's she done?'

'Nothing as far as I know. My enquiries are on behalf of her relatives who are naturally very concerned.'

'Oh, I just wondered. Wouldn't put anything past that one. She was a thorough bad lot. If it hadn't been for her, our Polly would never have left home.'

'In what way did she influence your daughter?'

'They met when we were doing a penny gaff at Magdalen Green. We often called on members of the audience to do a turn and this Kathleen was persuaded by her uncle, or whoever he was, that actor chap, to do some bird calls.' And grudgingly, 'They were very good. She could have made a name for herself in the halls and seemed to have a liking for the travelling life. But she was ambitious and lazy and went back to the weaving after a day or two. Polly told us she had some well-off gent in tow who had promised to better her. We all know what that meant, of course,' he added scornfully.

'What happened then?' Faro ignored the implication.

'Our Polly just walked out of the circus. Went with her. Left home.' His sobs renewed. 'They'll never convince me that she took her own life. Oh, dear God, dear God. That police doctor told me that she wasn't in the family way. As if any lass of our would kill herself for that,' he said scornfully. 'There are no unwanted bairns with us. All are welcome however they were come by. Welcomed, aye, and loved.'

'When did she leave home exactly?' asked Faro gently.

'About two months since, it would be. She had heard that there was money to be had in Dundee. The building of this bridge and so forth. There would be lots of chances for young lasses getting employment with Deane's.'

'And that was the last you heard of her?'

'Oh, no. She came home a couple of times.'

'But there was no other communication?'

The man frowned. 'Communication?'

'I mean did she write at all?'

'We don't go much on writing, sir. Moving around all the time doesn't give much time for scholars. As long as we can count up the pennies that's all is needed. Last time we saw her was – I don't remember exactly – a few weeks ago.'

'That isn't very long. Did she perhaps go to London with her friend?'

'London? There was never any mention of London.' He made it sound like the ends of the earth. 'She was staying in Dundee and she promised faithfully to come home for her brother's wedding. When she didn't arrive we knew there was something wrong.'

'It might have been difficult for her getting back – if she did go to London.'

'London or Timbuctoo, what difference does it make? She would have come home for the wedding. A tinker lass's word is her bond. 'Sides she'd never have gone all that way to a foreign place without telling her family.'

Refusing Faro's offer of fare for a carriage back to Carnoustie, or for the train, as they neared Paton's Lane Briggs said proudly: 'Legs were made to walk on, sir. Mine have been carrying me on longer roads that that for fifty years now.'

Watching him walk away, their despondent farewell brought acute memories of that other bereaved father on the railway platform. And Faro remembered his promise to McGowan.

Could that have been only yesterday?

Retracing his steps to the police station, Faro asked the sergeant in charge, Crail by name, if he might take a look at the accident log.

'Anything particular you're interested in, sir?' asked the sergeant, torn between helpfulness and curiosity.

'A lad, Charlie McGowan, worked on the bridge.'

'Oh, that one.' Flicking through the pages, he said: 'Here it is, sir.'

As Faro suspected, there was nothing in the entry to suggest it had been anything else but a platform that gave way on one of the piers. But turning over the pages for the last few months, he remarked:

'There do seem to be rather a lot of fatal accidents on the bridge.'

'What can you expect, sir? The Tay is notorious for high winds, it can pluck a body right off those pieces of iron, just as easy as winking.' Crail added with a kind of gruesome relish, and closing the logbook firmly: 'Anything else I can do for you, Inspector?'

Faro smiled. 'I'm curious to know why when I asked to see this particular entry you said: "Oh, that one." '

The sergeant raised his eyes heavenward. 'Oh, the poor laddie. We were all sorry about that, but his father just won't accept that it was an accident. According to him it was a personal vendetta between the lad and Deane's.' He touched his forehead significantly. 'Not quite right, you know. Grief gets them that way. We try to be sympathetic but what a trial he has been to us.'

'I understand his daughter-in-law, the lad's wife, also disappeared about the same time.'

Sergeant Crail gave a long-suffering sigh. 'Disappeared, left home. We put it on our missing persons list, of course, but when you've been on the force as long as I have, you know that if we stopped to investigate every case like that, we'd have no time left for crime. There's a dozen good reasons why a young widow should want to get away from it all and none of them very sinister.

'After all,' he added earnestly, 'perhaps she didn't care for her in-laws and we have only McGowan's word that she was happily married.'

Two missing women, two bereaved fathers mourning a son and a daughter, refusing to believe their deaths were accidental or self-inflicted but helpless to convince those in authority.

As for the girl Kathleen, he strongly suspected that she had never left Dundee either and all his instincts told him that Polly Briggs was a murder case. And that Dr Ramsey had his own reasons for silence.

He hated being baffled but any further investigations were the sole responsibility of Dundee City Police and as far as Detective Inspector Faro was concerned, the murderer's identity was of merely academic interest.

Too bad, but no doubt Vince would keep him informed of any interesting developments after his return to Edinburgh next week.

6 Faro had the rest of the day to himself and was surprised to find that Dundee's rush of wealth had, perhaps as a result of Sir Arnold Deane's benevolence, proved a boon to the common man. As he wandered through Overgait and Nethergait he noted that the shops looked prosperous. Although their windows were less elegantly dressed than those of Edinburgh's Princes Street, their prices for the goods on display were considerably lower.

In the Wellgait he bought some twist tobacco for $3\frac{1}{2}$ pence per ounce, while wistfully eyeing Finest Old Highland Whisky at 16 shillings a gallon, Winter Claret at seven shillings and sixpence per dozen bottles and Invalid Port at 27 shillings per dozen quarts. Mrs Brook will be mortified to know how much more economically she could run our household, he thought, gleefully making a note of prices and handing over one shilling for a pound of her favourite tea to take back as a present.

His wardrobe, or lack of it, was a subject of constant reproach from both Vince and Mrs Brook, which he scornfully dismissed, pleading lack of time for such trivialities. Now in an unprecedented burst of extravagance he marched into a gentlemen's outfitters and purchased a handsome tweed suit, two shirts and two pairs of cotton drawers. Delighted to find that he still had change out of three pounds, he completed this wild spree at Paraphernalia's Shilling Store in the Overgait with a new tweed cap.

Made suddenly hungry by such reckless spending, he tottered into the Old Steeple Dining Room and did full justice to an excellent three-course meal of soup, steak and potatoes, and rice pudding for seven pence.

Only one penny less for an evening's entertainment at sixpence for a seat in the stalls at the Theatre Royal, he thought, studying the poster outside. With a boast of 'Accommodating audiences up to 1200 in number at each of its three performances nightly', it offered varied future attractions 'to suit the Entire Family'. From grand opera to prize-fighters, to 'Alpha Omega's Magic Circus, in which M. Omega causes to vanish into thin air, tight-rope walkers, trapeze artists as well as performing poodles'.

Trudging back to Paton's Lane with his purchases as the shops were closing and gaslight flickered eerily across the piers of the now silent bridge, he found that Mrs McGonagall had lit a fire in his room.

Settling down to read before he went to the theatre, he took out the testimonials which McGonagall had pressed upon him.

We willingly certify that the bearer, Mr William McGonagall, has considerable ability in recitation. We have heard him recite some passages from Shakespeare with great force; and are of the opinion that he is quite competent to read or recite passages from the poets and orators in villages and country towns with pleasure and profit to his audience. We also believe him to be a respectable man . . .

And one signed by George Gilfillan, ending: 'he has a strong proclivity for the elocutionary department, a strong voice and great enthusiasm . . .'

Extraordinary, said Faro to himself, now almost eagerly anticipating the evening's entertainment as he struggled through the mass of people waiting to gain admission. He was heartily glad of his complimentary ticket.

Vince had been right, McGonagall's Macbeth was superb. Faro soon found himself transported beyond the shoddy set and threadbare costumes, the less than perfect performances of the supporting cast. He realised that this was in fact a one-man show and that McGonagall was quite capable of carrying the whole of Shakespeare's play single-handed.

With an audience who rose as one to give a standing ovation, Faro added his 'Bravo, bravo' to the calls and whistles and cheers as Macbeth staggered round the curtain. Sweat pouring from his forehead, McGonagall took his final bow.

As he walked back to Paton's Lane, Faro was still inspired, full of elation. Only one thing, he realised sadly, was missing to make the evening's enjoyment complete.

Even the world's best performance would have been bettered by the presence of a companion to share it with. If only Vince had been there. But at least the lad had seen it, they could discuss it together over a dram.

He was disappointed to find that the room was empty. Vince had not returned from his evening's engagement. The kitchen was occupied by a McGonagall daughter in charge of the sleeping infant.

No, her ma was out for the evening. So he was not even able to share his delight and congratulations with the actor's wife.

As he turned up the gas, the room, so threadbare and shabby, was dismal and cold too. His euphoria suddenly faded. There was something troubling him, at the back of his mind a shadow which threatened to loom large again.

This time it was something more personal and nearer home than the troubles of bereaved fathers and missing women. It was Vince. And as he tried to concentrate upon the newspaper he had brought in, his thoughts returned again to his stepson's new reticence.

In their Edinburgh days, Vince would normally have told him immediately what that 'previous engagement' was, especially as

Faro had the strongest suspicion that it concerned Rachel Deane.

Such reticence was odd and disquieting, even if he had to accept the fact that he was now dealing with a new version of his stepson, a man in love, a character previously unknown to him and in many ways one who would increasingly become a stranger, secretive, withdrawn.

'Life is not lost which is spent or sacrificed in the grand enterprises of useful industry.'

He was staring at the notice of the fatal accident Vince had attended yesterday, a fifteen-year-old boy crushed to death by falling masonry. Angrily he thrust the newspaper away.

What infernal pomposity. How dare those who knew nothing of the suffering and endurance of the poor make such heartless wicked statements.

Turning for sympathy to Mr Charles Dickens, who knew and understood such sentiments well, he began to read. After a few pages he realised he was not taking in one word. This shabby room was to blame, for his imagination was constantly imposing upon it the grandeur of Deane Hall.

Was that what was bothering him? Was his stepson in danger of making a totally unsuitable impossible marriage, a commitment to an heiress he could not hope to support?

Edwin Drood had no answer for him tonight and he sat down on the bed, took off his boots, undressed, washed in somewhat chilly water and got into bed. Grateful at least for Mrs McGonagall's warming pan, he turned away from the glare of the lights from the bridge which touched his window and fell into an uneasy doze.

He was drifting off at last when the window rattled in a sudden gale. Cursing, he got out of bed, fixed a piece of newspaper to steady the frame and wearily settled down again, longing for the absolute silence of his bedroom in far-off Sheridan Place where all life was subdued from ten thirty onwards. There even the dawn chorus was a frowned-upon intrusion into the residents' privacy and early morning birds embarked upon their song with respectful harmony and timidity.

For seconds only it seemed he dozed once more, to be awakened by a nearby public house disgorging its customers in a roar of noisy goodnights.

Dundee, it seemed, never slept. The street below was in a furore of activity all night long. The new day had not yet lightened the sky when he was roused by the tramp of boots as men began their day's work on the bridge. Soon any further hopes of sleep were made impossible by the screech of cranes, the clang of rivets and the shouts of workmen calling to one another.

Tiptoeing into Vince's room, Faro contemplated the empty bed and realised that it was many years since he had lost sleep wondering where his stepson might be. But Vince and the imponderables of his love life were no longer the only source of Faro's anxiety.

The strange events of the last two days refused to be banished and a set of melancholy tableaux paraded themselves through his mind.

Always the detective, although the solving of these particular mysteries was no concern of his, he found himself making mental notes and now that there was sufficient daylight, he produced the writing materials he never travelled without. Wrapping himself in a blanket, he began to write in the hope that his observations and deductions might yield something to aid the Dundee detectives.

Half an hour later, his mind cleared, his hands frozen, he yawned and plumping up his pillow fell asleep, to be awakened by Vince vigorously shaking his shoulder.

'Wake up, Stepfather. Wake up.'

A pale gleam of sunshine penetrated the window curtain. Vince was saying cheerfully: 'Come along, Stepfather, breakfast is ready.'

Faro was too relieved to see his stepson in such good spirits to feel resentment at having been, as he put it later, 'dragged from sleep'. Shaved and dressed he found Vince seated at Mrs

McGonagall's table beside Willie who was giving his first performance of the day, reading a review from the *People's Journal*:
' "I have long been attracted to the acting of Mr William McGonagall and it was many years ago when he first attracted my attention. He had such a grim and ghastly look about him that I was impressed with the idea that he at least looked upon acting as a rather grave and important occupation." Ah, gentlemen, how right he was.

' "He had likewise such an air of sorrow and melancholy about him that one could not help thinking there was some cankering care or secret sorrow gnawing away his peace of mind. And yet if you watched him narrowly, you could observe that when any leading members got hissed for not playing their parts too well, a Mephistophelian gleam of pleasure would flit across his countenance which would afterwards change into a settled and self-conceited expression, as much as to say: 'If I only had the opportunity of playing those parts, I would soon show you how they should be acted!' " '

And throwing down the paper he beamed upon Faro and Vince. 'True, how true. And it all came to pass.'

He was delighted, puffed up with pride at Faro's very genuine pleasure in his Macbeth. To Faro's question as to how he became involved with Shakespeare's plays, he smiled.

'Even as a child the books I liked best were his penny plays, more especially *Macbeth*, *Richard III*, *Hamlet* and *Othello* and I gave myself no rest until I obtained complete mastery over these four characters. This I did, gentlemen, by grim determination in the evenings after fourteen hours at the weaving. Life was not easy then, we were very poor, always on the move. But even then, gentlemen, I knew I had a calling.'

Vince had to leave for a morning surgery and Faro accompanied him down the road. 'Did you have a good evening?' he asked, unable to restrain his curiosity any further when the information had not been volunteered.

'Not really, Stepfather. A bit of a disappointment. I decided to call upon Rachel, sure she would be at home in the evening and eager to receive me. I was told she had retired early with a headache.' A tone of exasperation and something worse. Anxiety, uncertainty, had crept into Vince's voice.

'I told that odious butler to kindly relay my message, but was informed he had orders that Miss Deane was not to be disturbed. Would I leave a message? I reminded him that I had already done so and would he impress upon his mistress that as my stepfather's time in Dundee is short, I would therefore present you to her this afternoon without fail.

'I was intending coming straight home, but I didn't like the look of one of the three fellows who were injured last week on the bridge. He is in the infirmary so I decided to pop round. There were, as I expected, complications and we had to do an emergency operation.'

'Will he recover?'

'I hope so. It really is intolerable, especially as I find all my protests about not having proper safety precautions are being ignored, set aside as too expensive. It seems to me sometimes that only men's lives are cheap.'

As they reached the crossroads Vince said: 'I'd better see how my patient is. What about you, Stepfather, how will you spend the morning?'

Assuring Vince that he could amuse himself until the visit to Rachel Deane, Faro decided to take the ferry across to Newport and have a closer look at the bridge from the other side of the river.

There was a strong wind blowing in from the sea and the groaning of the iron columns above his head did little to reassure him.

As a casual observer, unfamiliar with the world of engineering, he felt that nothing short of a miracle could ever safely bridge the spans of the two piers across that vast and turbulent expanse of water and gales.

It had all looked extremely perilous on a mild morning when he had parted from Vince. Since then the day had deteriorated rapidly. Heavy clouds scurried across the sky making for a blustery stroll and he had to be content with a very brisk walk facing into an unpleasantly fierce wind whipping the river into a white foam.

As he feared, his return journey across the two-mile stretch of water was accompanied by all the less engaging qualities of open sea as far as his stomach was concerned.

Far above his head, creaking cranes and pulleys elevated baskets of enormous dimensions up the piers, presumably containing building materials. This activity was accompanied by warning shouts and directions from the workmen who bravely crouched on frail platforms where wooden screens served as shields to protect them from vagaries of wind and weather. On the sandbanks the seals, which Vince had told him to look out for, had wisely disappeared.

The rain began as he stepped ashore and decided him to indulge in a more luxurious meal than could be found in the Old Steeple Dining Hall. In the Glamis Hotel, encouraged by a handsome fire and sofas waiting invitingly in the main reception room, he was able to ignore the gloomy prospect outdoors.

Summoned to the dining room, he had just taken two spoonfuls of excellent Scotch broth when the walls reverberated to the sound of gunfire. The other diners promptly left their places and surged to the windows.

'What on earth is going on?' he demanded. 'Have we been invaded?'

Had something disastrous overtaken that Auld Alliance between France and Scotland in the short while he had been absent from Edinburgh? And staring over the diners' shoulders, he wondered if war had broken out although there had been no alert at the Central Office from England's network of spies.

'. . . four-five-six-seven . . .'

He was aware of the diners chanting at each explosion.

'Eight. Eight!'

The magic word was greeted by a cheer and a hurrah.

Seeing his solemn face one of the waiters said: 'Eight of them! Isn't that marvellous?'

'Eight of what?'

'Why, sir, eight whales of course. That's the *Excelsior* – one of the whaling fleet just returned. The gunfire is the signal of how many whales they've caught.'

'Oh, is that all?' said Faro returning to his soup. What an extraordinary place this was.

'Frightened me out of my wits. Can you imagine anyone in Edinburgh getting excited if a whaling ship came up the Forth?' he said to Vince when they met in readiness for the visit to Deane Hall, by which time the shoreline was already crowded with an enthusiastic group of townsfolk.

Vince smiled. 'You get used to it. Although I'd better warn you there'll be no sleep for anyone tonight. The inns will be packed, doing a thriving business. All the ladies of the town will be out in full force. I understand they come by boat from all up and down the east coast when the fleet is expected.'

Vince paused and then added, 'Talking of whalers, I've been thinking about McGonagall's girl. Perhaps she went off with the fleet, they do occasionally take their fancy women aboard. Although it's supposed to be forbidden, the authorities are pleased to turn a blind eye.'

'Well, we should soon see whether your theory is correct, Vince. If she walks into the house in the next day or two. I shall look to you to keep me informed about the missing Kathleen as well as any other developments in the case.'

Vince laughed. 'My dear Stepfather, don't look so doleful.'

'Doleful?'

'Yes, you really are addicted to crime, aren't you?'

'Perhaps so, but I shall have to restrain myself this time, since this is out of my territory.'

'And do I detect that you wish it wasn't?' When Faro shrugged, Vince continued cheerfully: 'Never mind, you will be back in Dundee very soon, remember. And your next visit will be a happy and memorable one. For our wedding. There's a family chapel in the grounds and that's where Rachel wants the ceremony to take place. Since you are not my real father, I would like you to be best man.'

'I would be delighted, lad. But surely there is some friend of your own age?'

Vince shook his head firmly. 'No one I would rather have than my very best friend – and stepfather.'

Touched and flattered, Faro asked: 'Have you fixed a date?'

'Rachel wants it as soon as she comes of age officially. It's incredibly near now, just a few weeks away.'

'No regrets or second thoughts, eh?'

'Not a single one, Stepfather. I am the happiest man in the whole world. Every day we are apart I find hard to bear. I want to be with her every moment. After our precious days and nights together, it is agonising that we should have to live apart again.'

The carriage swung round in the direction of Deane Hall. 'Especially with Rachel living away up here and me down in Paton's Lane,' he added. 'After all, we consider ourselves man and wife for we have exchanged the only vows that really matter.'

Looking out of the window, smiling shyly, he said softly: 'We are married, Stepfather, in every way but the legal formalities.'

As the carriage approached the lodge gates with their stone griffons Faro would have given a great deal to share in his stepson's happy confidence in a future that seemed to him fraught with problems.

The door opened promptly and the butler deigned to bow. 'Dr Laurie, sir. Mr Faro. Please come in. Miss Deane is expecting you.' Across the hall, he led the way to a handsome set of double doors. 'Would you please wait in the library while I announce you.'

Left alone with Vince, Faro whistled. 'What a room, what a

place to sit and read in.' He did not number among his vices, envy of other men's possessions. But these extravagant surroundings fulfilled the requirements of his wildest dreams, his hopeless ambition to possess a well-stocked library.

Each wall was stacked from floor to ceiling with oak bookshelves containing behind their glass doors a collection of handsome leather-bound volumes. A log fire blazed cheerily in a stone fireplace and two steps led up to a magnificent bow window whose padded seat overlooked a sloping garden. Beyond were spread out the hills of Forfarshire.

Faro had little time to do more than glance at the book titles and discover that most were first editions and many signed by the authors. As he sighed over a volume of *Heart of Midlothian* by Sir Walter Scott – 'To Arnold Deane with the author's compliments' – footsteps on the hall's marble floor announced the returning butler.

'Miss Deane will see you now, gentlemen.'

They followed him through the richly carpeted hall where two wings of an intricately carved oak staircase climbed graciously upwards beneath a handsome stained-glass window depicting Scotland's heroes, William Wallace and Robert the Bruce, flourishing broadswords.

At their approach two maids and a footman melted discreetly into the woodwork and Faro whispered to Vince: 'One would think we were royalty.' Privately he thought that the highly publicised manners and customs of their dear Queen had much to answer for. This new and affluent upper middle class had shown great alacrity in adopting such snobberies.

The butler opened double doors into a drawing room which was the size of a ballroom, a function Vince later told him it had fulfilled on many great occasions in the past before Sir Arnold's illness. And of course, it would do so again. When Rachel and he were married, this was to be the magnificent setting for their wedding reception.

Faro guessed as they walked across the floor that this room must cover the entire first floor level of the house. Windows faced south and west, dazzling crystal chandeliers tinkled above their heads, heavy Aubusson carpets cushioned their feet.

A huge fireplace well stocked with logs promised warmth to a girl who was dwarfed by the depths of the Carolean armchair and by the splendour of her surroundings.

She was smaller than Faro had imagined, her dark hair coiled on top of her head. And in the short time they were to be in her presence, Faro realised a deep sense of disappointment, and of revelation.

He had naturally expected that Vince would have chosen a beauty for his wife. His selection of young Edinburgh ladies had always indicated a preference for the loveliest of girls and only once, when he had been briefly infatuated with an older woman, the police surgeon's wife, had this preference faltered.

But this girl, who was to be his ultimate choice, was none of these. True, her hair was raven black and her eyes might well be violet but a screen behind the chair, presumably to keep her from draughts, also excluded any sun from the windows, sufficiently dimming the vast room's remaining light which might have served to accentuate her charms.

He looked quickly at Vince whose face was radiant with adoration. Well, well, beauty was indeed in the eye of the beholder, since his stepson's description had led him to expect a Helen of Troy or a Cleopatra, goddess extraordinary instead of a mere girl ordinary in the extreme. To his untutored eye, she appeared rather plain.

In the brief moments before she spoke, Faro, who was used to making rapid assessments of personalities since much of his work and often his life depended on swift judgements, decided that she must have some unknown qualities apparent only to a lover, that transformed her into an irresistible paragon of sparkle and animation.

I must not be so uncharitable, so ungallant, he told himself sternly. I should be delighted, gratified, since it appears that Vince has taken to heart my advice that there was more to love and a life partner than a pretty face.

But his initial disappointment was soon quenched by more important factors.

As Vince went forward to greet his beloved, Faro had remained at a discreet distance, easy to achieve in that vast room. He stared out of the window, admiring the view and allowing the lovers a little time to themselves.

· The girl's voice alerted him and turning he witnessed something stranger than the scene of sweet dalliance he had expected.

'I beg you to say no more, Dr Laurie. I can only presume that the urgency of your wish to see me concerns my grandfather's health. Pray be seated.'

Although the girl spoke softly her voice reached with a bell-like clarity to where he hovered waiting to be invited forward.

The words were either a joke or a bombshell. Faro looked across at Vince, who remained smiling tenderly down at the girl. A joke obviously, he thought with relief. A little game for lovers. She was pretending, teasing him. Well, well, was that the secret of her allure?

Still smiling, Faro moved nearer. But his presence had been forgotten.

Vince was no longer smiling. 'Rachel – dearest – for heaven's sake. What is all this about?'

Rachel Deane looked beyond Vince and saw Faro. 'Sir,' the appeal was directed at him. 'I received you both because Dr Laurie is my grandfather's physician. Indeed Sir Arnold thinks very highly of him. But when he knows how his trusted doctor abused his rôle to press his unwelcome attentions in this manner – and invade my privacy, I think he may come to change his mind.'

Faro looked from one to the other in bewilderment. If this

was a joke being staged for his benefit, then it was being played too hard and had gone too far for his taste.

He watched Vince spring forward and in an agitated manner attempt to seize Rachel's hands. He watched him sink on to his knees before her, saw her wrench her hands away, cowering far back in her chair.

'Sir – Mr Faro – please – be so kind as to remove this – this gentleman from my presence. Or must I call the servants.'

Faro went forward, put a restraining hand on Vince's arm. He noticed how it trembled.

'Vince, lad, what on earth has happened?' he whispered.

'I will answer that, sir,' said Rachel. 'This – this creature with whom you seem to have some acquaintance and influence, claims that I – that I am his betrothed, that we are to marry soon. This is preposterous, ridiculous. You have my word, sir, that although I have heard his name mentioned by my grandfather, I have never set eyes on him before in my whole life.'

7 'Rachel, for God's sake. Is this some kind of joke? You know perfectly well that it was through Sir Arnold that we first met. Oh, my dearest girl, you can't have forgotten that. You can't have forgotten Errol – ' his voice dropped to a whisper – 'the cottage where we stayed together.'

'The what? Are you mad? I never set foot in any cottage with you. Sir!' Again she appealed to Faro. 'You look respectable enough – can you not restrain this creature?'

'For God's sake, Rachel. Don't pretend not to have heard of him either. He is my stepfather, Detective Inspector Faro of Edinburgh City Police.'

Her eyes widened. The information seemed to take her by surprise, as indeed it must if she had never met Vince Laurie before.

'Then I presume you can vouch for this gentleman.'

Argument was futile. 'I can indeed, Miss Deane.'

She shrugged. 'At least I am not being confronted by a madman, for that was my first impression. But now I can see that he has been the victim of some wicked practical joke.'

'A joke you say. Is that all you can call it? All our – our days – our nights together.' Again Vince knelt before her, tried to seize her hands and was pushed away.

'Dearest girl, tell me the truth. Are the family forcing you to deny me, to deny that we are lovers? Is that what's the matter? Is it, is that all it is, my darling?'

Leaning forward he attempted to embrace her, but she half rose from her chair and seizing the bellpull tugged at it. The sound reverberated and the door opened with such alacrity that Faro could only conclude that the butler had been posted to listen outside.

'Please show these gentlemen out, Robson.'

'Yes, Miss Deane.'

'But Rachel – you can't – you can't do this to me.'

The butler had a firm grip on Vince's arm. It almost suggested that at one time he might have served with the police too. 'Come along, sir,' he said in the manner of one humouring a madman.

As Vince struggled, Robson gave Faro a helpless look. There was nothing he could do but bow briefly to Rachel Deane and follow his stepson from the room with as much dignity as was left to him.

At the foot of the stairs there was a short scuffle as Vince, recovering from that initial shock, made a valiant attempt to race back upstairs and confront Rachel. This time Faro showed no hesitation. He assisted the butler.

'Come along, lad.'

'But – but—' Bewildered, Vince was close to tears.

'There, there, lad.' The door opened rapidly, closed just as swiftly behind them. 'There, there. We'll think of something. Don't you worry.'

The Glamis Hotel was nearer than Paton's Lane, its surroundings soothing and impersonal, preferable to the bleak depressing bedroom and the risk of an encounter with the McGonagalls.

Faro thrust Vince up the steps. 'We wish to be private. Have you a room?' he asked at the desk.

'Across there, sir. We use it for private functions.'

'Excellent.' Following the bellboy, Faro propelled Vince into the room with its plush sofas and long table. The young man sat down meekly, still too dazed and numb to protest.

Faro ordered a bottle of whisky, much to the waiter's surprise. He clearly wasn't used to such generous orders.

'And two glasses.'

The waiter brought the order, his manner cautious and apprehensive as he stared at Vince, clearly wondering what these two gentlemen were up to. Were they in disagreement? Faro could see him nervously moving glasses and considering what was breakable in the room, as if anticipating an imminent bout of fisticuffs.

In any other circumstances he would have found it entertaining. And so would Vince. But neither had much heart left for amusement.

Faro poured out a generous measure. 'Drink it, lad. Go on. You'll feel better.'

Vince barely raised his head. 'Better? I never felt so vile in my whole life. I wish I was dead. She loves me. She is my wife – my wife, you understand. We have been lovers. And now – to deny it completely. To deny even knowing me. Oh dear God, what has come over her? She cannot be so cruel.'

He thumped his fist upon the table. 'What am I to do, Stepfather? How can I win her back? Tell me what to do, for God's sake – before I go mad.'

So saying he crashed down the whisky glass and began pacing back and forth to the window as if expecting some miracle in the shape of Rachel Deane to appear, his actions carefully watched by the nervous waiter who hovered by the private bar.

'Sit down, Vince. Sit down,' said Faro. 'I can do nothing to help you until we calmly consider all that has happened.'

'Calmly – how can I consider my broken heart, her cruel treatment calmly?'

'Because that is the way you have been taught to think, lad. It is the way you were reared, the way you have lived all your life with me,' said Faro sternly. 'If you are speaking truth – and I don't doubt that for a moment, then Miss Deane is lying. And if she is lying, then there has to be some reason. And we must find it.'

'She wouldn't lie. She is good and true—'

'Vince, listen to me. There is a mystery here and it has to be solved like any other mystery. And the sooner you calm yourself, the sooner we will find our answer.' Replenishing the glasses, he said: 'First of all, I want the evidence.'

'Evidence?'

'Indeed. I want you to tell me the whole story of your meeting with Miss Deane and what led to your further association. Rest assured I shall neither condemn nor condone but I beg you, leave nothing out.'

'It all began one day,' said Vince, 'when Sir Arnold was visiting the factory. Before his illness he came at regular intervals to inspect the working conditions and showed a lively interest in the workers. If a man or a woman had problems, he was never too grand to sit down and discuss their difficulties with them. He was, and is, greatly loved, a fine man.

'One morning during his perambulations he collapsed. Fortunately I happened to be on hand, since my surgery and my patients' records were something he might wish to inspect. He made a note of all details of accidents and in the case of deaths would write a personal note, with a few guineas, to the dependants.

'I could see at once that he had suffered a mild stroke. I took the necessary steps to revive him and he was grateful, insisted I had saved his life and asked that I should continue to attend him, as his personal physician was an old man who, Sir Arnold said, should have retired years ago.

' "I like having young men with young ideas around me."

'We got along famously and it was on one of my weekly visits to Deane Hall that I first met Rachel. As I was leaving she rushed downstairs to the hall and thanked me for all I had done for her grandfather. On my next visit I found I had to attend her as a patient. She had slipped on the stair and sprained her ankle. It wasn't serious but I think it was at that moment we looked into each other's eyes and we both knew what was happening.

'I know what follows sounds like madness, Stepfather, but you must be patient with me. She began visiting the factory, allegedly bringing clothes for some of the poorer workers, but she always did so when I was at my surgery. One day as she was leaving I took her in my arms and the next moment we were confessing our undying love for each other. I think I even asked her to marry me, although I hardly expected that a humble factory doctor would be seriously considered as a prospective suitor.

'On her next visit, she told me that she would be honoured and indeed proud to be my wife, but we must wait until she came of age, then she could do as she pleased. She told me that she longed for me, that such waiting time was intolerable and she had arranged with a friend, an old nurse, that we should visit her cottage for a few days. Did I think that was a good idea?

'Of course I did. I was deliriously happy at the prospect. We arranged to meet on Magdalen Green.'

He looked at Faro appealingly. 'Even then, I thought I was dreaming. I could hardly believe that she would be there, that it was true. But she arrived promptly in a carriage which she said was engaged to carry us to Dundee Railway Station. Errol she said was our destination—'

'Errol, did you say?' Faro interrupted. And when Vince gave him a questioning glance, he said: 'No – pray continue.'

'After purchasing our tickets, we sat in the train like two happy children playing truant. It was a short walk from the station before we turned through lodge gates into a vast estate where Rachel said her nurse's cottage was situated.

'I was a little taken aback, but enormously gratified, to find that there was no sign of any servants, or of the old nurse, who I had imagined would look after us and probably prove to be a stern chaperone. I had not the least idea then that Rachel intended to anticipate our marriage, that we were to become lovers.

'She had thought of everything. Before we met that day she had been into the Overgait and had purchased a picnic hamper, filled it with provisions, bread, wine, chicken, ham, a Dundee cake, enough for several days. We would certainly not go hungry and so we feasted, avoiding any of the estate workers as we walked in the vast woods. The house itself when we were near enough to inspect it, was shuttered. The family, she said, went to Italy each spring.

'At last it was over, we had run out of time. Time I had begged off from my surgery with the excuse of an urgent visit to Edinburgh. Time she had stolen to visit a sick friend in Perth.

'On the last day, almost tearfully we walked back to the station and took the train back to Dundee. I saw her into a carriage bound for Deane Hall and returned lonely and desolate, but full of hope for the future, to Paton's Lane. That night I wrote to tell you of my good fortune. But that is the last time I saw Rachel until our meeting with her this afternoon.'

Faro was deeply concerned with his stepson's story. The lad was too well balanced to have imagined the events of the last two weeks. He was not even romantic by temperament and had enjoyed great successes with the ladies until now without being under any obligation. Experienced where women were concerned, he was not of that nature who might in desperation mistake flirtation for serious intent.

Strongest of the evidence in Vince's favour was his natural antipathy towards the matrimonial state. It was Rachel's behaviour that was completely baffling. Why should a well brought up young girl in a strata of society which made the strictest demands of morality suddenly throw convention aside and elope with a young man she hardly knew?

'Did you have any reason to suspect her behaviour was at all – well, odd?'

'I am not sure what you mean.'

'Did she tell you anything in those few days about her background, her life as a child?'

Vince smiled into the middle distance. 'Only that she was often naughty. She hated being told what to do and – and—' He paused frowning.

'Well?'

'I remember recalling that her grandfather once told me that although he loved her dearly, she was his only grandchild, she was often wilful and naughty. A wild child, subject – subject to erratic fits. She would be over the moon as he put it, one minute, and the next sunk into deepest melancholy.'

Vince was silent now, looking at him as if there should be some ready answer. 'I wonder now could such fits be drug-induced, brought about by taking laudanum? As you probably know, Stepfather, lots of young girls take it for menstrual disorders and her grandfather once asked me to prescribe it for her, for exactly that condition.'

'Without you seeing the patient, Vince? Surely that is irregular?'

'I suppose it was. And had it been anyone else but Sir Arnold I would have refused. She did talk to me about this problem when we were in Errol, of course, so it was quite genuine.'

It was Faro's turn to be silent. 'Was there anyone who might have seen you together?'

'Only the guard at the station. I doubt whether he would remember us though. He hardly looked up when we handed in our tickets.'

'Estate workers then?'

'Well, we tried to avoid them wherever possible. After all, we were trying to be discreet. We weren't exactly eager to brazenly announce to the world that we were anticipating our marriage vows.'

And that fact didn't make sense either, thought Faro. What was all the hurry? Why didn't Rachel wait a few weeks until she came of age and could please herself in the choice of a husband?

In the few minutes he had been in her company he would have said that her reactions were exactly what he would have expected of the heiress of Deane. She certainly did not strike him as a lass who would throw her bonnet over the windmill and indulge in a passionate premarital love affair.

'Tell me something about this estate. Was there anything special that you could recognise again?'

'Of course I could find it. I have a map that Rachel brought with her. I carry it still,' he said softly, 'as a memento.' Producing it from his pocket book he spread it before Faro. 'See, there, the area ringed. That's where we stayed. It's just off the main road to Perth, at the signpost for Errol.'

Faro had a sudden feeling of triumph. 'Did it have twin lodges with tiny turrets and two spread eagles on the gateposts?'

Vince gasped. 'Exactly that. But how did you know?'

'Because, my dear lad, there is only one estate at Errol large enough to answer that description. And what is more, my friend Tom Elgin is gamekeeper on the adjoining estate.' He rubbed his hands gleefully. 'This is marvellous. Why, I stayed with him the night after Will Gray's funeral.'

'And you still remember the twin lodges?' said Vince in amazement. 'In your befuddled condition?'

'Old habits die hard, lad. Observation is second nature, and often an absolute necessity for my survival. And this time it is going to be invaluable, to prove that you were telling the truth.'

'You mean—' Hope flooded Vince's pale face.

'I mean that I shall visit Tom and see that cottage and the nurse.'

'The nurse of course. She'll tell you that Rachel contacted her.'

Vince's mood swiftly changed from gloom to optimism. For the moment, the account of his love affair had been in the nature of an expurgation. To his stepfather's suggestion that he might now wish to return to his lodgings, he said firmly:

'What on earth for? I'll only sit and brood and I've done enough of that for one day. Rachel may have spurned me for her own good reasons, but meantime there are other people who need me.' And consulting the wall clock, 'I have a surgery at the factory at five. Yes, I will be perfectly all right and I'll see you later this evening, I hope. Perhaps by that time you will have some evidence that will make Rachel admit that she loves me. It will make a change for you, this solving an affair of the heart, instead of a crime,' he added cynically.

Faro merely smiled. But he left wondering what was to be gained from the proposed visit, beyond the satisfaction of proving that Vince and Rachel had indeed visited Errol. And would it do the lad any good to learn that his beloved was a heartless liar?

As for solving enigmas of behaviour, whether criminal or in the human heart, there seemed little difference really. The puzzle lay deep in the labyrinth of personality, full of twists and turns and unsolved clues which German psychologists were only beginning to unravel.

At Paton's Lane Jean McGonagall was industriously scrubbing the front step.

'Oh, it's yourself, Inspector. I was just telling Willie, when I first saw you I thought you must be Dr Laurie's elder brother,' she added with a shy giggle. 'You look far too young to be his father.'

'His stepfather, actually,' he reminded her.

'Oh, is that it?' she answered vaguely as if she was still considering that possibility and would have liked to question him further. As he walked towards the stairs he thanked her for putting a warming pan in his bed and leaving warm water. Even if it was cold by the time he used it he realised it had to be got from a pump in the yard, carried up several flights of stairs and heated.

'I hope you are comfortable with us, sir,' she said anxiously. 'We haven't much as you know. We're that upset about poor Polly Briggs. Fancy doing herself in, the poor lassie. What on earth came over her to do a thing like that?' And with a sad shake of her head. 'I just canna take it in somehow.'

Her eyes filled with tears and she paused to wipe them on her apron. 'I expect our Kathleen will come for the funeral. Like sisters they were. I canna think that she would stay away.'

And Faro, listening, thought grimly, only if she too is dead. Out loud he said: 'Maybe she doesn't know, Mrs McGonagall. I mean, if she's in London, such news might not reach her.'

'Maybe so, maybe so. I'm right worried, sick with worry I am. I don't know where to turn.' And studying Faro's face hesitantly, 'Do you think you could help us? We were wondering if you might know someone in the police who could tell us how to go about finding our Kathleen?'

Faro refrained from replying that he and the Dundee City Police put together lacked the ability to work miracles. 'I will do anything I can, of course, but trying to find a missing person in London would be like searching for the proverbial needle—'

'In the proverbial haystack, sir.' The door behind them had opened and William McGonagall appeared. 'I've told you not to fuss, woman. Kathleen will turn up when she has a mind to do so. And now do go about your business, woman, and stop pestering Inspector Faro with our worries.'

As Jean went into the kitchen he said: 'A word in your ear, sir. About the girl. I am certain that she has found employment nearer home than London.' He winked at Faro nudging his arm. 'Delicacy forbids me mentioning the matter before Mrs McG. Women worry about their ewe lambs, but fathers like ourselves, we are men of the world. God gave us a deeper understanding.'

He glanced quickly heavenward as if expecting divine approval. 'For instance, there is the whaling fleet. A custom not freely known among respectable womenkind like my dear spouse, but the men do sometimes take lasses away on voyages with them. Lasses who are not their wives, if you get my drift.'

So Vince had informed him.

'Ah yes, sir, to be a man of the world is neither to condemn nor to condone,' McGonagall continued, 'a quality beautiful to behold among those of us who are thespians. We know the lure of the footlights. Kathleen was always stage-struck, with her bird calls and all. She envied Polly that travelling circus the tinkers lived with. She lacked a certain interest in the Bard,' he added with a regretful pursing of his lips, 'but with a little encouragement and training I could make her a great tragedienne—'

'Which reminds me,' Faro interrupted, 'that I have not thanked you for my ticket last night. I was enthralled by your performance.'

'Enthralled,' William repeated delightedly. 'You were enthralled. Alas, it was far from my best performance. The shock I had sustained earlier that day and so forth—'

'Mr McGonagall, take it from me, your Macbeth was brilliant!' Faro exclaimed. 'Even on the Edinburgh stage, and we get the London actors like Kean and Irving each year.'

'Is that true?' McGonagall beamed. 'Sir Edmund and Sir Henry. Well, well, sir, that is the greatest compliment you could pay me. I am most grateful to you, for an actor succeeding in living out a rôle is beautiful to be seen. I understand from Dr Laurie that you are also a worshipper at the shrine of the Swan of Avon. "To be, or not to be: that is the question: Whether 'tis nobler in the mind—" '

' "—to suffer The slings and arrows of outrageous fortune, Or to take arms against a sea of troubles, And by opposing end them?" '

McGonagall applauded, vigorously nodding approval and Faro hid a smile. He was being tested and McGonagall studied him keenly, thrusting out his lower lip.

'Indeed, sir, had you not chosen a life of criminology we might have made a tragedian out of you.' Standing back he looked him up and down. 'You have a fine imposing figure, an excellent profile and you belong as do us thespians to that category of men who carry their years lightly and grow better with maturity. By the time you are forty you will not yet be in your prime and at the age when an actor's voice has just reached its best.'

'I am forty and more,' smiled Faro.

'Then you are very fortunate, for you have worn extremely well.' Narrowing his eyes, McGonagall said, 'You have the tall Viking look. I can see you as one of the great Nordic heroes, even a Siegfried.'

Faro laughed. 'You know, I think I would prefer being a policeman. I don't think I was cut out for heroics.'

'Only off-stage, is that it, Inspector?' McGonagall laughed. 'You are too modest I fear. Let it be, let it be. You are not yet too old for the profession should you change your mind. We need mature actors for the Bard's great rôles, for Othello and Lear.'

When Faro repeated the conversation to Vince later, his stepson exploded into mirth. 'That caps all, Stepfather, really it does. You – an actor—'

Since McGonagall's claims, although far-fetched, had also been extremely flattering, as Vince doubled up with laughter, Faro said in injured tones: 'I don't think it was all that amusing.'

'I had a sudden vision of you in black face as Othello. I wish you could have seen it. Priceless, priceless.'

Faro felt his moment of hurt pride was well worth it, to see Vince able to laugh again. He had feared that with Rachel Deane's rejection something young and boylike might have been snuffed out for ever. Now he felt oddly optimistic as he considered what possible reasons lurked behind her denial of her own true love and of the idyll they had shared. And of what strange truths he might uncover during that visit to Errol.

And staring out of the train window as it headed towards Perth, Faro wished that he was at liberty to investigate Polly Briggs' 'suicide', Charlie McGowan's accident, the riddle of the two missing women, and to discover whether there was any connecting link.

Deciding that such a coincidence was playing one of his famous intuitions too far, with a sigh he realised that he must content himself with trying to solve the less dangerous but nonetheless intriguing mystery which was so important to his stepson: the enigma of Rachel Deane's extraordinary behaviour.

As Errol drew nearer his mood of optimism evaporated. Even if this visit proved that Vince spoke the truth, what difference could it make to his cause? Again he realised that proof of the cottage's existence could not force Rachel to admit that she had lied if she had deliberately hardened her heart to her former lover.

Faro had built up a mental picture of a girl who was subject to strange moods, to prolonged fits of melancholy. While Vince had accepted the medical theory, the full significance of her condition and its bearing on any permanent relationship between them seemed to have escaped him.

Faro's own conclusions were that Rachel had formed an infatuation for Vince and had embarked on an amorous adventure with him. When she returned to Deane Hall from their short idyll, she had either regretted her impulse or had been persuaded by her family that she was about to embark upon an unfortunate or even an impossible marriage.

Faro could sympathise with Rachel's family. Indeed be would have been the first to agree heartily. Evcn from his less involved point of view, it was obvious that a poor doctor was no suitable husband for an heiress.

But surely the girl could have been persuaded to choose a less cruel and heartless way of rejecting him?

The lodge gates were still there as he remembered them and as he walked down the drive towards the gamekeeper's cottage, he was relieved to see Tom Elgin returning with his gun under his arm.

His friend was surprised and delighted to see Jeremy Faro again especially as, at Will Gray's funeral, both had deplored that only on such melancholy occasions did they ever meet these days.

'You're the last person I expected to see. Don't tell me there's another funeral in the offing.'

Faro laughed. 'Not at all. As you know, I'm staying in Dundee and as my stepson is busy all day doctoring, I decided to take you up on your offer.'

As he took a seat at the fireside, Faro realised again that this typical estate cottage was similar to the one that Vince had described. Two panelled rooms downstairs, with a narrow staircase leading to two bedrooms with sloping ceilings and dormer windows.

Taking the whisky bottle from the cupboard, Tom Elgin poured out a couple of generous drams. '*Sláinte!*'

Lighting a pipe, he regarded his friend through the smoke. 'Well, well, Jeremy, so what brings you here, besides another crack with an old crony?'

Faro laughed. 'What makes you think I have a purpose in mind?'

Tom gave him a shrewd glance. 'Once a policeman, always a policeman. As soon as I saw you walking down the drive, scrutinising everything very carefully, I guessed that this was more than a social visit, pleasant though that would be.'

As Faro hesitated, Tom asked: 'Don't tell me the laird has been misbehaving himself?'

'Not at all, at least not that I know of. No, this is a personal matter and in strictest confidence.' And Faro plunged into the extraordinary story of Vince's love affair and its disastrous ending.

'How astonishing that the young woman should have denied it all. Even that they had ever met.' And frowning, Tom asked the inevitable question.

Faro had his answer ready. 'No, old friend, there is not the remotest possibility that Vince is not speaking the truth. I trust his word absolutely. I was there too, when she denied it.'

And without revealing Rachel's identity, he described Deane Hall and the way she had received them.

When he had finished, Tom looked thoughtful. 'There is another reason, of course, that has doubtless occurred to you. The lass may have been under considerable pressure from her own family. This grand room, what was it like?'

'The size of a ballroom.'

'Ah,' said Tom significantly. 'Could her parents have been listening somewhere nearby, out of sight? Just to make sure she was speaking as she had been instructed.'

Faro looked up quickly. Taken aback by Rachel's denial he had allowed bafflement and concern over Vince's violent reaction to blind him to the obvious.

'Once a policeman, always a policeman, as you said, Tom. And by God, I think you have something there, something I never even considered. The drawing room was huge and more dimly lit than was comfortable. There were plenty of chandeliers, so it did strike me that they were being rather frugal.'

As he remembered the scene he thumped his fists together. 'Dammit, there was even a large screen behind the armchair.'

Tom gave a nod of satisfaction. 'And I would wager, someone behind it too. Listening to every word.'

Faro shook his head sadly. For once his own much vaunted powers of observation had failed him. Undeniable proof that even experienced, well-trained detectives are capable of not recognising what is staring them in the face.

Eagerly he seized upon this idea of Rachel Deane being coerced by her family. Tom had given him new hope.

'Rachel – did you say that was the girl's name?'

'Yes.' It had slipped out, but never mind.

'Could that be Rachel Deane?'

'The same. You know her?'

'Only vaguely. I wouldn't recognise her now, but I knew her when she was a wee lass.' Tom whistled. 'The Deane heiress. Well, well, now I'm not altogether surprised at what you've told me.'

'Indeed?'

'Yes. I've heard tales of her odd behaviour before. A constant stream of governesses. Went through them like pounds of bannocks, according to her old nurse.'

'You knew her nurse?'

'Not knew – know her. Amy is still very much alive and kicking.' With a shake of his head, he added, 'And the way Amy tells it, she was the only one who could do anything with Miss Rachel. Her mother was a Balfray, you know, and their estate bordered on this one, the other end of the wood. I'll take you across if you like. Dougie, the factor, is an old crony of mine.'

As they climbed the stile, Faro had a sudden feeling of triumph. There was Vince's cottage with its apple tree, the tiny stream.

'That's it, that's it. Just as the lad described it.'

As they went closer, excitement turned to alarm. The cottage was roofless, its timbers blackened, a burnt-out ruin.

As Faro stood looking at it, Dougie approached. Greeted by Tom he was introduced with: 'Mr Faro was hoping to meet Amy.'

The factor pointed to the cottage. 'She's the luckiest woman alive, old chap. She's been living with her sister in Arbroath for more than a year now.'

Faro found it difficult making polite conversation after this further coincidence of another seemingly inexplicable accident.

'What happened?' he asked.

'Burnt down couple of nights ago. Thunderstorm. Reckon it must have been hit by lightning.'

'I hope there were no casualties.'

'No. It's stood empty since Amy went away. We were thinking of pulling it down. Storm saved us a job,' he said cheerfully.

Now he would never know if the interior had been as Vince described it, thought Faro. But having come this far, he decided to take a chance that Dougie had perhaps encountered the two young people.

Tom's eyes widened as he listened to his friend's bland explanation. 'Actually, I'm a detective, on the track of a pair of runaways. They were seen in this area, and it was thought they might be staying in an empty estate cottage. Tall young chap, curly fair hair, good-looking, early twenties. His companion is a slightly built girl with very distinctive raven black hair, twenty but looks younger.'

He paused to let the information sink it. 'You didn't happen to see them, by any chance?'

The factor shook his head. 'No, I didn't. But that's not surprising, seeing that my cottage is at the other end of the estate.' He tapped his chest. 'I had one of my bad bouts, bronchitis. I was in my bed for a week.'

Nudging Faro in the ribs, he chuckled. 'If they were elopers, I doubt they would be flaunting themselves anyhow.'

'I just hoped someone might have spotted them.'

'If they were here, then they were in luck, with the laird away to Italy and the house deserted. Most of the servants are allowed home too.'

When they left him, Faro said: 'Damn. Vince called it being discreet but I was sure that in the country stone walls have eyes and ears and foreigners in the district are noted carefully.'

'In the normal way you'd be right,' Tom agreed. 'There's nothing much goes on in the vicinity without it being a talking point in the servants' hall. Hedgerows have ears and empty windows have eyes all right. The folk here are as alert to the passing of strangers as any guard on duty outside Holyrood Palace.'

Tom was silent for a moment. 'Even if you found someone, what good would all this do, Jeremy? As far as I can see, it wouldn't make one iota of difference to your lad.'

'I realise that. I suppose all I want to do is to prove him right.'

'You've done that. Even if you had a roomful of witnesses that would only prove the Deane girl was a liar. But in the long run, that wouldn't make her change her mind about marrying your lad. And one word of warning, tangling with the Deane family means trouble.'

'So I have heard.'

'Aye, they are powerful enough to do anything they want by bribes or threats – or maybe worse – to close mouths of folk who might be trying to damage their saintly reputation.'

'Are you implying there is something I ought to know, Tom?'

'Perhaps. When I was on the force we had plenty of problems with the family that never reached the public's ears. The lass's mother took her own life, drowned herself in the estate pond over yonder.'

He shrugged. 'I should say that's what was supposed to have happened. But no one was absolutely convinced that she hadn't been given a helping hand. There were other scandals quickly suppressed, pregnant servant girls and so forth, false accusations substantiated by bought witnesses. I shouldn't be telling you this, Jeremy, but I wouldn't be a bit surprised if a lot of money passed hands to buy silences that were really miscarriages of justice.

'If you really want to put the Deane family under the microscope Superintendent Johnston is your man. He wouldn't do it for just anyone, but a senior detective has certain privileges.'

'I know him already. We have worked together on cases in the past.'

'Then he knows anything he tells you will go no further. It's well worth a try, Jeremy.'

The two old friends spent the rest of the visit in happy recollection of the past and of the remarkable advances in police methods of detection over the last twenty years.

As Tom saw him on to the Dundee train, Faro thanked him for all his help.

Tom grinned. 'You know what? I'm glad I'm not young and vulnerable any more. At least we've proved that your lad isn't suffering from some delusion caused by overwork, undernourishment and chronic infatuation.'

As the train slid out of the station, Faro found himself remembering Tom's words which again impinged on that other world, still closed to him. The workings of the human mind and its motives were becoming increasingly the concern of Vince's profession.

His own, the detection of crime, was somewhat more direct and based on tangible evidence and clues left at the scene of the crime or carried away by the criminal. A great deal easier to deal with, he decided, than sorting out the intricacies and vagaries of human behaviour.

Perhaps some day . . .

And he settled back to read the newspaper he had bought and had never had time to open.

'Man Falls under Dundee Train'.

With a sickened feeling of renewed horror, he saw the name Hamish McGowan staring up at him.

9 An elderly man, Mr Hamish McGowan of Groat Street, was fatally injured when he slipped and fell under the wheels of an oncoming train in Dundee Railway Station late last night. There were no witnesses to the accident but according to his widow, McGowan was well-known to suffer from dizzy spells.

When they reached Dundee, Faro called in at the station-master's office.

'Tragic, tragic, Inspector. But you were here yourself when we warned him.'

'Warned him?'

'Yes, indeed. About threatening Mr Wilfred Deane.'

'A moment, please – what has this to do with Mr Deane? Was he expected off the train?'

The station-master looked vague. 'Oh, I don't know about that, Inspector. Actually it wasn't a passenger train, it was the ten o'clock goods train McGowan fell under, but I expect he was lying in wait as usual.'

'What makes you think that?' demanded Faro.

'Well, he was pacing up and down the platform as he always did and I was trying to keep an eye on him.'

'That must have been difficult for you. Surely it was dark by then.'

'Oh, pitch black. But the platform is always lit by gas lamps.' The station-master frowned. 'Of course, it was very windy too. Perhaps he lost his balance,' he added hopefully.

'When was the next train due?'

'At ten thirty, the last one from Perth.'

It seemed unlikely that McGowan would be pacing the platform half an hour before the local passenger train arrived.

What had brought him to the station at that hour? Did he still intend to murder Wilfred Deane despite all his promises?

Faro frowned. He could have sworn that McGowan was a man of his word. So what happened that night to change his mind?

There was only one way to find out. He remembered the scrap of paper he had in his wallet. He would visit the grieving widow but first he must tell Vince the results of his investigations at Errol.

As he let himself into the dismal lodging, Jean McGonagall was waiting for him, her face flowing with suppressed excitement.

'There's been a constable here. Looking for you, Mr Faro.' She paused dramatically. 'You're to go to the police station directly.'

'Did he tell Dr Laurie?'

She shook her head. 'Couldn't, sir. He's not been in. Never came for his supper either. Probably an accident of some kind.'

Faro tried not to think of what that accident might have been or whether the victim in this case might be Vince himself. Cursing the brevity of the constable's message, which he felt had aged him several years, he hurried in the direction of the police station.

'Yes, Inspector Faro. The Superintendent is waiting for you, sir. He's in his office.'

Superintendent Johnston's smile was a trifle wan. He looked embarrassed as they shook hands.

'Sorry about all this, Faro.'

The Superintendent flourished a piece of paper. 'It seems that your stepson, Dr Laurie, has been in a bit of trouble. Taken into custody.'

'What?' If there was any sense of relief mingled with Faro's astonishment, it was that the lad was at least alive and unhurt.

'Here, read it for yourself,' said the Superintendent. With a sympathetic nod, he added: 'The young fellows these days. Impulsive they are.'

Faro quickly read the note signed by the constable on duty. He had been called to Deane Hall where Dr Vincent Beaumarcher Laurie had been restrained and subsequently put under arrest for 'violent behaviour and abusive language and threatening bodily harm to Mr Wilfred Deane'.

Faro cursed. 'My apologies, sir. This really is too bad. After all his promises of good behaviour too.'

'I gather the young man is enamoured of Miss Deane.' The Superintendent raised his eyes heavenward. 'We must make allowances for infatuations. We older folk have lived long enough to regard falling in love as a temporary state of insanity,' he added with a sigh.

Faro gave him a sharp glance. A married man with six children at the last count, Johnston no doubt spoke from a wealth of experience.

Leaning forward resting his elbows on the desk, the Superintendent said: 'Well, Faro, what are we to do? I am reluctant to have this go any further – the scandal and so forth. We don't want to bring this into the court and neither – to give them credit, for I gather this is not the first offence – do the Deane family.'

Rubbing his chin thoughtfully he added: 'If you could possibly guarantee his behaviour in future, the weight of your reputation will be enough to placate them, I fancy.' And when Faro looked doubtful, 'They are showing considerable patience and forbearance, you know. So is this young lady who is being constantly harassed. Do you think you could talk some sense into the lad?'

He frowned over the constable's note again as if there was something he might have missed the first time. 'I gather the damage to property included the smashing of a window and a valuable vase in the hall. Chinese it was, cost a hundred pounds—'

Faro groaned. What on earth had possessed Vince to behave in this ridiculous manner? 'I will settle the account. And you have my word that I will do my very best to ensure that my stepson keeps well away from Deane Hall in future.'

As they shook hands, Johnston smiled. He looked relieved. 'It was good to see you again, Faro. Look, let's have dinner together. I'll consult the wife and see what we have on. Staying long?'

'Alas, no. I'm due back at the Central Office early next week.'

'In that case we had better make it lunch at my club tomorrow. Pity you're going so soon.'

It was indeed, thought Faro, just three days to sort out the mess Vince was making of his life. Almost certain that Vince would lose his job over this fiasco and, what was worse, would not be given a reference, Faro realised there was a distinct possibility that he would not be returning to Edinburgh alone.

The real tragedy was that Vince's reckless behaviour might have cost him his future as a doctor, for Faro could not imagine Sir Arnold, once he heard about this evening's events, ever letting the young madman set foot across his threshold to threaten his family and terrify his granddaughter.

Accompanying him to the door, the Superintendent said: 'Until tomorrow, then?' And with a final sympathetic smile, 'As I said before, it's a pity you can't stay around until this business blows over. We'd all be happier if you were keeping an eye on the lad.'

'And so would I, but I can't be keeper to a grown man. He has to lead his own life. For better or for worse.'

'Caution him as best you can, Faro. If he does it again or makes a nuisance of himself in any way we'll have to put him inside. And if it comes to fisticuffs, as you well know, the scandal could finish him. Impress that upon him and for God's sake tell him to grow up. He'll soon meet someone else. There's better fish in the sea . . .'

But the time-worn cliché didn't console Faro or Vince, or put either of them in a better frame of mind.

Vince was pathetically eager to see him, a study in relief when he saw his stepfather walking down towards the cell where he was under guard.

Faro's hopes, however, sank to zero when his stepson emerged. Always so spruce and elegant, now unkempt, unshaven, and looking as if he hadn't slept for several days, he had obviously been drinking heavily.

Taking him firmly by the arm and saying, 'We'll talk later,' Faro marched him out of the police station. Once outside, he could restrain himself no longer. 'For God's sake, Vince, you look terrible.'

'And disgusting, don't I? Frankly I don't care what I look like, I don't care about anything any more. Particularly at this moment, whether I live or die—'

'That's your decision,' said Faro coldly, momentarily lacking his usual compassion and understanding. 'I've just come from a harrowing interview with the Superintendent.'

'So you know all about my shocking behaviour.'

He didn't sound contrite in the least. However, the expression on Faro's face as he looked in his direction halted him. As of old, he knew when he had gone too far.

'I'm sorry, Stepfather, really I am. Getting you involved like this.'

'And so you should be. You haven't given me a red face before anyone since your schooldays. And now I find myself having to guarantee your good behaviour. It really isn't good enough, after all your promises.'

'I've said I'm sorry—'

'Then I'd like to see you act like it, instead of being an impulsive young fool and getting the police into all this. If you hadn't had me on hand, you'd be cooling your heels in that prison cell with the door locked until your case came up before the court. Don't you realise what you're doing?'

Vince was silent and Faro stopped in his tracks, pulled him

roughly by the shoulders to face him. 'Look, lad, before we go any further I want your word, your solemn promise, now, before I leave Dundee, that you will stay away from Rachel Deane.'

Faro hadn't spoken so severely to his stepson since the latter was nine years old and had played truant from school. He might have grown up but that look of mutinous hostility carried Faro right back through the years. To the early days of his marriage to Vince's mother Lizzie when he had been faced by the implacable hatred of her illegitimate son.

Now almost as soon as he had noticed it, it was gone, replaced by Vince's most charming smile, albeit apologetic and a trifle wan. 'All right, Stepfather. I give you my word. Here's my hand on it. No more assaults upon Deane Hall. Although I'd like to kill Wilfred Deane. Smug smiling bastard. Oh, I'm sorry, Stepfather.'

'Being sorry is not enough. Did you ever look ahead for one moment and consider the fact that your infantile behaviour might cost you your post here with Deane's and seriously jeopardise any future one you might consider applying for? Can you in all honesty see them giving you a reference after such atrocious behaviour?'

Vince wilted under his stepfather's cold anger. 'I just wanted to try once more. That was all. I was very polite. But this time Wilfred Deane opened the door and said that Rachel was not at home and that if I continued these harassments then they would call the police.'

'Which he was quite at liberty to do if he felt they were being harassed.'

Vince ignored that. 'I argued with him, but I didn't lay a hand on him.' He clenched his fists, remembering. 'I could have choked the smug bastard, smiling at me, daring me to make a move. I called out Rachel's name, hoping she might hear and come and help me. Then the butler took over and between them they threw me out bodily. As for Rachel, she had never showed her face. Not a sign of her. But she was at home.'

'How do you know that?' Faro demanded sharply.

'They were lying. As I picked myself up from the drive, I saw her at one of the upstairs windows. Watching me. Never lifting a finger in protest. That was too much. I'm afraid I assaulted the front door and when no one came, I threw a stone through the window. You know the rest,' he said shamefacedly. 'Dear God, what am I to do?'

'Stay away from Deane Hall, for a start.'

Faro was furious. Anyone but Vince could see with half an eye that the girl no longer cared for him. Whatever motives had led her to that brief infatuation were now over and she deeply regretted her lapse from virtue.

Again he found himself wondering whether some quirk in her mind they did not fully understand had led her to seek an amorous adventure with her grandfather's handsome young doctor.

However, when she realised that his intentions were serious, she had coldly calculated, or had been made by her family to calculate, that she could not possibly exchange her life of luxury and plenty at Deane Hall for something which would seem to her by comparison only a little better than the squalor in which their workers lived.

As Paton's Lane approached, Faro said: 'You were speaking the truth. About the cottage, I mean. At least I've proved that. I've been to Errol for the day.'

Vince looked up, suddenly hopeful. 'You have? Oh thank you, Stepfather. Thank you. Did you see Rachel's old nurse? Did she tell you?'

Faro opened the door of his room. 'Sit down, lad.' It was very puzzling and to avoid arousing Vince's wrath with probing questions he had to proceed with great caution. At the end of his account Vince shook his head dully.

'I think I'll go to bed, Stepfather. Will you excuse me? This has been quite a day and I don't think I'm capable of coherent thought any more.'

As his stepson left, he embraced him: 'There, there, lad. Don't worry. We'll sort it all out.'

Vince smiled. 'Thank you, Stepfather. What was it I used to say when I was a little chap? I'll try to be a credit to you.'

'Something like that. Sleep well, lad.'

Putting his head round the door, Vince asked: 'Is it true? Must you go back to Edinburgh soon?' The question was followed by a look of disappointment and distress when Faro replied: 'Monday afternoon. Sharp.'

Vince swore. 'Now you'll never meet Rachel. Now you'll never know or understand how I adore her. And yet it's just as well. I guessed at that first meeting that you weren't terribly impressed,' he added with a shrewd glance.

'We didn't have much chance to get acquainted,' said Faro uncomfortably, heartily glad that it was unlikely he'd have the embarrassment of a second encounter.

In that as in so many things concerning Vince and Rachel Deane, he was to be completely mistaken.

10 Promises, it seemed to Faro just then, were easy to make and easy to break. However, it was a very shame-faced Vince he met at breakfast next morning.

'I promise not to get into any more trouble, Stepfather. You have my word.'

You have my word. McGowan had said that. Yet only twenty-four hours later he had been back at Dundee Station, pacing the platform, a madman stalking his quarry once again.

Perhaps it would be better to shrug off the whole incident, but Faro's sense of fair play demanded some sort of explanation for McGowan's rash behaviour which had cost him his life.

'How do I get to Groat Street?' And as Vince gave him directions he said, 'I'm hoping to see McGowan's widow.'

'McGowan? The man who was threatening Wilfred Deane?'

'The man who believed that his son's death was no accident and whose daughter-in-law has mysteriously disappeared.'

'I can well see that he felt justified in wishing to kill Deane,' said Vince grimly.

At the door, Faro turned. 'Have you half an hour to spare? Good. Would you care to accompany me?'

In Groat Street they climbed the winding stone stairs of a tenement similar in every way to the one they had left in Paton's Lane.

The door was opened by a young woman in mourning dress.

'I have come to pay my condolences to Mrs McGowan,' said Faro, wondering how he was to explain that he was a detective.

The young woman shook her head. 'Ma's no' very well. She's in her bed. I canna get her to see the doctor and her so poorly.'

Vince smiled and stepped forward. 'Perhaps I can help. I am the doctor at Deane's.'

'Oh sir, would you take a look at her? Her heart has always been bad but this shock of Da being killed—' She shook her head and left the sentence unfinished.

Mrs McGowan lay in the bed in the kitchen recess since the bedroom was occupied by her husband's coffin. Even to Faro's eyes she did look very poorly indeed. As Vince bent over her, he took a seat at the table opposite McGowan's daughter.

'Have you any idea how this dreadful accident happened?'

'All I could get from Ma was that he had someone to meet. He told her it wouldna' take long and that he'd be back for his supper. The next thing she knew was the police at the door.'

Her eyes filled with tears and she left him abruptly to refill the kettle at the kitchen sink. 'You'll both have a cup of tea?'

Vince, having completed his examination, said: 'She is very weak but there is no immediate cause for alarm. Plenty of rest and good nourishing food. I am sure you know better than anyone how to take good care of your mother,' he added with a smile.

The young woman shrugged, pouring out the tea. 'I may not be staying very long. I'm living in Liverpool now. It is just by chance that I happen to be here at all, on the way back from my young sister's wedding.' And glancing towards the bed:

'She's no' my ma. I was married to Charlie McGowan.'

So this was the missing widow.

'Your father-in-law was very anxious about you.'

'I know and I'm sorry about that. You see, I couldn't really tell them. They'd have been that upset. They thought Charlie and me were happy together, but that wasn't the way of it at all. I had already decided to leave him. I went a couple of days before the accident.'

She gave a shrug of distaste. 'He was going with another woman, some lass he worked with, and I'd gone back to my lad that I let down to marry Charlie. I left a letter, but he must never have told his folks. Too ashamed, because they thought the world of him.

'I only heard through my sister that he was dead. I got a shock, I can tell you. I didn't want to come here. I was too embarrassed to explain it all. However, when I was home this time, my folks told me that I should come and see the McGowans because they thought something had happened to me. Well, something had,' she added grimly, 'but not what they thought.'

She sighed. 'Now at least poor Pa McGowan will never know the truth about us. I'm glad he's been spared that.'

They left shortly afterwards, Vince promising to look in and see Mrs McGowan again.

'Well, what do you make of that, Stepfather?'

'One missing woman accounted for, and with a simple explanation for her movements.'

'After that, I shouldn't be in the least surprised if the fair Kathleen walks into Paton's Lane hale and hearty one day.'

Faro smiled. 'You will let me know?'

'I will indeed. At least this is one mystery happily solved.'

'One mystery that existed only in poor McGowan's mind.'

Was that the answer? Had McGowan meant to fall under that train, thought Faro as he walked to the club where he was meeting Superintendent Johnston for lunch, the one person who might be able to offer some discreet and helpful advice regarding the Deane family. At the end of a meal, with more sirloin of beef inside him than a starving Dundee family saw in a year, thought Faro guiltily, he realised there would never be a better moment to question the now mellow Superintendent.

As they sipped their brandy, he said, 'I wonder if you could give me some confidential information.'

'Willingly, if I can.' Johnston smiled benignly.

'It's about the Deane family.'

'Indeed.' Faro felt that a shadow of reserve had come over his friend's manner. 'What was it you wanted to know?' was the cautious response.

'Oh, just something of their family history.'

The Superintendent leaned forward. 'Are your people on to this?' he demanded sharply.

'I'm not sure what you mean.'

'Your special branch. Have they got wind of it?'

'Wind of what?'

Johnston leaned back in his chair with a sigh of relief. 'I'm not sure whether I should talk about this, even to you, although there's nobody I'd trust more in normal circumstances.'

He hesitated before continuing. 'I dare say it will all come out in the not too distant future but the position regarding Deane's is that we're investigating a massive case of fraud concerning the building of the bridge. We're in the very early stages and we don't want to scare anyone off.'

He laughed uneasily. 'It gave me quite a nasty turn when I thought the Edinburgh Police were on to it.'

Faro shook his head. 'No. My reason is rather more personal.'

'I should have realised that. Your stepson, of course.'

Faro broke a silence that threatened to be lengthy. 'Now you've aroused my curiosity, sir. I have always understood that Deane was the soul of respectability, a pillar of society and a public benefactor.'

'So did everyone else, until recently. As you know they have the contract for the bridge. Fought tooth and nail to get it, plenty of competitors too. Even without undercutting everyone else in the field, they were the obvious choice, with their background – the Baron of Broughty and all that sort of thing.'

Again he paused so long that Faro prompted him. 'Do go on.'

Johnston nodded in the manner of a man who comes to a sudden decision. 'Well, things seemed to be fine at the beginning and then there was a series of misfortunes. The bridge was to be finished in two years. Any fool could see that it wasn't possible, but lately there have been a staggering number of accidents.

'Vince is the factory doctor, so I know something of them.'

'Well, the accidents seem to have been due to shoddy materials and poor workmanship – gantries collapsing, piers sunk without careful knowledge of the rock formation. As you've maybe heard, the Tay is a tricky river at the best of times, subject to violent storms and high winds which haven't helped much.'

Faro smiled. 'I've experienced several kinds of remarkable weather in the few days I've been here.'

Johnston nodded. 'One of our detectives whose nephew was lost decided to take a further look, employing some plain-clothes men as navvies. The things the humble constable has to take in his stride. Anyway, he discovered that the sound materials which had been ordered and paid for had often been replaced by cheaper, less substantial and, indeed, often inferior ones.'

He tapped his fingers against his glass. 'In other words, Faro, someone has been making a hefty packet out of the enterprise. But this is no ordinary fraud, this is tantamount to murder when you consider the lives that have been endangered.'

It was a shocking story and confirmed what McGowan had told him of his son's discovery.

'This man McGowan who fell under the train—'

Johnson nodded and Faro continued: 'He told me that his son who worked in the finance department suspected fraudulent dealings.'

'Precisely. It was from him we received our first inklings.'

'Were you not suspicious then, when he so conveniently met with an accident on the bridge?'

'Of course we were. First the man Simms and then young McGowan. The two prime witnesses in a fraud enquiry.'

'Then why didn't you do something about it?' asked Faro angrily.

'Look, Faro, you know the rules as well as I do. They were both dead and we had nothing yet to prove our suspicions. But if we stormed in with accusations at this delicate stage, we'd alert whoever was guilty. Then Simms and McGowan would have died in vain.'

His reasoning didn't please Faro. This wasn't the way he worked even if there was a kind of logic about it. 'Can nothing be done about the bridge at this stage?'

'Not without tearing down the whole structure and starting again. And we'd certainly never be able to convince the shareholders that we were acting in the passengers' best interests. Or that poorer materials than those ordered had been used and that careless measurements had been made. They would simply laugh at us. After all, they have big money at stake. And that is what counts. Not human lives, Faro. Money and secure investments.'

'But if this goes on and the bridge is ever completed, you realise the danger. A trainload of passengers. My God, to sit back and do nothing is quite unthinkable.'

'We could all be wrong, you know. It is maybe not as serious as it sounds. We can do nothing meantime but if this fraud is proved then we will certainly insist that the work so far be properly reinforced to make it doubly secure.'

'Let us hope that it isn't too late and that your bridge isn't already doomed.'

Johnston frowned. 'Of course, it will cause a lot of bother. Delaying completion for a few more years will greatly distress the shareholders.'

'Damn the shareholders. What do their feelings matter when the whole bridge may fall in the first storm and take a full passenger train with it?' Faro shuddered. 'Dear God, it doesn't bear thinking about.'

'We've already been warned about that.' A moment later Johnston added casually, 'Not psychic by any chance, are you, Inspector?'

'Not that I admit to.'

'Then you needn't worry. My mother was Highland and I get the odd quiver now and again. One of our famous citizens was the Seer of Gourdie.'

'Yes, I've heard of him.'

'He was remarkably accurate about his own and other people's lives, foretelling his own death and other major, less personal events.'

'And he predicted that this rainbow bridge would fall. I heard about that.'

Johnston nodded. 'Of course, everyone laughed at such an idea. Took refuge in the knowlege that old Patrick Matthews was born in the eighteenth century. What could a man with old-fashioned ideas possibly understand about the marvels of modern progress and science?' Johnson paused and regarded him grimly. 'I just hope he's wrong.'

'And if he's right, that there's no train going across at the time it falls,' Faro repeated in worried tones, for the enormity of Johnson's revelations had thrust all else aside.

While the waiter replenished their glasses, Johnston asked: 'How is your stepson today? Has he recovered from his temporary experience of police hospitality?' he added with a grin.

'I hope so. I gave him a good talking to and extracted a promise that he would keep away from Deane Hall.'

Johnston sat back in his chair. 'Poor lad. If it isn't too late I'd implore him to steer clear of Rachel Deane. Forget about her.'

'How so?' demanded Faro sharply.

The Superintendent shrugged. 'Because the lass isn't – well, stable, let's say. She had a family history of mental illness; her mother and father were first cousins and Mrs Deane committed suicide while the lass was still a bairn.'

'One of my friends, Tom Elgin, whom you may remember, told me about that when I was visiting him.'

The Superintendent nodded. 'As is often the case in these

close-knit families, they waver between producing brilliant sons and simpletons.'

'Do you know Miss Deane personally?'

'We've visited the house socially through the years. And I've never been left with a very good impression. Rude, wild, and liable to throw the soup at the maid if it didn't please her. The kind that makes you grind your teeth and if there wasn't the excuse of some kind of mental disturbance, then you'd be tempted to take the hairbrush to her backside.'

'Has she ever been under restraint?'

'You mean put away? No, that possibility has never been raised. Not strictly necessary in her case since she had never been a danger, so far as I have heard, to anyone but herself. If she'd been in poorer circumstances there might have been some reason, but fortunately for her, Deane Hall is a big place. When she has these erratic outbursts from time to time, I gather she can be effectively put under restraint at home.'

'But this girl is the heiress, the whole of Deane's fortune comes to her as the only offspring.'

'That has been taken care of. Wilfred Deane, her second cousin, is in charge of the family finances and in fact is virtually top man since Sir Arnold's illness. He wants to marry her. Did your stepson mention that?'

'No. First I've heard of it.'

'Well, give the girl her due, she is not to be pushed into marriage either. Just as well,' said Johnston.

'You mean—'

'If this embezzlement business is proved, Wilfred Deane is likely to be spending some years behind bars.'

What an unholy mess. Faro walked back to Paton's Lane feeling considerably upset. How could he tell Vince that Rachel Deane had obviously escaped her supervised seclusion in Deane Hall only long enough to indulge her appetite for romance? Perhaps any man would have done just as well. The butler for instance.

But how to tell his lovesick stepson that his first great love, the consummation of his passion, had been with a girl with a family history of madness. A girl he could never hope to make his wife, even if she had not denied ever knowing him.

Johnston's revelations explained her violent reaction but how could he tactfully warn Vince? He rephrased over and over the words he would need and discarded them all as totally inadequate consolation for Vince in his present state of mind.

Gloomily aware that by now his stepson might have another pressing problem, in the form of dismissal from his situation as factory doctor, he climbed the stairs to their lodging.

Vince bounded towards him, beaming with delight. But the letter in his hand was the last that Faro expected.

'Guess what, Stepfather. I've had a note from Rachel. I knew – I told you – it was all her family's doing. And I was right. She wants me to meet her. I knew she still loves me. And she does.' He flourished a piece of paper. 'Read that. Read it. Now you'll be convinced.'

And Faro realised that any words of warning he might care to offer were now too late.

11

Dearest Vince. Meet me at Magdalen Green (where we met once before by the bridge) at 7 this evening. I will explain everything then. Do not fail me. I love you. Your Rachel.

Faro handed the note back. He was speechless.

'Well, Stepfather. What do you think of that?' demanded Vince triumphantly.

Highly suspicious were the first two words that occurred to Faro. He could not bring himself to respond to Vince's enthusiasm and utter the encouragement expected of him. Somewhat hesitantly, he said, 'I presume there is no doubt that this is Rachel's handwriting?'

'Really, Stepfather,' was the scornful rejoinder, 'I do know her handwriting. For heaven's sake, this is their crested notepaper, too. And I have other notes from her. Here,' he added taking out his pocket case. 'Read them if you wish. Check them carefully,' he added stiffly.

'No need for that, lad.'

'Thank you.' Vince's words were tinged with sarcasm as he replaced the notes, but on his lips was a dreamlike smile. Now that he believed Rachel Deane loved him, he was ready, even eager, to forget all the indignities she had heaped upon him. It was as if the last two days had never happened and Vince was about to rush headlong into the fantasy world they, or most likely he, had created.

'I can hardly believe it, after all that has happened.'

Neither can I, lad. Neither can I, thought Faro gloomily. 'It's like a miracle.'

A miracle or another cruel trick to destroy his stepson, he thought, listening to Vince now full of plans and speculations, all highly romantic and, Faro decided, highly impractical.

'Her grandfather dotes upon her and I have not the least doubt that she has persuaded him to let us marry. Don't you agree?' And not waiting for a reply, 'That swine Wilfred must have been the stumbling block. No doubt she will tell me all about it—'

Faro cut him short. 'Wait a moment, lad. Why all the secrecy? If she has the family approval, surely she or her grandfather might have invited you up to the house?'

He had to do his best to warn Vince that all might not be as he anticipated. He succeeded, for Vince looked suddenly thoughtful.

'Yes, that is a possibility I hadn't considered. Another is that she is making her escape from Deane Hall and wishes us to elope. That is something we have discussed before, in happier days,' he added wistfully. 'After all, she will be of age in two weeks' time—'

The more Faro listened, the more convinced he became that the note from Rachel and the whole situation it conjured up were deeply suspicious. A situation that Vince, in a sane mood, would have regarded with the utmost caution.

Watching his stepson prepare for the meeting, whistling happily, filled Faro with ominous dread that this time Vince himself might be in danger. When he emerged shaved and well groomed, wearing his best suit and cravat, every trace of any recent despondency had vanished completely. Young and handsome, he was revitalised by his lost love returned.

At six thirty the sky clouded over. The weather had changed, a squally wind followed by heavy rain indicated that a storm was blowing up the Tay.

Vince mistook his stepfather's sombre countenance for anxiety about the weather. 'How exasperating!'

It was just a few minutes' walk from Paton's Lane to Magdalen Green but on a night like this, with forebodings of disaster pricking like daggers in his mind, Faro came to a sudden decision. 'We'll need to take a carriage. And I'm coming with you.'

'But – but there is absolutely no necessity—'

'It's all right, lad, I promise not to intrude. I shall remain discreetly inside the carriage.' And in a flash of pure invention, 'You see, it's just occurred to me that if you're eloping, the assistance of a third party might be extremely useful.'

'Well done, Stepfather. It never entered my head. You do think of everything, don't you?'

Hiring carriages on the busy main road from the railway station were readily accessible. At five minutes to seven they reached Magdalen Green. As the road near the bridge offered little shelter but a large quantity of mud underfoot, the cab driver agreed that for another shilling they might wait inside the carriage.

Those last few minutes were an eternity for Vince and a gnawing anxiety for his stepfather. The bridge was empty of workmen now, with gaslight flares to help the night-watchman in his task.

The swaying lanterns reflected the ghostly dark shapes of the piers of the bridge. No longer echoing with the sound of daytime hammerings, the creak and groan of cranes and pulleys as they elevated their heavy baskets to the higher platforms, only the wind whistled eerily, rustling up a tide which tugged and dragged at the half-finished girders.

Seven o'clock struck and faded away, but there was no sign of Rachel.

As for Faro, he became more convinced with every passing moment that Rachel herself would not appear, as his sinking heart told him that this had been yet another cruel practical joke at Vince's expense.

Nevertheless, he was now watchful, alert to possible danger. If that note had been a ruse to lure Vince to this lonely place, then the lad might be in mortal peril, with paid assassins lurking in the dark shadows of the bridge.

They were in for a surprise, he thought grimly, feeling triumphant and thankful that he had spoilt their plan by accompanying Vince to this assignation. He and Vince had been in many similar scrapes and they had acquitted themselves nobly, more than a match for their adversaries. Wishing he had not left his pistol in Edinburgh, he now looked for something that might be used in defence as well as their own fists.

In the flickering gaslight, he could see by Vince's eager face that he had not the least suspicion that anything was amiss. Hopeful, his spirits buoyant, he whistled under his breath.

'This carriage was a good idea of yours, Stepfather. We would be getting very wet indeed, wouldn't we?'

Through the window which they had reeled down, they could see the darkness of the river speckled with white horses and Faro remembered ominously Shakespeare's 'Seas do laugh, show white, when rocks are near.'

The rain had ceased, revealing a full moon drifting through occasional breaks in the clouds. Faro glanced at Vince. Was he remembering its effects on lunatic patients? And a voice inside whispered: 'How then will it affect Rachel Deane?'

Now the occasional boom of sea lapping the shore competed with an eldritch wind, rattling here and there some loose segment on the piers above their heads.

Seven fifteen struck from a church clock nearby and Faro was about to suggest that they wait no longer, when Vince seized his arm:

'Listen.'

A closed carriage approached.

Faro leaned forward expectantly. Could it be Rachel?

'There she is. There she is.'

But the carriage swept past them and stopped twenty yards further down the road near the bridge.

'It must be her. Of course, she was expecting me to be on foot.' He leaped out. 'Rachel, Rachel. Over here.'

Faro watched from the window as Vince ran down the road to greet the girl who emerged from the carriage.

Now she was close enough for Faro to observe in the wavering gaslight that she was in a state of considerable excitement, or distress, or apprehension. Considering the inclement weather she was most inadequately clad, he thought. A light shawl only partially covered a plain dark dress, her hair hidden under a tall bonnet tied firmly under her chin. And that fretful wind, tearing at her gown, revealed light slippers.

Faro sighed. She carried only a small reticule over her wrist, hardly the luggage of a young lady intending to elope. Here was no triumphant mistress, blessed with family approval, coming to meet her lover. Appearances hinted that her departure from Deane Hall had been in some confusion and haste and that she wished to keep her assignation secret.

Vince had reached her side, arms outstretched in a lover's embrace. But again all was not well. Over Vince's shoulder she was staring at the carriage. She had caught sight of Faro and he saw her thrust Vince away so savagely that he staggered off balance and slipped on the wet road.

'Get away from me,' she cried. 'Leave me alone.'

Taken aback by the violence of the girl's reaction, Faro was never quite certain what happened next. Even as he sprang from the carriage to assist Vince to his feet, Rachel Deane ran swiftly down the road.

Vince was doubled up, winded, clutching his stomach. It was obvious, thought Faro grimly, that the innocent Miss Rachel knew something about self-defence too.

'Oh God, why did she do that? I didn't mean to upset her. Where is she? Tell her to come back.'

The gas flares illuminated her flight down the road towards the bridge. Once a cab came along and for a moment she seemed to be trying to make it stop. Then changing her mind she ran alongside the wooden fence. Some six feet high, its purpose was to keep at bay inquisitive children and deter any unauthorised persons from exploring the unfinished bridge.

As they followed her, even the elements turned against them.

With heavy rain renewed and driving into their faces, by the time they reached the gate and discovered it was locked, Rachel Deane had found another entrance.

A tiny figure in a billowing gown, she was already high above their heads, climbing steadily the swaying ladder on the bridge's first pier.

As Vince shook the gates, shouting: 'Rachel, Rachel, come back,' Faro examined the padlock.

12

'She didn't go in here. There must be some other way in.'

They found it easily. A few yards away, a broken plank in the fence. A narrow gap that only a very slender girl could have contemplated.

As Vince and Faro tried to squeeze through, a night-watchman, alerted by the voices raised above the gale, appeared from his hut. He carried a lantern and was yawning, obviously just awake.

'What's going on?' he demanded sleepily. 'No one's allowed to come in here.'

'Let us in. Open the door, I am a doctor,' said Vince.

The man glared at him and shook his head obstinately. 'Whatever you are, I canna open that gate without proper authority. More than my job's worth.'

'So is sleeping on duty,' snapped Vince.

'Is that so—'

'Stop arguing,' Faro interrupted. 'Look over there, a girl is climbing on to the bridge.'

'A girl? You must be mistaken. No one's come in here without me seeing them—'

'Use your eyes, man. Over there!'

The watchman raised his lantern. 'She canna do that,' he cried indignantly. 'It's not allowed. She'll get into an awfa' row for that—'

'Use your eyes, man. Over there!'

'For heaven's sake, man, don't you see, she's in danger. She could fall to her death, if we don't stop her. Now will you unlock this door?'

As the man withdrew his set of keys, he said: 'I still don't see how she got in—'

'She came through a hole in the fence. Down there.'

The watchman sidled down towards the gap and inspected it, frowning. 'Well now, I'd better get that fixed. Some laddies must have been up to mischief. There'll be trouble when Mr Deane finds out. Very safety conscious, he is.'

'For God's sake, will you open this door,' said Vince.

'Steady on there, sir. Steady on.' And misinterpreting Vince's desperation he said: 'Been at the bottle, have you, laddie? Go home and sleep it off.'

As Vince shook the gate savagely once again, he added sternly, 'Now, now, damage Deane's property and I'll need to get the polis to you.'

That was the key. Cursing himself for not having thought of it before, Faro said: 'I'm an Inspector of Police, and Superintendent Johnston will vouch for me. Dr Laurie here works for Deane's.'

The watchman, who was considerably smaller and slighter than the two men who faced him, now held the lantern high and peered into their faces. 'Dr Laurie. So you are. So you are, sir. You should have said so. I expect it'll be all right to let you in.'

And unlocking the gate, he added sympathetically, 'One of your escaped patients is it, sir?'

But Vince and Faro had pushed past him and were already in headlong pursuit of Rachel. His vociferous protests followed as he tried vainly to keep up with them.

'Wait a minute, gentlemen. I'll need to come with you. I'm not supposed to let anyone on the bridge. It's more than my job's worth.'

But neither heeded him.

'Look. Look. Up there.'

In the gaslight's feeble flare they saw Rachel Deane, now thirty feet above them, a tiny windswept figure clinging to the ironwork. She had reached the first platform of the pier.

'Rachel. For God's sake, come back—'

For a moment she paused, a pale face looked down at them.

'Stay there, Rachel. Don't move. I'm coming up.'

Horrified, Faro caught up with Vince at the base of the ladder. Rachel had discarded her satin slippers to make her climb easier, abandoning her reticule to free her hands. Vince thrust the slippers into his pocket and Faro seized the reticule as they began their ascent of the frail ladder.

'Come back, come back,' shouted the watchman. 'It'll no' hold the lot of you. You'll all be killed.'

Vince remained where he was looking upwards. Rachel had disappeared momentarily, concealed by the frail wooden shield erected to protect workmen from the worst of the weather.

'Wait there, Rachel. It's all right. I'll be with you—'

Even as Vince spoke, she reappeared and began a steady and rapid climb towards the second platform some eighty feet above their heads.

'Rachel, Rachel. Stop, for God's sake, stop.'

But Vince's plea, even if she heard it, did not deter her from her purpose. Now far behind Vince, Faro sighed with relief as he saw her reach the second frail shelter in safety.

'You can't go any further, Rachel. Please stay there.'

He heard the terror and agony in Vince's voice as with one faint cry, Rachel hurtled downwards past them.

Clinging to the ironwork, they felt the violent movement of air as her dark gown billowing out transformed her into some gigantic winged bird.

A second later, the turbulent waters of the Tay blossomed into a white rose of death to receive her. Then the blackness closed over once more and all was still.

Knowing that she could stay alive only seconds in those icy

waters, both men began sliding, scrambling down the ironwork, oblivious of torn clothes, bruised and bleeding hands.

On firm ground again, Vince cried out, 'Oh God – oh God—' and discarding his coat raced towards the water's edge.

Faro followed, his mind working coldly, his intention at all costs to prevent Vince from plunging into that swift-moving river with some mad idea of saving Rachel Deane. She was past saving. She could not have survived that terrible fall. As for Vince, an indifferent swimmer at the best of times, any attempt at rescue and he too would be a dead man.

'Let me go to her, damn you, damn you.' But Faro held him firm.

'No. No, I beg you – don't.' As they struggled, Vince cursing, Faro pleading, imploring, the watchman panted alongside.

'See, there's a rowing boat down yonder. Take it. I'll go and get help,' he yelled.

Vince and Faro sprang down the pebbled beach, pushed out the boat, leaped in and seized an oar each. Even with two strong men rowing for dear life, the river almost won that bitter struggle. At last they were near the spot where Rachel had fallen. Or had jumped into the dark waters.

Steadying the boat against the vicious tide, they circled, calling her name.

'Rachel. Rachel.'

But even Vince now knew that the battle was lost. Even if she had survived the fall, too much time had now elapsed. There was no longer the faintest possibility of finding her still alive.

A shadow floated towards them. A body, thought Faro for one heart-stopping moment, as he leaned over and fished out a shawl.

Wordlessly he handed it to Vince who clutched that pathetically sodden garment Rachel had worn. Hugging it to him, he sobbed, whispering her name over and over.

'Rachel, Rachel. Why – why? In God's name – why?'

And still with all hope vanquished, they could not return to the shore. Round and round they rowed the boat, stopping now and then to stare at the waters, at some imagined floating object.

Time had ceased to exist. They were both numb with cold and speechless with shock and horror, when Faro became aware that other vessels had joined them in the search.

A voice called from the dark shadow of a deck above their heads. The lifeboat from Broughty Ferry. 'We'll take over, lads. You return to shore. It's too dangerous. There's a gale blowing up.'

Vince shook his head, shouted: 'No. No. We are going to find her.'

Faro, dazed, realised that his feet and trouser legs were sodden. The boat was already half full of water. He began to steer for the shore.

'We'll get another boat, lad. Yes, we'll go on searching. But not in this one. See, we're sinking rapidly.' Raising his voice against the wind, he shouted down Vince's protests.

As they struck the pebbled beach again, he glanced up at the bridge. It was no longer deserted, there were many lights now as workmen in overalls swarmed over the girders holding flickering torches to assist in the search.

Two workmen in overalls were approaching the very spot where Rachel had fallen, from all appearances carrying out a minute inspection.

Faro cursed. And no doubt getting rid of any damning evidence as to what had caused Rachel's death-fall, he thought, following Vince along the river edge in quest of another rowboat.

Suddenly a shout from the lifeboat about twenty yards from the shore. Torches moved in closer and they watched, sick with horror, as a sodden shapeless mass was pulled aboard.

The lifeless body of Rachel Deane.

'Rachel,' Vince screamed, lunging towards the water.

'No. No, lad,' said Faro and held his stepson, sobbing, while the boat with its dread burden drew ashore.

A small crowd had already gathered and Vince wrenched

himself free of his stepfather's restraining arms. Head held high, he waded out into the shallows. From the boatman he gently took Rachel and carried her across to the greensward.

She looked so small, thought Faro, as if death had already diminished her. Tiny feet and hands, the gown clinging to the outlines of a childlike body, the bonnet drenched and shapeless but still tied firmly beneath her chin.

Chafing her hands and feet, Vince put his hands into his pockets and drawing out the satin slippers she had abandoned for that fateful climb, he tried to replace them on her feet, so stiff and cold and unyielding.

The alert had been given, the police van and an assortment of carriages were arriving as Vince bent over her and with considerable difficulty tried to untie her bonnet strings.

At last he succeeded and tenderly he spread out her dark hair, like a mantle about her shoulders. And it seemed to Faro, fighting back his own tears, that ruffled by the wind it was the only part of Rachel Deane that moved and lived.

Suddenly the watchers were pushed aside.

'Let me through. Let me through.'

Faro recognised the newcomer as Wilfred Deane, who took one look at the still form of Rachel and dropped on his knees beside her.

'Oh dear God – dear God,' he cried as thrusting Vince away, he took over, trying in vain to chafe life back into her cold hands.

Vince watched him. 'Too late. You are too late,' he said dully.

Deane looked up, recognised him and sprang to his feet. 'Damn you, Laurie, this is all your doing. I might have guessed you had a hand in it. If you'd left her alone, none of this would have ever happened. Dear God, to take her own life.'

Deane swayed where he stood, his face ghastly in the pale light as two constables came forward with a stretcher.

'I will go with her,' said Vince.

Deane seized his arm. 'Oh no, you will not. You have done enough, damn you.'

'I'm a doctor—'

'A fine doctor. More like an executioner. Her murderer, that's what you are.' His voice rose to a screech. 'A callous brutal murderer. And, mark my words, you would hang for this night's work, yes hang, if I had my way—'

His face contorted with hate, Deane lunged forward. Faro seized Vince's arm and Deane's fist hit thin air.

'Gentlemen, gentlemen, I beg you. This won't get you anywhere,' he said desperately. 'Try to be calm, for God's sake.'

Deane turned on him ferociously. 'We tried to warn him that my poor cousin was unbalanced.'

'She was not—'

'She was unbalanced,' Deane said slowly, 'and has been subject to fits of irresponsible behaviour since childhood. We all knew about it and tried to keep her from emotional involvements.' With a shake of his head, he added: 'We were warned long ago that such could throw her over the brink into madness—'

'You lie – you lie,' screamed Vince. 'I don't believe it – I won't—'

Deane laughed harshly. 'Then you had better try to believe it. Because you're going to have to live with this night's work for the rest of your life. You were in love with a madwoman.'

And turning on his heel to follow the stretcher back through the crowd to the police van, he looked at Vince and said sadly: 'We have that in common. So was I.'

The crowd moved nearer with sympathetic murmurs. 'Best get yourselves home. Out of those wet clothes. Catch your deaths. Aye, a good dram or two to warm ye.'

A police carriage rolled up and Faro thrust Vince inside. Then he retrieved the pathetic slippers and put them hastily out of sight in his greatcoat pocket.

But Vince had seen nothing. He lay back, his eyes closed, his face with its bruised black shadows the face of death itself.

Faro shuddered. There would be a reckoning for this night's work. That was for sure.

Somehow he got Vince upstairs and out of his wet clothes, while he forced several drams down his throat. Mrs McGonagall, alerted that they had tried to rescue a suicide, without thankfully having to be told the grim facts, had warming pans in their beds.

Her husband stood watching, his clichés and profundities on the tragedy falling on deaf ears.

Faro took a sleeping draught from Vince's bag and, hoping for the best, administered it full strength. Once he was breathing deeply, Faro retired to his own room.

Removing his greatcoat, he took out Rachel's slippers and laid them reverently side by side on the windowsill. From his other pocket he removed her reticule. Strangely heavy, it contained only one object, that both surprised and alarmed him. A large flat stone.

Suddenly all thoughts of sleep had vanished. Astonished that he could be so detached and think so incisively at this time of grief for Vince, Faro felt almost guilty in his clinical recapitulation of Rachel Deane's death plunge.

As he reconstructed those last minutes in exact detail, remembering how tragically small and vulnerable this poor mad girl had seemed, he sought an answer to the enigma of her sad possessions.

And for some time he sat still, weighing them in his hands as if in some vain hope they might yield a meaning of deeper significance than a madwoman's whim.

After a night of horrendous dreams of which awakening reality was worst of all, Faro overslept that morning. **13**

It was ten o'clock and he had decided against breakfast when Mrs McGonagall announced that he had a caller.

'He's waiting for you outside. In his carriage.' She sounded impressed.

Faro drew aside the lace curtain. The carriage bore what looked like the Deane crest. Tiptoeing into Vince's bedroom he saw that his stepson still slept.

'Let him sleep, Mrs McGonagall. If he should awaken tell him only that I had to go out and will be back soon.'

Wilfred Deane opened the carriage door. Greeted with a sympathetic glance, Faro decided that Deane also looked the worse for a sleepless night, tired and older than his thirty years, with all of his debonair self-confidence vanquished.

'Would you be so good as to spare me a few moments, Inspector Faro – I believe that is how we properly address you,' he added with a wry smile.

'That is so.'

'If you would care to accompany me to Deane Hall? And of course your stepson too, if he wishes.' Gazing across at the house from which Faro had emerged, he shook his head. 'What we have to discuss touches him most nearly. I am almost afraid to enquire as to his condition.'

'He was asleep when I left. I gave him a sleeping draught last night, it seemed the best thing to do—'

'Indeed, in the circumstances that was a wise decision.' As the carriage moved off, he leaned back against the fine leather upholstery. 'I realise this is a very early call. Perhaps you have not yet had time to breakfast,' he added tactfully with an understanding glance at Faro's unshaven face.

Rubbing his chin, Faro smiled: 'I am afraid I had little inclination towards food this morning.'

That sidelong glance of understanding made them allies. 'I have left instructions with the servants that we will partake of breakfast together while we talk.' A sudden dazzling smile brought a measure of charm. 'My valet is at your service too, if you wish to freshen up.'

Remembering the chaotic stunned effects of sudden bereavement in normal homes, Faro expected to see some evidence of deep mourning and was somewhat taken aback to find none.

On the surface Deane Hall's normal activities were quite unruffled and Wilfred Deane's excellent valet performed the function of barber with smooth aplomb. The man made no reference to the house's young mistress having tragically died a few hours before and betrayed not the least curiosity as to Faro's presence at breakfast. It was almost, thought Faro, as if he were well used to the needs of his master's visitors.

Feeling considerably refreshed Faro went down the long staircase and into a panelled dining room bearing a forest of disembodied stags' heads on the walls.

Warming his hands before a welcoming fire, Faro indulged in some mental measurements and decided that this room might have cheerfully accommodated the whole of 9 Sheridan Place.

Wilfred Deane entered and indicated the seat opposite. 'Eat now, Inspector. We will talk later. We will both feel considerably better then, I hope.'

Instead of the humble porridge upon which Faro normally

broke his fast, the huge sideboard displayed silver chafing-dishes bearing bacon, eggs, kidneys, sausages and two kinds of fish, kippers and kedgeree.

Taking a modest helping Faro wished that he had more of an appetite. Wilfred Deane, he observed, was not in the least put off his food by the night's terrible events.

Apart from the obligatory mourning touches in Wilfred's attire, always readily at hand in large and affluent houses, there was no indication that he had lost the girl he loved and had hoped to marry.

As they set aside their plates and Faro refused a third cup of tea, Deane's gesture dismissed the hovering table-maids.

'I hope you feel a little restored now, Inspector.'

'I do indeed.'

'Good.' Pausing, Deane tapped his fingers lightly on the table in the manner of one who is giving careful consideration to what he is about to say.

'I owe you an apology for last night, Inspector. My behaviour was quite abominable—'

'You were not in the least impolite – to me.'

'I was to your stepson. And considering all he had been through. Being – being there when it happened. I must have seemed damnably callous.'

'Shock can bring out the worst in all of us, sir.'

Deane sighed. 'I hope some day he will forget my dreadful words. Unfortunately they are true. I spoke truth when I said that we had something in common – that I too loved Rachel. I would have done anything – anything for her. But there was one thing no one could do, no amount of devotion could cure. Her poor sick mind.'

He paused deep in thought. 'I would even have married her, you know. Not to live with her as man and wife, but as her friend and companion. Someone to take care of her during her fits of instability.'

They were interrupted by the sound of slow footsteps and the door opened to admit a tall man with a patriarchal beard. This was the head of the family, Sir Arnold Deane, still recognisable as the man who had been the charisma and life blood of Deane Enterprises.

Faro observed that unlike Wilfred Deane's, Sir Arnold's mourning went further than the clothes he wore. Here was the countenance one would expect to see in such dire circumstances, ashen, bewildered by grief.

'Heard you had a visitor, Wilf.' Although he leaned heavily on a stick, there was nothing lacking in his strong grip as they were introduced. By the intensity of his gaze, Faro realised that here was a man, like himself, who had the extraordinary and often life-preserving gift of summing up friend or foe in thirty seconds.

'Are you sure you are well enough, sir—' Wilfred Deane began.

'Well enough, young fellow. What's that got to do with it, may I ask? How can I be well enough? I've lost my only lass.' He sat down heavily and stared across at Faro, silent for a moment. Turning his head sharply in Deane's direction, he said, 'You've told him about her – her trouble?'

'Yes, sir.'

Sir Arnold sighed. 'Sorry your stepson had to be involved in our problems. He's a fine young chap and an excellent doctor. He'll go a long way but—' he paused and shook his head, 'some day, you, sir, and your lad, may thank heaven that he did not marry her.'

Letting the words sink in, the old man continued: 'Wilf here tells me that when Dr Laurie called at the house she did not even recognise him. You were with him?'

'I was.'

'Very distressing, very distressing. But this peculiarity in her behaviour was not unknown to us. Even in her own family circle, there were days when she pretended she did not know us and that we were strangers to her. Is that not so, Wilf?'

'It is indeed, sir.' And to Faro: 'It was like some vicious little game of let's pretend, or as if her mind was split in two.'

Wilfred Deane looked searchingly at Faro. 'I assume there is a certain amount of trust tantamount with your profession, sir, and what we are telling you is in the strictest confidence. In the past we have tried, and mostly succeeded, to keep Rachel's condition from becoming public knowledge. Pride in the family name—'

'Pride be damned,' Sir Arnold interrupted. 'If pride were all. You forget, I loved the lass. She was all I had left—' and Faro saw how Wilfred winced as the old man added, 'after my David died.'

Sir Arnold's only son had died in a riding accident when Rachel was a child. Was the old man about to mention the strange coincidence that the girl's mother had also committed suicide by drowning? But sighing heavily, he added:

'There is another perhaps more pressing reason for silence. It would also have a very adverse effect on our shareholders' confidence if they thought there was some – well, instability, in the firm who had contracted to build a two-mile-long bridge.'

So that was it, thought Faro. That was the reason, the financial stability as well as respectability. Two good reasons for silence. With commerce possibly the more urgent.

'I realise that Dr Laurie was probably speaking the truth about their assignation. Rachel was missing for a day or two. Slipped out of the house. It was not the first time, was it, Wilf?'

Deane nodded. 'Indeed it was not. When she came home or more often was found and forcibly returned, she relished the secret of where she had been, with a childlike delight in keeping us in the dark.'

'Fortunately we mostly knew where to find her.' Sir Arnold smiled tenderly at the memory. 'With her old nurse in Errol. There was no need for concern on those occasions.'

'As far as we know, sir, or were able to find out,' contributed Wilfred.

A heavy silence followed as this information was left to settle with Faro.

'It would have been a great help to my stepson,' he said, 'if you had taken him aside and explained some of what you have told me.'

'I realise that now, and if we had had the slightest idea that—'

Sir Arnold, suddenly overcome, stood up, seized his stick and said: 'I cannot bear this. I am ill. You must excuse me.' He looked dazed, shocked as if realisation had just dawned.

Wilfred Deane touched the bellpull and the butler appeared. 'Sir Arnold will return to his room now.'

The old man brushed aside Faro's outstretched hand and stumbled from the room, dashing the tears from his eyes. They could hear him sobbing aloud as the door closed.

For a moment the two men stared at each other, unable to find the right words. When the sound of footsteps faded Deane continued:

'I realise we should have warned your stepson. Believe me, we would have told him. But how were we to know that he was to be trusted? He might—' He shrugged. 'He might have decided to make some capital out of it.'

'Blackmail, is that what you mean?' demanded Faro sharply.

'Indeed. It has been tried before,' said Wilfred softly. 'There have been other young men. We managed to keep it from Sir Arnold but Rachel was eager for romance and adventure. There was constant danger that she would take up with anyone – and I mean any man,' he stressed the words significantly, 'just for a passing whim.'

Suddenly he put his hands over his eyes. 'Dear God, we should have had her committed. But we couldn't face that, the thought of having her a prisoner for the rest of her life in one of those awful bedlams.'

And Faro found himself recalling Superintendent Johnston's words, that even in the most talented families who produce financial wizards, fate has its little joke and allows genius to spawn the occasional simpleton.

'We tried to do the best we could. This is a large house and we could keep her safe with us, with so little evidence of restraint that I doubt whether even the servants were aware of what was going on. And in those often long sane times, when she was sweet and loving, we foolishly thought that the demons inside her were quelled for ever. She was very clever, you know, and even in her darkest days she could show diabolical cunning. She could outwit us all.'

Wilfred leaned back in his chair. 'And now it's all over. I wish I could say thank God she's at rest. But I can't and I never will.'

There seemed nothing more to say and as Faro stood up to leave, Deane said: 'There will be a funeral, by the way, next Thursday. A small private family affair. If you wish to come — and of course, Dr Laurie.'

'Alas. I am afraid my return to Edinburgh is imminent. I have pressing matters awaiting me there.'

'I quite understand. Nevertheless, if Dr Laurie wishes to be present — at the graveside, there will be no attempt to prevent him so doing. And if he wishes to pay his last respects at the house here, we can promise him our sympathy and understanding.'

As they shook hands he added: 'Will you please convey my sympathy to your stepson. We are both in the same boat, alas, we have both to recover from a broken heart, if you believe such a condition exists.'

And opening the front door: 'There is one more thing, but it may be of some comfort to Dr Laurie. Tell him, as far as Deane's is concerned, that his post with us is secure. There is no question whatever of his being dismissed. We are happy to retain his services as our resident doctor.'

Faro left Dundee hoping only that this was the end of Vince's unfortunate love affair. But in that, as in all else concerned with the events of the past few days, he was mistaken and Vince's involvement with Rachel Deane was to have far-reaching and terrible consequences for all of them.

14 In the days that followed Faro could not rid himself of the guilty feeling that he had abandoned Vince at his most vulnerable. Although his sympathetic breakfast with Wilfred at Deane Hall and Sir Arnold's magnanimous attitude towards his young doctor made nonsense of such notions, the certainty that Vince was in mortal danger persisted.

His return to Edinburgh was marked by the anticipation of bad news. None came, only a letter from Vince apologising for the delay in writing. He had been very busy and there had been yet another fatal accident on the bridge:

> The watchman who tried to help us must have missed his footing on the ladder during one of his late-night inspections. He was not discovered until next morning. I cannot begin to tell you how this sad event, recalling as it did so vividly all that is still personally so unbearably painful, has upset me.

Faro felt a shudder of dread, wondering if Vince had also absorbed the more sinister implications of the watchman's death. Besides Faro and Vince, he had been the sole witness of Rachel's suicide. The hand of coincidence seemed once more to have been seriously overplayed.

As he wrestled with another of Edinburgh's sordid domestic crimes, Faro's thoughts turned constantly to

Dundee and the notes he had made on Polly Briggs' suicide and the apparently unconnected death of Hamish McGowan.

Once again he took up *The Scotsman's* report on the tragic death of Rachel Deane:

Miss Dean took a lively interest in anything connected with Deane Enterprises. Of particular interest to her was the progress being made in the building of the railway bridge and she often dropped in on the bridgeworks to utter words of encouragement to the workers and have a lively chat with her grandfather's engineers.

Faro was impressed by the reporter's active imagination that had completely missed the irony of an evening visit when work had ceased. On this melancholy occasion, Miss Deane had not only dropped in but had also dropped off the bridgeworks to her death.

To Faro, the lies that had been told, white enough to protect the firm and soothe its shareholders, were so transparent he was astounded that intelligent minds could let them go unquestioned. Was this then the hidden tyranny of Deane's, the ability to buy or enforce silence?

Like a festering sore, the incongruities of the events he had witnessed in Dundee grew deeper, stronger in his mind. Many years of training to observe and deduce from given facts could not be swamped by face-saving lies, especially when he had been there, a witness.

And so it was, as the weeks turned into months, that he still found himself on the threshold of sleep reliving those last horrific moments of Rachel Deane's life. In vain he tried to console himself that the girl was mentally unsound, as Wilfred and Sir Arnold had stressed. For only such a sorry fact could justify her mad dash to her death to escape her erstwhile lover and his stepfather.

Faro reconstructed again and again those horrendous scenes,

trying to find some grain of sense in Rachel's irrational behaviour. Had she seen Vince and himself in some distorted mirror of her imagination as pursuers? Pursuers who meant to recapture and return her to her imprisonment in Deane Hall. Had her poor sick mind indicated that no one would have the courage to follow her on to the bridge?

Two questions for which Faro would have given much to have answers he believed now must remain for ever unresolved. Did Rachel lose her balance and fall or did she voluntarily decide to quit this life by leaping to her death?

Although Faro now realised that this was one of the conditions of her mental disorder, he would have given much to walk about inside Rachel Deane's mind and discover when Vince's rôle as lover and intended husband of her lucid moments changed into that of mortal enemy.

Did that satisfactorily explain why she had so viciously attacked Vince after asking him to meet her at Magdalen Green? Why she had rushed out of Deane Hall without changing her footwear into something more adequate for heavy rain?

Again and again he saw Vince's pathetic attempts to replace those frail slippers on her feet when he tried to revive her, to warm life into her still body.

But most disturbing of all was the presence of a large round stone in her reticule – and nothing else. Did this indicate a desperate notion that it would help her to sink to the bottom of the river? If so, this clearly implied she had premeditated suicide before leaving Deane Hall. In that case why had she dropped it beside the discarded slippers?

Faro could not get rid of the alternative notion. That the stone had been intended for a more sinister rôle, as a weapon of self-defence, should any attempt be made to divert her from her deadly purpose.

And he shuddered with dread, when he realised how fatally

effective it could have been, aimed at a pursuer. Namely Vince, coming up the ladder directly behind her.

Another picture recurred and remained poised, solid and unshakeable.

As the boats searched those dark waters, suddenly illuminated in the flares, the figures of two workmen in overalls inspecting the place from which Rachel had fallen to her death.

One was tall, well built, the other smaller, more like the night-watchman in build. Their instinct of shielding their faces was natural, but it seemed in retrospect that they stepped back hurriedly, guiltily, as if agitated at being observed or recognised.

What were they doing there? Were they taking their work seriously, hurriedly repairing or replacing some evidence of neglect or malfunction that might have caused Rachel's death?

Another thought crept in. Had they been her executioners? Had a trap been sprung to make it look like suicide?

After another dawn of birdsong which defeated his attempts to continue sleeping or make sense of the notes sprawled about the bed, Faro realised he was getting nowhere. One pointer remained: since the tone of her note to Vince indicated that their meeting was to be secret, it seemed hardly likely that Rachel had advertised her intentions of going to the bridge at Deane Hall.

It followed that if no one had known of her purpose and no one could have foreseen that her flight would take her to the bridge, how then could that fatal trap have been sprung?

Unless she had confided in someone in Deane Hall.

Faro sighed wearily. That didn't make sense, but still the picture of the two men in overalls refused to be banished.

Remaining uneasy, anxious on Vince's behalf without ever quite knowing why, he was relieved as well as delighted to receive a letter informing him to expect his stepson home on a brief visit:

My old friend Dr Sam has recently taken up a post as assistant to the police pathologist and is getting married. I am to

attend the wedding. You will be interested to learn that since
I last wrote you the McG. have had word from the missing
Kathleen. She did not care for London and is now working
in a milliner's shop in Rose Street (yes, Edinburgh). The
McG. are jubilant at the news and plans are afoot to visit
her. I have promised to find time to call in and pay their
compliments . . .

Going downstairs to the kitchen to give Mrs Brook the glad
tidings, Faro was relieved to know that there was now a happy
ending to what seemed like the ominous disappearance of the
two young women. Charlie McGowan's widow had returned
for her father-in-law's funeral with a perfectly logical reason
for her absence. Now Kathleen Neil was safe and sound in
Edinburgh.

Faro remembered having decided many years ago that suspicions without foundation were chronic and incurable diseases
of the detective's imagination. But he had also discovered in
twenty years with the Edinburgh City Police that, left alone, time
often provides simple explanations for the darkest and most
baffling mysteries.

Perhaps it was mere curiosity that directed him towards Rose
Street as the shops were putting on their shutters. As he stared
into a milliner's shop window, he observed a pretty fair-haired
young woman arranging bonnets.

This must be 'the fair Kathleen' and on impulse he opened
the door, bravely determined not to be overwhelmed by such an
entirely feminine establishment.

To his enquiry, the girl shook her head. 'I wish I was Miss
Neil,' she said wistfully. 'I only work for her.'

Disappointed, Faro left with the distinct impression that
Kathleen Neil must have her own private reasons for concealing
from the McGonagalls that her position was grander and more
affluent than she had led them to believe.

Faro now awaited his stepson's arrival with pleasure not untinged with misgivings. Remembering the shattered condition in which they had parted company, he was not quite sure what to expect. Although confident that one day Vince armed with the natural resilience of youth would pick up some of the pieces of his life, Faro would not have speculated with certainty that he could also put them together again.

Remembering how long it had taken him to sort out his own life when Lizzie died, he expected Vince to be inevitably changed by the bitter experience of loss.

On the surface, he was relieved to see that his fears and gnawing anxieties were groundless. Here was the cheerful, well-balanced young man, his impish sense of humour undiminished.

Only in sudden silences, a sentence left unfinished, did the cracks below the surface reveal themselves and a sudden bleakness in his eyes showed that Vince's mind had drifted again to that sad shore where he had lost his Rachel Deane.

It was not, however, until they sat at supper together that Vince drained his glass of claret and sighed heavily: 'Well, Stepfather, how long does it take to recover, would you say? I cannot forget her, you know. I see her everywhere.

'The Deanes have been unfailingly kind and considerate. I was wrong about them, I know that now. They were trying to protect poor Rachel from herself. Wilfred was very decent to me at the funeral and asked me to dine with them at Deane Hall. He told me much the same story as I understand he told you. And Sir Arnold too.'

With a sad smile he added: 'Seems that my services as doctor are well thought of, at least. Although I had behaved so outrageously, they were prepared to forget the past. All very heartening, Stepfather, especially as they have seen fit to accompany their goodwill towards me with a substantial rise in salary.

'I was very touched when the old man said there was no one they would rather have seen Rachel marry, as he thought very highly of me both as a doctor and as a young man with excellent qualities.'

He darted a look at Faro. 'Are you pleased? I was.' And without waiting for an answer: 'I am now a constant visitor to Deane Hall, free to use the library too. You would love that. Once a week I go and examine Sir Arnold, listen to his heart and that sort of thing. Then afterwards I have dinner with Wilfred and a game of billiards or a hand at cards. Who would have thought it?'

Who indeed, wondered Faro somewhat cynically, feeling uncharitable for his newly aroused suspicions that Vince too might have been bought by Deane's. Hiding his thoughts, he merely smiled, remarking that he had recently encountered Wilfred Deane on Princes Street on his way to a business meeting.

'Yes, I gather he comes fairly often, so he has very good reasons for wishing that accursed bridge was complete.'

'So he said.'

'He didn't mention me?' Vince asked.

'We were both in a hurry, we only had time to exchange the civilities.'

Faro would not easily forget his reaction to recognising Deane emerging from a carriage outside the Royal British Hotel. That familiar figure jolted him back to their last unhappy meeting and wishing heartily that this encounter could be avoided, he realised that this was impossible. Since one had to step aside to allow the other passage, a lack of acknowledgement would have amounted to rudeness.

It had to be said for Deane that Faro saw in his fleeting expression of annoyance and even embarrassment, an equal eagerness to avoid this meeting. But the politenesses had to be observed.

Both men bowed, raised their hats, wished each other good day, enquired earnestly about each other's health and agreed that the weather was abominable.

Deane went further. He felt obliged to explain: 'I am here for a meeting with our Edinburgh shareholders. More frequently than I would wish with that infernally tedious train journey in both directions.'

But each saw in the other's face how even indirect reference to the unfinished Tay Bridge touched unpleasant memories. And it was with considerable relief that they bowed and parted once more.

Vince sighed. 'The fact that we both loved Rachel is a bond between us. It keeps her alive for us.' His eyes suddenly filled and he shook his head. 'I'm not in any danger of ever forgetting her. As I told you, I see her everywhere. At first – after the funeral, I was in a daze, those early days.

'Can you imagine, I used to follow perfectly innocent young ladies in the Overgait, terrified them by my approaches. I just wanted to speak to them, be comforted, if you like, because there was something, the way they walked, or the set of a bonnet, a laugh or a cloud of dark hair that reminded me of Rachel. Even such glimpses were oddly consoling. I can see now that I was always searching – and will continue to do so, alas, for that lost happiness.'

He shrugged apologetically. 'I know this isn't making sense, Stepfather.'

It was Faro's turn to be sympathetic. He knew all about such reactions as a phenomenon of loss, and had entertained a persistent belief that Lizzie must still be alive somewhere if he could only find her again.

'After your dear mother died, lad, I found myself looking for her in shops, walking down the High Street, haunting crowded places, staring into strangers' faces, just longing to see someone who reminded me of her so that I might relive a tiny fragment of our life together.'

'That's it exactly. I thought I was going mad.' Vince sounded relieved. 'Does the search ever end, I wonder? At the moment, I imagine going on to the end of my days trying to find someone exactly like her and yet knowing deep down that I never will.'

They were interrupted by Mrs Brook's arrival to draw the curtains and attend to the fire. When she departed Vince told him about the wedding at St Giles and added: 'There is something I have promised McGonagall. I must find time for this.'

He took from his pocket a brooch in a velvet case. 'This belonged to his grandmother who was Kathleen's great-aunt.'

The brooch was of diamond and pearl in the shape of a shamrock. 'I suspect it's been the lifeline of the McGonagalls, in and out of pawn, but things are looking up now and he wants Kathleen to have it. Says it will bring her luck. Have you seen the shop, by the way?'

'Aye, and very smart it is too. Prosperous. She should do well in there.'

When next day Vince returned from visiting the Rose Street shop Faro was very glad he had kept his suspicions about Kathleen's modest establishment to himself. His stepson, at least, was oblivious to any interesting possibilities as to how she might have suddenly acquired a thriving millinery business.

Faro wondered if in fact Vince was aware that Kathleen was the owner not the employee when his thoughts were diverted by a happy glow long absent from Vince's countenance.

'I must say, Stepfather, that she is quite a stunner. I was quite captivated. I'm only sorry we did not meet earlier, when she was in Dundee,' he added ruefully.

And Faro that night felt more cheerful than had been the case for many a day, for Vince could talk of nothing but the fair Kathleen.

'I should have liked to have taken her to the wedding. I fancy she would have enjoyed that. She would have been a sensation in one of her delicious bonnets too. Oh, incidentally, there was one familiar face. Remember Dr Ramsey?'

'I do indeed. The dour young police surgeon at Dundee.'

'The same. He was Sam's best man. Seems they are cousins.

And let me tell you, away from those doleful surroundings, he is anything but dour, quite the contrary.

'As for the fair Kathleen, I haven't much time now but I'm hoping to be better organised when next I come home for a weekend. And, of course, there is always the possibility of her visiting Paton's Lane to see the McGonagalls. She did mention that.'

Faro was intrigued. 'I should very much like to meet her.'

'And so you shall, Stepfather. I thought we might have luncheon at the Café Royal before I leave.'

Faro had a table near the window and as the couple approached and he shook hands with Kathleen he suppressed a smile. His first impression was that Vince had in fact succeeded in his search. Whether consciously or not, he had found a girl who reminded him of his lost love.

True, on closer acquaintance he realised that any resemblance to Rachel Deane, whom he had met so briefly and under somewhat trying circumstances, was quite superficial. And during the meal it faded completely as he studied this pretty girl, so shy and overwhelmed by her surroundings that they had the effect of rendering her almost inarticulate.

When later he mentioned those first impressions, Vince shook his head firmly. 'They are not in the least alike, Stepfather. But I do know what you mean. Perhaps that's what attracted me to her when we first met. I can't explain it, except that they are basically the same type, rather than anything more definite.

'I had only seen her photograph at Willie McGonagall's and that was taken when she was very young. She's much prettier now.'

A now buoyant Vince departed for Dundee, leaving his stepfather gratified by promises of fairly regular visits home in future, for which Vince was even prepared to endure cheerfully that abominable train journey. To be near his new love, thought Faro, seeing through any other excuses Vince had readily available.

And so the day came when Vince threw casually into the

conversation that he was seriously considering the possibility of a situation in Edinburgh again.

As Faro suspected, the fair Kathleen was the main reason.

'Who knows, Stepfather, perhaps in the not too distant future I may be able to achieve the circumstances which would allow me the right credentials to set up successfully as a family doctor,' he added with a shy smile.

'Are congratulations in order?' Faro asked, his first feeling of delight mingled with gratitude that Vince was making a spectacular recovery from his tragic infatuation for Rachel Deane.

To Faro's question regarding his intentions, Vince **15**
grinned sheepishly. 'A bit early for that, Stepfather. But
I have hopes. I mean, Kathleen is always glad to see me,
never refuses an invitation. And of course, the McGonagalls would be delighted.'

'Scarcely a valid reason for choosing a wife, is it, lad?'

'I know that perfectly well, Stepfather. I haven't asked
the lady formally but her attitude has given me every
reason to believe she will accept me.'

Observing Faro's veiled glance, he added hastily: 'No, no,
Stepfather. Nothing like that. No unbridled passion this
time. This is quite a different courtship, if that's what
I might call it. And I'm very glad it is so. All very proper and up to now nothing more has been exchanged between us than a chaste goodnight kiss – on the cheek. But,'
he added cheerfully, 'sometimes I suspect – and hope,
dammit – that my chaste fair Kathleen has hidden fires.'

Faro received this information on the progress of
Vince's courtship with mixed feelings. Did the cautious
reserve on Kathleen's side involve the ownership of the
milliner's shop and confirm his own suspicions regarding
the possibility of a protector, a secret lover?

Vince was smiling happily. 'I'm glad that there has
been this restraint between us. It has given me time to
sort out my own feelings. I shouldn't like Kathleen
to discover – or even to imagine for one moment – that
she was my second choice.'

'Does she know about Rachel?'

Vince shook his head. 'I didn't consider that was necessary.'

The likelihood that he himself was a second choice had not occurred to Vince's unsuspicious nature. Direct and honest in his dealings, if he had a fault it was to believe that as he always spoke truth, then so too did others.

'I shall certainly tell her, if she consents to be my wife. That would only be proper.'

'I detect a certain reluctance. Are you afraid that your unhappy love affair might influence her?'

'At this stage, perhaps I am.' And with a heartfelt sigh, 'Let's face it, Stepfather, I can now see quite clearly that whatever my feelings about Rachel and hers about me, marriage between us would have been a complete disaster. Her fits of unreason – insanity, let's give it an honest name – were going to get worse.'

He paused and then added, 'The heightened emotions and physical demands of married life would have increased her instability. In such cases the bearing of children is a further hazard, quite capable of throwing the young mother over the edge.

'This is not conjecture on my part, it is, alas, a proven medical fact, and something not at all infrequent in unbalanced young women. Paul Ramsey, my new friend, lent me a very interesting book on the subject just last week.'

Was this all Vince needed to prove to himself that he had loved not wisely but too well? thought Faro cynically.

'There would have been little in the way of family life for us and a sad bleak prospect for any children we might have brought into the world. We would have been wise to make the decision to remain childless and I know now that willing as I was to marry her, eager for her to be my wife, my rôle would have been increasingly that of attendant doctor rather than husband.'

As Vince left for Dundee, Faro said: 'Let me know in time when you are coming again and I'll drop in a note inviting Kathleen to dinner.'

'What a splendid idea.'

From Faro's point of view, hoping for a glimpse of Kathleen's hidden fires, that evening two weeks later was unremarkable and even, for him, a little boring.

Kathleen again seemed overwhelmed by her surroundings and spent a lot of time gazing around her and admiring the furniture. Otherwise he found her once again more inarticulate than he thought accountable from shyness and a certain awe of Vince's famous stepfather.

Reserved and retiring in company, with little to say for herself, Kathleen was also, Faro reminded himself, the shrewd business woman, whether as manager or owner of the Rose Street establishment.

That second meeting also confirmed her lack of sexual attraction. He realised from his limited experience that apparently shy women are capable of stripping off a colourless personality with their garments once the bedroom door is closed. But in Kathleen's case, the idea of her being anyone's secret mistress became increasingly absurd as the evening dragged to its weary close.

Only once did he succeed in raising her animation. In the drawing room was a grand piano belonging to the previous owner of the house, which Faro had acquired with other furniture. Apart from his daughters' visits when they taxed its grandeur with scales and pianoforte exercises, it remained untouched.

Observing that on several occasions Kathleen's wistful glance had strayed towards it, he asked in sudden hope: 'Do you play?'

She shrugged. 'A little and not well.'

'Mr McGonagall mentioned that you sang very sweetly and were very talented,' Faro said encouragingly.

She laughed. 'He told you about my "Song of the Forest", did he?'

'Your bird calls?'

'Yes.'

Vince beamed. 'I say, Kathleen, won't you give us a rendering?'

She looked at Faro for approval, but when he added his plea, she shrank back in her chair: 'Oh no, I don't think – really—'

Vince stood up, took her firmly by the arm. 'Come along, Kathleen. No use hiding your talent under a bushel. Now it's your turn to sing for your supper.'

She played a few chords hesitantly and then gathering courage, suddenly lost her shyness and trilled happily through the blackbird's call, the laverock and the nightingale and an assortment of wild birds, ending with the humble robin's song.

Faro and Vince applauded, their response instinctive. It was really quite remarkable. McGonagall had been right. Here was a girl with an astonishing gift.

As she closed the piano lid, Faro said: 'You could have made a very good career for yourself on the stage.'

Kathleen shook her head. 'I have little ability as an actress and I have been a great disappointment to poor Uncle Willie. He despaired of me when I couldn't learn all those long speeches in Shakespeare. I was always more at home with wardrobe, making costumes. That was how I first became interested in creating my own millinery.'

And that, as far as Faro was concerned, was her longest speech of the evening. Having bowed over her hand, as Vince escorted her back home to Rose Street, he closed the front door thoughtfully.

Vince, he decided, had exchanged the enigma of Rachel Deane for the enigma of Kathleen Neil with her downcast eyes, modest glances, and long silences.

Faro was disappointed. Oh dear, dear, this was not at all the wife he had hoped Vince would choose. He had always envisaged his stepson with a young woman of spirit, his intellectual equal, one who would respond to and enhance the camaraderie between the two men with her own wit.

Ideally, he realised, he was hoping for a stepdaughter-in-law who would grow as close to him as Vince. Now he recognised sadly that he was hoping for the impossible. Did such a girl even exist beyond the realms of fantasy?

Well, since his Lizzie died, he had but once thought he had encountered such a perfect woman.

And deliberately he thrust those sad thoughts aside.

To more practical matters, he knew that once the engagement was announced and the wedding date fixed, he had best set about moving out of Sheridan Place and finding himself another home.

He smiled suddenly, realising he was back at precisely that same hurdle where he had been four months earlier, when Vince had written to tell him of his forthcoming marriage. During the interval between Rachel's death and his decision to propose to Kathleen Neil, while summer had bloomed and faded into golden autumn, time had also gone about its business dulling the pain in the human heart.

So much had changed since then. Only on Tay Bridge, it seemed that little progress had been made. Passengers from both cities who had anticipated an easier journey between Edinburgh and Dundee grumbled more than ever and with reason. Older folk wondered whether they would live long enough to see it finished.

Stage comics made jokes about it. And pithy sayings were springing up, parodies of Robert Burns:

> My love is like a red, red rose . . .
> And I shall love you, dear, always,
> Till the first train steams over the Tay Bridge.

If Vince's courtship of Kathleen Neil gave Faro cause for concern, then he was also delighted that Vince had made new friendships in Dundee, with the young police surgeon Dr Ramsey and, more surprisingly, with Wilfred Deane. On several occasions the two had travelled to Edinburgh together in Deane's carriage, a welcome relief to the abominable train journey.

Faro chided himself on his own base ingratitude. Vince could hardly be blamed for choosing a wife who did not meet his stepfather's requirements. Kathleen Neil might be somewhat lacklustre, but she had been capable of repairing the damage and reconstructing some happiness from those sad ashes of Vince's first love.

At first, Faro had regarded the entry of Kathleen into their lives as perhaps holding some vital clue to Polly Briggs' disappearance and subsequent death. But Kathleen was vague on the subject of Polly except to say that she didn't know where she went after they parted in London. Her refusal to be drawn into any discussion amounted, Faro thought, to almost callous indifference to her friend's fate, which in any other person than Kathleen Neil might have aroused his suspicions that she was involved in Polly's demise.

He had long prided himself on being a shrewd assessor of character but as he failed completely to get beyond those mouselike qualities of timidity and shyness, Kathleen did not strike him as being capable of calculated murder.

The further explanation was simpler. The friendship which Jean McGonagall had described as 'so close, like sisters' but which Briggs had described as 'a bad influence' had been on Polly's side rather than Kathleen's.

And Polly Briggs must remain an enigma, while the mysterious circumstances of her death were strictly the concern of the Dundee City Police. Faro still had hopes of learning the truth some day. In the words of Voltaire he was fond of quoting: 'Love and murder will out.'

They did not fail him now.

On one of his visits home, Vince told him that Dr Ramsey, in his cups, had confided certain disturbing medical facts about his post-mortem on Polly Briggs.

'Paul is certain that she didn't take her own life and that she was already dead before she was put into the water.'

'What are you suggesting?'

'Drowning, as you know, Stepfather, is death by asphyxia, caused by air being prevented from reaching the lungs. Whether or not suicide is intended, the body instinctively reacts with an initial struggle during which water is gulped into the lungs. Eventually they become waterlogged and this weighs the body down enough for it to sink. The unmistakable sign we look for is a fine froth in the mouth and nostrils but the main internal indication is a ballooning of the lungs as a result of distension with water.'

Vince paused dramatically. 'Paul has been seriously concerned about his findings.'

'Which were?' Faro demanded.

'The signs of death by drowning were absent. There was every indication that the girl had been dead for several hours and rigor had already set in before the corpse was disposed of by throwing it into the water. Paul's further examination revealed a contusion at the base of the skull, not immediately obvious because of her thick hair, but this he firmly regarded as being the fatal blow.'

'And what were his conclusions?'

'In his opinion the girl did not drown. She was murdered.'

'Then why in God's name hasn't he done something about it before now?'

'He did. All that he told me, and I believe him, was written in his report. He left it on his desk in readiness to send to the Procurator Fiscal. Then, in the middle of the night, two men arrived at his lodgings. There had been an accident, would he come quickly.

'When he got outside they bundled him into a cab, beat him up and advised him if he wanted his family to stay healthy and his career likewise, then he had better accept that Polly Briggs committed suicide.'

'Naturally, he did as he was told,' said Faro contemptuously.

'Naturally. Not all men are brave, Stepfather. Some value a

future and a peaceful life. He has a wife and two young children. And now not only are they in danger, but also if at this late date he reveals all to Superintendent Johnston, he will no doubt lose his position as police surgeon.'

'So what has he decided?'

Vince shrugged. 'He is suffering enough, haunted ever since by assisting this miscarriage of justice and several times he has attempted to make a clean breast of it. On that day when he visited the mortuary, soon after he was beaten up, he was absolutely terrified.'

Observing his stepfather's expression, he said: 'I am only telling you because the case of Polly Briggs is beyond your jurisdiction. Otherwise I would have remained silent, respecting Paul's confidence, and I must ask you to do the same.'

'Tell me one more thing, if you please?'

'And what is that?'

'Has your friend any suspicions of the murderer's identity?'

'Oh yes, indeed. He suspects that this was no jealous lover's *crime passionnel*. The fact that his confidential report on the post-mortem was read and action so immediately taken, suggests to him that Polly Briggs' murder is part of a much larger crime, carried out by an organisation so powerful that they have spies in the police department.'

'Deane Enterprises, in fact,' said Faro slowly.

'Possibly.' Vince made the admission reluctantly.

'And how does this affect your friendship with Wilfred Deane?'

'Not at all. Why should it? I doubt whether Wilf has ever heard of Polly Briggs,' he added loyally. 'Besides, Stepfather, there are others who might wish to buy silence. The shareholders of the gentlemen's select clubs, for instance.'

As autumn spread a golden glory of sunsets over Arthur's Seat and leaves fell like drops of blood on the banks of the River Tay,

Faro found his hands full with two particularly brutal murders and a plot to assassinate a royal personage (neither of which have any place in this chronicle).

One day, looking for notes he had made on an earlier case with some similarities, he was searching through a trunk in the attics of Sheridan Place. Once the property of his late father, Constable Magnus Faro, this receptacle had become the last resting place for clues and objects relating to unsolved murders. When he moved from Sheridan Place into a smaller establishment, it would be prudent to discard this detritus of twenty years with the Edinburgh City Police.

As he pushed back the lid, there were the slippers and reticule belonging to Rachel Deane. Long since past any hope that they might conceal some amazing truth that had escaped him, he might as well begin his clearing-out operations by consigning these to Mrs Brook's rubbish bin.

Weighing them in his hands, he wondered why he had retained these mementoes of that distressing event, storing them with this battered collection of clues that had not led anywhere. Was it only a faint hope that one day he might still find an answer? Why had he not got rid of them immediately he unpacked in Edinburgh and discovered them in his luggage?

He had kept them secret too long. He could not produce them now without renewing for Vince the terrible emotions of Rachel's death. Replacing them, he closed the lid hurriedly. But their presence in the trunk upstairs continued to haunt him, arousing emotions for him too. Emotions of dissatisfaction. Certain of a mystery concerning Rachel's suicide, he felt that somehow he had failed Vince and himself.

In view of Dr Ramsey's confession to Vince, Faro also felt guilty that he had failed Polly Briggs' father and it was no consolation to tell himself that there was nothing he could do, since Dundee crimes were none of his business.

But Faro was not used to failure, it left a bad taste in his mouth. Considering that he had a high success rate with people who meant nothing to him at all, it was very humiliating that results were dismally lacking in a case involving those near and dear to him, particularly his stepson.

He wished he could wipe clean the slate of the nightmare that persisted of the suicide he had witnessed and had been so helpless to prevent. An indelible scene that must for ever link his memory with that short disastrous visit to Dundee.

Vince's next visit brought news that William McGonagall **16**
was to appear in Edinburgh, at an open air production
before Her Majesty the Queen in the park adjacent to
the Palace of Holyroodhouse.

This was to be a gala variety and an elegant version
of the penny gaff circus. Her Majesty was well known to
have a surprisingly unsophisticated, even childlike taste
in entertainment. And circuses, it seemed, were irresistible to her. She had approved a programme including
clowns, a juggler and a magician called Alpha Omega,
but clapping her hands with quite unqueenly glee, had
asked especially for lions and trapeze artistes.

Her Majesty, it was observed, had a penchant for
watching other mortals risking life and limb on the high
wire or with wild animals. She had a wistful partiality
for brave lion-tamers in leopard-skins. This savage form
of amusement did not go unmarked by her courtiers,
suggesting as it did wry comparisons with a less tender-
hearted, sentimental monarch, the Emperor Nero
feeding Christians to the lions in Ancient Rome. Her
Majesty's wish granted, the lion act was found and commanded to appear, although no setting was less like the
Colosseum than Queen's Park overlooked by the grandeur of Arthur's Seat, its slopes resplendent in a purple
blaze of autumn heather.

On the other hand, all was far from sweetness and
light in the Central Office of the Edinburgh City Police,

feverishly drafting in extra constables from outlying areas. Faro listened patiently to Superintendent McIntosh's grumbles about the considerable expense involved.

As senior detective, protecting the Queen on twice-yearly visits was Faro's responsibility and constant headache. He could well have done without the hazards involved in mounting this additional event.

The Superintendent smiled grimly. 'Sometimes I think that Her Majesty is either remarkably courageous or lacks imagination.'

Faro, who had only recently foiled an assassination attempt, opted for the latter. 'To Fenians and others with deep-seated grudges, or who are simply mad, we might now add escaped lions.'

The Superintendent gave him a hard look as he continued: 'And wild beasts are also a threat to the lesser mortals of her realm, like all the Edinburgh citizens who will be drawn to this circus to please their children and for a glimpse of royalty, as well as those aforesaid lions.'

McIntosh groaned as Faro pointed to the plan on his desk. 'Let's make no mistake about it, sir, we will need a great many extra safety measures. Measures which you will recall are difficult enough to put into effect when stone walls are involved and massive buildings with guarded entrances.'

After the Queen's recent escape, the idea of her sitting in a frail circus tent in a huge park surrounded by a dense crowd of people, from which a shot could be fired and an assassin make his escape in the confusion, did nothing for Faro's nerves as grimly he supervised elaborate security measures.

These included a specially constructed Royal Box which could be under constant police guard and which had no access from underneath as had the tiers of wooden seats.

It was with some relief that he scrutinised the programme. McGonagall was to recite 'The Battle of Bannockburn', calculated to enhance his credits and boost his further bookings with the information 'As performed before Her Majesty the Queen and the Crowned Heads of Europe', some of that bevy of relatives he hoped would be accompanying her.

Vince, who had heard McGonagall's Bannockburn, expressed doubts about such a choice. 'It just may not kindle the Queen's heart with kindness when she hears the heroic stanzas regarding English King Edward's sorry defeat.'

The McGonagalls duly arrived in Edinburgh and hastened to Kathleen's flat above the milliner's shop. There they would stay for the weekend, Jean having been prevailed upon to leave her little brood to bask in the vicarious glory of her husband's triumphant appearance before royalty.

She whispered that she was hoping – just hoping – that she might be presented and, with this in mind, had purchased a new bonnet and cape. New to her that was, for it had cost two and sixpence from one of the ladies in Dundee who sold cast-offs for the wealthy wives of the jute lords in Broughty Ferry.

Faro received all this information from Vince, who was to escort Jean and Kathleen on the gala evening. As they proudly took their seats, those special seats of privilege opposite the Royal Box reserved for guests of performers, Jean McGonagall was a happy woman.

Further she confessed to Faro that both she and Willie were delighted since Vince was 'like one of our own now'. It was obvious through the visit that they took every opportunity of beaming fondly upon the couple in the manner of those who believe an announcement of a romantic nature is imminent.

His presence in the guest box necessary in the line of duty, Faro took his seat beside Jean, Kathleen and Vince. As the performance began he was amused to notice that, in common with most of the members of the audience, Jean and Kathleen were more interested in observing the royal party, whose jewels outsparkled the performers' many glittering costumes.

For Faro too, acrobats and clowns took second place as he watched the Royal Box, not from motives of curiosity but of acute anxiety for any unscheduled moves in that direction. Sharp-eyed, constantly alert, his hand never left the pistol in his greatcoat pocket.

The bareback riders, the performing dogs, Alpha Omega's magic went down very well. And then the safety net was placed between the audience and the ring for the entrance of the lions and their tamer.

Safely behind bars but bringing with them the smell of wild animals and an exciting but scaringly alien whiff of the jungle, the lions in their ornate cage arrived behind plumed circus horses, also less than happy at the burden of ferocity they escorted.

Part of the act no doubt, but impressive. The roars were convincing enough to replace smiles with whimpers of fear from the more sensitive children and shivers of tremulous excitement from their elders.

Faro looked across at Her Majesty, clapping her hands enthusiastically as the Great Tonga (born Tony Brown in Coventry) bowed before her. His magnificent frame was only partially covered by a leopard-skin presumably from one of his charges who had refused to obey him.

Muscles rippling, the Great Tonga skirmished playfully with his lions, assisted by a long pole to keep them conveniently respectful. With this light armour he prodded the more sluggish performers who had a tendency to yawn while others leaped up and down on boxes obligingly showing their teeth.

At last came the moment the audience had been waiting for. The animals were shooed into their cage and bundled away by the clowns. One solitary lion remained.

'Absolute silence, if you please,' demanded the ring-master. 'It is essential for the safety of Monsieur Tonga that we have absolute silence. Any sudden noise which might frighten this savage animal could be fatal. I beseech you, ladies and gentlemen—'

After a roll of drums, Tonga opened the lion's mouth and stuck his head inside. Seconds later he withdrew it, patting the lion as if he had no more harm in him than a pussy-cat by the fire.

Faro was near enough to see that he had hardly been in any real danger since the poor beast was toothless, elderly, had mange and was probably fated to die of tranquil old age.

Along with compassion he felt a rising tide of anger. He could not abide zoos, or the sight of wild animals imprisoned. His dislike of caged creatures, animals or birds, was regarded with wry amusement by his colleagues at the Central Office. And why not, since his everyday activities had succeeded in putting so many human malefactors behind bars.

After the lions came McGonagall in borrowed but handsome robes depicting Robert the Bruce in chain mail, with magnificent flowing velvet cloak and a splendid fiery red wig which took several years off his age while adding an agreeable several inches to his stature.

Slowly he emerged from the curtained entrance and in stately slow measure gained the centre spotlight. After bowing to the Queen, he immediately thrust forward his left leg and raised his right hand – more, thought Faro, as if working a pump handle than handling his cardboard sword to any purpose.

Mouth forming a complete circle, round as a cannon's mouth and with the ardour of a warrior who fights for glory, he plunged full tilt into 'The Battle of Bannockburn':

> 'Sir Robert the Bruce at Bannockburn
> Beat the English in every wheel and turn,
> And made them fly in great dismay
> From the field without delay . . .'

Faro lost count of the verses which led to the flight of the English army. It seemed that Her Majesty, now whispering to one of her ladies-in-waiting behind her fan, shared his confusion:

'... King Edward was amazed at the sight,
And he got wounded in the fight:
And he cried, Oh heaven, England's lost, and I'm undone,
Alas, alas, where shall I run?
Then he turned his horse, and rode on afar
And never halted till he reached Dunbar.'

It was over and McGonagall, acknowledging polite applause, promptly announced that seeing his little poem had been so well received he might have the honour of addressing one to Her Majesty, especially for herself.

'Most August Empress of India, and of Great Britain the Queen
I most humbly beg your pardon, hoping you will not think it
      mean
That a poor poet that lives in Dundee
Would be so presumptuous to write this poem unto Thee.
Most lovely Empress of India, and England's generous Queen,
I Send you an Address, I have written on Scotland's Bard,
Hoping that you will accept it, and not be with me too hard,
Nor fly into a rage, but be as Kind and Condescending
As to give me your Patronage.
Beautiful Empress of India and England's Gracious Queen
And I think if Your Majesty likes it, right pleased you will be
And my heart it will leap with joy, if it is patronised by Thee.
Most Mighty Empress of India, and England's beloved Queen,
Most handsome to be seen.'

Mild applause, some exchange of amused glances, but not a great deal emanating from the Royal Box, thought Faro sadly. McGonagall had taken a liberty in presuming to address Her

Majesty and he doubted whether that would do him any good. Poor Willie was irrepressible, although Faro decided he should stick to acting as he had no great future as a poet.

Now the ring was taken over by more magicians, performing dogs leaping through rings and on and off the horses' backs, clowns tumbling and throwing buckets of water over one another. Some tight-rope walking and trapeze swinging, then the ring-master announced the climax of the evening's entertainment. They were to see a death-defying trapeze act, at the end of which the beautiful Selina would swing above the lion cage and dive into a tank of flames.

The high-wire performance was unremarkable until, after mild applause, the ring-master again begged for absolute silence. A lion's cage, high-sided but roofless, was wheeled in, the safety net dragged away by the clowns, the tank pulled forward and torches thrown in.

Flames leaped high causing the lion to pace his cage with angry frightened roars of protest.

'Poor beast. It's terrified of fire. That shouldn't be allowed,' Faro whispered to Vince.

But his protest fell on deaf ears as all eyes turned to the apex of the tent forty feet above their heads, where the trapeze swung lazily with Selina, a pretty girl in spangled tights, barely visible through the pink smoke.

Back and forward she swung and at the last moment to an accompanying roll of drums she leaped on to the platform and plunged through the smoke above the lion's cage and into the burning tank.

There was a horrified roar from the audience as the crowd surged to their feet. But before panic could break out, a roll of drums, a spotlight on the trapeze high above their heads. There bowing to the crowd was Alpha Omega and the beautiful Selina, with not a singe mark or a whiff of smoke to tarnish her spangles.

A sigh of relief, an outburst of cheering. Then as the brass band played the National Anthem, the audience remained on their feet until the royal party left the box.

Vince and Jean were still applauding while Faro sat rigid in his seat with Kathleen beside him, her hand grasping his arm, her face white with terror.

A strange excitement, like the lifting of a shutter in the photographer's camera, surged through him. As they followed the crowd swarming out of the tent, Jean was asking Vince:

'But how did he do it? Why, we all saw her fall. Have you any idea?'

Faro looked at her. 'Oh yes, I know now how it was done. I should have seen it at once. Fool that I was.'

'Do tell, do tell us.'

Suddenly aware of them again, Faro turned away from the tent. 'It's just a simple magician's trick. I won't spoil the magic for you.'

One of the clowns had come over and was speaking to Kathleen. She seemed to know him and he was being introduced to Jean and Vince.

'I must go. I'm still on duty,' said Faro.

'Join us later, won't you, Stepfather?'

As Faro hurried in the direction of the royal party, now boarding their carriages, he glanced back wondering if Kathleen's establishment also provided wigs for the clowns and costumes for the circus performers.

'Stepfather's very jaunty tonight,' Vince whispered to Kathleen as Jean chatted animatedly to the clown.

Kathleen smiled. 'Isn't he always?'

'I shouldn't be in the least surprised if he spotted a criminal in the crowd. I know that look of his. Like a bloodhound on the trail. Yes, he's definitely on to something.'

Having seen Her Majesty safely restored to Holyroodhouse and his men dismissed, a very relieved Faro walked homeward through the now almost deserted Queen's Park, where the circus tent was already being dismantled.

As he sauntered past, the clown whom he recognised as the one known to Kathleen, hailed him.

'Inspector Faro, isn't it? Thought I recognised you in the front row, sir. You didn't know me, of course.' And as he dragged off wig and false nose, Faro found himself looking into the countenance of Polly Briggs' father whom he had last encountered outside the police mortuary in Dundee.

Briggs brushed aside Faro's congratulations on the evening's performance. There was something else on his mind and Faro guessed that this must concern his dead daughter.

'I see you had that Kathleen with you. She's done very well for herself with that rich man, by the look of things. Was that him with you?'

'No, that was my stepson, Dr Laurie,' said Faro in a tone of annoyance.

'I see,' said Briggs, a mocking smile indicating that he saw all too clearly. 'Jean hinted that there was love in the air.'

Faro found scant comfort in the knowledge that he had been right about Kathleen's rich protector, apparently common knowledge to everyone but his stepson. Shrewd and intelligent in many ways, honest himself, Vince would never be so unchivalrous as to doubt a lady's word or her virtue.

As Briggs continued to regard him with veiled amusement, Faro cursed Jean McGonagall. 'The fact is,' he began coldly, trying not to sound as angry as he felt, 'my stepson is merely escorting the young lady to the circus.'

And changing to a safer topic: 'The show was excellent, the clowns were particularly fine. Where do you go next?'

'Down to the Borders, then across to Galloway. Willie of course was just here for the one night, especially for the Queen. What a nerve to make up a poem for her like that. Didn't you think so?'

'I thought he did very well. It was very brave of him.'

'I suppose so.'

Faro was relieved to end the conversation as someone called Briggs' name.

Turning on his heel Briggs suddenly swung round to face Faro again. 'They never found why my lassie drowned, those Dundee police.'

'So I understand.'

'I will never rest until I find out why she did it. And if there was a man involved, I'll kill him.' Briggs studied Faro intently as if trying to read his thoughts. 'The police say the case is closed.'

Guiltily, Faro remembered Ramsey's post-mortem, and how the doctor had certain knowledge that Polly had been murdered but was powerless to do anything about it. He hated lying to Briggs but there were too many innocent people involved and he had given his word to Vince.

'I expect they did their best,' he said lamely.

'I doubt that their best is good enough. And it doesn't bring my lassie back. Pity you hadn't been on the case, Inspector. I hear that you always get your man.'

'Well, not always, Briggs. Just sometimes,' he added sadly.

There was no more to be said and with a brief salute Briggs went back to the circus tent.

Faro watched him for a moment, noting the weary defeat of his shoulders. Briggs looked stooped and old and Faro felt suddenly ashamed that he had been angry with him. Angry with himself, too, and wishing that he had been asked by the Dundee police to help find Polly's murderer, who was probably still at large.

As was the murderer of Rachel Deane. There was not the least doubt in his mind about that.

Vince was at breakfast next morning, reading *The Scotsman*, when Faro put in an appearance. He had slept badly.

'That was a splendid party afterwards, Stepfather. Pity you missed it, you should have been there. All this chasing of criminals is very well, but not when it seriously interferes with a chap's social life.'

And pointing to the newspaper: 'Willie got a mention here for his performance. He'll be pleased about that.'

Faro said nothing, pouring himself a cup of tea. He didn't feel particularly hungry.

Vince smiled across at him. 'What, no breakfast? Anyone would think you had had a high old time, wining and dining last night. Is there something you aren't telling me about? A secret assignation?'

Faro grimaced. Obviously Vince was back again in his old teasing manner. He should be grateful for that.

Vince had returned to his newspaper. 'Good Lord. Good Lord. Sir Arnold is dead. Here it is. Late notice. Died in the early hours of this morning.' He looked across at Faro. 'He's been very poor ever – ever since—' He still found difficulty in alluding to Rachel's death. 'A bit wandered, poor old man.'

He sighed. 'Wilf will be in full charge now. I don't suppose it'll make any difference to me, but I'm sorry. I shall miss Sir Arnold. He's been good to me.'

Faro dreaded that Sir Arnold's funeral, coming so soon after Rachel's, would reopen that well of sadness for Vince, only now healing.

17 Vince returned two weeks later, full of information about Sir Arnold's funeral, one of the largest Dundee had ever seen.

'Brought it all back to me, so soon after Rachel. The graveside, the vault. All that sort of thing,' he said sadly.

As usual he spent the entire weekend with Kathleen. After the first rather uncomfortable evening, Faro had not renewed his invitation for her to dine with them at Sheridan Place, although he realised guiltily that he must do so soon.

However, it was a very subdued Vince who returned from taking Kathleen out to dinner on the Sunday evening.

'I will be taking the 6.25 train tomorrow morning, Stepfather,' he said, looking in to say goodnight. And opening his bedroom door: 'By the way, I might not be home again for a little while.'

At Faro's questioning look, he said: 'I made up my mind tonight to ask Kathleen to marry me.'

'And—?'

'She declined my proposal.'

Faro felt a curious sense of relief as Vince continued:

'Everything seemed so right and it would have made the McGonagalls very happy—'

'You don't marry someone to make their relatives happy, dammit,' Faro said sharply.

'I know that. But I am rather disappointed.'

Disappointed he might be, thought Faro shrewdly, but hardly heartbroken. There was nothing here to resemble his grief at losing Rachel.

'Did she give any reason?' Faro asked.

'The best. She has a lover already. That explains so many things, doesn't it? Seems to have been going on for quite some time. In fact, he set her up in the milliner's shop.'

Here then were Faro's own suspicions of the rich protector confirmed, first by Briggs and now by Kathleen's own admission, which he felt considering the ardour of Vince's courtship was somewhat overdue.

Mistaking his stepfather's expression, Vince said: 'It isn't as immoral as it sounds.'

'I didn't say it was. You should know by now, lad, that I'm quite unshockable.'

Vince nodded. 'She says he loves her and in her own words, once his present circumstances leave him free to propose, and he gets his life sorted out, they intend to marry.'

'Is there a wife already?'

'Sounds like it, although she was very reserved about discussing his affairs. Said she had promised him never to tell anyone and she was only telling me because she knew she could rely on my discretion.'

His glance invited affirmation and when Faro was silent, he went on: 'Apparently he's quite high up – her words – and it would be disastrous for his position in society if all this was made public. At least it explains her "touch me not" attitude. She confessed that she was very attached to me and that in normal circumstances, she would have been honoured to be my wife, etc., etc.'

Pausing he added bleakly, 'Or so she said last night.'

Faro put a hand on his arm. 'I'm sorry, lad. You seemed quite smitten.'

'Not to mind, Stepfather. There are more fish in the sea, as you once reminded me,' was the pseudo-cheerful reply. 'Actually we didn't have a lot in common, you know, I see that now. Not enough for a lifetime, at any rate.'

And as an afterthought: 'Perhaps the real reason I was attracted to her in the first place was that I was looking for another Rachel. And she did remind me of her, at first sight. But that wore off after the first meeting.'

And observing his stepfather's anxious look, he smiled. 'Not to worry, I'll be all right this time, I promise. Who knows, two rejections, maybe it'll be third time lucky.'

'I hope so, lad.'

Vince was silent, studying the doorknob gravely. 'Oh, by the way, talking of proposals and so forth, I have another bit of news that will surprise you. Now that Wilf has inherited, his engagement to Lady Clara Wilkes will be announced shortly.'

He smiled. 'He told me very confidentially as we drove down together, but I'm sure he won't mind you knowing, since you are the soul of discretion. Lady Clara is an heiress of ancient family whose estates are in Fife.'

'This is all very sudden.'

'Oh, yes, totally unexpected, Stepfather. She's a remote cousin. Her husband ran off with another woman, an Italian princess, I understand. Wilf and she were childhood sweethearts and have been secretly engaged for some while, with Sir Arnold's blessing. Now that her divorce has come through they are to marry quietly, without any fuss, since the Deanes are officially in mourning.'

'A very well-kept secret.'

'Oh, indeed. And it explains what I could never understand. Why someone as eligible as Wilfred hadn't married long ago. Even for dynastic purposes.'

But Wilfred Deane's newfound happiness was not destined to last.

*

Two days after the announcement in *The Scotsman* Faro was summoned to the Royal British Hotel where a man had been found dead in his room.

On Princes Street the church bells were summoning worshippers to morning service, while inside the hotel Sergeant McQuinn was waiting for him and a uniformed constable kept curious hotel guests and alarmed staff at bay in the corridor.

Inside Room 102, the police surgeon Dr Holmes knelt beside the corpse who lay wide-eyed and staring as he had fallen.

'Haven't touched a thing, Inspector. I've just arrived, waiting for you to make your inspection of the room.' He pointed to the body where a tiny red rose of death had bloomed and congealed on the immaculate white shirt-front.

Faro looked around. It was an almost tidy scene of death, no visible bloodstains, only a chair overturned and a broken ornament near the door. The bedcovers had apparently been dragged off in some sort of struggle but the bed itself had not been slept in, for its pristine pillows were undented.

As Holmes began to examine the body, Faro leaned over.

'Anyone found the murder weapon? A knife with a stiletto blade, I would say, since there is so little blood about.'

'Correct, Inspector. Stabbed once, a bull's-eye straight to the heart. Died instantly.'

McQuinn and the constable had followed Faro inside and were methodically searching the room. An easy task since the drawers and wardrobe were empty, the dead man's travelling bag unpacked.

'No evidence of the knife, so far, sir. Guess the murderer carried it away with him.'

'How long has he been dead?' Faro asked the police surgeon.

'Oh, by the condition of the body, I would say at least twelve hours. Between ten and midnight last night.'

McQuinn handed Faro a piece of paper. 'According to reception, the deceased is one of their regulars. He had no visitors last night. His wife usually comes with him, but he was alone this time. Just as well for her, perhaps.'

And looking over Faro's shoulder: 'He's a Mr James Burnett, a businessman from Arbroath. That should be easy to check, sir. At least we have an identity for him.'

Faro looked at the body. 'I think you'll find that Mr Burnett isn't his real name.'

McQuinn whistled. 'So it's not going to be a simple case after all.'

Faro smiled wryly. 'After all your years with me, McQuinn, I shouldn't have to tell you that murder is never simple.'

'Any ideas, Inspector?' asked the police surgeon as he drew a sheet over the body.

'Yes. I know this man. His name is Wilfred Deane.'

'Of the Dundee Deanes?'

'The same.'

'Good Lord. This will cause a sensation.'

'Didn't I read that he was about to be married?' said McQuinn. 'Then I wonder—'

'I think you'll find that the lady calling herself Mrs Burnett was not Lady Clara Wilkes,' said Faro, examining the room.

Apart from the bedcovers on the floor, the lack of a struggle suggested that Deane had been easily overpowered and that death had come to him as a surprise.

'That stiletto stabbing suggests an Italian job to me,' said Sergeant McQuinn. 'There's a lot of them about in Edinburgh these days. Could be a vendetta. Fallen foul of one of their families.'

When word reached Superintendent McIntosh, he was mortified that an illustrious and prominent Dundee citizen should have been murdered in his territory.

'Dundee Police are sending a detective. He's already on his way but you will be in charge of this case, Faro.' A pause. 'Any ideas?'

*

'Any ideas?' asked Detective Sergeant Elliott. He arrived that evening at Sheridan Place off the same train as Vince, who came in his official capacity as Deane's doctor, horrified to hear of his friend and employer's brutal murder.

Both men exchanged grumbles about the atrocious rail journey. Both were in agreement about one thing. 'High time they got that bridge finished.'

'This wasn't a murder for theft,' said Faro in answer to Elliott's question. 'Nothing of value was taken. His pocket case was full of bank notes, his watch and rings intact.'

'Bad business,' said Elliott. 'Any suspects?'

'Just one. Woman calling herself Mrs Burnett, his only regular visitor. As they knew her well, she did not bother to register. But the bellboy met a heavily veiled woman making her way to Deane's room on Saturday evening. When he said: "Good evening, Mrs Burnett," she ignored him. He thought perhaps he had been mistaken.'

'Or she was anxious not to be recognised,' said Elliott slowly.

'Did anyone see her arrive or depart?' Vince asked.

'No one,' replied Faro.

Elliott looked crestfallen as only a detective can when deprived of evidence to link the main suspect with the murder.

'Any other ideas, sir? I understand you both knew the victim.'

'We had a slight acquaintance,' said Faro.

'Good, that is a great help. For motive, and so on.'

'I think I can assess from the state of the room how the murder was accomplished and from the evidence, this case has all the marks of the *crime passionnel*.'

'A woman's crime, is that it, Stepfather?'

'Do I take it you have hopes of an early arrest, Inspector?' Elliott interrupted. And seizing upon Faro's non-committal response as affirmation: 'Excellent. Well, well, I never expected this kind of progress. You are certainly living up to your reputation, sir.'

Faro smiled wryly. 'First catch your murderer, Elliott.'

'I would say it's an open and shut case.'

'Yes indeed,' said Vince enthusiastically. 'Ten to one it is the missing Mrs Burnett.'

'The hotel staff were very eager for a bit of gossip. Apparently Mr and Mrs Burnett were never seen in the dining room like any other married couple, honeymooners apart. Had all their meals in the upstairs suite,' said McQuinn. He had been very busy, very thorough with his interviews at the hotel.

'And being wise after the event, the manager said he thought it highly suspicious that a gentleman allegedly from Arbroath should choose the weekend to conduct his Edinburgh business and receive visits from his wife.'

'I expect Sergeant Elliott knows that Mr Deane had recently become engaged,' said Vince.

'Indeed yes. The Wilkeses are very well thought of, a highly respectable family. There is going to be one hell of a scandal when we have to investigate Lady Clara's alibi. Ever met her, Dr Laurie?'

'Not yet.' Vince looked at his stepfather. 'I suppose it is just possible—'

Faro shook his head and said to the detective, 'You're wasting your time. I think you will find that the lady is completely innocent and can account for her movements that night. Also it will come as a considerable shock to her to learn that Deane had a mistress in Edinburgh.'

'A shock to everyone who knew him, Stepfather.'

'And neither lady with any inkling of the other's existence,' said Elliott thoughtfully. 'So if Lady Clara is innocent, all we have to do is find this other woman.'

'That could be quite a poser,' said Vince. 'But I'm sure my stepfather is up to it.' He smiled. 'He is probably one jump ahead of us right now.'

'We need only go as far back as Deane's engagement. I fancy

that came as a startling surprise to Mrs Burnett. And fortunately I know exactly where I can lay hands on the lady who calls herself by that name. If you would care to accompany me.'

He turned and looked at his stepson who was listening eagerly. 'You too, Vince lad.'

Vince laughed uneasily. 'Why me?'

'Because you know the way better than I do.'

'You don't mean – Oh no, Stepfather. You can't—'

'I do. And I'm afraid I must.'

18 It was a very silent quartet who were deposited by the police carriage in Rose Street. First, Detective Sergeant Elliott and Sergeant McQuinn, to take notes in case an arrest was made, then Vince, shocked into stunned silence by the information that he was to step inside the shop and behave in a casual fashion.

Last to emerge was Faro, clutching a parcel whose contents he did not see fit to divulge. 'Best wait outside, lads.'

'We don't want to alarm her,' said Elliott firmly. 'We don't want any unnecessary violence. But we had best be prepared, Inspector,' he added, patting his greatcoat pocket significantly. 'Let's try to act as normally as possible, Dr Laurie.'

It was doubtful, thought Faro, whether anyone could regard that white stricken face as normal, and he gave his stepson a rallying pat on the shoulder.

As Vince walked to the counter, Faro hovered by the door while Elliott and McQuinn looked through the window keeping the scene under careful scrutiny while trying to remain inconspicuous. It wasn't easy, two tall men and a uniformed constable, who was the driver, all gazing with elaborate concentration at a windowful of ladies' bonnets.

They saw the pretty young assistant step forward, shake her head.

'Come along, Elliott,' said Faro and threw open the door.

As they spread themselves before her, the assistant eyed them with alarm.

'No, I'm afraid Madame is not at home to anyone.'

'I am a friend of hers,' said Vince.

The girl considered his companions doubtfully. 'Madame is indisposed.'

'She will see me,' said Vince winningly and striding purposefully behind the counter opened the door leading upstairs to the flat.

'You can't do that,' protested the girl. 'Wait – I'll lose my job for this.'

Elliott and McQuinn pushed past her up the stairs. Faro paused before a tray of milliner's accessories then he followed them.

They found Kathleen slumped in a chair by the window. There was something in her attitude which touched an unhappy memory for Faro. She looked up at them with a wan smile.

'I've been expecting this visit, gentlemen.' She turned her gaze to Faro, said softly, 'You've come to arrest me, haven't you, Inspector?' And nodding vigorously, 'Yes, I did it. I killed Wilfred Deane.'

Faro heard a sigh of relief from Elliott. There was going to be no violence, just a confession and a peaceful arrest.

'I'm glad you've come,' she said, rising wearily, supported by her hands on the arms of the chair. 'Strange, it's better to be taken by friends.' Looking intently at Vince, 'By people who care about what happens to you rather than by impersonal constables who are merely doing their duty.'

'Have you the murder weapon, Kathleen?' asked Faro. 'You used a long hatpin, like this one,' he added, flourishing that same article used by ladies to stab their hats into submission, which he had picked up from the counter downstairs. 'Am I right?'

Kathleen's face paled, her hands flew to her throat as if she felt the rope around it. For a moment he thought she was about to faint.

'Will they hang me?' she whispered.

'Sit down, lass,' he said not unkindly. 'We'll do the best we can for you. It was self-defence, after all, was it not? May I?' And leaning forward he pulled aside the silk scarf she wore. On her neck, on either side of her throat, were two ugly bruises.

Vince swore. 'Did he do that to you?'

Before she could reply Faro said, 'Be so good as to pour a glass of water for her, will you please.' And to Elliott, 'You see I was perfectly sure that when Miss Neil visited the hotel room that evening as Mrs Burnett, she had not the least intention of murdering her lover. He had summoned her as usual, but this time with the express motive of getting rid of her.'

'Surely that's a bit steep,' said Elliott. 'I mean, if he was just breaking it off—'

'Bear with me, if you please. Deane had excellent reason for not "just breaking it off" as you call it. He had to shut Miss Neil's mouth for good. Believe me, gentlemen, his whole future was at stake. And if anyone had murder in his heart that evening, it was Wilfred Deane. And when he attacked her, so brutally and unexpectedly, she used the first and only weapon to hand – the long pin which had secured her bonnet.'

He paused and looked down at Kathleen. 'Perhaps you would like to tell us in your own words what happened, lass.'

As Kathleen spoke, she threw occasional glances of appeal and apology in Vince's direction. 'When I first met Vince I told him—'

'If you please, lass, we'd like to hear it right from the beginning. How and where you first met Wilfred Deane. This will all need to come out in court,' Faro added to McQuinn who had taken out his notebook in readiness.

'I met Wilfred Deane when I was working with Uncle Willie McGonagall in the factory. He isn't my uncle really,' she said, 'just a remote cousin who was very kind after my mother died. Anyway, he got me a job in the jute factory, hoping to train me for the stage. He wanted me to be a Shakespearean actress. But I was never any good at that.

'One day when Wilfred was visiting the factory he came and talked to me. I felt very flattered. He came often after that and I guessed that he was taken with me. Of course I played up to him, he was a wealthy man.'

She paused. 'To cut a long story short, after we became – intimate – he bought me this shop in Edinburgh. He didn't want anyone to know and I was to pretend that I had gone to London. I didn't mind, I would have done anything for him. Anything.'

The word was a whisper, her sigh remembered. 'He asked very little in return. Just that he might come and visit me when he was able to do so. He often had business meetings to attend here. I agreed. Who wouldn't? After life in the factory, it was a very good exchange. And after my early life in a Dublin slum,' she added bitterly.

'When Sir Arnold died and Wilfred inherited I presumed the family opposition to his marrying me that he talked about would be at an end. No one could disinherit him now for marrying a former factory girl. The whole of Deane's was his now. I had a note – I have it here somewhere – to meet him as usual for the weekend at the Royal British Hotel.'

From her reticule she produced a crumpled piece of paper which she handed to Faro. 'But this time I was in for a shock. I wasn't prepared to find out that everything he had told me and had promised was a lie. He told me to prepare myself for bad news. He could not marry me, first of all. He had to marry this Lady Clara, but this was to be a marriage of convenience. He needed Lady Clara's money to keep Deane's afloat, but he did not love her.

'I was to rest assured that I was his one true love and there was no reason why we should not continue as before, this arrangement had worked so well. Of course I was very upset and disappointed. I wept. I had waited all this time for him to be free to marry me. I had no wish to remain in the backwater of his life as his mistress, seeing him only when he could visit Edinburgh.

'We never went outside the hotel in case we were recognised. I was always heavily veiled. What kind of life was that? I wanted to be at his side – as his wife, living at Deane Hall. I wanted children too,' she added bleakly.

'When I told him all this, he kissed me, assured me that I was worrying unnecessarily. Do you know, he never once lost his temper. So patient with me, smiling, understanding.'

Taking a deep breath, she continued painfully. 'As he held me, he removed my bonnet, loosened my hair. As he usually did before – before—'

Her sudden pause, eyes wide, relived that moment. In panic she was suddenly aware of this audience of men.

'We quite understand, lass,' said Faro hastily.

She shook her head tearfully. ' "Never worry, my dearest. We will think of something. Rest assured of that." And those were his very last words to me. He shook down my hair, let it fall about my shoulders, put his hands round my throat. I thought he was about to caress me. I closed my eyes.'

Her voice faded and her hands trembled towards the bruises. 'But his grip grew tighter and I saw in his eyes reflected in the dressing-table mirror that he meant to kill me. The room was growing darker. I struggled frantically. I'm quite strong really and I pushed him hard, he let me go. But as I tried to reach the door he came at me again, knocked me down with his fist.

'I fell beside the bed, put out my hand to struggle to my knees and felt my bonnet – with the pin still sticking out of it. He turned me to face him, his hands tight around my throat again and I struck at his chest with all my might.

'You know the rest,' she ended wearily and, sobbing, buried her face in her hands.

As Faro went forward, put a hand on her shoulder, she looked up. 'I've sat here for the past two days, trying to summon up courage to give myself up. The waiting was worse than seeing you coming up the stairs, I can tell you. I'm glad you came. Now I can be peaceful. Will they hang me, Mr Faro?' she asked again.

'I think when all your story is known, no jury will convict you, Kathleen? There would be a public outcry against any such verdict. Especially as you saved the hangman a job.'

'I don't know about that, Faro,' said Sergeant Elliott.

'Let me finish,' said Faro. 'A public outcry, since Wilfred Deane is himself a murderer—'

'Hold on, Faro. Attempted only—' Elliott protested.

Faro shook his head. 'Deane has already committed murder and escaped justice. As Kathleen well knows.'

It was Kathleen's turn to protest. 'I don't know anything about that, sir. Honest I don't.' But there was panic in her voice, terror in her eyes.

'I think you do. You see, I believe all your story. Except for the first part. You weren't being quite straight with us, were you? About Deane's reasons for not marrying you? Oh, it is true he was going to have to make a marriage for business reasons with a woman whom he did not love. But you knew about that right from the beginning. He made no secret of it.'

'I never did. I never did,' she cried. 'I swear I didn't know of Lady Clara's existence until I read it in the newspapers.'

'Ah, but it was not Lady Clara he told you he was being forced to marry when he confessed his predicament to you originally. It was nearer home. Much nearer.'

Kathleen bit her lips and turned away sullenly as Faro looked across at Vince. 'It was Rachel Deane, as we both know. He told us so that night she died. How much he loved her.'

'He never loved her,' Kathleen shouted. 'That was a rotten lie.'

'It was indeed,' said Faro, 'for love didn't enter into his cruel calculations. It was money again. Money he desperately needed to save himself from jail.

'Time was running out. He knew there was already a fraud and embezzlement enquiry under way regarding the inferior building materials that had been substituted for the more expensive ones contracted for the Tay Bridge.'

Elliott nodded. 'So you knew about that too, Faro?'

'Superintendent Johnston told me in confidence.'

'These enquiries are the main reason why this damned bridge is taking so long in the building. It was no secret with us. We all knew about that on the force. Go on, Inspector.'

'Wilfred Deane was desperate to lay his hands on Rachel's fortune. He might have succeeded but she fell in love with someone else, someone she had just met briefly. Her grandfather's doctor, namely Vince here. And that was when he decided to murder her.'

'But that can't be true, Rachel took her own life. We saw her,' said Vince. 'Good God, Stepfather, you were there.'

Faro shook his head. 'Would you do something for me, Kathleen?'

When she looked doubtful, he said: 'It might well strengthen your case, save your life.'

'All right,' she agreed sullenly.

'Would you please remove your shoes.'

'My shoes? If that's what you want.' As she kicked them aside, Faro withdrew from the bag he carried a pair of ladies' slippers.

At his side, Vince's cry of painful recognition was added to Kathleen's gasp of alarm.

'Those were Rachel's,' said Vince. 'She wore them that night – and you've kept them all this time,' he added accusingly.

'I know, lad, I know. And I've kept them with good reason, for just such an occasion as this. Kathleen, if you please.' Kneeling down he took her foot and slipped on first the right slipper and then the left.

And looking up triumphantly, 'As I suspected. They fit perfectly. Made for this lass. Gentlemen, I've waited for months to find this particular Cinderella.'

'Are you mad, Stepfather? That's a mere coincidence. Those were Rachel's shoes,' Vince protested.

'Then why didn't they fit her? You tried them yourself when she was recovered from the river. They kept falling off. The reason, although we were both too distressed to note its significance at the time, was that they were several sizes too large for her.

'Why? Because they were Kathleen's shoes and it was Kathleen who ran away from you that night and climbed the ladder on the bridge.'

'But how – how—'

'Hear me out. It was Kathleen who climbed the ladder. But it was Rachel who plunged or was thrown to her death in the River Tay.'

19 Vince stared open-mouthed at Faro. 'What are you saying, Stepfather? We saw Rachel jump—'

'No, we didn't. It was not Rachel. And she did not drown. She was probably already dead—'

'But we were there when they took her from the river.'

'Oh yes, two hours later. Time enough for her to give all the appearance of having drowned. A post-mortem, however, might have revealed that she was heavily drugged.'

Vince continued to shake his head in bewilderment, gazing at his stepfather as if he had taken leave of his senses.

Faro put a hand on his arm. 'Vince, lad, I know this is going to be terrible for you. But believe me, Rachel was probably already dead when her body plunged into the Tay. Drugged, carried up the iron pier by Deane in one of those huge baskets the workmen used for transporting materials from one level to another—'

'But the letter I received,' Vince interrupted, having found his voice at last. 'That was from her. I knew her writing. I had other notes, dammit.'

'Oh yes, indeed. She wrote the letter. I haven't the least doubt about that. She had been kept prisoner in the house since she returned from Errol. Carefully watched from the moment she announced to Deane that she was going to marry Dr Laurie. And what was more her grandfather would have been delighted when she told him.'

Ignoring Vince's groan of anguish, Faro continued: 'Deane
was desperate, so he shut her up in her room, explaining to
everyone that she was suffering from one of her periodic bouts
of madness. Vince, lad, Rachel was never mad. Wilful, difficult
but more spoilt than anything by being a rich man's only granddaughter. But mad, no. The madness was dreamed up by Wilfred
Deane. That was his invention.

'He realised he couldn't keep her prisoner for ever. Time was
running out for him. Rachel would inherit on her birthday.
Meanwhile the police were investigating a possible fraud. And if
he could not replace the vast sums of money he had been
systematically embezzling from the firm, then he would be dis-
graced and go to jail.

'He had to have Rachel's money to set the accounts right. He
couldn't drag her to the altar unwillingly or without her grandfather's permission, especially as the doting old man was prepared
to accept her choice, namely the young doctor he had taken such
a liking to.

'There was only one way out. And so he decided to kill her,
make it look like suicide. He didn't anticipate much difficulty in
then getting the money from Sir Arnold on the grounds that a
sick old man was incapable of handling the firm's finances.
Everyone was sympathetic and the shareholders had known for
some time now that Deane's was being run by Wilfred.

'Perhaps he had been considering getting rid of Rachel also
for some while. Certainly from that first moment he saw Kathleen
in the factory and noticed that there was a resemblance.'

Pausing he looked directly at Kathleen. 'Was that when he
began to formulate what must have seemed like a clever but
extraordinarily foolproof plan, using you as an innocent
accessory?'

When she turned away, he went on: 'But to return to that
fatal evening on the bridge. He went to Rachel, said he had had
a change of heart. He had decided to let her marry you after all,

Vince. But she must go that night, elope, before anyone could stop her.

'How eagerly then she must have written that note to you. Dear Wilfred was being so helpful, he even brought her one of the maid's dresses and a cheap shawl, a uniform garment which could easily be obtained for Kathleen too.'

Looking at his stepson's white face, he said: 'I'm sorry, lad. This is very distressing for you. Because the moment Rachel wrote that note she had unknowingly signed her own death-warrant.

'Deane then administered the drug, most likely in a cup of tea to fortify her for the journey, or by some other seemingly innocent means. Then he took her out in his carriage until the drugs took effect. He knew about Dr Ramsey's discoveries concerning Polly Briggs and so Rachel had to be kept alive to make it look like drowning for the Procurator Fiscal's report.

'On the bridge the workmen had gone and it was already dark. He had bribed the night-watchman to look the other way while he carried in Rachel's body and deposited it in the basket. The watchman little realised that Deane would make sure he never lived to enjoy that substantial bribe, though I doubt if even he – unless he was a very good actor indeed – knew the contents of the basket he was helping his master to elevate by the pulleys up to the top platform.

'Deane then climbed the ladder himself and began his vigil. There was one more assignation to keep before his plan could succeed.

'And this is where you came in, Kathleen. What was it? How did he persuade you? Just one more impersonation.'

'One more? What do you mean – one more? I swear—'

Faro held up his hand. 'I mean this was the second time you had pretended to be Rachel Deane. The first was at Deane Hall when she denied ever having met Vince.'

When she didn't reply, he said: 'I am right, am I not? Come

along, Kathleen,' he added sharply. 'It's all gone too far to go back now. And you won't help anyone, least of all yourself, by concealing the truth.'

Kathleen stared at him mutinously as if about to refuse. Then suddenly defeated, she said: 'All right, I'll tell you what happened. But I swear to God I'm innocent of Rachel Deane's death. I knew nothing of what he intended when I agreed to appear as Rachel Deane that first time for Vince's benefit. Only that he had made a wager with one of his friends.'

She smiled. 'Wilfred loved gambling, he couldn't resist it. That was how he got heavily into debt. I didn't think his request was strange, because he often wagered on daft things. This one was that he could pass me off as Rachel Deane, to fool this friend who would be hiding behind the screen with him. It was, he said, all a bit of a lark, but if he won the wager, a thousand guineas, then I should have as my reward my milliner's shop – this place.'

'Paid for, as you now realise, by Rachel Deane's death,' said Faro grimly. 'Have I been right so far?'

She shrugged. 'Yes, and I wish to God you hadn't. I would do anything to undo what happened that night.'

'Pray continue.'

'I never guessed that the reason he was first taken with me was that with dark hair instead of fair, he thought I could be made to look like Rachel. Then at a Saturday night social he heard my "Song of the Forest", realised that as a born mimic I could probably imitate a human voice as easily as bird calls.'

She sighed. 'I loved him right from the start. He convinced me that this impersonation was all a harmless joke to trick his friend, but I would have done anything for him, anyway. Whatever he asked without question.'

'Did you ever meet this friend?'

'No. I doubt now whether he ever existed. Just another lie,' she added with a bright bitter smile.

'Did you ever go to London?'

'No, that was for Uncle Willie's benefit, so that they wouldn't worry. I was to stay in Deane Hall. Of course in order to impersonate Rachel I had to spend some time with her. There was no difficulty.'

'Did you never meet anyone?'

'Sometimes I saw a maid in the distance who looked the other way – or dived into the linen cupboard, the way the gentry treat their servants.'

'How was your presence explained to Rachel?'

'Oh, that was easy. I was a dressmaker and milliner and very good at making wigs too. I ran a very exclusive establishment and only visited clients in their own house. I could be recommended. Rachel welcomed me. She was a trusting gentle creature, pretty and a bit vain.

'She liked the idea of having a wig made too. It was quite usual in her station in life. She was as much a fool as I was. I stayed several days to give her fittings and by that time I could do an exact imitation of her voice. It wasn't too difficult after bird calls – the human voice, I mean.

'Wilfred was very pleased. Although in a strong light I couldn't have fooled anyone, in a dimly lit room, with Rachel's voice, he said the result was quite uncanny.'

'And as long as you didn't stand up,' added Faro, 'since you are two inches taller but more slightly built. Your face might pass muster but not the rest of you. And your feet and hands are larger too.'

Pursing his lips, he studied her for a moment. 'That was another thing that bothered me. Why, in all that heat of passionate denouncement when you said you had never met Vince before in your life, you never once got up from that huge armchair, not even to ring the bell.'

'I thought the difference in our shape would be noticeable.'

'And of course, you couldn't hope to make these appearances too often.'

'Wilfred had said only once at Deane Hall. Later he told me that it had been a dress rehearsal. The friend was making a fuss about a thousand guineas and was unwilling to pay it. He thought I had done very little. So there was to be one more appearance. The friend wanted something more daring before he would pay up.

'He wanted to see Rachel Deane on the bridge in moonlight. I was scared at first, but Wilfred said it was quite safe and so I agreed. I would meet him on the bridge, wearing a bonnet to conceal my hair. He also insisted I wear a plain dress, like a maid's. And a plain bonnet. I couldn't think – and he wouldn't tell me – why he wanted two exactly the same.'

'Because it was essential for his plan that you and Rachel were dressed alike. And of course you couldn't wear a wig this time. It might have fallen off. Then all would indeed have been revealed. When you attacked Vince, you entered the yard by the broken fence—'

'Wilfred had arranged that, I knew exactly where to look for it.'

'So you ran to the bridge, kicked off your shoes to make the climb easier. Tell me, why did you carry a stone in your reticule?'

Kathleen looked uncomfortable.

'Was that to deter Vince should he succeed in following you?'

'I think that was what Wilfred intended,' she whispered, her eyes downcast.

At Vince's horrified gasp she turned to face him. 'Don't look so shocked,' she said viciously. 'I never loved you. It was always him I wanted. I would have done anything for him. Anything. You meant nothing to me.' She snapped her fingers. 'Not even that much. Nothing at all.'

She began to weep noiselessly as Faro continued: 'May I tell you what happened next? When you climbed to the second platform behind the pier, you ducked back. Wilfred came forward and heaved Rachel's body from the bridge.'

'I swear I didn't know that was what he was going to do. I

was sick with fear. He told me later that she had to die or go into the bedlam. She was quite insane and he was doing her a kindness. I swear I would never have agreed, if I'd known it was just her money he was after. And that everything he had told me was a pack of lies.'

There was a pause and Faro said, 'After it was done, you both waited until we ran down to the river. Then you both put on workmen's overalls and while all attention was diverted to the search for Rachel's body, you came back down the ladder. Two workmen who had been inspecting the scene of the accident.

'Wilfred then discarded his overalls and reappeared as if he had just arrived. As a matter of interest, what did you do?'

'I went to the station and took the morning train to Edinburgh.' Kathleen wrung her hands. 'I was horrified by what had happened. You have to believe me, I never had any idea until that night that he intended to murder Rachel.'

'Although you knew he had murdered before. When he got rid of Polly Briggs.'

Her face flushed guiltily. 'I don't know anything about that.'

'You might as well admit it, Kathleen. It will all come out in court. But this time you were not involved. Although you must have had your suspicions.'

'Oh all right then. Polly Briggs was jealous when she saw that Wilfred liked me. She was determined to get even so she struck up with a fellow high up in the office. Charlie something-or-other.'

'Charlie McGowan?'

'Yes, him. She told me he wanted to marry her but he had a wife already. And the wife had found out and was going to leave him. Then she told me an extraordinary story that Charlie was hoping to go into partnership with Deane's. He was very clever at his job, but he had also found out something that would give him a hold over Wilfred Deane.'

'And you told him?'

Again she coloured. 'Of course I did. I thought it was only proper to warn him. I didn't want him to go to prison. I would have done anything to save him from that.'

'How did you feel when you heard that Charlie McGowan was dead?' Faro asked coldly.

'That was an accident, Wilfred told me.'

'And you believed him. What about Polly?'

'I thought she had committed suicide, because of Charlie. Perhaps she was in the family way.'

She saw by Faro's expression that he didn't believe that either. 'You're very clever, Inspector. But how did you guess all this?'

'I assure you I did not guess. Those are not my methods at all,' said Faro sternly. 'I observed and deduced and came to what I am far from happy to realise was the right one. The only conclusion I could make in the sorry mess you have made of your life.'

With a grim smile, he added: 'But you very nearly got away with it. I was completely baffled. Oh, I had clues all right but nothing that fitted or made sense. You have your Uncle Willie to thank that you were found out.'

'Uncle Willie? How on earth did he know?'

'He didn't. But if we hadn't been invited to his performance at Holyrood the other evening—'

'I don't see what—'

'Of course you don't. But when I saw the magician's trick with the girl who apparently dived into the flaming tank and then saw her resurrected, unscathed, back on the trapeze, I realised that two girls were involved. That was the piece that had been missing all along from my calculation. Once it was in place, I knew exactly how Rachel's death had been stage-managed.'

As they watched her led away, she turned to Faro a last time.

'Will Uncle Willie and Aunty Jean be involved?' she asked anxiously. 'They have been so good to me. Like parents. I wouldn't want them to be hurt.'

'I'll do my best.'

Afterwards Vince said to him, 'Do you know, Stepfather, I think she was lying. That she knew he intended to kill Rachel but was prepared to look the other way. Her story is fairly thin in parts.'

'I dare say we will have it all in detail before the trial is out.'

'There must be some good in her. I mean, she was worried about the McGonagalls, about a scandal for them.'

Faro suppressed a smile. 'Scandals never hurt an actor, lad, they thrive on it. Sensational news will simply add lustre to his notoriety. And notoriety is something always to be welcomed. Only being totally ignored can damage an actor like William McGonagall.'

Epilogue

The Deanes are fictitious, but the tragic consequences to be paid for dubious dealings concerning the Tay Bridge is a true story.

Sunday 28 December 1879 dawned unseasonably mild but with an unnatural stillness which amateur astronomers put down to the brief eclipse of the moon due just before sunset. At 4 p.m. it began to rain heavily and retired admirals and sea-captains who resided in handsome villas on both sides of the Tay disgustedly laid telescopes aside.

Barometers were consulted and the sudden fall noted while in leafy avenues and parks, gardens were crushed as if a giant foot had stepped upon them and great trees bent under the weight of the rain.

By 5 p.m. the east wind had increased to gale force. As the first roof slates and chimneys crashed to the ground those about to depart for evening service had second thoughts. Rattling windows and sounds of broken glass as conservatories were demolished recalled uneasy memories of the gale twenty years earlier. It had flattened entire forests and whisked out of the earth ancient trees of enormous proportions.

In Edinburgh although the weather had worsened considerably the 4.15 'Edinburgh Express' left Waverley Station on time, reaching Granton twenty minutes later. After a particularly ferocious voyage across the Firth of Forth the passengers reached Burntisland where Engine 224 prepared to leave at 5.20. Relatively new, built in 1871, it pulled four five-compartmented carriages. One first class, one second and three third. Last of all came the luggage van.

The description of 'The Edinburgh' as an express was optimistic since it stopped at every station. However, the increasing gale did not slow down its leisurely progress across Fife.

Meanwhile Dundee's Tay Bridge Station was in the full grip of the storm. There was consternation as the wind roaring through the tunnel had burst out with a violent explosion, carrying away part of the handsome glass roof and leaving a trail of destruction. A similar tale was being reported from Dundee's main streets, littered with plate-glass windows blown out of shops, while the normal Sabbath quiet of the suburbs was shattered by a crescendo of flying chimney pots, tiles and uprooted trees.

At 5.50 the local Newport train crossed the Tay Bridge. Carriages rocked alarmingly from side to side and seemed to lean over in the full blast of the storm. The sparks which flew from the wheels convinced the terrified passengers that the train was on fire. The guard assured them that this sparking effect was quite common in such weather, caused by the wind pushing carriages so that the flanges of the wheels ground against the guard rail.

With sighs of relief from passengers and railwaymen alike the train safely reached the shelter of the now shattered Tay Bridge Station. The happy ending of one story was the prelude to tragedy, for the passing of the 5.50 had pushed the bridge to the very limits of its endurance.

In the words of one observer there was 'a continuous roar punctuated at intervals by ferocious blasts' as the gale hurled itself upon the bridge. It tore and relaxed its grip momentarily, tore and relaxed again, a gruesome tug o' war over the iron girders and the battered, beseiged columns.

At 7.13 the 5.20 from Burntisland rushed towards the bridge.

The gale pounced upon it, roaring like some savage animal devouring its helpless prey. The train seesawed dangerously, trembling and the high girders hung by a thread.

In Tay Bridge Station, a few intending passengers and railwaymen paced the platform impatiently. The Edinburgh Express had been signalled as it entered the bridge. It was now 7.23 and something was amiss. The telegraph was dead. The signalbox was over the Esplanade and a signalman rushed to meet them. Yes, there were still signal lights on the south end of the bridge where the train had entered. Perhaps it had stopped for some unknown reason but the telegraph lines were down.

They ran back towards the station where two men said they had seen fire falling from the bridge at about 7.15. Another had seen great spumes of water rising from the river at about the same time. Two railwaymen set off to walk the bridge.

At 9 p.m. the training ship *Mars*, which had been anchored near the bridge, approached. A wave of expectation, a whisper of 'survivors' rippled through the now large crowd.

A few bewildered crewmen came ashore. The deck watch had seen the train on the bridge, had observed its lights entering the high girders. His attention distracted momentarily by the storm, when he looked again, the moving lights strung out in a line had vanished and there was apparently a long break in the bridge's outline.

The Newport ferry arrived. It had been grounded since 6 p.m. by low tide. Here was the first link with the south shore and the possibility of survivors, but because of the storm and difficult currents, the ferry had been unable to get anywhere near the bridge.

Mailbags had been washed up at Broughty Ferry, plus reports of debris along the shore all the way from Ladybank to Monifieth.

Provost Brownlie shook his head. 'I'm afraid the bridge is down then; no doubt about it. And the train's gone too.'

Dundee newspapers were already setting up tomorrow's

headlines: 'Terrific Hurricane – Appalling Catastrophe – Tay Bridge Down – Passenger Train Hurled into River – supposed loss of 200 lives—'

'The scene at Tay Bridge Station tonight is simply appalling. Many thousands of persons are congregated around the building, and strong men and women are wringing their hands in despair . . .'

As newspaper reports go, this was a restrained piece of journalism.

On Monday 29 December the sun rose at 8.47 a.m. Slowly the bridge began to take shape, a giant monster unbending from sleep and a great sigh arose from watchers lining the shores from Broughty Ferry to Magdalen Green. All night long, praying that rumour lied, they had awaited this moment and the irrefutable evidence of their own eyes.

Now the cruel morning light revealed the central piers, 'like columns of some majestic ruin of antiquity', all that remained of the high girders.

The Queen had sent a message. 'Inexpressibly shocked, we feel most deeply for the two hundred passengers and all those who have lost friends and relatives in this terrible accident.'

The agent who had checked tickets at the last station before the bridge arrived. He clutched fifty-seven tickets, told of two season tickets and perhaps a dozen more passengers travelling past Dundee; seventy-five dead was substituted for the estimated number who travelled regularly by that same train on weekdays.

The news flashed across the nation by electric telegraph and swamped headlines on the Afghan war and the storming of Sherpur. It brought to readers everywhere a chilly sense of national betrayal and disbelief that Imperial Britain who ruled the waves and half the civilised world – with pretensions towards the other half – and could build anything better than any other nation, had been caught out.

The desks of harassed editors were littered with indignant

letters: how could Britain be let down in the eyes of the world by a bridge that dared to fall? Other letters from cranks believed it was God's judgement on people who used wheeled transport on the Sabbath.

And so Hogmanay, the greatest day of celebration and inebriation in the Scottish calendar became just Wednesday 31 December, on which divers discovered the train. It had plummeted down with the girders, like a bird trapped in a cage. The engine's throttle was still open, the brakes unapplied, proof positive that the train had just entered the high girders when they fell. Any bodies would have been washed away towards the sand flats and five pounds reward was offered by the Council for every body recovered. Search parties patrolled night and day, their torches eerily pricking the darkness with pinpoints of light while whalers, superstitious to a man, shook their heads. Seven days must pass after a drowning before the river god would release his victims for Christian burial, on the eighth day.

The body of one victim, Ann Cruickshank, was recovered. A maid from Kilmaron, unimportant and obscure in life, at her funeral with every honour. Dundee buried all seventy-five of the Tay Bridge disaster victims.

A Court of Inquiry decided that the bridge had been badly designed, badly constructed with shoddy materials and maintained with shoddy workmanship. Twenty men had died in its building and seventy-five men, women and children in its fall. The first contractor died before his contract could be taken up, the second went insane and died.

The disaster fund had raised two thousand pounds, with a generous £250 from Sir Thomas Bouch. His bridge with its unlucky thirteen girders had got him a knighthood and brought death and disaster to Dundee. Elected scapegoat, it was with some satisfaction that the citizens learned the design of the Forth Bridge in Edinburgh was to be taken away from him, pending enquiries, and all work upon it was to cease.

Bouch survived only four months after the report destroyed him. His melancholia advanced into madness and when he died on 1 November the Tay Bridge disaster had claimed its last victim.

One of the chief characters, however, had a surprising resurrection. Engine 4-4-0 No 224 was not permitted to end her days a rusting wreck, a constant memento of Dundee's greatest tragedy. She was gathered together, repaired, refitted and put back into service, where she remained for another forty-five years. Not without reason, she was known as 'The Diver'.

The high girders too were lifted from the river bed. Sold as scrap to a company of locomotive engineers in England and made into railway engines, each bore a small plate recording the origin of its metal. Many continued into the twentieth century.

The last word must go to William McGonagall, for Inspector Faro was right in his predictions. Long forgotten as a tragedian, dubbed by posterity 'Scotland's Worst Poet', he is remembered for his 'Beautiful Railway Bridge of the Silvery Tay'.

> Good Heavens! The Tay Bridge is blown down,
> And a passenger train from Edinburgh,
> Which filled all the people's hearts with sorrow,
> And made them to turn pale
> Because none of the passengers was saved to tell
>   the tale
> How the disaster happened on the last Sabbath
>   day of 1879
> Which will be remembered for a very long time.
>
> It must have been an awful sight
> To witness in the dusky moonlight,
> While the Storm Fiend did laugh, and angry did
>   bray
> Along the Railway Bridge of the Silvery Tay,

I must now conclude my lay
By telling the world fearlessly, without the least
    dismay,
That your central girders would not have given
    way,
At least many sensible men do say,
Had they been supported on each side with
    buttresses,
At least many sensible men confesses,
For the stronger we our houses do build,
The less chance we have of being killed.

To Kill A Queen

To my dear Aberdeen friends,
Anne and James Logan;

and the 'Culter Gang':
Sheila and Rodney Jones
Joan and Pierre de Kock
Gwen and Angus McLeod
Françoise and Donald Macdonald
Evelyn and John Steele
Joyce and Ron Wright

and many more!!

As the train steamed into Aberdeen station, the promising morning of glittering sunshine was under threat from a shroud of mist creeping in from the North Sea.

The foghorn's dismal note did nothing to dispel the persistent chill and was less than welcoming to the two men who emerged wraithlike from the smoke enveloping the platform.

Both were fair-haired and blue-eyed but there all likeness ended. The elder had a countenance curiously in keeping with the legends of Viking raiders in the north of Scotland. Tall leanness concealed considerable strength. A somewhat arrogant face defied the popular fashion for beards. High of cheekbone and nose, only a mouth full lipped and well shaped conceded to curves and hinted at a gentler disposition than first glance suggested.

As for his companion, a frivolity of blond curls sought to escape from the tall hat he clasped firmly against a shrilly unpleasant wind. It cut like a knife, moaning through the open roofs, making its presence felt day and night. With a countenance curiously innocent and vulnerable, this younger man could have passed for seventeen.

But the appearance of both men was deceptive. Closer acquaintance might have detected tight-drawn precision, an ability to make rapid and often life-saving decisions about the younger man's almost cherubic countenance. And in the elder, a certain steeliness about the eyes told a tale of authority, of power and hidden springs coiled taut and ready for instant action. Here was a man used to danger, a man who could be loyal friend, or deadly foe.

His name was Detective Inspector Jeremy Faro. His companion who constantly deplored the lack of evidence of a maturity more befitting his chosen profession was somewhat surprisingly, considering the still youthful appearance of the elder man, his stepson, Dr Vincent Beaumarcher Laurie. He had just been appointed as locum tenens to the resident doctor at the Prince Consort Cottage Hospital at Beagmill on the edge of the Balmoral Estate.

Carrying their light luggage, they walked smartly towards the far end of the station where, almost invisible behind a platform high in wooden boxes, the train for Ballater was being loaded. Both men pressed handkerchiefs to noses. Even the strong breezes were no armour against the pungent aroma around them.

'High in coffined kippers,' muttered Vince.

'Aye, with everything boxed but the smell,' Faro added and Vince looked at him enquiringly.

'Did you write that?'

Faro shrugged. 'No. Read it somewhere.'

'Fortunate that you aren't here on business, Stepfather. Any self-respecting Central Office bloodhound would be put off by the scent, his nose permanently put out of business, I shouldn't wonder. Ugh!' Vince added, as they hurried aboard the waiting train.

The kippers were a delicacy destined for the Royal breakfast table at Balmoral, where Her Majesty was very partial to Aberdeen's famous export. In one of the estate cottages Faro and Vince would partake of less redolent fare, notably the traditional porridge provided by Aunt Isabel, or Bella as she was known, a grand old lady on the eve of her ninetieth birthday.

Faro's mother was never slow to remind him of family obligations and her original intention had been to travel down from Orkney for this important occasion, bringing Rose and Emily to be reunited with their father on Deeside. She had shown great enterprise by reserving accommodation in one of Ballater's excellent hotels on the excuse that Aunt Bella's cottage was quite inadequate for a whole family which included two grown men. But as they prepared to set out disaster had struck. Mary Faro wrote that the two girls had gone down with chicken-pox.

Faro was bitterly disappointed. Chances to see Rose and Emily were rare and ninetieth birthdays were even rarer. He had no desire to add to his aunt's distress by the absence of her heart's darling. Himself. Her favourite nephew, treasured by her as the son she had never had.

Throughout the years Aunt Bella had been his constant refuge in times of stress, providing a retreat whenever he was convalescing from illness, or from injuries resulting from violent encounters with criminals. Faro had many but, as his enemies grumbled, he bore a charmed life.

As for his children, he bore enough guilt and suffered enough sleepless nights for his neglect, real or imagined, of his motherless daughters, whose rightful place, according to Mary Faro, was with their father in Edinburgh. Diplomatically he tried to justify himself in the face of her reproaches – without ever revealing the constant dangers of his life with Edinburgh City Police.

He was a marked man, frequently the target for incidents from which he had narrowly escaped death, making light to her of broken limbs and gunshot wounds. But criminals were no respecters of a policeman's family and he knew from past experience that the presence of two small girls could add a nightmare vulnerability to his daily life.

His thoughts were distracted by Vince reeling up the carriage window and settling back into his seat gratefully.

'I suppose all you have to do is enjoy yourself for a few days, Stepfather. How do you fancy a life without crime for a change?'

'Exceedingly well. Let's hope there is nothing more unlawful than whisky illicitly stilled and salmon illegally gaffed.'

Unbuttoning his greatcoat, Faro took the brim of his tall hat between two fingers and spun it adroitly on to the rack above.

'How do you do that?' asked Vince in admiration.

'Trick of the wrist, lad. Something my late uncle taught me long ago at Easter Balmoral. Quite deadly, I assure you, with the skean-dhu. But I wasn't considered old enough then for sharp knives.'

'I must say I'm looking forward to seeing Great-aunt again,' Vince sighed. 'I fancy a comfortable pastoral hospital where the patients are few and the population healthy. And uncomplicated. For a change.'

A slight tremble in his voice, another, deeper sigh, told all too bitterly how his own happiness had been recently blighted.

Faro regarded him sharply. Vince was staring out of the window. His eyes, suddenly bleak, reminded Faro, in the unlikely event of his ever forgetting the tragic details, how the lad's appointment as factory doctor in Dundee had been marked by heartbreak and near breakdown.

The lad was still looking far from well, but putting his faith in youth's resilience, Faro was confident that Vince would soon find the new job much more agreeable. And he hoped he would also find a more enduring love.

Meanwhile he was convinced that the splendid Ballater air would do the lad a power of good, with Aunt Bella's cosseting close at hand as an excellent substitute for Mrs Brook, their admirable housekeeper.

He hoped Mrs Brook was enjoying her few days' holiday in Perth. Deliberately he pushed to the back of his mind the ominous shadow that now hung over 9 Sheridan Place. He shuddered from the turmoil that must ensue should Mrs Brook's invalid sister, recently bereaved, need her constant attention.

A widower in a large family house, at the mercy of inefficient servants, he saw himself seeking board and lodgings nearer the Central Office.

Staring out of the window he gazed at the magnificence of

an undulating landscape which suddenly replaced his gloomy thoughts with the excitement and pleasurable anticipation of long-lost boyhood. For if there was any place on earth he could call his spiritual home, then it was Deeside. In that sad childhood summer after his policeman father Magnus Faro was killed, he had found healing with his aunt, and with his uncle a passion for fishing, albeit of the net and jar variety.

Gradually, he began to relax as every mile distanced him from a battle of wits with the villains who lurked behind the noise and grime of Edinburgh's High Street and continually harassed the Central Office.

There Superintendent McIntosh tended to be absent-minded about his chief detective's right to have holidays.

Grumbling as always, he had stared moodily out of the window. 'A deuced inconvenient time, I might say, Faro. I'm away to a family wedding in Aberdeen.'

McIntosh's expression had then changed to one of suspicion. 'Easter Balmoral, did you say? Near Crathie, isn't it?' And snatching a paper off the pile on his desk, he added, 'I thought so. Came this morning. Woman murdered.'

Pausing for reaction and finding none forthcoming, he demanded, 'Wouldn't have anything to do with your sudden desire to go up there, would it?'

Assured that this was a holiday and family occasion only, McIntosh sighed. 'Ah, well, in that case, I suppose if you must.' His impatient gesture signalled that permission was given somewhat grudgingly and the interview at an end.

About to leave, Faro turned. 'This murder case . . .'

'Person or persons unknown. That's the verdict. But between you and me, the evidence points to a jealous lover,' said McIntosh. 'Nothing you need concern yourself about.'

'Where exactly did it happen?'

'I was just reading it when you came in.'

But as Faro stretched out his hand towards the papers, McIntosh quickly covered them.

'Never you mind, Faro. You are on leave, remember.'

'I know that but—'

'But nothing. Case is closed and you stay out of it, Faro. We want no meddling, if you please. It's out of our province and the Aberdeen police won't thank us for poking our noses in. You know the rules,' he added sternly. 'Inspector Purdie from Scotland Yard is up there right now. Called in because of the proximity of Balmoral Castle, I imagine.'

When Faro mentioned this to Vince, the latter had smiled. 'Doesn't sound as if that one would be difficult to solve even for the local constable. The old *crime passionnel* again.'

'But presumably without enough evidence to hang him.'

'It happens.'

As stations flashed by and the Dee Valley unfolded its backdrop of grandeur, the two men were soon absorbed in the passing scene: gurgling streams, a gleaming ribbon of silvered river, and through lofty treetops a tantalising glimpse of turreted castle. Houses great and humble were overshadowed by the Grampian Mountains and Lord Byron's 'dark Lochnagar', its secret crevasses, even in summer, white-scarred with snow.

And everywhere towered the Scots pine, sole survivor of the most ancient woodland in Britain, the Caledonian forest, from which the bowmen of Flodden had taken their arrows and more than a thousand years before them, the Roman army had built their war chariots.

A pastoral scene, no doubt, but behind grey castle walls ancient when Mary Queen of Scots had visited the area, murder had been done. The bloodied pages of history opened everywhere. Here Montrose camped with his troops on the way to the sack of Aberdeen. There Jacobites rode out for Prince Charles and a cause already lost, to die savagely on the battlefield at Culloden.

Now it seemed the butchery was limited to sport. As the Ballater train steamed into intermediate stations, carriages bearing coats of arms of noble houses awaited descending passengers.

This was the heart of the shooting season. A few weeks and it would be over. Golden October would cover the land, the guns would be silent and deer, freed from man's ritual slaughter, would again go about the business of survival.

These sombre hills would echo by moonlight to that most eerie and primeval of sounds, the crash of antlers, the bellowing roar as King Stag went into the rut, a fight to the death to maintain his territory and his harem against the young bucks who annually threatened his supremacy.

When Faro spoke his thoughts, Vince's dry response was 'Sounds remarkably as if your old monarch of forest and mountain gave lessons to humans. Seeing that the deer were probably here first.'

There was no answering smile from his stepfather, suddenly aware of a more vulnerable monarch and the periodic attempts on the Queen's life. The fact that there were fewer at Balmoral, where she was considerably more exposed, never failed to surprise him.

Earlier that year in London a youth named Arthur O'Connor had pointed an unloaded pistol at the Queen, the idea being to scare her into releasing Fenian prisoners. Prince Arthur had made a weak attempt to jump over the carriage and save his mother. But John Brown was quicker; he seized the 'assassin', and was rewarded by his grateful sovereign with a gold medal, public thanks and an annuity of £25.

The Prince of Wales, who did not like Brown and enjoyed any chance of discrediting his mother's Highlander among his siblings, complained that his brother had behaved with equal gallantry and had been rewarded with only a gold pin.

As for O'Connor, the Queen greeted his one-year imprisonment with dismay and told Gladstone to have him transported, not out of severity but to prevent him trying again when he came out of prison. O'Connor received this verdict magnanimously, his only stipulation being that his exile should be in a healthy and agreeable climate.

The attempts reported in the newspapers had now reached six. It was a sombre fact, as Faro knew, that there had been many more. Never admitted to the popular press, such outrages were confined to the secret files of Scotland Yard and Edinburgh's Central Office, where Her Majesty's visits were Faro's responsibility and a constant source of anxiety.

'She is either the most foolhardy or the most courageous woman we have ever encountered,' he had told Vince.

'Puts her faith in the divine right of kings as sufficient protection, does she?'

'Possibly.'

'There is another explanation.'

'Indeed? And that is?'

'I'd hazard a complete lack of imagination,' was the short reply.

Faro shuddered as he now thought of that distinctive imposing figure, a boon to the caricaturists and eminently recognisable even at a distance. Stoutly clad in black dress with white streamered widow's cap, the Queen presented a perfect target for a desperate man with a gun.

And here she was at her 'dear Paradise' oblivious of danger. Most days found her traipsing happily about the lonely Deeside hills regardless of weather, without the small army that any cautious monarch would consider necessary. Her security guards, Captains Tweedie and Dumleigh, were sternly commanded to remain behind at the Castle where they idled away many boring hours with nothing better to exert their wits on than playing cards as Her Gracious Majesty set forth accompanied only by her two favourite ghillies, Grant and John Brown. A formidable pair doubtless on their own terms, but no match for a determined assassin.

The Queen's only real protection, Faro knew from his aunt, was that in the country every newcomer was scrutinised and gossiped about via a bush telegraph system in many ways swifter and more efficient than the electrically operated version in

Ballater. It was the simple truth that strangers could not walk these country paths without being observed, their presence questioned, remarked upon and neighbours alerted.

'Safe as houses she is,' Aunt Bella had said on his last visit. 'Ye ken there's not a blade o' grass stirs, not a new tree grows that isna' observed.'

When he had smiled at this exaggeration, she went on, 'Look out o' yon window. Naething but space ye'd guess? Aye, a body would ken that the whole world is empty. But it's no', that's no' the case at all.'

And sweeping her arm dramatically in the direction of the hills, she said, 'Fair seething wi' watchful eyes, it is. There's naught else for a body to do but mind ither folk's business. That's what.'

Upon that and upon the devotion and loyalty of her Scottish subjects and servants, the slender thread of the Queen's life and limb and the future of Great Britain and its colonies depended.

'Here we are at last, Stepfather,' Vince interrupted Faro's reverie and he saw that the vista of hills had been transformed into a town by a cluster of grey roofs and tall spires.

As they emerged from the station there were few remaining passengers unclaimed by the waiting coachmen. Faro was suddenly aware that he and Vince earned some curious glances, lending a comforting verisimilitude to his aunt's remarks.

At the station entrance a man saluted, came forward. 'Ye'll be for Mistress MacVae's place.'

'Indeed yes,' said Faro in surprise as the man took their bags and put them in the cart.

As they drove off, Faro glanced back over his shoulder. Among the faculties of self-protection developed through years of battle with violent men was a sixth sense warning him when he was under careful scrutiny, and he knew that he was being watched.

Now one solitary passenger remained. A heavily veiled woman was cautiously emerging from the station.

At the sight of him, her footsteps had faltered. And as he

looked back for a moment he was certain that he knew her although her face was well hidden.

He laughed. What an absurd idea. He had obviously embarrassed the poor woman by staring so rudely. And her in mourning too. Gravely, politely, he raised his hat in her direction. There was no acknowledgement although her swift movement of turning her back suggested a guilty anxiety not to be recognised.

Faro glanced quickly at Vince but saw that the lad's attention was distracted by the handsome houses and shops as the cart trotted its way through Ballater's main thoroughfare.

Faro sighed, for a moment obsessed by memories as Vince's words regarding his own late unhappy love came back to him.

'I see her everywhere, Stepfather. I have to restrain myself from accosting innocent young women because they remind me, in a walk, or a smile, of her.'

Faro straightened his shoulders, suppressing a shudder of distaste. He must take warning from Vince's experience, since his own infatuation was now an inexcusably long time ago.

Vince was smiling at him. 'Well, we're on our way.'

'We are indeed,' Faro replied, casting aside his sombre thoughts.

And so the two men set forth, one intent upon dreams of one day being Queen's physician and the other with dreams of a peaceful few days doing nothing more strenuous than a bit of fishing.

For Faro, however, a relaxing holiday on Deeside had in store a dreadful alternative.

Their road led them past Knock Castle, a grim fortress staring down through the trees. Ruined and ancient, rooks flew forlornly around its desolate walls. A sad unhappy place, deserted, as if still haunted by the blood feud in which the eight sons of Gordon of Knock were extinguished in one day by their Forbes rivals.

Then a mile away from their destination at Easter Balmoral, through dappled trees, they glimpsed Abergeldie Castle. Rose-red walls enfolded a history of Jacobites in its dungeons and the spectral presence of French Kate burnt as a witch. But no ghosts tormented its present owner, the Prince of Wales, or the guests who attended his lively shooting parties.

Beyond the castle someone with an inventive turn of imagination had come up with an ingenious device of aerial transport. A strong cable stretched across the river. On it was a cradle in which two people were propelling themselves laboriously across to the opposite bank at Crathie, thus saving the walk round by the bridge which gave access to the main Deeside highway. Their efforts were being enthusiastically applauded by a band of shrill young people.

'Shouldn't fancy that myself,' said Vince.

Faro agreed. And as they travelled close to the river bank, he observed that Edinburgh's recent drought had also affected Deeside and the waters, normally noisy and frequently in spate, had their boiling foam tamed to a sluggish stream.

Even with hopes of fishing diminishing, Faro sighed pleasurably. Each visit to Ballater impressed him with the growing affluence he found there. Once the rich had come to the famed watering place at nearby Pannanich Wells, but the building of a railway and the added attraction of the Queen at Balmoral Castle had extended prosperity to Ballater. And the railway shareholders, aware of this growth in potential, had begged Her Majesty to allow the line to be extended as far as Braemar.

She would have none of it, however, unwilling to let her shy retreat be invaded any further, preferring to keep at some distance those holiday-makers from home and abroad anxious to follow the fashion set by the Queen of Great Britain.

As Faro silently approved her resolve, their driver drew aside and doffed his cap respectfully, giving way to an open carriage approaching rapidly down the narrow road.

'The Queen, gentleman,' he muttered.

Faro and Vince just had time hastily to remove their hats as Her Majesty swept by, her widow's streamers dancing gleefully in the breeze. A pretty young girl with downcast eyes sat at her side. Princess Beatrice, Faro guessed, who looked as doleful and unhappy as the two ladies-in-waiting, their complexions somewhat blue with cold.

Standing on the carriage box, an imposing figure in Highland dress, rosy in countenance and obviously impervious to weather, was one of her Balmoral ghillies.

Chin tilted, the Queen moved a graceful hand and permitted herself a gentle smile in acknowledgement of the other vehicle.

'I'm certain she recognised you, Stepfather,' said Vince.

Faro felt that was extremely likely, for they had shared several encounters while he was in charge of her security in Edinburgh.

He smiled after the retreating carriage. The population thought of their Queen as stern and unbending, but Faro had noticed an almost coquettish tendency in her dealings with men, particularly if they were young and handsome.

This behaviour had not escaped attention – in particular her reactions to Inspector Faro, who fulfilled all the conditions implied by the word attractive. In addition to towering over her physically, he could also make her laugh.

He was always taken by surprise by that hearty guffaw. It was startling in its almost masculine intensity and considerably more wholehearted than the genteel merriment, if any at all, one might have expected to issue from the rather formidable Royal visage.

Remembering that laugh gave Faro cause to ponder as to whether there might be something after all in the press lampoons.

Vince asked, 'Would that be John Brown with her?'

'It would,' replied Faro. Could there be a grain of truth to justify the sneering epithet 'Mrs Brown'?

Memories as always came flooding back as the carriage climbed the steep hill to Easter Balmoral. In common with the Queen, Della had been a widow for more than ten years. Her husband Ben had been ghillie at Balmoral in its humbler days before the present castle was built, when it was home to Sir Robert Gordon, who sold it to the enthusiastic Royal couple, the then young Queen and her adored Prince Consort.

Good Prince Albert had not lived long to enjoy his new home, but the Queen still preferred her Highland retreat, the 'dear Paradise' she and Albert had created, to Buckingham Palace. Because of this rumours were rife that Her Majesty was in danger of becoming a recluse and a hermit. This did not pass unobserved in London. The gossip distressed and annoyed Mr Gladstone and the elder statesmen, in addition to presenting a ready target for the anti-monarchy faction.

The carriage turned a corner and there, nestling against the gentle foothills of Craig nam Ban, sat the familiar cottage. Smoke issued from its solitary chimney, wafting the haunting smell of peat towards them.

But the breeze also carried a more acrid odour. Twenty yards distant was a burnt-out ruin. The two men turned, stared back at it.

'That was Nessie Brodie's cottage,' said Faro.

Vince sniffed the air. 'Must have been quite a blaze.'

'And recent. I hope no one was hurt.'

The road was rocky and uneven and the driver failed to hear his question. Doubtless Aunt Bella would regale them in some detail. But as they stepped down, the door flew open and down the path to greet them came Tibbie, whom Bella had adopted when she was a little lame girl many years ago.

There was no welcoming smile as she ushered them indoors.

'Yer auntie's no' here, Jeremy. She's in the hospital.'

And before Faro could do more than utter a shocked exclamation of concern, Tibbie went on, 'She's no' ill. Naething like that. She had an accident. Naething broken, thank the Lord, a few scrapes and burns. Did ye no' get ma letter?' Faro shook his head. 'I posted it myself twa-three days sine. When Dr Elgin told her it wasna' likely she'd be fit to be home for her birthday. She was that upset. Said I was to write to ye straight away. I dinna ken why ye havna' got it.'

Her rising indignation refused to take into account that most letters from Aberdeen to Edinburgh, let alone Deeside, took at least a week to arrive at their destination.

Vince and Faro exchanged glances. How exceedingly fortunate that Mary Faro had insisted that her visit with the children remain a surprise, otherwise the disappointment would have been doubly hard to bear.

As Faro sat down at the kitchen table, the atmosphere overwhelmed him. He was ten years old again and nothing had changed. Walls steeped in a hundred years of peat smoke, sheep's wool for weaving, the daily baking of bread and bannocks, all

combined to open a Pandora's box of memories, happy and sad.
'What happened to Auntie?' he asked Tibbie. 'Was she on
steps cleaning out the cupboards again?'

'No, indeed she wasna'. Worse this time. She went plunging
into Nessie's cottage. Ye'll have seen it as ye came by. Or what's
left of it. Bella saw the fire from the window here and awa' she
went, fast as her legs would carry her, to rescue poor Nessie.'

'I presume she succeeded.'

'Aye, she did that,' said Tibbie proudly.

'At ninety,' said Vince in shocked tones, 'she should have
known better.'

Tibbie turned a bitter look on him. 'She doesna' think she's
ninety, ma laddie. She's that spry onyways, it's hard to credit.
Why, I mind well—'

'Just tell us what happened,' Faro asked with desperate
patience.

'She got Nessie out but a beam fell, mostly missed her, the
Lord be thanked. Flying sparks gave her one or two burns and
she got a few bruises. Nothing serious, as I've told ye, but her
breathing was bad.'

'Shock, of course,' said Vince firmly.

'Aye, like enough. Onyways, the doctor thought she was better
in the hospital considering her age and the like . . .'

'And Nessie?'

'Och, she's in the hospital. There's the pair of them in beds
next to each other. Nessie's getting on fine. Nothing more than
a dunt on her puir head. But she has a bad heart, ye ken. Bella's
fair desperate to be home for her birthday. But there's no telling
whether they'll let her out in time.'

She looked at them sadly. 'I doubt ye've come all this way for
nothing though. If only ye'd got ma letter—'

'Not at all. We would have come anyway,' said Faro hastily.
'Vince has business here.'

'Business? What like business?'

'I'm going to work at the hospital. Help Dr Elgin.'

Tibbie greeted this news with delight. 'She'll be right glad to see the both of ye. She's that proud of Vince here. Always telling everybody what brains ye've got. And as for ye, Jeremy Faro,' she added turning to him, 'ye were aye her favourite.'

And nodding vigorously, 'Aye, it's providence ye came. For she needs a wee bittie cheering. The nurses are having a hard time of it, I hear, she's that energetic. Having to keep to her bed is a sore trial.'

As Tibbie bustled about setting the table with remarkable speed for one so lame, she carried on a breathless non-stop monologue, one that neither Faro nor Vince had any possibility of turning into the remotest semblance of a conversation.

'—and what sort of a journey had ye? What like in Edinburgh?' Before Faro could do more than open his mouth to reply she had shot off again, answering the question for him.

By the time soup and bannocks appeared on the table, Tibbie was forced by the necessity of feeding her guests to let a few words pass their lips. Her occasional comments on their journey allowed their narrative to reach as far as Ballater.

'And we met the Queen on the low road,' Vince interposed smartly, thereby receiving an admiring look from his stepfather.

'The Queen, was it? Well, well.'

When he mentioned Princess Beatrice, Tibbie sighed. 'Bless her dear heart, she's that shy although she's past seventeen. Never has a word to say for herself when she comes visiting with her ma. The Queen still calls her Baby. I hear tell she doesna' want her to get married. Wants to keep her at home for company.'

'There was a ghillie with them, tall fellow with reddish hair and a beard?'

'That would be Johnnie Brown.'

Tibbie's attention was momentarily diverted by the need to remove bannocks from the oven and Faro, consoled that his aunt was in no danger, asked, 'What about this murder, Tibbie?'

'Och, I was just coming to that. Ye should have been here,

Jeremy. Morag Brodie, niece to puir Nessie. Or so she claimed. Stabbed, she was—'

A sound from outside and Tibbie turned towards the window. 'There's Johnnie Brown now. The verra man himself,' she said excitedly. 'Goodness gracious, he's coming here.' Darting a fleeting glance in the one mirror to see that her mutch was tidy, straightening her apron and staring wide-eyed from Faro to Vince and back again, she prepared to open the door.

'What on earth can he be wanting? The Queen was in for her visit and a cup of tea just before the accident.'

The visitor who entered seemed to fill the whole room. Brown was a splendid figure of a man, in the Highland dress of kilt and sporran-purse (bearing the head of some fierce beady-eyed animal), with great strong legs in hose and brogans, and a plaid thrown carelessly across his shoulder to serve as robe or bed, where necessity arose. Perched on his red-gold hair was a Balmoral bonnet.

Gazing from John Brown to his stepfather, Vince decided that even in a much larger gathering, these two men could easily overshadow everyone else by their presence.

He recognised not only a physical similarity but felt as if the giants of old had materialised as they solemnly shook hands and took stock of each other. Both men, he guessed, had in common that rare quality of being shrewd observers of character. Perhaps both knew or had been brought up to the old adage, 'Look well on the face of thy friend, and thine enemy, at first meeting, for that is the last time thou shalt see him as he really is.'

Vince was surprised to see that Brown had been followed into the room by a young man of his own age. Black-haired and blue-eyed, he would have been handsome but for the look of disquiet on his features.

'No, not disquiet,' Faro was to remark later, for it was a look he recognised. 'He reminded me of a sullen guilty schoolboy, grown-up but defiant still. And afraid.'

Introduced as Lachlan Brown, as they shook hands, Faro

presumed the lad was kin to the newcomer. Was he John Brown's son, despite there being little resemblance between them?

Perhaps aware of their thoughts, Brown explained. 'Ma ghillie. Ye're no' needed here, lad,' he added.

And Lachlan Brown, thought Faro, was very relieved indeed to take his departure. Throughout the visit as Brown accepted a dram from Tibbie and answered her bombardment of questions, Faro found himself intrigued by the identity of that oddly unhappy and watchful young man.

He had encountered many like him in his long career: those who, guilty or innocent, are made extremely uncomfortable and often rendered inarticulate by the presence of the law.

Why was Lachlan like that, Faro wondered? Certain that they had not met before, Faro felt there was nevertheless a haunting familiarity in Lachlan's appearance, an attitude, a gesture he seemed to recognise from a long way off. As if he was watching someone he knew well, distorted by a fairground's 'house of mirrors'.

Disturbed by the futile attempt to remember, he turned again to John Brown. Meanwhile his own lack of attention had been noted by his stepson who was busily comparing the two men.

Studying Faro critically, Vince again noticed his lack of sartorial elegance. The detective had deplorably little interest in clothes; they were to him at best a necessary covering rather than a prideful luxury.

Vince knew from his duties among the Edinburgh poor that all they could afford or ever hope to possess was one set of clothes, and that probably fourth- or fifth-hand. But why Faro should wish to emulate such unfortunates was beyond him. In a vain bid to fit his stepfather into the manner of life his position in society demanded, Vince had taken it upon himself to offer advice, which was accepted with good-humoured resignation and a complete lack of application.

Take the matter of boots. Faro failed to recognise that in his profession, which entailed an extraordinary amount of walking, a second pair was almost a necessity of survival. But Faro loved his old boots; the older they were the more he loved them, and the less willing was he to part with them.

Suddenly Vince realised why Faro had remained standing, partly hidden by the table. He was in his stocking feet. The new boots which Vince, ashamed of him, had insisted he 'break in' for the Deeside holiday had been removed and thrust aside, aching toes and a blistered heel thus relieved.

Vince now watched with interest and amusement what must happen next. Faro could not with politeness remain standing while John Brown was about to accept a seat and the refreshing of his dram. He must step forward and reveal all.

But even parted from his boots which lay accusingly distant, Faro was in command of the situation.

'You must excuse me.' He pointed. 'New boots, you know. Confoundedly painful.'

John Brown laughed, held up a hand. 'Man, think nothing of it. I ken fine the feeling. See these auld brogues o' mine. Ten year, I've had them. I love them like a lassie,' he chuckled. 'Man, the agonies I suffered breaking in yon new pair I must wear in Her Majesty's presence chamber and in her blasted drawing-room. Wummin, wi' their dainty feet and their dainty ways, they canna ken what we men suffer.' With a loud guffaw he slapped his bare leg delightedly.

And that was that. Suddenly, all embarrassment gone, both men were grinning at each other like apes, thought Vince.

Chortling happily, touching dram glasses, bound by common recollections, vying with each other on the matter of uncomfortable and abominable footwear, they stretched out their feet to the blaze.

Vince felt his presence was superfluous although John Brown tried politely to draw him into the conversation, putting him at his ease by talking softly and carefully, as if yon puir young Edinburgh laddie didna' understand the Highland speech.

Faro listened with some amusement, realising that they had the advantage since the Gaelic and not Lowland Scots was John Brown's native language.

As for Vince, he merely sighed. This was an all-too-familiar sore point, recalling the manner in which his Dundee patients treated him: as if he was still a wee school laddie and unaware of the ways of the world. If only they knew.

The next moment, Brown seemed to remember the reason for his visit. All jollity was suddenly wiped from his countenance, and he slammed down the empty glass on the table, refusing a refill.

'Inspector Faro, Dr Laurie,' he said, 'ye are doubtless wondering what has brought me to your doorstep with all haste the minute ye've arrived.' Pausing dramatically he looked from one to the other. 'Gentlemen, I am here on the Queen's business.'

Finding himself included, Vince sprang to the immediate and happy conclusion that there was in the offing an invitation to lunch or dine at the Castle. For Her Majesty's benevolence to the tenantry was well known. She was ever eager to dispense good works of a religious nature and for those unable to read, flannel petticoats and plentiful practical advice on child-rearing, a subject on which she was undeniably an authority. The statesmen and aristocrats of the realm would have been shocked to be present and to hear their monarch addressed thus informally:

'Sit yeself down, Queen Victoria,' or 'Ye'll tak one o' ma bannocks and a wee bittee crowdie cheese, Mistress Queen.'

In humble thatched cottages, the Royal gifts were received with no more awe or reverence than had the Queen been fulfilling the rôle in which she liked to cast herself, as laird of Balmoral.

While Vince and Faro waited for Brown to continue, Tibbie was hovering by the table, listening intently. She was the first to break the silence.

'And how is your mistress the day, Johnnie? She was verra

gracious just afore the accident. We had a wee visit, ye ken, and Mistress Bella gave her a jar o' pickles to take back home to the Castle wi' her. She had admired them that much.' And with a shake of the head, 'The Queen will be that upset to ken Mistress Bella's in the hospital the now.'

'A sad business, Tibbie. But she's on the mend—'

'Aye, she is that, but—'

Faro listened helplessly. His curiosity about Brown's visit thoroughly aroused, he longed to get to the point. But unable to stem the tide of conversation by which Tibbie had diverted her visitor's attention he occupied himself with some minor observations.

The timing of Brown's visit suggested urgency since after setting down his Royal mistress at the Castle he must have picked up the lad Lachlan and set off immediately for Easter Balmoral.

The inescapable conclusion was that 'the Queen's business' was vitally important. Faro also suspected – if their earlier encounters were anything to go by – that it was likely to prove both uncomfortable and unpleasant.

He was right. Brown finally managed to extract himself from Tibbie's well-meaning chatter by standing up abruptly and snatching his bonnet from the table.

'I have words for your ears, Inspector. Perhaps you'd be good enough to step outside a minute.'

Thrusting feet hastily into boots, Faro followed Brown into the tiny garden. Before Brown carefully closed the door behind them, Faro had a glimpse of Vince's startled and rather crestfallen expression as Tibbie declared:

'Good gracious, lad. I hope everything's all right up at the Castle and that no one's been pilfering the silver—'

Brown heard it too. At Faro's enquiring glance he shook his head. 'More serious than that, Inspector. Much more serious.'

Was Brown about to discuss the Crathie murder? Or was the Queen in danger?

As he thought rapidly about how he could deal with such an

emergency single-handed, Brown continued. 'Aye, this matter concerns the Queen's twa wee dogs.'

'Dogs, Mr Brown, did you say?'

'Aye, man. Dogs. Twa o' them wandered off and were found dead, still wearing their collars. Shot.'

Brown paused, regarded Faro intently. 'The Queen's verra upset. Verra. I'm at my wit's end, Inspector. Made all the usual enquiries but we canna' find their killer. The Queen will be verra severe on him. Royal property and the like, *lèse-majesté* and so forth.' With a shake of his head, he added, 'I wouldna' be at all surprised if it was the jail for him when we get him. And that, Inspector, is where you come in.'

'Me?' Faro's voice quavered a little.

'Aye, you, man. Who else? When the Queen saw you on the road back yonder she says to me: "There, Brown, there is your answer. Inspector Faro. How very fortunate that he is here. He will know exactly what to do. He is a policeman, after all. He will find out who killed our precious darlings." '

Faro stared at Brown in stunned silence.

Should he feel flattered? Was he actually being asked . . .? Nay, the Queen didn't ask, she commanded, and he was being commanded to investigate disappearing dogs that got themselves shot.

In constant danger of losing the crown off her Royal head by wandering unconcerned within the sights of madmen's guns, the centre of sinister plots emanating from a dozen different European countries, here she was demanding that the deaths of two household pets be investigated by Scotland's prime detective.

He had a sudden desire to laugh out loud at the absurdity of the task. At the same time he was seized by a considerable eagerness that none of his colleagues in Edinburgh's Central Office should ever be made aware that Faro was now searching for dog-killers. Even Royal dog-killers.

Brown stroked his beard, regarding Faro's silence thoughtfully. 'Too difficult for ye, Inspector?'

Faro pulled himself together with some effort. 'I shouldn't think so. But I thought it was the Crathie murder you wanted to discuss.'

Brown opened his mouth, closed it again. 'And why should I want to discuss that in particular?' he demanded suspiciously.

'I am a detective, sir,' Faro replied trying not to respond with the indignation Brown's questions warranted.

'That matter is closed. The lass is dead and buried. No one knows who killed her. Person or persons unknown. That was the verdict.'

He put heavy emphasis on the last word and continued sternly, 'I have been directed here, Inspector, by the Queen to bring to your attention the matter of her twa dogs.'

'What kind of dogs were they?' Faro asked, repressing a sigh.

'King Charles spaniels. Peaceful brutes, if that's what ye're getting at, Inspector. No' the kind to threaten any puir body. Or take a nip out o' a passing ankle. No' like some,' he said with a dark look at his bare leg on which a closer inspection might have revealed a profusion of ancient scars suspiciously like those of canine encounters.

Faro nodded. King Charles spaniels. How like Royalty. 'What were their names?' If he had to conduct a murder enquiry presumably Royal dogs merited the same methods as mortal victims.

Brown thought for a moment. His frown deemed this a somewhat unnecessary question. 'Er, Dash and – Flash. Aye, that's it. Grand at following the guns.'

Faro considered this statement. And no doubt it was the most likely cause of their unfortunate end. He pictured them growing stout like their Royal mistress, slow-moving. Too slow-moving to get out of the way of exuberant grouse-shooters.

'Male or female?'

Brown thought about that too. 'Och, we dinna worry. There's always more men than wummin, ye ken.'

'I beg your pardon. I meant the dogs, not the guns.'

'Och, man, you should have said what ye meant,' was the reprimand.

'Dogs or bitches, we call them. These twa were bitches.' And with a defiant stare, 'And no' in heat, if that's what ye're getting at.'

Faro was disappointed at this deflation of his second logical conclusion for the disappearance of bitches. 'Shot by mistake obviously. Got too close to the birds. Or the sheep,' he added lamely.

Brown shook his head. 'No,' he said firmly. 'I havena' told the Queen, I didna' want to upset the puir lady but they were shot through the head. And from the powder burns I'd say at very close range.'

'Where and when were they discovered, Mr Brown?'

'Twa hundred yards from the Castle. On the path by the river. Night after the Ghillies' Ball.'

The estate was vast, thought Faro despairingly. The dogs buried and nearly two weeks later there would be few clues, that was for sure.

Regarding Faro sternly, Brown continued. 'Look, man, all this isna' of much importance. It's no' where it happened, the Queen wants to know. We all ken that. It is who would deliberately shoot the Queen's favourite dogs.'

It was at this stage of the conversation that Faro decided that Brown, excellent fellow though he was, would never make a detective. The first question was 'Where and when?' Which almost inevitably led to the second, 'Why?' and lastly, the all-important 'Who?' For in that sequence lay hidden the precise clues to the killer's identity.

Early in his career Faro had hit upon the almost infallible theory that the criminal inevitably leaves behind from his person some tangible piece of evidence, be it a thread of torn clothing, a footprint, or some small possession lost in the death struggle which might be used to link him with his victim. And in the same manner, he reasoned, the murderer also carried away on his person by accident some substance identifiable with either the victim or the scene of the crime.

This theory had rarely let him down in his twenty years with the Edinburgh City Police. He held it in such high regard that he saw no good reason to abandon it when considering dogs instead of humans.

'I should like to see the exact spot, if you please.'

Brown shrugged. 'They are buried in the pets' cemetery, among all the wee birds, dogs and horses that have served the Queen loyally. She is sentimental about such things—'

'You mistake my meaning, Mr Brown,' Faro interrupted. 'I wish to see where the dogs were found.'

Brown regarded him a little contemptuously. 'As you wish, Inspector. But take my word for it, there's nothing there. Ye'll be wasting your time.'

'Nevertheless,' said Faro firmly.

'Verra well, verra well. If you insist. And it's a fair walk – Inspector,' he added in the pitying tone reserved for the born countryman's idea of the town-bred traveller.

'And I'm a fair walker, Mr Brown. You have to be in my job, you know, tracking down criminals.'

Brown seemed surprised at this information. He responded by nodding vigorously and withdrawing a handsome gold timepiece from his waistcoat pocket, 'It'll need to be the morning then. I'm on duty at the Castle within the hour.'

'Tomorrow it is, then.' Faro walked with Brown to the gate. 'I am about to visit my aunt in the hospital at Beagmill.'

'Beagmill.' Brown smiled. 'Lachlan has the trap at the road end, so if you'd care to accompany us, we'll set you down there.'

Glancing down at his boots, hastily retied, Faro bowed. 'My feet are obliged to you, sir.'

Brown gave him a sympathetic nod and Faro added, 'Is there room for Dr Laurie?'

'I dinna see why not.'

Faro signalled to Vince who was staring out of the window. And as they walked ahead of him on to the roadway, Brown was unable to suppress his curiosity. 'Yon's a fair dainty young man.'

'My stepson, sir.'

Brown seemed surprised. 'A real physician, is he?' His tone implied awe.

'He is indeed. He takes up the post of locum tenens at your hospital tomorrow.'

'Well, well.' John Brown didn't greet this information with any enthusiasm. 'He looks awfa' young. No more than a bairn.'

'I warn you not to be misled by appearances, sir. He's a good man to have around in a fight, I assure you. And what is more, he is my most trusted assistant. His help has been invaluable in solving many of my most difficult cases.'

'Do you say so? Well, I never.' Brown's response implied disbelief and Faro, glancing back, realised from the scarlet colour that flooded Vince's ears that he had overheard Brown's hoarse whisper.

He looked at his stepfather and mouthed indignantly, 'Of all the nerve.'

As they walked down the steep hill to where Lachlan and the dog-cart waited, with a desperate need to change the subject, Faro asked, 'Is Lachlan your son?'

'Nay, Inspector. I'm not wed. He's a fostered bairn wi' one o' my cousins. Been away at the college, studying.' He made it sound a formidable task.

As they boarded the cart, he continued, 'Brown's a common name hereabouts. From the days when the clans were proscribed and the laird's kin took something a little less dangerous then their Gaelic surnames . . .'

Clattering wheels and the bumpy texture of the steep track made further conversation impossible. The scenery, however, was enchanting and Faro was quite content to gaze at the panorama of mountain and stream and breathe in the wine-clear air, already sharpened like his appetite by the hint of autumn waiting in the wings. Far above their heads another flash of gold.

'Yon's a golden eagle, Inspector. Has his eyrie on Craig Gowan.'

The eagle soared, the sunlight on widespread wings turning him into that bird of fiction, a phoenix rising. Along the line of the mountains rose sharp triangles of stone. Brown followed Vince's gaze.

'Cairns, Doctor,' said Brown in answer to his question. 'Monuments put up by Her Majesty to mark some memorable event in her family's stay at Balmoral. Yon's Beagmill.'

Lachlan reined in the cart opposite a handsome granite building set back from the road.

'Until tomorrow, then, gentlemen. We will look by for you at nine.'

Faro and Vince walked up the drive to the main door. Embedded in stone letters: 'The Prince Consort Cottage Hospital. 1860'. Inside a wooden board with a Royal coat of arms declared the establishment 'dedicated to the alleviation and treatment of illness and disease among Her Majesty's loyal servants and tenants'.

The hospital had two strictly separate wings, whose entrances bore the words 'Men' and 'Women' also carved indelibly in stone, the sexes sharply and properly divided.

Although undeniably small, Faro observed that the wards were a considerable improvement on the housing conditions prevailing in many a Scottish town.

For the poor of Edinburgh's High Street with their squalid tenements and wynds supporting ten of a family in one dreadful room, such cleanliness and orderly comfort would have prompted thoughts that they had died and gone to heaven.

Prince Albert's main concern had been the health of the young: too many infants died at birth or succumbed to the many diseases of infancy. Among Britain's poor, to have survived forty years was to have reached old age, and many were consigned to earlier graves by neglected illness and hard work. Ironic, was the whisper, that for all his good words, the Prince had died at forty-two of typhoid and, some hinted, of medical mismanagement.

A decade later, residents were either extremely healthy or regarded hospitals with suspicion. Wards were rarely more than one-quarter filled and patients fell into categories of broken limbs, amputations (through horrendous accidents with farm equipment) but rarely the old and infirm.

The latter were something of a rarity, usually incomers or foreigners to the district, since hardy local folk never gave up, and old Balmoral servants preferred to die in Royal harness. Or in extremities of age, they drifted into a happy second childhood under the careful and loving attention of the younger members of the family.

The Prince had provided the hospital with a doctor and three nurses. He had liked his doctors to be young and imaginative, perhaps even a little rebellious in the cause of medical progress. The present incumbent, who was approaching his seventieth year, had been prevailed upon to take a short holiday and to employ a young assistant.

While Vince's Dundee appointment as factory doctor eminently qualified him for such responsibility, the unhappiness in his personal life had also taken toll of his never-abundant self-confidence. He had it on good authority, however, that should he prove worthy of the hospital appointment and Dr Elgin's esteem, then he might be offered a permanency.

Was it the Balmoral connection that attracted Vince, a step nearer his ultimate dream, the goal of Queen's physician? Faro wondered. He entertained some misgivings about his young stepson hiding himself away in a country hospital instead of a large town where he could gain experience and expertise in medical diagnoses.

The hospital seemed ideal for a family man, a middle-aged doctor and a countryman at heart, rather than a young man at the beginning of his profession. Vince, Faro suspected, would soon become bored.

'Dr Elgin,' the nurse-in-charge informed Vince sternly, 'was not expecting your arrival until tomorrow. He is now off duty for the evening and is only available in case of an emergency.'

'Then please do not disturb him on my account. I have lodging for the night and will present myself tomorrow.'

Consulting notes on the desk, the nurse said, 'Not before eleven, if you please. Eleven o'clock is when Dr Elgin completes his morning rounds,' she added, directing them to the ward where Aunt Bella received them rapturously with hugs and kisses.

At last all three, rather damp about the eyes, settled back and with assurances that Bella would be home in time for her birthday, they smiled at each other as happily as the stern hospital atmosphere would allow.

The only other occupant of the ward was an old lady with a bandaged head who seemed to be asleep.

'That's Nessie Brodie. It was her cottage burned down. Puir soul,' whispered Bella. 'Ye ken her, Jeremy?'

Faro did vaguely. His aunt would enjoy having a sympathetic companion and a captive audience. For if that blameless lady had a solitary fault it was being a compulsive talker.

Talk was to her like breathing. The house resounded with ceaseless chatter between Tibbie and Bella, though Faro suspected that neither heard one half of what the other was saying. And on the rare occasions when Bella thought she had the house to herself, she was quite happy keeping her vocal cords in excellent trim by talking to herself.

Now her sole disappointment at going home was the knowledge that her beloved great-nephew was to be Dr Elgin's assistant.

'If that isna' an awfa' coincidence,' she cried. 'And me not to be here to keep an eye on ye.'

The old woman in the next bed stirred, muttered something and closed her eyes again.

'Puir Nessie, she's no' been the same since the night I dragged her out of the fire.' Faro and Vince listened patiently, unwilling to tell her that Tibbie had already stolen her drama in the detailed account of the cottage in flames and Bella's daring rescue.

'Och, I'm just fine,' she assured them cheerfully. 'Ma legs are still bandaged, ye ken, but I'm getting on grand. Just a few scratches.'

With a sigh, she continued, 'They wouldna' consider letting

me bide in ma own home. Said I was to come into the hospital where I could be looked after properly. Ma stairs are a wee thing steep and narrow, and puir Tibbie's no' able to heave me up and down. Lassie's that frail hersel'.'

'You were very lucky, Auntie,' Faro said.

Her smile was pure content. 'The Good Lord looks after his own. I have every faith that ma prayers will be answered and I'll be home for ma birthday.' And with a tender look, 'I prayed that ye would manage to come as well, Jeremy lad. And Vince too. I am blessed. It wouldna' be the same without you. If only your dear mother and the wee bairns—'

She listened to Faro's explanation with concern. 'Those puir wee lambs. Let's hope they dinna have their bonny faces marked—'

'No, dear. That's smallpox not chicken-pox.'

That assurance came from Vince and she looked at him gratefully. 'Afore I forget, Jeremy, ye'll be sad to hear—'

There followed a gloomy recapitulation of all the people who had died since Faro's last visit. Again he listened, holding her hand and squeezing it encouragingly as he put in the occasional exclamations of concern that were required of him.

This splendid show of interest was quite beyond Vince whose face, except when Bella's glance fell upon him, set in an attitude of confusion and growing despondency.

But Faro was prepared to be patient. One casual question was guaranteed to bring forth full life histories for the whole district. With Aunt Bella he knew that he had on hand a fount of more valuable information than Inspector Purdie, with headquarters at the Crathie Inn, walking or riding up miles of farm roads with his exhaustive enquiries would gain in a whole week of painstaking detection.

'What about this murder, Auntie?' Faro asked.

'I was just coming to that. Kin to Nessie, the puir lass,' she said rather loudly.

This had the required effect. As if waiting her cue, Nessie

opened her eyes, looked at the two men and struggled into a sitting position, picking up the conversation with such alacrity that Faro wondered how much she had already overheard.

'Aye, Mr Faro. Am awfa' tragedy. Ye ken, the lassie was my niece,' she added dramatically.

'Only by marriage, Nessie,' said Bella sternly, as if resenting this rôle of importance bestowed on her neighbour. 'Nessie, as ye'll recall, used to be an upper servant at the Castle—'

'Aye, and ever since I retired I've been sewing for the Queen, petticoats, and alterations to her gowns.'

'And she's good at it too,' said Bella, reluctant to relinquish her part in the story.

'Had to be, Bella. Especially as the Queen's grown stouter and it's been no easy matter keeping in step with all the extra inches without drawing her attention to it.'

'One would have assumed that the Royal coffers would run to new linen for such a contingency,' said Vince.

'True, true. But the Queen is well known to have her head turned fast against wastefulness.'

Faro suppressed a smile. It was common knowledge from his experiences at the Palace of Holyroodhouse, that she kept a tight hold of the Royal purse strings.

'Anyway, getting stout would depress the poor lady, especially as she likes her food—'

'And her drink too, I hear,' said Bella in a cautious whisper. 'After all, she hasna' much else to console, her puir lady, being a widow and having sic' responsibilities.'

'You were telling us about this unfortunate lass,' said Faro in a kindly but determined effort to direct the conversation.

Nessie frowned. 'From Aberdeen way. Must have been on Dave's side o' the family. He left home when he was thirteen, and I was fair flabbergasted when Morag walked in six months ago. Or was it seven. Let me see—'

With Bella's help this was at last sorted out to Nessie's satisfaction. The flow of duelling words was interrupted by a nurse with the information for Dr Laurie that Dr Elgin had learned of his unexpected arrival and would be delighted to receive him.

Vince accompanied her willingly, kissing his great-aunt and promising to take care of both patients.

Goodbyes were said and Faro, looking at the momentarily speechless ladies, urged them on: 'You were saying. About Morag. Do go on.'

Nessie needed no further encouragement. 'Seems she was orphaned long since and had found some letters. When she saw that we lived on Balmoral Estate, she had heard so much about Ballater being a great place for holidays, she decided to see if she could get work in one of the hotels. She came to me first, and I did better than that for her.

'Bonny, a wee bittie wild, but I kenned they were needing kitchen servants at the Castle and Johnnie Brown put in a word for her. He took a right shine to the lass. So did Lachlan.'

Pausing, she sighed. 'We all had hopes there. And we were, well, surprised when she told us she was to marry a footman.'

Suddenly she began to cry, 'It's awful, awful. I can hardly believe it. I blame myself, Mr Faro. Really I do. When she didn't come home, I thought nothing of it. She was often kept late at the Castle. And now for this to happen. I canna believe such wickedness.'

'Murdered,' Bella said to Faro. 'Stabbed she was. Body found over Crathie way, in a ditch. Just up past the signpost to Tomintoul.' She sighed. 'Twa-three days after she nearly drowned, too—'

'I was coming to that, Bella,' Nessie interrupted reproachfully. 'Aye, it wasna' the first time that devil had it in for puir Morag. When she was crossing over on the Abergeldie cradle wi' her footman – the quickest way o' getting to Crathie, all the servants use it,' she explained to Faro, 'they both fell into the water.'

'Everyone was a bit fu', ye ken,' said Bella, 'but Brown's laddie dived in and saved her. Puir James—'

'The footman, Jimmy Lessing,' put in Nessie.

'Oh, he was drowned, puir laddie,' Bella continued rapidly, in case this interruption should divert the telling of the tale to her companion. 'His body smashed to bits at the mill race. Terrible it was. Terrible.'

'And our puir Morag only knew him from the ring she'd given him—'

'Dreadful, dreadful,' said Faro sympathetically.

'Then Nessie's cottage burnt down,' said Bella, her voice heavy from significance. 'The night after the Ghillie's Ball.'

'A Saturday it was. I hadna' seen Morag that week. She mostly came by on a Thursday to bring me the Queen's sewing, or she'd look in on a Saturday for a wee chat. But she never came that week at all.' Nessie sounded bewildered, her voice fretful with anxiety.

'I'd never ha' managed the twa o' ye the night o' the fire,' said Bella. 'But as luck would have it Morag wasna' there.'

Faro felt cynical about luck being involved. It seemed that the girl had been singularly unlucky. Even through the frantic retelling of the story pieced together by the two women, his mind worked fast sifting the unimportant from the significant.

'I ken one thing fine,' Bella said mysteriously. 'The lass was probably expecting. Matters are different in the country. Nature will have its way wi' young folk. I used to be a nursemaid and I ken what I'm talking about. Most marriages hereabouts are from necessity. With so little siller about couples tend to delay until there's a bairn on the way. No one thinks ony the worse of a lass for that. Except the Queen, of course.'

'What has the Queen to do with it?'

'She's that firm and respectable, lad. Covering up the legs of the piano and talking about a limb of chicken or lamb. Maids and footmen are no' supposed to meet in the grounds either. That wasna' much help to poor Morag, bless her.'

'He'll try it again,' said Nessie. Her voice suddenly excited, she put her hands to her face. 'They'll get her yet. And she'll no listen to anyone. Morag knew. She told me,' she shouted and stabbing a finger in Faro's direction began to sob noisily.

'Nessie, Nessie, dinna' take on so,' said Bella and to Faro she whispered, 'Tak' no heed of her, puir tormented soul. It's that dunt on the head did it to her. She has nightmares. Thinks someone's trying to harm the Queen, but no one will believe her.'

Faro felt an ominous chill at the words. He regarded the patient in the other bed thoughtfully, alarmed at the sudden change from normal conversation into hysterical denunciation. Perhaps her mind was wandering. That must surely be the medical and the logical explanation.

But – was it? Was there something far more sinister, a link between the killing of the pet dogs and the girl who called regularly at Nessie's house to deliver the Queen's sewing?

Was he on the threshold of a plot of much greater magnitude, one that might threaten the life of the Queen herself?

But there was no possibility of further questioning. Nessie's head had sunk on to her chest and the bell for the end of visiting hour having already rung, he gave his aunt a farewell hug.

In the entrance hall he saw Vince, now accompanied by Dr Elgin, whose rotund figure and rosy complexion testified to good living and belied his seventy summers.

He greeted Faro with a charming friendliness that must have been a boon to his patients.

'We have a room in readiness for Dr Laurie.'

'And an early start tomorrow,' said Vince.

'Six o'clock,' added Dr Elgin cheerfully.

Faro saw Vince's eyes roll heavenward. A sluggish riser, he was never at his best in the early morning.

'Since your time with us is short, Mr Faro, we must spare Dr Laurie to you as often as we can.'

'Thank you, sir.'

Then he added, 'Perhaps you would care to join us for a little light refreshment before we retire.'

'Thank you, no, sir. It has been a long day.'

As Faro tactfully made his excuses, Dr Elgin said, 'Please feel at liberty to visit your aunt whenever you wish. Our strict visiting hours do not apply to such an illustrious visitor.' He smiled. 'You have my permission to ignore them. I shall tell the staff that you are to be admitted at any time.'

At the door he added, 'You have a vehicle to take you back to Easter Balmoral?'

'Alas, no. But I am used to walking.'

Faro, acutely aware of his new boots, was grateful when Dr Elgin continued, 'May I recommend the livery stables a hundred yards down the road. Willie keeps late hours and as the season is almost over, he may be able to accommodate you.'

Thanking him, Faro left the hospital feeling much happier about Vince's prospects. He was sure there would be a rapport between the two doctors. Suddenly conscious of how tired he was, footsore and weary, the prospect of hiring a pony-trap for a few days seemed an excellent idea.

At the stables the 'pony' turned out to be an ex-racehorse.

'He used to be a good runner in the Abergeldie stables in his prime, belonged to the Prince of Wales,' said Willie proudly, explaining that he had been a jockey in his young days. 'We've both got too old for that, of course, but should you care to ride, there's a saddle. He's a biddable beast, ye ken.' And patting the horse's head affectionately, 'There's only one thing, sir, he needs stabling, a proper night's lodging.'

'There's a barn at Mistress MacVae's—'

'I ken it fine. There'll be no problem there,' said the stableman, throwing a bag of oats into the cart and giving Faro full instructions on the care of this valuable animal, whose name it seemed was 'Steady'. Or had he misheard, Faro wondered, when at first it refused to 'Trot on' as instructed.

By the time they had reached Aunt Bella's cottage, however, Faro and his new companion had achieved a brisk pace plus a mutual respect and understanding. Steady seemed to have no complaints on being introduced to his new stabling and blew into Faro's ear affectionately.

Faro slept well that night, and welcomed the almost forgotten sensations of waking sleepily to cock-crow, bird song and warring blackbirds outside the window. Even the raucous din of a full-going rookery was music to his ears.

As he opened the casement window, distant sounds emerged, sheep bleating on the hill, indistinguishable from the white boulders, and a dainty herd of hinds following their lord and master down to the stream to drink.

He sighed with pleasure. If only life could be always like this, if he could keep this moment and carry it with him like a letter, or a faded rose. For these scenes thrust him back vividly into the days of his childhood, now almost obliterated by years of city life.

Breathing deeply, he filled his lungs with the pure air and hurried downstairs, lured by the appetising smells of cooking.

Tibbie was taking bannocks out of the oven. She smiled a greeting and as he sat down at the table with sunshine flooding the room, life seemed very good indeed.

It could be perfect, he decided, if only people stopped murdering one another.

4 At the hospital he found Vince awaiting his arrival. Dr Elgin had been good to his promise and with few patients to attend, he had been given the morning off.

Impressed and relieved to see his stepfather equipped with a pony-trap, he said, 'How clever of you. And invaluable in the circumstances. Should keep you one trot ahead and save wearing out the precious boot-leather. He moves faster who has a horse and cart.'

'He also moves faster who can ride.' And as they set off Faro related Willie's tale of Steady's distinguished early days.

They had reached Abergeldie Castle when Vince said, 'We will certainly be in good time for John Brown – perhaps even for a couple of Tibbie's excellent bannocks before he arrives,' he added wistfully.

Faro smiled. 'How's it going, lad? Settling in all right?'

'Yes, indeed, Stepfather. You know I think I'm really going to enjoy being here. Food apart.' He sighed. 'Dr Elgin is a splendid fellow, such stories to tell. You should have stayed to supper,' he added reproachfully. 'You would hardly credit what medicine used to be like in the old days. Makes me thankful I didn't take it up before the advent of chloroform. A course in butchery would have been more useful than a medical training.'

His mood had turned sombre. Clinging to his seat as they negotiated the sharp bend, he asked, 'About this murder, Stepfather. Aren't you intrigued?'

Faro related the version he had gathered from Nessie and Bella. At the end, Vince frowned.

'A rum do, I'd call it, Stepfather. And everyone very keen to get the corpse off stage and the enquiry closed as quickly as possible. The fact that Lachlan Brown was sweet on the girl may be of some significance.'

'My thoughts exactly.'

John Brown was already waiting for them outside the cottage, the silent Lachlan at his side, whose presence Faro now considered with more attention than at their first meeting.

Impressed by the Inspector's enterprise in arranging his own transport, Brown nodded approvingly. 'If ye'll just follow us, then.'

The estate grounds were vast and towards the main drive, with a glimpse of the Royal residence across wide lawns, Lachlan led the way down a narrow path through the trees.

In sight of the river, they alighted and walked to the path where, only a footfall away, the Dee sparkled and burbled on its way to the German Ocean.

Brown pointed with his foot to a stone. 'That's where we found the dogs.'

Vince and Faro immediately crouched down to make a careful study of the area, parting the grass and examining it carefully. Brown watched this procedure with wide-eyed astonishment. To Faro's question he replied: 'Aye, this was exactly the spot. Isn't that so?'

Lachlan, so addressed, merely nodded. Silent and withdrawn, Faro was beginning to wonder whether the lad was shy or had some vocal handicap.

'Did it rain, by any chance, on the night the dogs disappeared?'

Brown thought about that. 'No, not that night. But we had a storm the night before.'

'And there has been no rain since?'

'Nary a drop. A dry spell is usual for this time of year.'

So the low water in the river had indicated. Faro was pleased with the accurate timing. There should have been imprinted on the dried mud paw marks, bloodstains and tufts of dog hair.

There were none.

The grass was undisturbed. No scuffle marks, no bruised grass, nothing to suggest that the dogs had been resting and had been surprised by their killer.

Faro stood up, certain of one thing: that they had been killed elsewhere and their bodies carried to this spot for discovery.

But why?

Brown meanwhile watched the antics of the two men as if they had taken leave of their senses. Consulting his watch gravely, he said, 'I must leave you, gentlemen.'

Vince had walked a little distance away, stepping through a tangle of weeds to what had once been a handsome watermill, now falling into neglect and crumbling ruin.

'Ye'll no' find anything there, Doctor,' Brown called after him. 'It's here the puir beasts were killed.' And to Faro, 'I'll tell the Queen that ye're looking into it, conducting an enquiry. Isn't that what ye call it?'

And with a flicker of amusement as Faro bowed in assent and made to follow Vince, 'That hasna' been used since the new mill was built the Crathie side o' the river. The Queen bought the miller's land here to add to the estate.'

'Was it intended for some useful purpose?'

Brown looked up at the empty windows. 'It was just in the way, ye ken. Untidy-looking. Buying it was almost the last thing Prince Albert did before he died. And somehow Her Majesty hadna' heart to do anything about it after that. Like everything else, it was left to lie exactly as it was on the day when she and Prince Albert looked it over together and decided to buy it.'

Moving towards the path again he said, 'I'll need to go, Inspector.' Pointing to the pony-trap, he added, 'No need for ye to spend yer money on that. Tell Willie ye need it for yer investigations and the Queen will pay the bill.'

'I'm most obliged to Her Majesty for her generosity.' Faro had already decided that the Royal task he had been set was doomed to failure and with it, any hopes he had been cherishing of a quiet fishing holiday.

'Before you go, Mr Brown. Have there been any similar incidents reported?'

'In what way similar?'

'Anything like this business. Violent deeds, damage to property,' he said helpfully.

Brown scratched his beard, frowning. 'Let me see. There was the fire at Mistress Brodie's croft. But that was an accident. The puir woman is in the hospital—'

'Yes, I met her last night.'

Brown frowned. 'That was how your auntie got injured, ye'll ken that. Nothing mysterious about it. Barns often go on fire.'

'What about the murder of Morag Brodie? Did that not raise a stir in the neighbourhood?' The question seemed superfluous. In a rural community, if his Aunt Bella was a typical resident, no one would be speaking of anything else for months to come.

Lachlan was very still, and when Brown replied he did so reluctantly. 'Aye, the lass who got herself killed.'

And Faro, thinking that was a curious way to express it, as if Morag Brodie had deserved death, asked, 'Where was her body found?'

'In a ditch over yonder. Crathie way.' Brown's eyes slid across Lachlan. 'That case is closed.'

'A murder without a murderer, whatever the verdict, is never closed as far as I'm concerned, Mr Brown.'

Brown looked him straight in the eyes. 'But then ye're not concerned, are ye, Inspector?' he fairly crowed. 'And Detective Inspector Purdie – from Scotland Yard,' he added significantly, 'is satisfied with the verdict.'

'I understood that the lass was a servant at the Castle?'

'How did ye guess that?' Brown's glance was suspicious, and

although his question was chilly, it was asked with elaborate carelessness.

'I didn't. My aunt was full of it, of course.'

Brown's sigh of relief was audible as he once more glanced at the silent sullen Lachlan. 'I must awa'. If you want any more information about – about Morag Brodie, why d'ye no' ask the Inspector. Or Sergeant Whyte, our local lad.'

The moment of danger was past; he was prepared to be affable, even expansive. 'Detective Inspector Purdie is acquainted with these parts. Like yeself he used to bide here for holidays when he was a wee lad.'

Turning to leave, he came back. Facing Faro squarely, hands on hips, he said, 'Ye should know, Inspector, that we're trying to keep all this business from the Queen. As much as possible. We dinna want to distress her.'

His voice defiant, he added, 'It must be obvious to ye that we do our best to give her a restful holiday and spare her as much as possible from anything sordid or unhappy.'

Or anything concerned with the real world, Faro added silently. A brutal murder would obviously tarnish her vision of Balmoral as the 'dear Paradise' she and her beloved Prince Consort had built.

'We are proud to have Her Majesty at Balmoral and we like to keep her happy and content with us. This is her only place now where she feels at home. It's her refuge. We dinna want to spoil that for her.' It was quite a speech. 'The puir woman has had that much grief,' he added desperately.

But Faro was unmoved. Considerably less grief than most of her subjects, he thought bitterly. And surely the Queen should be more concerned about the possibility of a murderer living in the midst of her rustic tenantry than the unfortunate death of two pet dogs, however beloved.

Neither man spoke. Observing Faro's guarded expression, Brown moved unhappily from one foot to the other. Then consulting his watch, he looked over his shoulder towards the Castle. Touching his bonnet briefly, he took Lachlan by the arm and walked rapidly in the direction of the Royal apartments.

Faro watched them go, his mind on Morag Brodie.

'Stepfather. Over here.' Vince waved to him excitedly from one of the upstairs windows of the ruined mill.

Faro picked his way through thorn and briar that would have done justice to the Sleeping Beauty's Palace and did nothing for his trousers and coat, or his temper. Opening the creaking door into shuttered semi-darkness, he shivered.

As his eyes became accustomed to the gloom he saw that this had once been the kitchen. The heart of family life, it had known laughter and prosperity. Now the sense of desolation rushed out, clawing at him. Cheerless and forbidding, it was not a place in which he would care to linger. And although it was still sturdily roofed, he would have no wish to seek its sanctuary on a stormy night.

Vince gazed down at him.

'Up here, Stepfather.'

'Found something, lad?' said Faro climbing the open staircase.

'Yes, look around you. What do you make of this?'

Signs of domesticity, blankets and sheets, even a tablecloth, two mugs and plates, and a vase of wilted flowers indicated that this room had been recently occupied.

'And over here,' said Vince. 'Bloodstains.'

Faro studied the marks on the floorboards. He could see a dark area at the top of the stairs, which continued downwards, streaks on steps and stone walls. Bending down, he picked up a small clump of brown hair.

'From the dogs?'

'Perhaps, Stepfather. And on the bed. Spaniels shed a lot of hair. I would hazard a guess that they were both shot in here and their bodies carried out to the river path.'

Pausing, Vince looked around the room. 'Are you thinking the same as I am, Stepfather?'

'Precisely. That this place has been lived in recently. And by someone who was no passing stranger seeking shelter. And no tinker. Tinkers care little for sheets and fine blankets. They don't put flowers in vases, either.'

'But girls do. Especially girls who are entertaining a lover.'

'Ah, now we're getting somewhere, lad,' said Faro as he examined the fireplace. 'Let us reconstruct the scene. This was a clandestine meeting. No fire was lit, for that would bring attention to the fact that the ruined mill had an occupant. The bedlinen and tablecloth indicate a lass of refined taste.'

Considering for a moment, he said, 'I think if we gathered these together and took them to the Castle, we would find they originated from the same source in the linen room. Purloined by Morag Brodie for the special occasion which, alas, was to cost her her life.'

'So you think she stayed here.'

'Undoubtedly. She spent the night she was killed here and perhaps one night before. But no more than that.'

'How can you tell?'

'Fine linen sheets like these crease badly and have to be changed frequently. Consider their almost pristine condition. And the two pillowcases, lad. Only one has been used. I would say that only Morag slept here and that she waited in vain for her lover. And when he finally arrived, it was not to sleep with her, but to put a knife in her.'

Faro wandered back to the stairhead. 'But not in the bed,' he said. And eyeing the scene narrowly, 'Probably here. Where the blood has soaked into the floorboards. But for some reason it was inconvenient to dispose of her body, and while he was awaiting his chance the Queen's inquisitive dogs came on the scene. He realises his danger, shoots them and carries their bodies on to the river path. Does this suggest anything to you?'

'Only that the murderer might have been someone employed at the Castle. A fellow-servant?'

'Or a ghillie,' was the reply.

'And if your theory is correct, Stepfather, he is still lurking about, his crime undetected. Another good reason for not spreading alarm and despondency in the Royal apartments.'

'And for apprehending him before he strikes again. In the light of our discovery, I think it might be prudent to look in at the local police station. See what new material, if any, Inspector Purdie has come upon.'

There was a moment's silence before Vince said gently, 'Stepfather, I thought I heard you say that Superintendent McIntosh had warned you off.'

'Indeed yes, but perhaps the good Inspector will have something to offer on the subject of murdered dogs,' said Faro innocently. 'But first of all we must return you to the hospital and pay our respects to Aunt Bella.'

'It is as well you have Dr Elgin's blessing. I was given to understand most firmly that visiting times are strictly adhered to, despite the current lack of patients.'

As they drove briskly in the direction of the cottage hospital, Faro was silent, his mind still exploring the scene they had left behind at the ruined mill.

'More theories?' Vince asked, finally breaking the silence. 'About the dogs, I mean?'

'One is at a considerable disadvantage not to have had a sight of the bodies. The murdered girl and the dogs all neatly buried. Having to take it all on hearsay is very inconvenient. And irritating.'

'Taken that all we were told of the discovery of the dogs was correct,' said Vince. He had concluded that Brown would be a reliable witness and, in common with his stepfather, a man who could be guaranteed to miss little. 'It has just occurred to me – might not slaying the Queen's pet dogs rate as a treasonable crime?'

'Indeed, yes. Damage to her personal property, *lèse-majesté* and so forth would undoubtedly merit a heavy jail sentence.'

'And one she would see to personally, I don't doubt, and the Royal displeasure is enough to strike terror into the heart of any prospective dog-slayer,' said Vince.

'That makes sense, lad, but let's consider what doesn't. Why go to all that trouble, leaving the bodies around? Why not just bury them, throw them into the river, or carry them across the river in that excellent and convenient cradle? Dispose of them well away from the scene of the crime as no doubt was the case with the murdered girl?'

'That thought had occurred to me, Stepfather. Perhaps their killer was interrupted in the act—'

Faro made an impatient gesture. 'Do not let us miss the real point. We have built up a picture of what we think might have happened. But why? For if the dogs' deaths are coincidental and unconnected with the girl's murder, although the timing would seem to indicate the contrary, what else could they have done to merit death?'

'Not everyone is fond of dogs. Perhaps they made a nuisance of themselves. Took nips out of the servants,' Vince suggested.

'Vince, these are the Queen's pets. For the servants, having nips taken out of their ankles would be an occupational hazard.' Faro sucked in his lip. 'There was only one reason. A threat to the murderer's safety. That is the only logical reason why anyone would go to the extent of incurring Her Majesty's extreme displeasure – and we can all guess the consequences of that. Remember. You cannot blackmail a dog,' he continued. 'Perhaps they knew their killer and he panicked.'

Vince thought for a moment. 'Let's suppose that a farmer had shot them for sheep worrying, for instance. Then he wouldn't have carried them back here, Royal collars and all, as a mark of defiance, would he?'

'Any farmer who had marauding dogs on his land, Royal or no, would have a legitimate cause for indignation and the assurance that right – and the law – was on his side. But we have Brown's words that these King Charles spaniels were the most docile of animals.'

'Of course, one dog shot could have been an accident.'

'Got in the way of an indifferent gun? True, there are many around at this time of year.'

'That would be a possibility, Stepfather. Especially if he was afraid of the Queen's wrath.'

'But not two dogs, lad. Not shot through the head at point blank range. We are dealing with a much more complex situation here than an irate but scared farmer who didn't see the Royal collars until too late. Or an unlucky sportsman.'

The hospital gates were in sight. As he stepped down, Vince said suddenly, 'Isn't this all a bit far-fetched, Stepfather? After all there could be another simpler, quite coincidental explanation.'

'Then I'd like to hear it. Go on.'

'Well, they could have been sniffing about that mill regularly after rats and scared a poacher who panicked. Nothing to do with Morag Brodie's murder.'

'Let us hope you are right, lad,' said Faro fervently. But he was unable to stifle the growing fear that the murder of Morag Brodie was but a prelude to something much more important their killer had in his sights. And that the dogs had somehow been in danger of revealing all.

As they entered the hospital, approaching them from the direction of the wards were two uniformed policemen and one in plain clothes.

Faro stopped. 'Detective Inspector Purdie, I presume.'

'Indeed, yes.'

'Faro, from Edinburgh City Police.'

'This is a pleasant surprise. Your exploits are well known to us.'

Faro shook hands with the tall, burly detective. His face was luxuriously bearded, and keen eyes regarded him from behind gold-rimmed spectacles. His appearance implied that this would be a good man to have around in a fight.

'Sergeant Whyte of the local constabulary,' said Purdie, indicating the elder of the two who saluted smartly.

'And Sergeant Craig.'

'Extra staff for the duration of Her Majesty's visit,' Whyte put in, indicating that his own seniority was not in dispute.

'Sergeant Craig is here to assist me. I particularly requested someone who has experience of murder investigations and also knows this area.' Purdie's apologetic look in Whyte's direction suggested an awareness of discord between the two officers. The elder and more experienced had obviously been made to feel insecure by this appointment.

Eager to impress, Craig's smile was supercilious. Here was a young man very pleased with himself. Something familiar in his bearing hinted at the ex-soldier, while a new uniform and boots indicated recent promotion. Faro decided Craig was not in any danger of allowing anyone to forget it.

'There isn't much crime in the area, as Sergeant Whyte here will tell you,' said Purdie. 'Normally this case would have been dealt with by Aberdeen.'

'I understood that the case was closed now.'

Purdie eyed him pityingly. 'From my experience, a verdict of murder by person or persons unknown is never satisfactory. Especially with the Queen in residence, every precaution must be taken to ensure her safety. That's why they called in Scotland Yard.'

His shrug was eloquent. It indicated that this was a complete waste of time. 'Dr Laurie tells me your aunt has made a good recovery and she will probably be ready to go home tomorrow. She was looking very fit and cheerful. A great age, but Whyte tells me ninety is not all that unusual for country people. And your aunt still has all her faculties.'

Pausing he smiled. 'She was delighted by the chance of a few words with passing strangers. It was she who told us that Mistress Brodie's important visitors were relatives from Aboyne.'

'You didn't talk to Mistress Brodie then?' asked Vince.

'Alas no, we chose an inconvenient time. When we arrived she already had two persons at her bedside. The nurse implied that this was the limit and a great dispensation outside the official visiting hours.'

'I'm sure we could have arranged—' Vince began.

'Thank you, but I would not dream of disrupting the hospital's routine.' And turning to Faro, 'A stroke of luck meeting you here, Inspector. I have just arrived but when Sergeant Craig told me you were in the area, I could scarcely believe my good fortune.'

Vince, encountering Faro's triumphant look, was saved a reply as a nurse hurried towards him. Bidding them a hasty farewell, he followed her down the corridor.

Faro hesitated a moment, then decided in the circumstances of Purdie and his colleagues having been turned away, it would be tactless to insist upon seeing his aunt.

At the entrance a carriage awaited Purdie. A not-too-cleverly disguised police carriage, which the Inspector from Scotland Yard was important enough to have placed at his disposal. It was, Faro thought, a conveyance calculated to hinder a discreet investigation, alerting every citizen guiltily concealing an illicit still or poacher's trap and sending waves of alarm and despondency into the surrounding district. Its repercussions would undoubtedly be felt even in those areas where law was administered both rarely and reluctantly by the portly, easy-going Sergeant Whyte.

Looking back at the hospital, Purdie said to Craig, 'We will return later.' And to Faro, 'We have delayed it as much as possible until Mistress Brodie was considered fit to respond to our official enquiries about the fire.' He sighed. 'This is the second of our mistimed visits since we linked our endeavours to those of Sergeant Whyte, who has failed to make any progress.'

Both men looked at the unfortunate Whyte, who shuffled his feet miserably.

'We thought she might be able to throw some light upon the murdered girl's last hours,' said Purdie. 'Being kin, and so forth.'

Considering whether he should, at this point, reveal his discoveries in the ruined mill, Faro decided to await a more opportune moment. 'My aunt tells me Nessie Brodie has been very muddled since the accident.'

Craig shook his head disapprovingly, and patted his notebook pocket with military precision. 'The first time we found her fast asleep when we looked in. It was Inspector Purdie's decision that we should return later.' His pitying glance conveyed the impression that his superior officer was too soft-hearted by far and that he, Craig, wouldn't have had any hesitation about waking the old woman up.

'After all, this is an official enquiry,' he added to Whyte, creating an impression that the elder policeman was no longer up to his job.

Purdie beamed upon Faro. 'Mistress MacVae was most helpful, Faro, a positive mine of useful information. No doubt you inherited your flair for detection from her.'

It was Faro's turn to smile. He must remember to tell Bella, she would love that.

'We had been toying with a theory that the fire might have been deliberate, perhaps in the mistaken idea that the girl Morag was visiting. However, your aunt told us that Mistress Brodie was well known for her kind heart, allowing tinkers to sleep in her barn and if the weather was bad leaving food and drink there. Just in case any benighted stranger needed shelter or was caught in a storm.'

'Was there a storm on that night?' Faro asked Whyte.

'Not exactly a storm, sir. A fine mist and cold for the time of year—'

'Very well.' And to Craig. 'I presume you have combed thoroughly through the charred ruins.'

'Yes, sir. As a matter of fact Inspector Purdie had a piece of luck. He picked up what looked like a clay pipe.' Craig darted an admiring glance in the Inspector's direction.

Purdie shrugged. 'Doubtless belonged to one of Mistress Brodie's nocturnal visitors. Too many drinks, our tinker fell asleep, pipe in hand, and when he woke and found he had set the dry hay alight, he panicked and bolted.'

'That's right, sir,' said Whyte triumphantly. 'There are always plenty tinkers about around this time of year. Ghillies' Ball brings them down like vultures, looking for pickings.'

'Have you questioned the tinker camps?' Faro asked.

Whyte looked uncomfortable under the scrutiny of Craig and Purdie.

'They had all gone this morning. Fly-by-nights. And pursuing them is a waste of time. I've had years of it. The sight of a uniform and they either close up like clams or tell a pack of lies.'

Faro sighed. There was a running war between country constables and tinkers who were all too ready to appropriate possessions they regarded as discarded and useless. As this extended to misunderstandings about clothes innocently left to dry on washing lines, the crofters' resentment was understandable.

'About the girl, Morag Brodie. What do the servants she worked with have to say?' he asked Craig.

'They can all account for their movements. First place I checked. Naturally.' Craig sounded mildly indignant at this interrogation.

'Even though Morag was a foreigner by rights,' Whyte intervened, 'the servants found her a sprightly but biddable lass. Only complaint about her I ever heard was a fondness for the bottle. And the lads.'

'Her background has been investigated,' said Craig. 'And everything she told them about herself, which wasn't much, was reliable information. I checked it myself.'

Craig was beginning to sound exasperated and Purdie said

patiently, 'These are just the normal routine enquiries after a murder, as I am sure you are aware, Faro.' Pausing he added, 'I don't think you need worry over this one. We're pretty certain we've got our man. A few more loose ends to tie up and I expect to make the arrest within the next day or two.'

'Oh, indeed.' Faro waited hopefully for Purdie to reveal the suspect's name. Instead he merely shook his head mysteriously, without offering any further information.

'I gather you have very few crimes like this one round here,' Faro said to Whyte. 'It must have caused quite a sensation.'

It was Whyte's turn to smile pityingly. 'They're a peaceful lot in these parts, Inspector, not like your city mob. Must be fifty years since the last murder.'

'Were you the first to examine the body?' Faro asked.

'Aye, sir. Jock, from Duncan's farm, found her in the ditch. Came straight for me. Never touched a thing.'

'What were the nature of her injuries?'

'She was stabbed to death, sir.'

'Were there many wounds?'

'No. Just the one.' Whyte touched his chest. 'Just here. Right to the heart. She must have died instantly.'

'Indeed? Now that is very interesting. Tell me, have there been any other incidents in the neighbourhood?'

'What kind of incidents had you in mind, sir?'

'Incidents involving loss of life, let us say.'

Faro realised he was going to have to spell this one out. Giving Whyte time to think, he watched Purdie who, clearly bored with the conversation, was trying to light a pipe. This was no easy task in that unsteady carriage, but one he managed with great expertise and without removing his leather gloves.

'What about the river in spate?' he asked Whyte. 'Doesn't that claim a victim or two? There was a poem I remember when I stayed here as a lad – went something like "Blood-thirsty Dee each year needs three, But Bonny Don, she needs none." '

And to Purdie, 'Perhaps you remember it too.'

Purdie frowned, shook his head while Whyte's response was to regard Faro blankly.

Deciding to prompt the sergeant's memory, Faro continued, 'My aunt told me that just a few days before the murder, Morag Brodie was nearly drowned, falling out of the cradle crossing to Crathie. The fellow with her who was drowned was also a servant at the Castle. A footman.'

Whyte looked mutinous and said reproachfully, 'That's all past history, Inspector. Lessing's dead and buried, poor laddie. Nothing to do with the case,' he added huffily.

'We've been all over this ground, Craig and myself. Very carefully, I assure you,' Purdie intervened gently. 'Believe me, we've explored every possible avenue.'

'I do apologise,' said Faro abruptly.

'Not at all, we're delighted to have your keen powers of observation on our side—'

'Now that you ask for it, sir, here is another observation which I am sure has already occurred to you. Is it not strange that the lad who went to the trouble of rescuing her from drowning should have then risked his neck to murder her? I gather from your unspoken comments and other information that has come my way that your prime suspect is Lachlan Brown.'

'That is correct,' said Purdie. 'The Brodie girl had jilted young Brown for the footman who was drowned.'

'Jilting implies that there was talk of marriage.'

Purdie shrugged. 'Country matters, Faro. Let us say rather that the two had been on intimate terms.'

Faro was silent, remembering the evidence of a lovers' assignation in the upstairs room at the mill. With the footman Lessing dead, who else but Lachlan Brown could Morag have been waiting for?

'I should have thought that the answer was rather obvious,' Purdie continued. 'Consider the workings of human nature, if you please. When Brown rescued her and at the same time let her lover drown,' he added emphasising the words, 'he had hopes. When she refused to go back to him, with heaven knows what reproaches, well then, that was that,' he concluded, with an expressive gesture across his throat.

And Faro realised that the Inspector's speculation fitted perfectly his deductions at the mill.

They were in sight of Bella's cottage. 'This is where I leave you,' he said.

A handsome closed carriage stood in the roadway outside the gate.

'Ah,' said Purdie. 'I see you have a visitor.'

Faro shook his head. 'Someone enquiring after my aunt, I expect.'

'We're on our way to Bush Farm. Brown's place.' Purdie paused significantly. 'Bush Farm is very close to where the girl's body was found.'

And as Faro stepped down, he continued, 'I was hoping I might persuade you to accompany us. Take part in a little private investigation, if it would amuse you.'

Faro was tempted but his conscience prevailed. He thought about the Queen's dogs. That was his most urgent priority.

'Perhaps tomorrow, then?'

Inside the cottage was the last person he had expected to see: Superintendent McIntosh patiently awaiting Detective Inspector Faro's arrival.

His presence spelled out one word.

Trouble.

5

Superintendent McIntosh dominated the tiny parlour where his huge bulk was being viewed with polite anxiety by Tibbie as he settled uncomfortably, overflowing from one of Bella's diminutive armchairs.

Greeting Faro's entrance with relief, she bobbed a curtsy and hurried into the kitchen with promises of a pot of tea and some fresh pancakes.

Watching the door close, McIntosh said sternly, 'I am here incognito, Faro. This is strictly off the record.' And glancing round the walls nervously as if they might conceal a listener, 'I travelled by carriage from Aberdeen immediately after the wedding—'

A chronicle of trials and tribulations followed, sufficient to convince the uninitiated that in the manner of bees to honey, Superintendent McIntosh attracted disaster.

As for the incognito, Faro thought cynically that a closed carriage outside Bella's cottage would have already become an urgent topic of conversation in every kitchen in Crathie and surrounding areas. The entire populace would now be exchanging theories and speculation about who might be calling on Mistress MacVae. And her away in the hospital.

'I thought it wise not to use the telegraph on this occasion.'

Faro was again grateful for this thoughtfulness, seeing that private messages were an impossibility. All communications were avidly read and their contents subject to endless discussion long before fourth- or fifth-hand they reached their destination. Only those to the Castle under the Queen's personal code were necessarily treated with any reverence.

'It must be something very serious to bring you out of your way, sir.'

McIntosh smiled grimly. 'It is indeed. The wedding made that awful train journey a little easier to bear. The sooner they get that damned Tay Bridge built the better.' He sighed. 'I found myself having to kill two birds with one stone. If you will forgive the inappropriate simile, since it is my most urgent desire to prevent a second bird falling to the gun. A disaster that would be. A national disaster.'

McIntosh was addicted to his mixed metaphors and all Faro could do was listen patiently.

'Do I take it your visit concerns Balmoral and a member of the Royal Family?'

McIntosh seemed astonished that Faro should have made such an obvious deduction. 'Indeed, yes. Her Majesty, Faro, no less. We have just heard from sources at Scotland Yard that there is to be an attempt on her life. Here, before she leaves at the end of the week.'

Faro had a sinking feeling that his intuition had been right. That there was more involved in the servant girl's murder than a jealous lover. It also explained the real reason for the presence of a detective from Scotland Yard.

Two deaths, both conveniently buried and accounted for. Two of the Queen's pet dogs shot. Faro thought rapidly. Could all four put together in the right order add up to the Queen's life in danger?

'About this girl who was murdered. Is there a connection?'

'Highly unlikely.' MacIntosh shook his head. 'You're to stay out of that, Faro. I've warned you. They've got Scotland Yard on the case. We must be careful not to create any ill-feeling,' he added nervously.

'I have just made Inspector Purdie's acquaintance.'

'Have you indeed? Then remember it's the Queen's safety you are to concentrate on, Faro. There have always been attempts and rumours of attempts. Not only in London either. As you well know, we've been plagued by them in Edinburgh. Fenians with guns, mostly out in the open. This time it is different. This time it is to be an inside job.'

'You mean in the Castle itself?'

'I do. And by someone close, with access to Her Majesty.'

Dear God, the thought made him shudder when he remembered the informality of the daily life at Balmoral. An assassin just had to get lucky once, be in the right place at the right time.

'We have been led to believe that all staff are closely vetted by her security guards.'

McIntosh chortled. 'Captain Tweedie and Captain Dumleigh, known popularly, I understand, as Tweedledum and Tweedledee.'

Faro smiled at this allusion to the instant popularity of Lewis Carroll's sequel to *Alice in Wonderland*, a particular favourite of his two daughters.

'Can you imagine,' McIntosh chortled, 'two big watchful ex-policemen trying hard to look like footmen or pretending to be personal assistants to equerries?'

'Surely all the known Fenians and anarchists have been accounted for? And that last troublesome batch are now safely behind bars.'

'True, Faro, true. We have an excellent secret service in operation and it would be very difficult, given their present sources of reliable information, for any known undesirables to be "slipped" into Balmoral. But this is a new one on us. A domestic assassination.'

Pausing he regarded Faro solemnly. 'The Prince's Party, they call themselves. Recently sprung to our notice. Supposedly they are the staunchest of patriots, their cause the good of England, their message that Queen Victoria neglects her duties and should retire as she is no longer fit to reign over us. She should abdicate and let the Prince of Wales take over the throne.

'They'll go to any lengths, believe me. I'm not saying, between you and me,' he added again with that nervous glance around the room, 'that it might not be a bad thing for the country. Many of the Queen's disgruntled statesmen – and her subjects – would agree with them.'

Once upon a time, Faro would have disagreed strongly. His Royal Highness had a reputation for wildness and the frequent scandals surrounding him were suppressed with difficulty and great expense. Only marriage to an excellent virtuous Princess had tamed him.

He was very popular in Deeside and the indiscretions that many of his nobles had condemned would, when he was King, be dismissed light-heartedly.

'A dam' fine fellow, just sowing his wild oats, y'know,' is what they would all say. His past was one many a less illustrious elder son and heir to a noble house would emulate, as the natural thing to do.

'I see by your expression that you don't understand what all the fuss is about,' said McIntosh. 'But we have good reason to believe that there's a sinister motive behind this group who are using the Prince as a front. And once they have him on the throne, then they'll twist him around their little fingers. By fair means or foul,' he added slowly.

When Faro gave him a hard look he nodded grimly. 'You get my drift.'

'Blackmail?'

'The same. They'll soon make it obvious that they are in real terms far from being passionate patriots. The opposite in fact. What they stand to gain is that they will use their power to take over the country. And between us, His Royal Highness has left evidence of indiscretions, letters and so forth, enough to merit a national scandal if they were made public.'

'This is incredible. Whatever he did in the past, we're talking about matricide, sir. It's well known that he doesn't get on with his mother. But matricide . . .'

'It's been done before – Medicis, Borgias.'

'That was in the Middle Ages, we're living in civilised times.'

'Are we? I wonder. Before you get virtuous about it, the Prince, we are informed, has no idea that they plan to get rid of his mother. He would not unnaturally be glad to inherit, but irritation with a parent is a long way from killing them off. If that was the way of it then most of us would be orphans. Nationally, there was never a better time for the Prince's Party,' McIntosh ended gloomily.

'In fact,' he added in a treasonable whisper, 'I doubt sometimes whether she would even be missed. The country as you well know if you read your newspapers is very anti-monarchy just now. They take badly to her preoccupation with Balmoral. And, dare I say it, with John Brown.'

Faro had met the Prince of Wales and was relieved to hear that he was not personally involved in this treasonable plot. Apart from a high-spirited reputation for being both susceptible and unreliable where a pretty face was involved, Faro found him witty, roguish and intelligent. He didn't doubt that Bertie would make an admirable and responsible king some day.

'The plan, if plan there is, is being presented to the Prince by a body of his admirers, earnest well-wishers and loyal Englishmen.'

'And Englishwomen perhaps?' Faro added. He could see it was just possible that the Prince might be manipulated by the ambitions of one of his current aristocratic mistresses.

'You have a point there, Faro. The theme is that the country is being mismanaged under the present Government by a monarch who has so little interest in her subjects, she hardly ever deigns to appear in public. She prefers to hide away most of the year with her wild clansmen in the Highlands of Scotland.

'And to many Englishmen anything north of the Tweed means that people still live in caves. The only interest most of the wealthy have is in buying land, estate and titles. They don't see the real country.'

It was true. In ever increasing numbers they came up twice or sometimes only once per year to shoot over their vast estates, have a continuous house party for several weeks and then disappear back to the Home Counties. These were, in fact, the notorious absentee landlords whose advent spelt ruin and desolation to the Highlands of Scotland.

McIntosh drained his glass. 'And, of course, you must see the drift of this plan. If they succeed and the Queen is got rid of then the Prince will inevitably be full of terrible remorse. Worse than that, he will only ever be a puppet king. They will make sure of that. They will make the laws, he will sign the State documents but one step out of line and they will need only to whisper one word in his ear.'

'What do you want me to do, sir?'

'Word is that the Queen must be in London for the State Opening of Parliament next Monday.'

'But that's less than a week away.'

'Exactly.' McIntosh counted up on his fingers. 'We can expect her to leave here on Friday or Saturday at the latest. So you have four days to find the killer before he strikes.'

'But that's impossible—'

'Nothing's impossible, Faro,' said McIntosh sternly. 'Use your much vaunted powers of observation and deduction on this. We're putting you on extended leave. You stay here until the Queen is safely back at Buckingham Palace. Understand?'

Rubbing his chin thoughtfully, he added, 'The fewer people who know you're here the better.'

Realising Bella's talent for gossip, not to mention Tibbie and the eagle eyes of all the locals, Faro said vaguely, 'I expect it may have got around that my visit is purely social. For my aunt's ninetieth birthday.'

'Keep it at that, if you can. I understand Purdie's a top man at Scotland Yard. Normally this would have been a case for the

Aberdeen police. Fact is with the murdered girl having been a servant at Balmoral, etc., etc. It's all in the letter I had from the Chief Constable. Take Purdie into your confidence, Faro. In the unlikely event that he doesn't know all about this already.

'Get his help,' he added desperately. 'Don't be too proud to ask. Between the two of you, you should be able to thwart this attempt. Get John Brown on to it too. He's loyal and devoted, by all accounts. You've met him, of course.'

'The day I arrived—'

Reluctantly Faro told the Superintendent about the Queen's dogs, but the reaction he had dreaded wasn't forthcoming. McIntosh merely dismissed it as somewhat eccentric behaviour to be expected of a Royal personage.

'Whatever next, Faro?' he said brusquely. 'But do not be sidetracked. This other matter is vital. Prevent the murder, Faro, without trampling on too many Royal toes, or outraging too many duchesses.'

'That won't be easy, sir.'

'Use your influence with Brown, indulge him about the dogs. Enveigle yourself into the Castle as much as you can. Look around. You're sharp-eyed. Good heavens, man, I don't have to spell it out to you.'

He paused. 'Incidentally, it's well known that the Prince hates Brown.'

'So does his brother Prince Alfred. The Queen was furious when he once refused to shake hands with a commoner, a mere ghillie,' said Faro.

McIntosh shrugged. 'Possibly that would go for most of the Royal children. In their eyes Brown is a peasant with an overblown idea of his own importance. Moorcock turned peacock is the Royal whisper. Have you heard the latest?' Without waiting for Faro's reply, he went on, 'He's now extended his power over the Queen by introducing her to seances. Seances and spiritualists, if you please. Putting her in touch with Prince Albert.'

'I wonder who was behind that piece of inspired skullduggery.'

'Indeed. And who do you think goes into a trance and speaks in the Prince's voice, calling her "Liebchen" and giving her tips on how to rule the country?'

'Not Brown surely.'

McIntosh nodded. 'The same.' He looked at Faro curiously. 'What's the chap like? I mean, to exert all this influence over Her Majesty?'

'Sound as a bell, I'd say, loyal to the soles of his brogues. I hope you're not going to imply that he's involved.'

McIntosh smiled into his beard. 'Not at all, Faro. That never crossed my mind. It was something quite different I had in mind. Er – do you think, I mean . . .' His eyes roved the room, searching for the right words to phrase that burning question. 'Is there any truth in the rumour?'

'What rumour?' said Faro innocently, deciding not to spare the Superintendent.

'Dammit, man, you know perfectly well. That he and Her Majesty are, er, well – to put it delicately – infatuated?'

Faro laughed. 'Don't tell me you are being influenced by the popular press, sir. She needs a strong man, another Prince Consort, a father figure, but that's all. Someone with all the trappings of pomp and self-interest stripped away. Someone who would die for her if necessary but is much happier to live for her.'

'I thought her Prime Minister performed that function,' said McIntosh, clearly disappointed. 'How does Mr Gladstone take all this adulation of Brown, I wonder?'

'You must realise from your perusal of the newspapers, sir, that she cannot stand the man. He treats her with awe and reverence. She was overheard and quoted as saying, "He treats me like a public meeting." ' Faro shook his head. 'No, she needs a friend, not a lover. Someone she can be a woman with, let her hair down, take a dram, for heaven's sake.'

With a sigh, McIntosh picked up his gloves, smoothed them

with his large hands and looked wistfully in the direction of his empty glass. 'And that is damned fine stuff.'

'It is indeed. Made at our local distillery up the road. A little more, perhaps?'

'Mm. Thank you. You were saying—'

'John Brown makes her feel like a woman, not a Queen Empress.'

'Rumour has it that he even chooses her wardrobe. Isn't that going a little far, don't you think?'

Faro smile. 'Not at all. After all, this isn't the first time a Queen has been mesmerised by a commoner. Take Mary Queen of Scots and Bothwell—'

'Bothwell was an earl,' McIntosh exploded. 'Brown is a mere ignorant peasant. A ghillie, dammit.'

'A ghillie he may be but ignorant, no. He's a dominie's son, well read—'

'I suppose you're going to tell me this is a situation not unknown. Seems to arouse, er, um, passion in a woman of breeding, being wooed and won by a common soldier or servant   '

Faro glanced at the Superintendent and wondered what kind of literature he read in his spare time. 'On the subject of clothes,' he said hastily, 'Her Majesty has no interest in gowns. Hasn't had much since Prince Albert died. Tends to wear the same black satin in Edinburgh every year.'

'It has been noticed,' said McIntosh drily.

'I'm not a man fond of dressing up myself,' said Faro uncomfortably, 'but I insist upon being clean and tidy and I feel shabby black is hardly in keeping with the Royal image.'

McIntosh nodded. 'There's a story circulating that this Brown fellow was overheard saying to her, "Now what's this you've got on today, woman?" He didn't approve of what she was wearing.'

He guffawed. 'Apparently she listened to his criticism and meek as a lamb went back and changed into something more suitable. Can you credit that?' And slapping his thigh delightedly, he added, 'Man, it would be more than my life was worth to criticise Mrs McIntosh's gowns.'

Faro suppressed a smile, for the Superintendent's wife was known in the Central Office as 'The Tartar', managing to keep her large husband well and truly under her tiny thumb.

As Faro walked down the road to where McIntosh's carriage waited, the Superintendent said, 'Any chance of an invitation to lunch or dine at the Castle?'

'Not so far.'

'Pity. Couldn't you get Brown to arrange a meeting, talk about those dogs – lost, weren't they?' he added vaguely.

'Shot, sir. Dead.'

'Oh yes.' McIntosh was not an animal lover and obviously wondered what all the Royal fuss was about. 'Try to impress on Brown that Her Majesty owes you an audience. And it would be an excellent chance for a little quiet investigation.'

On the step, he turned once more. 'There's one question you haven't asked me, Faro.'

'And what is that, sir?'

'Who is the brains behind the Prince's Party?'

'I haven't the least idea.'

McIntosh laughed. 'You should, Faro. He's an old enemy of yours.'

'Really? I have accumulated a vast number of those through twenty years with the Edinburgh Police.'

'But not many as clever or as wily as this one.' And watching Faro's expression eagerly, he said, 'This time we think it is Lord Nob's handiwork.'

Lord Nob. Noblesse Oblige. A devil with a dozen names and a dozen faces, whose background was noble perhaps, rumour had it, even Royal, but whose true identity no man had ever cracked and lived.

Their last encounter had been in what Faro's notes described as 'The Case of the Killing Cousins'.

On a stormy clifftop in Orkney he thought he had seen the last of his adversary. Faro groaned inwardly.

Closing the carriage door, McIntosh leaned out of the window. 'I see you recognise the gravity of the situation. This is one of national peril. This isn't something you handle alone, Faro. Get Purdie on to it, d'you hear,' he repeated. 'Believe me, you are going to need all the help you can get. We're relying on you, Faro, See to it.'

6 Faro found Tibbie in the barn. She had taken under her slender wing the welfare of Steady. Loving animals great and small, she announced proudly that he had been given his dinner.

With the rest of the day to himself until visiting time at the hospital, the idea of sitting with his fishing rod by the banks of the Dee now appalled rather than appealed. Especially as he brooded upon the fact that every boulder might now conceal the hidden presence and watchful eyes of his old adversary.

Considerably more in keeping with his temper was the challenge presented by marching out to confront danger. And by solving the sinister mysteries looming around him perhaps he might finally outwit Noblesse Oblige.

Horseback was an excellent alternative to exploring the countryside on foot in search of clues. A rider could not only move faster, he could also penetrate less accessible areas than one in a pony-cart.

Steady seemed to agree with him and made no resistance to being saddled up. If it wasn't too idiotic, thought Faro, he appeared to be smiling knowingly. The cause, he discovered, was a slight malformation of the upper lip due to a couple of missing teeth.

As they trotted off down the lane, the pleasure of riding through a golden, crisp-aired day with the sun still at its zenith brought a delightful sense of well-being.

Ten years ago, before the advent of horse-drawn omnibuses in Edinburgh, this had been his usual method of travelling into the countryside on the track of criminals. But in town he never felt safe in the narrow crowded streets and wynds of the High Street and its environs. In that vast criminal underworld where lurked many hazards, a man on horseback was particularly vulnerable.

With a half-formed plan in mind he found himself drawn towards the area across the river where Morag Brodie's body had been found. He did not doubt the efficiency of Purdie and Craig and realised there was little hope of any overlooked clues – especially as he suspected the girl's body had been taken from the ruined mill on the Balmoral Estate, to be discovered on the road which, according to Purdie and his map, led to Bush Farm.

Was this obvious deduction the right answer? That this had been to divert suspicion to the discarded lover, Lachlan Brown?

Climbing the steep brae, with its twists and turns, he had an unexpected stroke of luck. The sound of creaking wheels and a farmhand emerged driving a haycart.

Faro drew Steady in to let him pass.

"'Tis a fine day, mister.'

Faro replied in kind.

The man was middle-aged, cheery-faced. 'Ye've missed the Mains road, Doctor.'

'Doctor?'

The man eyed the horse and Faro's tweed suit reflectively. 'Aye, sir, ye'll be visiting the maister. Een o' the bairns has the croup.'

Faro shook his head. 'Alas, I'm not the doctor, and I fear I'm lost.'

The man's curiosity was thoroughly aroused. 'Stranger to these parts, are ye, sir?'

'Not quite. I'm biding with my aunt Mistress MacVae at Easter Balmoral.'

The farmhand was immediately interested. 'That was an awfa' business about the fire—' Suddenly he pushed back his bonnet, scratched his brow. 'I ken who ye are, mister,' he added stabbing a finger in Faro's direction. 'I wasna' far out in thinking ye were the new doctor.'

'He is my stepson.'

'And ye must be Mistress Bella's nevvy, the policeman,' was the triumphant response.

'Correct.'

The man chortled delightedly. 'We've heard all about ye, sir. Solving all these mysteries.' And leaning forward confidentially, he added, 'Did ye ken that there was a murder hereabouts?'

'I did hear something of the kind,' said Faro vaguely.

'Aye, sir,' was the excited response, 'and what is more, I could show ye the exact spot, if ye'd care to see it.'

Leaping down from the cart, he led the way back and stopped by a bramble-filled ditch some twenty yards distant.

He touched the verge with his boot. 'Here, sir, this is where she lay. I'll no forget it in a hurry, sir. For it was me that found the puir lass,' he said proudly.

'You must be Jock?'

'The same, sir.'

This was indeed an unexpected piece of good fortune.

'Early morning it was, I was on the way up to the fields here. And there was this bundle of rags, I'm thinking. Then I saw it was a woman. Och, a drunken tinker, her hair was over her face. When I tried to wake her up,' he gulped at the memory, 'I thought it was mud dried on her dress. Then I saw it was dried blood. She had been stabbed in the chest.'

'Did you touch anything?'

'Nothing, sir. I ran and telt the maister. He's an invalid, puir body, been in a wheelchair for nigh on twa' years. He was right upset about it, told me to saddle up and ride into Ballater to get Sergeant Whyte. And Dr Elgin. There's been an inspector, a top man from London,' he added in tones of awe. 'He asked me a powerful lot of questions – and the maister too. He has it all written down, just exactly like I've telt ye.'

Faro did not doubt that. 'Did you know the lass?'

'Everybody kenned Morag Brodie,' Jock said slowly. 'A foreigner, no' frae these parts, working up at the Castle. The Crathie Inn was een o' her haunts wi' the rest o' the servants.' Again confidentially he whispered, 'Aye, a fair bucket o' drink they took, but kept themselves to themselves, o'course,' he added with a wry smile. 'Superior to the rest o' us.'

He stopped to watch the distant figure of a woman, carrying a basket.

'That's ma missus. Brings ma piece to the end o' the road.'

The haycart trundled off down the lane. Five minutes later Faro emerged from the ditch without any new evidence but with an abundance of scratches from the close-packed bramble hedge.

At that moment he was thankful that this particular case was not his responsibility and that Purdie had the killer already in his sights.

Why then did it continue to trouble him? Was it the vague possibility that the murder of Morag Brodie had its origins in a plot to kill the Queen?

He sighed. His search for whoever killed the Queen's pet dogs seemed even more ludicrous in the light of Superintendent McIntosh's monstrous revelations.

From the distant hill, the echoes of gunfire, the faint plumes of smoke and clouds of birds rising indicated that the sportsmen were still busily engaged in the morning's activity.

Shading his eyes he stared across the river and wished he could see inside the mind of the assassin who at this moment lurked somewhere behind the granite walls of Balmoral Castle, tranquil in afternoon sunlight.

He turned Steady's head, briskly trotting downhill until they reached the river bank and the bridge which gave access to the Castle gates. As they entered the drive, a landau approached carrying four passengers.

Faro recognised General Ponsonby, the Queen's secretary, and Prime Minister Gladstone. Sitting opposite them were two large gentlemen. With only the most cursory observation, stolid countenances and military bearing betrayed them as the security guards, Captains Tweedie and Dumleigh.

The General, who knew him, bowed and obviously identified Faro for the others, who now turned and regarded him intently.

As they disappeared he found himself close to the spot where the Queen's dogs had been killed. When his presence in the grounds was revealed to Her Majesty she would, he was certain, express her impatience if he did not have some substantial progress to report to Brown within the next day or two.

If word of the Queen's dissatisfaction with his investigations reached the popular press, then his whole reputation might be under threat. He could imagine Her Majesty's scornful reactions on her next visit to Edinburgh: 'Inspector Faro, you say. Have you no one else? Why, he could not even discover who killed our precious dogs.'

Suddenly aware that he was running out of time, he shuddered. He had at most four days to discover the dog-slayer and avert a plot to murder their Royal mistress.

This was Tuesday. At the end of the week the Queen left once again for London.

If she was still alive.

As he rode towards the Castle, the drive appeared to be deserted and he realised how easy it was to gain access to the Castle. No guards, no policemen. Just as the Queen wished it to appear, a normal country house.

Dear God, that it was so.

He looked up at the windows, all empty, close-curtained in tartan. He turned away, frustrated, helpless to avert the catastrophe taking shape within those walls.

As he started back down the drive the sound of loud barking presaged the appearance of three liveried white-wigged footmen, leading a selection of assorted dogs.

At the sight of his horse the dogs became even more agitated, while Steady greeted the tirade with remarkable calm, snorting a little but remaining aloof.

The footmen meanwhile with great difficulty and much disentanglement of chains at last succeeded in quieting their charges.

While Faro expected to be challenged on his right to be riding about on Royal property, they merely regarded him sullenly. Touching his whip to his hat in brief salute, he trotted past and out on to the road leading to the bridge, suddenly elated by the encounter.

Did the footmen normally walk the dogs? If so, had this been one of the duties of Lessing, Morag Brodie's drowned lover?

He was to find the answer to that sooner than he expected when, a few hours later, with Steady again saddled to the pony-cart, he set off once more for the hospital.

Bella greeted him cheerfully: 'I'm being let home tomorrow for ma birthday—' The door opened to admit a somewhat breathless Vince. 'I was just telling him the grand news—'

'You go on one condition, Great-aunt,' said Vince sternly. 'That you promise to take care and not do too much.' And turning to Faro, he added, 'Dr Elgin has given me the evening off. I wonder, could we have supper together? I'm told the food is excellent at the inn.'

'No need for that, lad. Tibbie'll give ye both a bite to eat.'

'That's all very fine, dear. But we're not going to impose on Tibbie. Besides it's time I made the acquaintance of the locals. Agreed, Stepfather?'

'Agreed.'

'Forgive me carrying him off, Great-aunt. He will be all yours, I promise, from tomorrow morning.' And to Faro, 'Ten minutes, at the entrance?' And turning back to Bella, 'I'll look in and see you two ladies later.'

In the next bed Nessie remained motionless, apart from her heavy breathing.

Bella looked towards her anxiously. 'The puir soul. She gets that upset, cries a lot about Morag. And the Queen's sewing. Always was a worrier, ye ken. The nurse had to give her something to make her sleep. Puir Nessie, she's upset at me going. She wants home too.'

'But where will she go?'

'She can bide with me, of course,' said Bella indignantly. 'No one goes without a roof over their heads hereabouts, Jeremy. There's always good neighbours. And cottages falling vacant on the estate. The Queen's a kind caring body, never forgetting them as has served her.'

She smiled at him, picking up a ball of wool and needles from the bed. 'Now off you go and' have yer supper, lad. I have the heel of my sock to turn and then it'll be bedtime. See and come early for me in the morning.' He hugged her fondly, promising to do so.

Vince was awaiting him in the lobby and greeted the pony-cart with delight. 'No more walking today, thank heaven. It's not a very big hospital, but the corridors seem uncommon long. Especially as I have to attend both men and women patients and when Prince Albert designed the dratted building, he omitted to make any communicating door between the two wings. I cannot imagine how it hasn't killed Dr Elgin years ago.'

The coaching inn was busy, obviously extremely popular with locals and visitors alike. They found a corner table near a cheerful log fire and over an excellent meal of broth, roast beef and Athol brose, Faro told his stepson of his conversation with Purdie and the two policemen, and his meeting with Jock at the murder scene.

McIntosh's secret visit and the plot to kill the Queen, he left until the end.

Vince whistled. 'This is incredible, Stepfather. What a hornet's nest you've stumbled on this time. But you know, I'd wager that Inspector Purdie knows about it. And that's the real reason for his presence here.'

'My thoughts exactly. And the sooner we put our two heads together the happier I'll be.'

'Three heads, Stepfather, if you please. Don't forget about me. I want a part of this too.' Vince sighed. 'You've realised of course that time isn't on your side!'

'In this game, Vince lad, it never is,' said Faro grimly, glancing at his watch. 'Talking of which, since it's now past ten o'clock I had better make a move in the direction of the bar if we want to be served with any more drams.'

Pushing his way through the crowd, trying to claim the attention of the harassed barman, he was greeted by another customer, similarly employed.

'We have met before, sir.' At Faro's puzzled smiled, the man laughed. 'You fail to recognise me without the wig.'

'The wig? Ah, one of the footmen—'

'Correct. I apologise for the dogs' unruly behaviour this morning. Horses can get very uppity.'

'Not at all.' And as both men received their order, Faro said, 'Perhaps you would care to join us. At the table over there.'

'Thank you, I have already eaten. I had arranged to meet some friends.' And looking around, 'I don't see them anywhere. I've just arrived and at this hour it is impossible to find a seat,' he added, following Faro through the crowd.

The footman had an English accent, and on closer acquaintance he was not so young as Faro had first thought. Perhaps about his own age, touching forty, with a pale rather melancholy face and quite startlingly pale eyes.

Holding out his hand he said, 'Peter Noble's the name.'

'Mr Faro. Dr Laurie.' Faro's warning glance in his stepson's direction established his wish to remain incognito.

'This is our favourite haunt,' said Peter, settling himself comfortably and lighting a cigar. 'Can't tell you what a relief it is to be warm for a change and to escape all those restrictions at the Castle. Oh, I beg pardon, do have one, gentlemen.'

Vince who had not acquired the smoking habit declined. Faro

would have preferred his old pipe but felt it would be churlish to refuse and the chance of an excellent cigar rarely came his way. A moment later he was glad of his decision, appreciating a high-quality Havana obviously in keeping with the Royal household.

'Her Majesty is a regular tartar about this sort of thing,' Peter continued, puffing happily. 'Can't abide smokers or the tobacco habit. I don't think I'll be telling tales out of school for it's fairly common knowledge. The strict rule is all cigars and pipes are banished to the smoking-room. Even illustrious guests are so treated. And that isn't the worst. By Her Majesty's order, that particular door is locked promptly at midnight.'

He laughed. 'It breeds a camaraderie among the guests and servants, I assure you. A kind of conspiracy which does add a furtive enjoyment to their illicit activity. Some have been overheard saying it beats being back at Eton or Harrow. Especially as smoking is forbidden even in the privacy of their own rooms.'

The waiter approached and Peter accepted the large dram that Faro had ordered. He drank it gratefully and as Faro and Vince made their excuses, saying that the hour was late, and prepared to leave, Noble stood up and bowed.

'I do thank you both for your hospitality. Your table by the fire was well chosen. Indeed, I am most reluctant to leave, but I should go and join my friends.'

Faro observed that the footman swayed somewhat as he added, 'Shall I tell you something, Mr Faro?' And without awaiting a reply, 'You can't imagine how deuced uncomfortable the Castle is. Even in summer, if summer ever exists in this northern clime, for there are no fires then in the guest rooms. The windows admit draughts and I am told that getting into bed is like drowning in ice cold sheets. Her Majesty regards such niceties as warmth as a loosening of the moral fibre.'

He looked from one to the other. 'That's how it is for the

guests. I leave it to your imaginations, gentlemen, what it is like for us poor underlings.'

At the door, Faro offered him a lift back to the Castle.

'I'm obliged to you, sir, but as a group of us come down regularly we take a hired carriage.'

As they waited politely for his friends to assemble, Faro wondered how he could get around to the question poised most urgently in his mind.

'Do you usually walk the dogs?'

'No, sir. But we are one short. I'm the newest arrival, so I inherit that lowly task. Last chap unfortunately got himself drowned.' He grimaced.

'Fellow called Lessing, wasn't it?'

'The same.' Peter looked at him curiously and Faro was saved any further comment by shouts from the darkness.

'Yes, over here. I'm coming.'

And with profuse thanks he ran a somewhat zigzag course towards the carriage where his arrival was greeted with shouts of encouragement and urgency.

When Faro returned to the hospital next morning with the pony-trap in readiness to take his aunt home, Vince was nowhere to be seen. A pretty nurse told him: 'Dr Laurie is with a patient just now—'

'It's all right, nurse, I can find my way.'

In the ward he found Bella in tears. Putting his arms around her he wished her many happy returns of her birthday.

'It'll no' be that, lad. No' without Nessie.'

Faro looked at Nessie's empty bed.

'Where is she?'

At his words she broke into noisy sobs.

'Oh, Jeremy, lad. It's awful, awful. I canna' believe it.'

'Why, what's happened? Where is she?'

'Dead. Dead. Last night. And her so well. I just canna' believe it. And it all happened while I was here, in the next bed. And her not a day over seventy, so strong and well until yon fire—'

Faro put a hand on her arm. 'Auntie, people do die from delayed shock. Vince will tell you that,' he added as his stepson appeared around the door.

'This is a bad business, Stepfather. So unexpected. Heart failure.' Vince looked puzzled as he turned to Bella. 'It's been a shock for you, but you'll feel much better once you're in your own home again. I'll look in and see you later. Promise now, not to overdo things. Take care.'

'I will that. But oh, I'll miss Nessie. We've been close friends for thirty years or more.'

As Faro put a comforting arm around her shoulders, she patted his hand. 'The Good Lord be thanked I have you at such a time.'

Over Bella's head, Vince nodded to Faro. 'I'm attending to a patient. We'll leave you to get dressed, dear. Do you need any help?'

'I can manage fine, lad.'

Outside the ward, Vince led him out of earshot to the nurse who was going off duty.

'Thank you for waiting, Nurse Roberts. If you would be so good as to tell my stepfather about Mistress Brodie's visitor last night.'

'Inspector Purdie, you mean, Doctor? He came after visiting time and said he had to see Mistress Brodie urgently. He had a message for her from Balmoral.' She smiled. 'Some delicacies from the Queen for her old servant.'

'What kind of delicacies?'

The nurse frowned. 'He was carrying a box, tied with ribbon. Sweeties, I expect.'

'You would, of course, recognise the Inspector again? He might come by – er, to see me,' Vince ended lamely.

The nurse looked puzzled. 'We-ell, I didn't get a very good look at him. It was dark and, as you know, Doctor, the hospital is strict about lamps at night when most of the patients are asleep. Lamps and candles can be dangerous unattended, if sick patients try to get out of bed—'

'Of course, of course,' said Vince.

Faro smiled. 'As a matter of interest, what does the Inspector look like?'

The nurse thought for a moment. 'Tall, clean-shaven. Seemed to feel the cold. Wore his muffler and greatcoat collar high.' She paused indicating her chin. 'And he kept on his hat.'

Vince exchanged a significant glance with his stepfather who asked, 'What time was this?'

'About nine o'clock, sir. We had just completed the evening rounds.'

'Where were you during this visit?'

'At the table there.' She pointed to the far end of the ward.

'You were present all the time?'

'Not every minute,' Nurse Roberts admitted reluctantly. She was beginning to sound exasperated at his questions. 'I mean, Inspector. Someone sent by Her Majesty personally. It seemed, well, most impertinent, especially when he had requested a screen for privacy.'

'A screen? Isn't that somewhat unusual? Do you normally provide screens for visitors?'

'If it is specially requested, we do. You know, husbands and wives, we like to give them a little privacy. Especially if there is someone sharing the ward.'

Seeing his look she continued hastily, 'Nothing improper, I assure you, Inspector. The screen was Dr Elgin's idea, but although the patient is hidden from the inquisitive eyes of the other patients, they are clearly visible to the staff,' she added sternly.

'How long were you absent from the ward?'

'Five – ten minutes. I had things to check in the linen room and when I came back he had gone. I went to remove the screen immediately. I was very quiet as I presumed in the dim light that Mistress Brodie was asleep. It wasn't until I made my last round at midnight that I discovered she was dead.'

She darted a helpless look at Vince. 'It could have happened any time, whether I was there on duty or not. Her heart gave out, doctor.'

'Of course, nurse. No one is blaming you,' said Vince.

'Before you go, what happened to the box of sweeties?' Faro asked.

'It was empty. We threw it away when we cleared out her locker.'

'Just one thing more. Had you met Inspector Purdie before?'

'No. Never. This was his first visit.'

'How do you know?'

'Well, he asked me to give him directions.'

'Thank you, nurse. You have been very helpful,' said Vince. 'See if Mistress MacVae is ready to leave, if you please.'

Watching her walk towards the ward, Vince said, 'Of one thing we can be quite certain, Stepfather. Nessie's visitor was someone impersonating Inspector Purdie.'

'And taking a great chance that the real Inspector Purdie wasn't known to the night-nurse,' said Faro. 'I would very much like to examine that empty box of sweeties.'

'Too late. It would have gone into the incinerator this morning with all the other hospital rubbish.'

Faro swore and Vince continued, 'Look, I was with Dr Elgin when he examined Nessie's body. There was nothing to indicate it wasn't natural causes.'

'But we both know how easily heart failure can be induced in a frail old woman. Stoppage of breath could be achieved by putting a pillow over her face.'

'But why? What on earth had she done to deserve being murdered?'

'It was not what she had done but what she knew.'

At Vince's puzzled shake of the head, he continued, 'I would swear that this has something to do with the murder of Morag Brodie. And I'd be prepared to wager a hundred golden guineas that the reason for Morag's murder is that she knew about the Balmoral plot and talked too much. Bella told us that Nessie had raved on about the Queen being in danger.'

Faro swore again. 'We should have been prepared for something like this. They had already tried to kill her by burning down the cottage.'

'They?'

'Oh yes, Vince. We are well out of the realms of the *crime passionnel* now. We are into political assassination.'

Vince's eyes widened in horror. 'You mean—'

'I mean the Prince's Party. I'd stake my life on it. And we have to find our bogus inspector and quickly. Because his next victim is the Queen. And this time, we have to battle against the clock. He has to play his cards quickly.'

John Brown had confirmed that the Queen had to return to London for various State occasions. The first and most important, as McIntosh had said, was the State Opening of Parliament on Monday next.

'She doesna' give much notice,' Brown had grumbled. 'Often tells the servants, "We leave tomorrow." Then it's all hell let loose.'

Faro took his aunt home and her conversation rolled over his head as he reviewed the rapid turnover of events since his arrival. And he no longer doubted that another fragment of the puzzle, the slaying of the Queen's dogs, fitted neatly into his conclusions.

7 Bella was speedily settled in her favourite armchair, among birthday tributes including an Orkney shawl from Faro's mother and lace mittens from his daughters, Rose and Emily. The shawl was to be pinned with an amethyst and pearl brooch from himself and Vince.

But the occasion which had been so eagerly anticipated was marred by Nessie Brodie's death. Bella could speak of nothing else and the now tearful Tibbie added her lamentations at their neighbour's untimely end.

'Tell Tibbie about Nessie's last visitor,' Faro said, curious to hear the story in Bella's own words, and managing to get in a word between the sobs and exclamations of the two women.

'That inspector, you mean. Nessie knew him well. He bided with them one summer when he was a wee lad. They were talking and joking together. Quiet-like but I heard every word. At least most of it,' she said apologetically. "How's your poor hand, Davie lad?" was the first thing she asked him—'

Faro suppressed a smile. Bella's excellent faculties did not include sharp ears. She was growing increasingly deaf but hated to have it noticed. He concluded she would make a poor witness as she continued:

'Of course, I didn't want to seem nosey especially when I saw that screen being put up between us,' she added huffily. 'So I pretended to be asleep—'

She was interrupted by a new arrival. Tibbie had opened the door to Inspector Purdie.

'Care to accompany us to Bush Farm, Faro?'

On the doorstep Faro made a point of introducing the new-comer to his aunt.

'You are Inspector Purdie?'

'I am,' was the cheerful reply.

Bella's baffled expression held a multitude of eager questions and as they walked down the path Faro glanced back over his shoulder. She was watching them intently, standing very still, a hand shading her eyes against the light.

Her reaction put the stamp of certainty on Faro's suspicion that she had never seen the Inspector before.

In the carriage, Purdie said, 'Craig has gone on ahead.' Smiling, he added, 'Glad you got your aunt home safely, Faro. A remark-able old lady. Which reminds me, I must go in and see Mistress Brodie at the proper visiting hour this evening.'

So he hadn't heard.

'I take it you didn't go in last night.'

'Last night? I'm afraid not. Craig and I went into Braemar for dinner which became rather an extended affair. And I don't like breaking rules, Faro, even hospital rules. Or wielding my author-ity unnecessarily,' he added sternly, 'unless it's life and death. And interviewing a woman whose house has burned down hardly fits into that category.'

'In this case it's a pity you were so conscientious. You might have saved her life.'

'Saved her life? What on earth do you mean, Faro?'

'I mean that she's dead.'

'Oh dear, how very unfortunate. But in the circumstances, I suppose we mustn't be too surprised. She was old and had sustained a considerable shock.'

'I rather suspect that she was murdered.'

'Murdered?' Purdie whistled. 'By what means?'

'Smothered most likely, if the box of sweets her visitor brought wasn't poisoned.'

'Faro, you astonish me.' Purdie looked at him as if he had taken leave of his senses. 'Do you realise what you're saying? Are you sure of your facts?'

And without waiting for an explanation, he continued, 'I hardly need to tell you that one has to be careful in our profession not to regard every sudden death as suspicious. After all, what reason would anyone have for murdering a harmless old woman?'

'That we have still to find out,' said Faro grimly.

'Then I presume you have good grounds for your suspicions.'

'I do indeed. She had a visitor last night. Someone pretending to be you.'

'Me—?'

Faro cut short Purdie's angry protests. 'Hear me out, if you please. Since our bogus inspector took the trouble to have screens put around the bed, I suspect either poisoned sweetmeats or a soft pillow was the method used to hasten the cause of death certified by Dr Elgin as heart failure.'

'Good Lord. This is dreadful, dreadful. And I don't much care for someone impersonating me. What was he like?'

Purdie listened grimly to the description as recounted by the hospital nurse. At the end he sat back and sighed deeply. 'We've got to find him, Faro. I have a personal stake in this one. What makes it worse is that I knew the old lady. Stayed with her once. She wouldn't remember me, of course, it's more than thirty years ago. And I've changed a bit since then,' he added wryly.

'On the contrary, she remembered you well. She talked to my aunt about you. She was very proud of your distinguished career.'

Purdie sighed. 'How extraordinary.' He looked out towards the hills. 'My family farmed here a couple of generations ago. What amazing memories these country folks do have.' He sighed. 'We had better get Craig to start the usual procedures.'

'No. In this case, I think not.'

'But that's highly irregular, if you suspect murder.'

'What I want is to prevent another murder,' said Faro.

'How so?'

'By alerting our man that we're on to him.'

'Go on.'

'My theory is that if Nessie Brodie was murdered then it is because she knew something dangerous about her niece Morag's associates at Balmoral.'

As the carriage climbed the steep hill leading to Bush Farm, Purdie considered the landscape thoughtfully. 'Our visit here is not unrelated to the case then. We have almost all the evidence necessary to make an arrest once the Queen has left Balmoral.'

'Why wait until then?'

Purdie shrugged. 'Because I have been so instructed. The Prime Minister's instigation, I gather, that I am to keep as much as possible from the Queen.' And turning to Faro, 'Your guess is, I am sure, as good as mine as to who killed the girl.'

'I never guess in such matters. Matters of life and death, I prefer to be certainties, sir. Matters of conviction, supplemented by foolproof evidence.'

Purdie laughed. 'Come, come, Faro. You can do better than that. Even the most rudimentary training in police procedure must have taught you that the first place you look for your murderer is in the victim's family circle. Who has something to gain? Who hated her, etc., etc.?'

'Precisely. But in this case there wasn't much to be gained in the monetary way. She had no family but her Aunt Nessie—'

'And I don't think by any stretch of imagination could that dear kind soul, God rest her, be a suspect.'

Purdie's expression was suddenly bleak. 'So where else do we look, Faro? Who have we left? There are not many contestants and Morag Brodie was known to have rejected Lachlan for James Lessing, a footman at the Castle, who subsequently drowned in a tragic accident. Logically then, our suspects are down to one,' he added grimly.

'But Lachlan did save her from drowning—'

Purdie held up his hand. 'I know your argument, Faro. Why save her just to murder her? I think we have worked that one out. He saves her, believing gratitude will restore her love for him. But she refuses him. He goes berserk.'

Pausing he regarded Faro's doubtful expression. 'For heaven's sake, this is the standard *crime passionnel*. Happens all the time. You of all people should know that.'

'Let us say I have some reservations about the nature of the killing. In my experience, one stab to the heart rarely indicates a frenzied attack.'

'Is that so?' Purdie sounded exasperated. 'From the evidence so far, I don't think there is the slightest doubt that Lachlan Brown is guilty. Everything so far points to him. But this case must be handled carefully. We are on delicate ground here, the lad being kin to John Brown, and John Brown close to the Queen.'

Faro thought cynically about those in authority trying to keep the facts of life and death from the Queen, desperate in their anxiety that her 'dear Paradise' should remain unsullied. On the other hand, he was not at all sure that Her Majesty's somewhat morbid preoccupation with death could not deal with a local murder. She might even relish it.

Opening the carriage door, Purdie regarded him intently. 'You get my drift, I think, without any further elaboration.'

Faro hesitated before replying. 'There is one further point, sir. My mysterious visitor whose carriage you observed yesterday was Superintendent McIntosh of the Edinburgh City Police.'

'I know the Superintendent—'

Faro finished his brief account of McIntosh's visit and his fears for the Queen's safety with, 'He thought you should be told. If you don't know already.'

His searching glance of his companion's face told him the worst.

'I do know, Faro. And now that the cat is well and truly out of the bag, if you hadn't deduced it already, you will understand the real reason for Scotland Yard putting me on to this case. As I told you when we first met, your presence here was an almighty stroke of good fortune.

'And even before your disclosures regarding our old adversary Lord Nob, where you have the advantage over me, in a personal encounter, I was considering enlisting your help. Ah, here is Craig now,' he added, putting a finger to his lips. 'We will keep this information to ourselves, if you please.'

'If you are intent on making an arrest, you would have more chance of finding Lachlan at the Castle with Brown at this time of day.'

'Ah, we are ahead of you there, Faro,' said Purdie with a mysterious smile. 'At precisely this moment he should be on the hill with the Queen's picnic party. I thought we might seize the opportunity of his absence to search his cottage.'

Craig approached them, his face bright with triumph. He held up a knife, its long blade worn with constant use and sharpening, and in the horn handle a cairngorm stone.

'Here is your evidence, sir. Look what I've found.'

Purdie took it gingerly.

'That looks like blood to me, sir,' said Craig excitedly, pointing to dark stains on the blade.

Purdie nodded, a little non-committally, thought Faro. 'Show us exactly where you found it.'

Craig led the way to a woodpile at the side of the bothy. 'It was hidden, sir. Down at the back. I nearly missed it.'

'May I?' Faro examined the knife briefly.

'What do you think, Faro?' asked Purdie.

'Surely you recognise the skean-dhu, sir, the all-purpose knife every Highlander prides himself on wearing in his hose? I would suggest that its murderous appearance is perfectly in keeping with its normal function.'

'And that is?'

'It's used by ghillies for disembowelling deer, skinning rabbits and the like. In a society less preoccupied with etiquette it was used as table cutlery. To cut meat and the throats of its owner's enemies.'

'So this could be the murder weapon?' said Purdie eagerly.

'It could. Except that one would expect to find one identical in every Scots household from here to the Canadian Rockies and beyond.'

Craig was not to be outdone. 'But look at the stains, sir,' he insisted.

'I hate to disappoint you, but I suspect they are of animals' blood,' said Faro.

'Why should he hide it then?'

'I think it was less likely to have been hidden than accidentally mislaid.'

Craig looked mutinous, clearly disappointed. He turned to Purdie for support. 'What do you think, sir?'

'I think Inspector Faro may have a point. But there again, the knife might have been used for a more macabre task. So we must retain it as possible evidence, until we make further enquiries.'

And watching Craig rewrap the skean-dhu in a piece of sacking, he continued, 'Well, Faro, are you still willing to accompany us?' And observing his reluctance, 'I would feel happier if you could overcome your scruples on this occasion. It may be of crucial importance to our enquiry.'

'Very well.' As they walked towards the bothy Faro asked, 'What else do you expect to find besides a knife that may or may not be the murder weapon?'

Purdie shrugged aside the question. 'When the Queen leaves Balmoral she sometimes takes with her members of her staff especially recommended. There is a rumour that Brown is anxious for the lad to go to London to continue his studies. A fact not without some significance.'

'Get him away from past indiscretions, is that what you mean?'

'And particularly the scene of the crime.'

'If he is guilty.'

'I am more inclined to "as" he is guilty, Faro. I shouldn't put too much credence on that word "if". You surely realise that we cannot risk a possible murderer leaving under cover of Her Majesty's entourage.'

'How do you propose to stop him?'

'Let's say we won't make it public. We will simply restrain him under lock and key until the Queen leaves.'

'What if John Brown protests? I can't imagine him taking that lightly.'

'John Brown or no John Brown, I shall formally charge Lachlan with the murder and have him escorted to prison in Aberdeen. Craig is ready to take care of such arrangements.'

Purdie smiled. 'Once Brown is convinced of Lachlan's guilt, he will accept the implications of allowing freedom to a murderer who, having got away with it once, might be considered excellent material for recruitment by some sinister organisation.'

'The Prince's Party, for example?'

'The same, not to put too fine a point on it.'

Perhaps Purdie was right, thought Faro. The game was too big and too dangerous to take chances.

Lachlan Brown's bothy stood in the annexe to the main farm building, a barn before its more recent conversion into a labourer's cottage.

As was the country custom, the door's only fastening was a latch. There would be little to search, two rooms where Faro expected the only evidence to be of a young bachelor's indifference to tidiness.

Instead, he was startled by the presence of a piano occupying a large portion of the living room. Obviously it was not for show amid such simple white-washed walls. Music sheets of Schubert, Brahms and Bach indicated that it was in constant use.

The rest of the bothy was similarly surprising. Lachlan seemed to have exercised considerable care in choosing one or two small pieces which, like the piano, might be equally at home in Balmoral Castle.

The bookshelves displayed a variety of books which testified to Lachlan's taste in literature and suggested to Faro that their young owner deserved a better life than that of a Balmoral ghillie.

At his side Craig was examining the books curiously.

'See all this crime stuff, sir,' he said to Purdie.

'That our suspect is interested in reading about crimes doesn't mean that he also commits them.'

'But here – this is an axe murder case.'

'Craig, come away,' said Purdie patiently. 'I read such material regularly, as I am sure Inspector Faro does,' he added and when Faro smiled, he said, 'There now, be assured, Craig. It has given neither of us an overwhelming desire to murder anyone. Other than recalcitrant constables, that is. Now, come along.'

As Craig joined them in the bedroom, there were more surprises in store. A postered bed with a patchwork quilt took the place of the usual straw pallet; other refinements comprised a press for clothes, a wash-stand with toilet articles and an escritoire. On the white-washed walls, the paintings included a small Landseer.

Good taste abounded and, over all, a surprising air of opulence. Had this not been a farm bothy, its furnishings would not have shamed the lodging of a young man of quality.

One thing was becoming abundantly clear: John Brown's protégé was no simple village lad. And Faro stood by, ill at ease, suppressing a natural distaste for searching through even a murder suspect's personal possessions.

As Purdie and Craig showed more enthusiasm for the task which they conducted with police thoroughness, he noticed with dismay that neither had been schooled in the same methods as himself. By Faro's rules, the search completed, all items should be carefully replaced to give an appearance of never having been disturbed.

Craig suddenly turned from the escritoire and said, 'What's this, now?'

He held up a thick wad of banknotes. Faro and Purdie watched him thumbing through them. 'Four hundred – five hundred pounds.'

'And where do you think he might have got such a sum?' Purdie said to Faro.

Craig whistled. 'A small fortune, sir.'

'A fortune it might be,' said Faro. 'But one I see little reason to link with Morag Brodie's murder. Unless—'

'Exactly, Faro,' said Purdie slowly, as Craig replaced the banknotes in the drawer. 'Unless. And I think we might conclude from this particular evidence that we're on the track of something much bigger than a rustic murder.'

And for once Faro had to agree with him.

As they were leaving the bothy, Purdie swore.

There was John Brown coming along the lane. He was alone and as he approached his greeting was tinged more with alarm than curiosity.

'Ye're wanting to see me?' he asked Purdie. Then he noticed Craig with the sackcloth bundle under his arm.

'Well, what's that ye've got there?'

Purdie disregarded his pointing finger and pretended to misunderstand the question. 'It is Lachlan we have business with.'

'What sort of business would that be?' Brown demanded suspiciously.

'When can we expect to find him at home?'

Brown shrugged. 'He's awa' visiting. Ballater way. That's all I can tell you.'

Purdie's usually bland face registered the dismay of a hunter thwarted of his prey. 'When do you expect his return?'

'Late tonight. Mebbe not. I canna tell ye.' He grinned. 'The lad is mebbe courtin', ye ken. But I'll let him know ye called. Ye can depend on that.'

And touching his bonnet, he opened the gate, his eyes sliding anxiously towards the sackcloth bundle. Then to Faro he said, 'Have ye any information yet for Her Majesty?'

'I'm afraid not. These things take time.'

Brown's shrug was disbelieving. 'Her Majesty is getting gey anxious. She's wishful to have the criminal apprehended afore she leaves.'

Watching Brown's retreating figure, Craig said, 'Shall we go into Ballater, sir?'

'For what reason?'

'To apprehend Lachlan Brown, of course. I'm sure the proximity of a railway station has not escaped you, sir.'

'Come, come, Craig. You can do better than that. He would hardly disappear without taking his belongings. Or more important, his five hundred pounds.'

'But we have the knife.'

Purdie shook his head. 'We have, but he doesn't know that yet, does he?' And at Craig's anxious expression he went on, 'I don't think we need worry about him eluding us. He will be back. You can bank on it.'

On the way back to Crathie, Faro recounted to Purdie his quest for the Queen's dog-slayer and his suspicions that Morag Brodie had been murdered in the ruined mill and her body then transported over to Crathie.

Purdie looked very thoughtful and as Bella's cottage came in sight Faro rapidly added his account of his meeting with the dog-walking footmen and of his subsequent encounter with Peter Noble.

'Very interesting, very interesting indeed,' said Purdie. 'Especially that connection with Lessing. I think you might have stumbled on to something very significant indeed. And I must confess it does alarm me. I am more than ever certain there is not a moment to be lost.'

With a promise to meet later that day, they parted.

Inside the cottage, the tiny parlour was already crowded with well-wishers and neighbours.

Bella greeted him excitedly and gave the answer he had expected.

'Jeremy, that wasna' Inspector Purdie.'

'I assure you it was.'

'Then that wasna' the man who came in to see Nessie.' And shaking her head, she added firmly, 'He didna' look a bit like that.'

8 Faro was finishing his third cup of tea and resisting a profusion of pies, scones, bannocks and Dundee cake, made by Tibbie and the neighbours to mark the grand occasion of Bella's birthday and welcome home.

Loosening the two lower buttons of his waistcoat he realised that he was out of practice in the marathon eating stakes. A week of this particular good life and he would be unable to get into his clothes, and as the latch was raised heralding a fresh influx of well-wishers into the already overflowing parlour, he decided on retreat.

Looking down over the stairhead, he saw the new arrival was Lachlan Brown. Greeting Bella he handed her a delicate china figurine which also looked as if it might have had its origins in Balmoral Castle.

'It has a tiny hair crack – here,' he said apologetically at Bella's pleasurable exclamations. 'I'm afraid the Queen threw it out—'

'Oh, laddie, laddie. It's lovely. Ye're that kind.' She hugged him delightedly.

'It is no better than you deserve. We're all glad to have you back with us, Mistress MacVae.'

'Ye'll have some tea. Or a dram.'

Faro hovered indecisively, watched him carry cup and plate towards the door. A moment later Tibbie climbed the stairs.

'So that's where ye are, Jeremy. Lachlan wants a wee

chat wi' ye. He's in the garden,' she added concealing her curiosity with utmost difficulty.

He found Lachlan on the wooden seat, staring out across the hill, looking if possible even more sullen and remote than he had at their first meeting.

Turning round he made no attempt to shake hands. 'I'll not beat about the bush, Inspector. I am here only because Johnnie insisted that I should see you. It's about Morag Brodie,' he said abruptly. 'I didn't kill her, whatever they are trying to prove. Yes, sit down, if you please.'

Faro regarded him narrowly. Black-haired, white-skinned, the lad was handsome enough on a good day to turn any lass's head; rebellious, with an arrogance that stemmed, Faro suspected, from being kin to the Queen's favourite.

'The point is, can you prove your innocence?'

Lachlan shrugged. 'She said she loved me. Then she met this other fellow. I don't see why they think that gave me good reason for murdering her.'

Suddenly the rain that had been threatening since morning began. Lachlan gave an exasperated gesture towards the drops that fell around them, heavy as coins. 'Is there somewhere we can talk?'

'Of course.' Faro led the way indoors to his room.

Lachlan sat down on the edge of the bed, considered his clasped hands. 'I did not kill Morag,' he repeated dully. 'I happened to be passing by when the accident happened. I jumped in and saved her – or haven't they told you that?' Without waiting for Faro's reply, he said, 'As soon as I got her on to the bank, I dived in again and tried to get Lessing. But I was too late.'

Lachlan sighed. 'Even if I had hated Lessing – and I didn't – I wouldn't stand by and watch any man drown.'

Faro was almost inclined to believe him, bearing in mind the surprising character of the bothy. From his vast experience of violent men, Lachlan Brown seemed too finely drawn and sensitive to have stabbed Morag Brodie in a blind and brutal fit of jealousy. Especially as the lad might have had the pick of a much wider range of elegant young ladies than the servants' hall at Balmoral could offer.

Suddenly he was curious to hear more of his background.

As if interpreting his thoughts Lachlan said, 'All right, Inspector. You had better have the truth. I expect it will come out sooner or later. I was only marrying Morag because she was having a child.'

So Bella had surmised, thought Faro, as Lachlan continued, 'Oh, it wasn't mine. But I was being paid handsomely for my trouble, a pension of two hundred and fifty pounds per year to give her child a name.'

Two hundred and fifty pounds a year was five pounds a week. The salary of an upper servant at Balmoral was the same, which might also mean that if Lachlan lived carefully he could exist in comfort for the rest of his life.

'And who was this generous benefactor?' Faro interrupted.

'Ah, that is a question I cannot answer.'

'Cannot or will not?' asked Faro softly.

Lachlan smiled. 'No, not from any delicacy or discretion. Just because I don't know either. The offer came from "A Well-Wisher" on Balmoral notepaper.'

'You have the letter in your possession?' asked Faro eagerly.

'Not even that. I was told to destroy it and that the bank in Ballater had been given instructions.'

'You were not in any doubt? You did not think that, for instance, it might be a hoax?'

'Not after I checked with the bank and found it correct in every detail.'

'Every detail. Such as?'

'There were no terms. Merely the payment. The first deposit of two hundred and fifty pounds had been made in good faith.'

It all sounded a little cold-blooded and hinted that whoever was responsible for Morag's pregnancy was a man of wealth and importance. As for Lachlan, he was taking this somewhat murky business remarkably well. He was either innocent or he was a very glib liar.

'All that was required of me was that I declared Morag Brodie as my wife "by habit and repute" before two witnesses in the Scots fashion.'

'A marriage that would never stand up in a court of law outside Scotland.'

'Exactly, Inspector, but it would preserve her respectability. So what had I to fear?' said Lachlan cheerfully. 'Besides Morag left immediately to return to her duties at the Castle. There was no consummation, the marriage was to be kept secret until the Queen left for London.' He shook his head. 'I never saw her again and I did not feel inclined to bring up the matter when I was questioned by the police. Johnnie advised me to keep quiet.'

Faro could understand why, since this dubious undertaking gave Lachlan an even more valid purpose for getting rid of Morag Brodie while retaining her mysterious dowry. Murders were regularly committed for far less monetary gain.

Inspector Purdie, he was sure, would be very interested in this new piece of information.

'Johnnie disapproved strongly, but he agreed to be a witness. And Dave Grant. Their discretion can be relied on implicitly,' Lachlan added, 'although they both did their utmost to talk me out of it.'

'I am not surprised.'

'I did give it some thought, truly. But the marriage was to be in name only. There was no further obligation. The money was the main temptation. I have been supported by the Brown family all my life until now. Gives me the chance I have always wanted to study the pianoforte.' He smiled sadly. 'A dream was suddenly a possibility.'

'Did you never wonder why you were chosen for this rôle in Morag Brodie's life?'

Lachlan shrugged. 'I have no idea. She was pretty, intelligent and I hope they get whoever killed her. I liked her well enough and I'm sorry she's dead. And not only because of the lost annuity.'

He laughed bitterly. 'Save your disapproval, Inspector. As a love child myself, abandoned by an unknown father, I realise that the state of idiocy known as being in love requires a measure of blindness. I prefer to keep my eyes wide open.'

His words brought to Faro echoes of his stepson's railing against his own illegitimacy – except that Vince's mother had been more fortunate in meeting Jeremy Faro.

'How old are you, Lachlan?'

'Twenty-two.'

Almost the same age as Vince, thought Faro, another parallel in two lives that were otherwise poles apart.

'Have you any family?'

Lachlan looked at him sharply, was about to speak and then looked out of the window. 'Uncle Johnnie is my family. All I have here. He isn't really my uncle, of course, although I should call him so. He is a kind of fourth cousin twice removed.'

His smile transformed his face with a shaft of familiarity. Where had he seen this lad before?

'How long have you lived here?'

'I was fostered by the Browns when I was still a small child. Orphaned, you know,' he added casually.

'Do you know anything about your parents?' Faro asked gently.

Lachlan's eyes shifted to the fireplace, his expression as bleak and implacable as its adornment of solemn china dogs.

'No.' And with a determined effort to change the subject, he added harshly, 'I had another reason for coming to see you, Inspector. I presume you were part of the police search of my home.'

'Reluctantly, yes. I don't approve—'

'Please don't apologise,' Lachlan cut short his excuses. 'I might have expected something of the sort. I have been told Inspector

Purdie is very thorough and quite ruthless in his acquisition of evidence. I have nothing to conceal and I might have let it go at that but Johnnie insisted that I tell you. I have five hundred pounds in banknotes in a drawer in the escritoire.'

Faro remembered it being counted.

'There is forty pounds missing. Perhaps you can throw some small light on that mystery.'

'No. I can only say that I was present when Inspector Purdie and Sergeant Craig counted the notes and the sum of five hundred pounds was intact.'

Lachlan nodded. 'Nevertheless four banknotes are missing. In case you are curious, this has nothing whatever to do with my, er – marriage settlement. It represents money I was given, a gift, recently.'

'How recently?'

'Very recently,' said Lachlan firmly. 'A legacy. From a source I am not at liberty to disclose.'

'Has Mr Brown any theories on the money's disappearance?'

Lachlan hesitated a moment. 'He is as puzzled as I am.'

'Some passer-by—'

'No.' Again the voice was emphatic.

'But your door is left unlocked. Tinkers, for instance?'

Lachlan laughed. 'Inspector, our doors are never locked and while tinkers might remove – and frequently do remove – objects outside, which they regard as under the sky and therefore any man's fair game, they have scruples – no, fears or superstitions would be more appropriate – about house-breaking. A term of imprisonment locked behind bars is worse than death to them.

'Besides, there have been no tinkers in the neighbourhood since my last visit to Ballater—' Biting his lip, he cut off too late the betraying words.

Faro's mind was racing ahead. 'I would like to help you,' he said, 'but unless you are frank with me . . .'

'I can tell you no more. I have already told you more than I should.' Lachlan stood up. 'I see my visit has wasted your time. I am sorry—'

'Before you go. Do you know anything about a lost skean-dhu?'

'A worn blade, horn handle with a cairngorm stone in the hilt?'

'The same.'

'Where did you find it?' Lachlan's eager delight made nonsense of this being the murder weapon.

'Sergeant Craig found it behind the woodpile.'

'So that's where it was. That is Johnnie's favourite dirk, given to him by Prince Albert. He lent it to me a couple of weeks ago when we were skinning rabbits. I mislaid it. Johnnie was very angry and we searched high and low. We did blame the tinkers. May I have it please?' he said, putting out his hand.

'I'm afraid not. It has been taken away by Sergeant Craig. As evidence,' he added heavily.

'Evidence?' At Faro's silence, he laughed softly. 'Och yes, I see it fine. It would have its uses as a murder weapon. After all, that was its original purpose—'

They were interrupted by the arrival of Vince, who threw open the door and announced that he had put all his patients to bed and was sorely in need of a dram.

Lachlan was disposed to be friendly to the newcomer. He talked about the best places to eat and the best places to fish. He was instantly transformed into a knowledgeable and enthusiastic countryman.

He left shortly afterwards, declining Faro's invitation to accompany them to the Crathie Inn where they were to dine, since Vince had little interest in the birthday party fare on offer. He would, however, accept a lift in the pony-cart as far as the Bush Farm road.

At their destination, Faro went over the day's events and the details of Lachlan's visit.

'He was right, Stepfather. Morag was pregnant, early stages.

Dr Elgin told me. That Scots marriage though.' Vince shook his head. 'Very cunningly thought out, don't you think? Could it be that the father was a member of the Royal entourage?'

Faro gave it some consideration. A well-known method of paying off discarded mistresses, the higher the lady's position on the social scale the more likely the gift would be accompanied by a title or an estate. But in the case of a maid at the Castle, the sum offered to some willing local lad would seem like a fortune.

'Known as the rich man's hasty exit from an embarrassing situation. I fancy that the Queen must be well aware of such matters.'

Vince laughed. 'Despite her pretence that servants do not exist below the waist and that the piano's limbs must be decently covered. You think Lachlan was speaking the truth about this mysterious benefactor?'

'I do. But I don't know why, lad.'

'I expect it has occurred to you that his reluctance to reveal the source of this money might well point to a more sinister connection with visits to Ballater.'

Faro nodded grimly. 'That Ballater might be the present headquarters of the Prince's Party. Is that what you mean?'

Vince nodded. 'And that Lachlan might be up to his ears in the plot. I think you should look very carefully into that young man's background, Stepfather, especially bearing in mind that he has just returned to Ballater after a long absence. A scholarship to Oxford, no less.'

'Really?'

'So Dr Elgin tells me. Can you beat that? What would a ghillie's lad be doing at Oxford? Why not St Andrews, or Edinburgh? Even I never aspired to Oxford.'

Faro suppressed a smile. Because I could never have afforded to send you there, he thought, even if the idea of an English university had entered my head. This was the 'lad o' pairts' with a vengeance.

Outside the cottage hospital, Vince said, 'I fancy Lachlan's absence would bear looking into, Stepfather, if it hasn't been done already.' Turning, he added, 'I don't suppose it has escaped your notice that his pale skin, so unusual in a country fellow, could be something else.'

'Prison pallor? Is that what you have in mind?'

'The same.'

Settling Steady for the night, Faro went into the darkened cottage. It was late and in due deference to Bella's great age and recent sojourn in hospital, the visitors had gone long since.

Creeping upstairs as quietly as he could, a board creaked under his foot and his aunt called out:

'Jeremy? I'm still awake.'

Turning up the lamp he saw she looked tired, but glowing and happy, like a small child at the end of an exciting birthday party. From underneath her pillow she handed him a silver cigar case.

'This was my dear man's. He would have wanted ye to have it. Been lying in a drawer for years. Tibbie came on it again when I was away, and she was cleaning. It was all tarnished.' She touched it lovingly. 'See what a bit of polish does. Vince told me ye smoke cigars sometimes. I want ye to have it while I'm still here and can see ye having the pleasure of it. Here, take it.'

Inside, under the Royal coat of arms, the inscription read: 'To Ben MacVae, a loyal servant. Albert.'

Thanking her with a hug and a kiss, he put the cigar case into his jacket pocket, resolving to fill it with fine Havanas at the earliest opportunity.

Faro's first visitor next morning was none other than the Prime Minister. An imposing figure with white hair and side-whiskers, Mr Gladstone bore an anxious expression which was either natural or induced by the gravity of his visit.

Ushered into the parlour by a curtsying Aunt Bella, Mr Gladstone accepted her offer of tea and bannocks.

'I would be delighted with a little refreshment. I have been up since six this morning and have already walked ten miles. At a measured twelve minutes per mile,' he added proudly.

He dismissed Faro's remarks of appreciative amazement. 'I trust you will not take it amiss that I am calling upon you informally. John Brown has alerted me to your presence, sir. Your name is not unknown to me in connection with the visits to Edinburgh by Her Majesty the Queen—'

His momentary pause, eyes lowered, almost amounted to genuflection, thought Faro with some amusement.

'—and with security arrangements and dangers to her Royal person averted. All of which you have managed so skilfully to handle. Most skilfully and courageously,' he added in a whisper.

Did he always speak like this, in the manner of a Member addressing the House or reading a carefully prepared speech? And Faro suppressed a smile, remembering that the Queen's aversion to Mr Gladstone was because of his subservience.

'I come to you, sir, on this occasion as a supplicant.' Mr Gladstone placed his fingertips together as if about to deliver a sermon. 'A supplicant, sir. In direst need. For time is of the essence. Her Most Gracious Majesty the Queen' (again the lowering of eyes and voice), 'Her Most Gracious Majesty's life is once again in mortal peril. Mortal peril.'

Faro felt a quickening sense of disaster looming ahead. 'You have reliable information to that effect, sir?' he interrupted sharply.

'Only the merest hint, alas. A young man who was an – er, employed in the capacity of – er, surveillance of the Queen's safety. Very much undercover, you understand, sir. Very much. Discovered a threat to Her Majesty in none other than the Royal Household.'

Pausing dramatically, his hand upraised, he let the words sink in. 'Other attempts in the open have failed or have been frustrated. But this was daringly planned to take place by the Royal fireside. Such audacity. Breaking the sacred sanctity of hearth and home—'

'This man, Prime Minister—'

'I am not at liberty to discuss his identity. Except to say regretfully that he is no longer with us.'

'Paid off?'

'Dead,' said the Prime Minister hollowly. 'Pray do not question me further, Inspector.'

Could this be Lessing, the drowned footman? Faro wondered. If so, that threw a completely new equation into the plot. He would have loved to ask, but had no option but to respect the Prime Minister's wishes.

'Does your information concern an attempt at the Castle?'

'Indeed, sir. Have I not made that abundantly clear?' Mr Gladstone added indignantly.

'I had presumed so. And that this attempt must be imminent.'

'Imminent, indeed. As Her Majesty leaves Balmoral at the end of the week for the State Opening of Parliament, time is of the essence and we have very little—'

Too little to waste in verbiage, Faro thought in exasperation, wondering how any urgent business ever got through Parliament past its Prime Minister.

'You suspect this will come from within, that it is to be a domestic murder attempt?'

Mr Gladstone winced visibly at the word 'murder'.

'And from someone close to the Queen? One of the servants perhaps?'

'Servants, sir. I can hardly believe that one of Her Majesty's staff would commit blasphemy by touching the Royal person. Besides, all the staff are hand-picked, with excellent references. And those at Balmoral are particularly reliable. Most come from families who have served the Royal household since the Castle was built.'

Drawing himself up to his full height he regarded Faro disapprovingly. 'Loyal to a man, sir. They would willingly lay down their lives for Her Gracious Majesty. As I would, sir. Willingly.'

Faro felt uncomfortably that these dramatics were rather over-played. 'I should like to see records of these servants. I presume that their particulars are on file.'

'Indeed. There is a register of when each one took up his or her position, plus the salary and any information regarding special qualifications for the Royal service.'

'Is it possible that I might have access to this information?'

'Indeed, yes. If you think it will help. I shall have it put before you.'

'No, Prime Minister, that would not do at all. This inspection must be sub rosa. If it is seen that I am carrying out an investigation then we lose out by alerting the assassin.'

Again Mr Gladstone winced at the word. 'If you wish, sir, but I thought that the true purpose of your visit here was being kept secret. That officially you were merely on a visit to your aunt.'

'That is what I thought, and hoped, a week ago,' said Faro with a sigh. 'My aunt, alas, is a dear good soul but is not renowned for her discretion. She is inclined to talk about her family and their preoccupations at some length.'

Mr Gladstone's face fell. 'That is a pity. A great pity.'

'Indeed it is. I expect that every movement I make is under observation.'

'In that case perhaps you will accompany me. We might make it look as if we had met by accident while I was taking one of my walks.'

'No, Prime Minister. That will not do at all. I would opt for a discreet social visit. In the evening perhaps when there are fewer prying eyes. And with your permission, I shall bring my stepson Dr Laurie, so that it looks as if we have arrived merely for a game of cards.'

'Capital, capital,' crowed Mr Gladstone delightedly. Then he added nervously, 'Do you play cards for money, by any chance, Inspector?'

'I would not dare, sir. There is an old adage about lucky at cards, unlucky in love. I seem to be lucky in neither, alas.'

The Prime Minister nodded eagerly. 'I have in my time tried to exert a little influence on His Royal Highness in the matter of gaming. At dinner at Abergeldie he invited me to play whist. I queried, "For love, sir?" To which he replied, "Well, shillings and half a crown on the rubber." Protocol demanded that I submitted, especially since the Prince's suggestion of such paltry stakes did show a nice point in manners.'

Faro was spared the search for a suitable response when Mr Gladstone continued, 'Perhaps I should bring to your attention that Sergeant Craig has inspected the servants' register recently in connection with the – er, unfortunate murder that Inspector Purdie of Scotland Yard is investigating.'

'The Inspector is aware of the Queen's danger.'

'Fully aware. But since he has not yet had the honour of protecting the Royal person, we consider that you have experience in the matter which might be invaluable to him. Especially as Her Gracious Majesty is acquainted with your methods.'

As Faro accompanied the Prime Minister to his carriage, he asked, 'What are Her Majesty's commitments outside the Castle before she leaves?'

'She plans a visit to Glen Muick tomorrow, a picnic followed by a salmon leistering later in the day. The fishermen attract the salmon to the surface by torchlight and spear them.'

Gladstone frowned suddenly as if the dangerous potential of that wild place at sunset had just occurred to him. 'Perhaps it would be advisable for you to accompany us. I shall arrange it.'

And leaning out of the carriage window, he added, 'I understand that you are carrying out a minor investigation at Her Majesty's behest concerning the recent decease of two of the Royal dogs.'

Faro nodded glumly and the Prime Minister continued, 'May I presume that you are on the track of some clues?'

'Alas, no.'

'A pity. A pity indeed.'

Faro did not like to depress the Prime Minister further by telling him that the identity of the Queen's dog-slayer and the prospective assassin were undoubtedly one and the same.

9 Inspector Purdie arrived ten minutes after the Prime Minister had left. Aunt Bella, whose supplies of warm hospitality were inexhaustible, offered tea and bannocks.

'If you would be so kind as to butter them, not too thickly, Mistress MacVae.'

Congratulating her on her recovery, Purdie commiserated with her on the loss of her neighbour. This threatened to bring about floods of tears and Bella retreated hastily.

'I am sorry. I did not realise—'

'They have been friends for thirty years or more,' said Faro. 'Nessie was like one of the family.'

Purdie sighed. 'Apart from the burned-out shell of the croft down the road, how little the place has changed since my boyhood visit. I do not remember ever meeting you then,' he added regarding Faro curiously.

'I was in Orkney a good deal.'

'A pity our visits never coincided. Your aunt has a remarkable memory for faces and names.'

Faro laughed. 'So good one is never sure how much is memory and how much hearsay. The old are like that.'

'I have thought so too. The young have more important matters to concentrate on.'

Tibbie carried in the tray, Bella at her heels. She said, 'I'll leave you gentlemen to your tea. Perhaps you'll pour, Jeremy. That pot is difficult until you get to know it,' she added with a warning nod in his direction.

Faro did as he was bid and Purdie tackled the modest repast with vigour and enthusiasm.

As Faro finished his account of Lachlan's visit and his mention of the missing banknotes, Purdie showed no signs of surprise. 'They will be returned,' he said grimly. 'I have the matter in hand.'

'Craig?'

Purdie nodded. 'He confessed. Didn't know what came over him. He was needing money urgently, overspent on his next week's wages. Apparently the unfortunate fellow has got into debt. Not too precise about details, but when pressed he admitted to gambling for large stakes at the Crathie Inn.'

Faro swept his excuses aside. 'This amounts to stealing, Purdie. I need not stress to you that this is a particularly serious matter.'

'I agree and I have reprimanded him severely.' Purdie's tone was light but Faro was not convinced. For a police officer in search of evidence to appropriate banknotes or any other possessions was a matter for instant dismissal with Edinburgh City Police.

'I have great faith in the lad,' said Purdie. 'This is the first time he has succumbed. He was hoping that in a few days he could replace the money or send it back anonymously.'

And determined to close the subject he said firmly, 'Now to business. Did the Prime Minister's visit throw any more light on the Queen's danger?'

Faro decided not to mention his inspection of the register in case Purdie took it amiss. 'Did you know they had an undercover man who gave them the hint about the Prince's Party?'

Purdie nodded. 'Lessing, you mean?'

'So it was him.'

Purdie smiled. 'Naturally, Faro, he was sent by the Yard as soon as we realised there would be an attempt at Balmoral. I gather he found something out but had his unfortunate accident before he could be of any further use.'

'In the circumstances can we continue to dismiss his drowning as accidental? Especially as it also sheds some light on the murdered girl.'

Purdie helped himself to another bannock. 'Unfortunately we will never know now whether he was recruiting her or whether she merely knew more than was good for her and was apt to be indiscreet when she had taken drink.'

Faro considered for a moment. 'There is another possibility which I am sure has occurred to you.'

'And that is?'

'That Lessing did not drown after all. That he was swept down river and that someone was waiting for him.'

'You mean, they hit him on the head or stabbed him—'

And Faro found himself remembering the bloodstained skean-dhu.

'—Then he was dumped in the mill race? Is that what you are saying?' Purdie shook his head. 'Far too much of a coincidence, don't you think, that the murderer should have anticipated the accident and have been waiting his opportunity downstream – at the exact moment?'

He dismissed Faro's theory with a shrug. 'No, Faro, I'm afraid that won't do at all. Let us not forget that the Prime Minister is inclined to exaggerate. I will maintain that Lessing drowned. However, you have succeeded in raising some uncertainties in my mind. In the circumstances a visit to the Castle would be well worthwhile.'

'Then you will be glad to hear that I have engineered an invitation to cards this evening. My stepson will accompany me and I have been promised an opportunity to scrutinise the servants' register. Perhaps you would care to join us.'

'Capital, Faro. As you know, I left that part of the investigation to Craig. As well as taking their statements. But now . . .' His sigh emphasised Craig's unreliability.

As Purdie was leaving he thanked Bella graciously. She watched him from the window while Tibbie gathered up the tray from the parlour.

Faro smiled. 'I don't get my bannocks buttered, Auntie,' he said teasingly. 'Nor am I allowed to eat without removing my gloves.'

'Ah, so you noticed, did you?' said Bella.

'That he only ever takes off one glove seems curious. What is wrong with his right hand, anyway?'

Bella held up her hand dramatically with the two middle fingers covered. 'That's what happened. On that holiday he spent with Nessie. She never forgave herself although it happened away from her cottage. He was playing with a saw.'

She sighed. 'It was the first thing she asked him when he came to visit her that last night.' And when Faro looked puzzled, she went on, 'The man she thought was him. No wonder she said she would never have recognised him again. "How's your poor hand, Davie?" He said he had managed fine all these years. "You can get over anything, if you work at it." '

This explanation provided another answer for Faro as the two men set off in the pony-trap later that evening. The fact that Purdie could light a pipe and keep his gloves on and his pride intact. To overcome such a handicap as a policeman and reach the height of his profession was admirable indeed.

Vince had sent a message that he would be found at nine thirty in the Crathie Inn, which put paid to his part as one of the card players. He would be disappointed at missing a visit to the Castle, thought Faro, as he and Purdie were received at the entrance.

A liveried footman led the way through a maze of carpeted and curtained corridors bedecked in the now familiar Balmoral tartan. Black, red and lavender on a grey background, it had been designed by Prince Albert himself.

The late Prince's influence was everywhere, from the bust

crowned in laurels to the permanent evidence of the Queen's melancholy veneration of widowhood. Death was the predominant theme. Their progress was overlooked by stags' heads gazing down at them in the last glass-eyed throes of mortal conflict while Mr Landseer's paintings depicted the dying agonies of stags and rabbits, and the bloody corpses of game birds.

The corridors were ill-lit too; Faro had imagined a more extravagant use of wax candles in a Royal residence. They followed the candelabra held high amid frequent warnings:

'Mind the steps, gentlemen, if you please. This is a bad one. Take care now.'

Such remarks suggested that there could be a succession of broken ankles for the unwary or the poor-sighted, conclusions echoed by Purdie's whispered, 'One needs sharp wits for the hazards of this journey.'

At last they were ushered into the Prime Minister's study where a fire of dismal proportions did little to enhance the pervading gloom of dark oak panelling, leather sofas and, for light relief, the soundlessly snarling tiger-skin rug.

The Queen's secretary Henry Ponsonby rose to greet them. Faro had met him before in Edinburgh and had great respect for the General, who combined efficiency with an admirable economy of the jargon of officialdom.

'Mr Gladstone is in audience. He sends his apologies for his absence.' He pointed to the desk. 'These are the registers you wish to inspect, gentlemen. I understand your concern is with newcomers, is that not so?'

'It is.'

Ponsonby opened the ledger, turned up the lamp. 'Then perhaps I might be able to save you some time. Most are footmen, casual employees taken on for service during the period of the Queen's residence. Such persons would have their credentials investigated thoroughly, of course.'

'And if they come from beyond Deeside?' Faro indicated two addresses in Perth.

'Then they would generally be recommended by other members of the Royal family, or other households. Such as Abergeldie, the Prince of Wales's residence.'

Faro exchanged a glance with Purdie. To build up a dossier on servants from far afield and find out whether they were who they pretended to be would take several days.

When he said so, General Ponsonby shook his head. 'The Queen either brings servants with her or in most cases employs tenants from the estate of Crathie. This is a small tight area, convenient on a temporary basis, so that they can return to their own homes when the Castle is closed. In some cases, you will observe, we are already into the second generation of servants from one family.'

He ran a finger down the list and ticked off various names: son of, daughter of. 'I can personally vouch for all of these.' Then raising his head he glanced across at Faro. 'You will have to look elsewhere for your criminal, sir.'

Faro was startled by his directness until he realised that Ponsonby presumed he was still engaged in the quest for whoever had killed the Queen's dogs.

'What about Abergeldie Castle?' asked Purdie.

'You mean the Prince of Wales's servants?' Ponsonby shook his head. 'That is the business of the Master of the Household. Besides, the Prince is not in residence and the Castle is empty meanwhile.'

At the door he turned. 'The Prime Minister informs me that you wish to be included in the Queen's outing to Glen Muick. That is so? Excellent. Pray be so good as to ring the bell on the desk when you wish to leave.'

The servants' register went back to the first Balmoral Castle. Many were retainers employed by Sir Robert Gordon, who had then passed into Royal service with the new building and its illustrious owners.

'Excellent character, trustworthy and dependable' were the usual marginal comments.

'I think we can safely dismiss these worthy souls from among our suspects,' said Purdie.

The list of newcomers and temporary staff did not take long to compile:

'Morag Brodie, lower servant, recommended by Mistress Nessie Brodie, seamstress to Her Majesty. (Deceased)

'Lachlan Brown, ghillie, recommended by Mr John Brown.'

And 'recommended by H.R.H. Prince of Wales', four names:

'Peter Noble, footman.

'James Lessing, footman. (Deceased)

'Captain Horace Tweedie, security guard.

'Captain David Dumleigh, security guard.'

Purdie crossed out Lessing and Brodie and indicated the footmen:

'One dead, one to go. Or are we on the wrong track? Who would you consider the most likely, Faro?'

'Noble has access as footman and so has Lachlan Brown as ghillie.'

'I am inclined to add two more to my list,' said Purdie.

'The captains?'

'Precisely. I consider anyone who has been in the Prince of Wales's service is worthy of careful attention and even now I am awaiting a full report from the Yard.'

Faro studied the list. 'If we learn that the two captains are beyond reproach, then the only newcomers are Lessing and Noble.'

'And as Lessing is marked deceased, that leaves us with Noble.'

Purdie shook his head. 'You are forgetting Lachlan Brown. And there is one other whose name is not on our list.' He sighed heavily. 'But that I think I will keep to myself until my enquiries bear fruit.'

Faro thought of Craig. Had Purdie reasons of his own for

suspecting his colleague? 'I trust your enquiries will not take too long. We have only three more days,' he warned.

'Two more, to be precise,' was the grim reply as Purdie rang the bell on the desk.

In the carriage, Faro decided that Purdie must be told about Lachlan's Scots marriage.

The Inspector was very impressed with this new information.

'Ah, Faro, at last, the perfect motive. Perhaps this is precisely what we needed.'

As they parted inside the inn, he declined Faro's invitation to a dram. 'It has been a long day and I have various notes to make.'

Watching him climb the stairs to his room, Faro hoped that he would have a chance to become better acquainted with the Inspector. His usual experience was of detectives and policemen working closely on a case, their lives often depending upon one another, yet parting afterward each with only the faintest inkling of the others' personal lives.

In the bar Vince had just finished supper. Thrusting aside his plate with a sigh of satisfaction he said, 'I fancy I shall be eating here regularly. Hospital food.' He grimaced. 'Reminds me too much of medical school. I do miss good cooking. Having been thoroughly spoiled by our Mrs Brook, I was expecting more of the same from Great-aunt.'

And accepting the dram Faro set before him, he asked, 'Now, what news?'

Faro outlined the events of the day, his visits from Lachlan and from Mr Gladstone, ending with the visit to the Castle. Considering the list, Vince said:

'I wonder about the footman drowned in the Dee. By the way, I wandered down to the kirkyard, saw his grave and Morag Brodie's. Thought it might inspire me with some splendid deduction and enlightenment. It didn't. Only to consider how ironic that the girl who was with him had survived only a few days, to be murdered. And that John Brown would not take kindly to his lad being under suspicion of murder.'

'Indeed, no. How would he be able to face the Queen again? Betrayal from within—'

'What are you hinting at? You surely don't think John Brown—'

Faro laughed. 'Heavens no. Brown in a plot to kill the Queen? That is beyond belief. Especially as Bertie has no love for his mother's favourite servant. Can you see the Prince's Party approaching him with such a proposition?'

'Not by any stretch of imagination.'

Then Faro remembered wryly that it was usually those who were beyond his stepson's stretch of imagination who had proved to be guilty in past cases.

'Do I detect you have a certain reluctance to consider Lachlan's guilt, Stepfather? Two hundred and fifty pounds per year to go through a form of marriage valid only in Scotland smells fishy to me. And that five hundred pounds could have been the pay-off from the Prince's Party for getting rid of the girl and Lessing. Surely Lachlan's presence at the drowning episode is highly significant? I am suggesting that he might well have engineered the whole incident, Stepfather.'

He paused, then with a disappointed shrug, said, 'You don't look very convinced.'

'I'm not. Not certain sure as I would wish to be. As I have to be on my own cases when I am in at the beginning and have viewed the bodies myself and studied their relation to the scene of the crime. There are raw edges here that nag. My instincts tell me that there is some vital factor missing.'

'At least we can rely on Inspector Purdie,' said Vince.

'True. But he was not here when it happened either. I have the strongest feeling that the motives are all too obvious and that far from apprehending the murderer, the Inspector is merely at the entrance to the labyrinth. At present I am convinced of only one thing.'

'And that is?'

'Morag Brodie's murder is linked, somehow, with an attempt to be made on the Queen's life. And we have only two days left, lad. Two days to avert a national catastrophe.'

As they parted, Vince announced that Dr Elgin, knowing that Faro's short stay in Easter Balmoral was drawing to an end, had freed him from duties until midday, after the early morning ward round.

'I was thinking we might take a drive up to Bush Farm,' said Faro collecting him at eight. Steady trotted along happily through roads dappled with sunlight. The hint of autumn touching the treetops with gold was dazzling in its perfection and difficult to reconcile with thoughts of sudden violent death.

As they reached Bush Farm, John Brown was emerging from the gate. Flustered and bleary-eyed, he was in that condition the Queen was pleased to call 'bashful'. More accurately, he was still suffering from the effects of a heavy night's drinking.

Rumour had it that the Queen quite often participated in such an activity and could match him dram for dram. But no one really believed that.

'Lachlan?' he said in answer to Faro's question. 'He's awa'.'

Vince's look of alarm indicated that Lachlan, guilty, might have taken flight.

'Away where?' asked Faro politely.

'Away courtin' – mebbe. I dinna ken,' Brown grumbled.

'Courting?'

'Aye, that's what I said. I dinna ken where. That's a man's business and I dinna question him. If he wants me to know, then he'll tell me.'

'Mr Brown,' said Faro. 'This information might be vital.'

At Brown's suspicious stare, he hesitated only a moment and then plunged on. 'The Queen's safety may be at risk.'

Brown looked astonished. 'Ye're no implying—'

'What I'm implying is that the Queen, and your lad Lachlan, may be in danger.'

Vince's admiring glance in his stepfather's direction said plain as words: Well, that's one way of convincing Brown to tell all.

John Brown shook his head vigorously in a valiant effort to gather together his thoughts. 'I dinna believe ye. No one would touch the Queen here. It's havers, man, havers.'

His laugh though scornful was not quite convincing. 'As for the laddie, he's awa' into Ballater. There's a lady he's acquainted with.'

'You've met her?'

'Once. She stayed a night at the farm here. Two-three years ago.'

'She isn't from this area?'

'She is not. A foreigner.' Brown sniffed disdainfully.

A coarser-grained fellow would have spat, thought Faro as he asked, 'You mean French or something?'

'Not at all. She's from up north somewhere. Doesna' speak the Gaelic at all.'

That covered a wide range of Scottish folk from the Borders to John o'Groats.

'She wouldna' be my choice for the laddie,' Brown admitted reluctantly. 'She's a wee bit older than himself. But then, an older lady is often verra attractive, even irresistible.' His expression softened as he looked across the river in the direction of the Castle and Faro remembered that the Queen also fitted the category of the older, 'irresistible' lady.

'May we take you down the road?'

'No. The carter passes this way in an hour or two. I'll no' delay you any longer.'

As Steady gained the main road with his two passengers, Faro urged him into a trot: 'I hope we're in time.'

'Time for what?'

'For Lachlan Brown.' Faro looked grim. 'I've been putting

together a few observations and deductions. Remember the veiled lady we met when we arrived in Ballater.'

Vince's face looked blank.

'Of course, you were too busy with the scenery. But now I am having some second thoughts and indeed, I would not be surprised to find that she, and not Lachlan, is our quarry.'

'The source of the five hundred pounds he lied about.'

'Exactly. On the same theme, I am surmising that it was she he met the other night.'

'Wait a minute, Stepfather. Are you hinting that she might be working for the Prince's Party? And the hired assassin?'

'Perhaps even that. If our quarry is Lord Nob, then he frequently works with a woman accomplice. And I am quite confident that nothing about our mysterious lady will surprise me in the least.'

But in that, as so often was the case, Detective Inspector Faro was to be proved wrong.

As the pony-trap trotted briskly into the station, the train from Aberdeen had been signalled.

Their destination was the waiting-room, which they found occupied by an old man reading his paper in one corner and by Lachlan sitting close to a woman swathed in veils.

He was holding her hand.

As Faro walked quickly in their direction, Lachlan and the woman stared up at him. She gave a little cry of alarm, poised for instant flight. She tried to dodge past him but Vince blocked her exit, standing firm between her and the station platform.

'No – no,' she cried.

Faro decided on the bold approach. 'Madam, before you board that train and before I take you and this young man into protective custody, I would beg you to reveal yourself.'

Still protesting she retreated behind Lachlan, gathering her veils closely about her face.

'Madam, have the goodness to remove your veils.'

'No, no.' Her voice was a faint whisper. 'I cannot.'

'Then, madam, you give me no alternative.' And stepping forward, Faro moved so quickly that she could not escape.

Lachlan struggled against Vince's restraining arms and the other solitary passenger opened his mouth to protest. Then considering the odds, he thought better of it, buried his face in his newspaper and tried to pretend they did not exist.

Pinioning the woman's wrists, Faro pulled aside the veil.

Words failed him utterly as he found himself staring into the last face in the world he had expected to see. The anguished and bewildered countenance of a woman well known and once well beloved.

It was the face of Inga St Ola from his homeland in Orkney.

'Inga! For God's sake. What are you doing here?'

'I can tell you what she is doing here. It's none of **10** your damned business.' And Lachlan took a threatening step towards him.

'No, Lachlan, please. Please, dear. I know this – this man.'

'You do?' Lachlan stared from one to the other.

'We are old friends.' Inga smiled thinly. 'From Orkney days.'

'Then we must tell him.'

'No.'

'We must. This has gone too far, Mama.'

'Mama?' Faro's voice was a whisper.

'Yes, Inspector. Lachlan is my son.'

Faro heard Vince's sharp intake of breath.

'He is my very well kept secret.' Inga continued to gaze at Lachlan fondly, squeezing his hand. 'I left him here more than twenty years ago . . .'

As Faro listened he was coldly aware of two things, Vince's heavy gaze and a sudden sickness in the pit of his stomach. In a great tide it threatened to overwhelm him, and in so doing, banished all other emotions, including the Queen's mortal danger and the possibility of lurking assassins.

Was it – could it be – that Lachlan was his own son? His and Inga's?

Taking the boy's hand again, she was saying proudly, 'Lachlan is one of my youthful indiscretions.'

'My father died before they could be married. A riding accident,' said Lachlan in defence of his mother's honour. 'Isn't that so . . .?'

Again Faro found himself watching their lips move but hearing no sound beyond the tumult of his own heart. Aware of Vince very still at his side, he flinched before his stepson's stare that, his guilty conscience told him, reviled and accused him.

Vince also shared the brand of bastardy. But at least there seemed to be no resemblance between them except in their unfortunate circumstances.

He turned his attention again to Lachlan, regarding him harshly, unable to see even a fleeting likeness to the face that he shaved before the bedroom mirror each morning.

But now he recognised that the black hair, blue eyes and white skin he had thought of as typical of the Celtic Highlander, Lachlan had inherited from Inga St Ola.

Whoever was Lachlan's father, he was no adopted child. He was Inga's flesh and blood. And Faro was astonished that he had been so blind, and that the familiarity taunting him since their first meeting had failed to bring Inga to mind.

Suddenly he longed to get her alone, ask her some vital, searching questions. Vaguely he heard the guard's whistle, the train's engine. How could he stop the pair boarding the Aberdeen train?

But that was not their purpose. Inga walked towards the guard's van where a large package had been unloaded.

She regarded it sadly. 'This was to have been my wedding gift. At least it will still be useful in your kitchen.' And tucking her arm into Lachlan's, she laid her cheek against his shoulder with a sigh.

Faro could think of nothing to say, and regarding the boy's stony face, mumbled, 'A tragedy indeed.'

Had Lachlan allowed Inga to believe this was a love match? And the revelation that Inga St Ola was his mother did not declare him innocent of murder. Much as Faro desired it should, it changed nothing.

Faro knew he must not, could not, allow any influx of personal feelings to influence his judgement. But the enormity of his discovery was too terrible to contemplate.

He knew now that the prime suspect for Morag Brodie's murder might well be his own son. But what right had he to expect a son's love, should Lachlan learn that his father had not been killed in a riding accident but was Detective Inspector Faro who had deserted his mother and Orkney to serve with Edinburgh City Police?

He shuddered with distaste. The revelation that he might have a son was bitter indeed. The detective's son who was a murderer, involved in a conspiracy to assassinate the Queen of Great Britain. The publicity would not go down well at the Central Office. It would spell the end of his career.

But Lachlan was a stranger to him, his name assumed.

No one need ever know the truth, a small voice whispered.

But Faro would. And he wasn't sure that he could live with that knowledge for the rest of his life. He was bitterly ashamed of his cowardice.

He might see his son tried for murder, found guilty and hanged by the neck until he was dead.

A cold shaft of premonition seized him. Had he always suspected that a child might be the reason for his mother Mary Faro's report that Inga had suddenly disappeared for several months after their love affair and his departure to Edinburgh?

It had always been a possibility, resting dangerously in the recesses of his mind. Now, after more than twenty years, had it come home to roost?

'Let us take some refreshment before we return.'

He blessed Vince for thus taking the situation in hand. And for gallantly leading the way ahead with Lachlan, who after one swift frowning glance at his mother, followed.

He was grateful to have Inga on her own, although she displayed a sudden reluctance for his company. As she seemed anxious and determined to keep up with the two young men, Faro put a hand on her arm.

'Stay, Inga. Talk to me, for God's sake. Talk to me.'

'What about, Jeremy? What would you like to hear? The weather I left in Orkney? This year's crops?'

'No, dammit. Other times and things. We are old friends. When did we last meet?'

'Only last summer,' she said sharply. 'No need to make it sound like the last century.'

He made a despairing gesture, able to think of nothing but the question mark hanging above Inga's son, Lachlan.

'So what is the weather like in Orkney just now?' he said with a weak attempt at humour.

Inga gave an exasperated exclamation, regarded him angrily. 'Just like it is here, Jeremy. You know that perfectly well.'

Her sweeping gesture encompassed the sleeping mountains with their burdens of sheep and boulders. 'Just like this,' she repeated, 'without the trees.'

'I didn't mean that—'

She laughed shortly. 'I know you didn't.'

'Are you really in mourning? Or is that part of the rôle you are playing, Mrs – what-is-it?'

She stopped in her tracks, stared at him defiantly. 'Saul died three weeks ago. Or has that news not reached you yet?'

Saul Hoy was the blacksmith at Balfray Island, to whom Inga had been housekeeper and more than that, she once confided, for many years.

'I've been away from Edinburgh. I am truly sorry. How did it happen?'

'He'd been ill for some time. I found him sitting in the kitchen in his chair one morning.' Her eyes filled with sudden tears.

'I'm sorry, Inga,' he repeated.

Slightly mollified, she sighed. 'I shall miss him.'

'What will you do now?'

She shrugged. 'That was my main reason for coming to Scotland. Lachlan and I have always been close. He was always begging me to come to Deeside. Saul left me comfortably well off so now I may be able to purchase a house for us.'

'A moment, Inga. Did you by any chance give him money? Five hundred pounds to be exact?'

'Yes, I did. Saul left it to him. But I don't see—'

Faro groaned. 'No, you couldn't. Please go on.'

'Ever since Saul first took ill and we both knew it was final, we discussed what might happen. Saul, bless his heart, worried so about me. He urged me to think about coming here to Lachlan. The wedding came as a complete surprise—'

'Saul knew about Lachlan?'

She smiled slowly. 'Oh yes. He was the only person in the world I trusted with my secret.'

Faro stopped in his tracks. 'Inga. Tell me. I have to know – is Lachlan – is he—'

She smiled up at him defiantly. 'Go on. Finish it.'

She wasn't going to spare him and Faro took a deep breath. 'Is he my son?'

Again she smiled. 'And if he is, Jeremy Faro, what then? What will you do about it?'

'I will marry you, of course,' he said sternly.

Inga doubled up with laughter. So sudden, so shrill was her laugh that Vince and Lachlan halted, looked back, hesitated, until Faro signalled them to proceed.

'Jeremy Faro,' she gasped, 'you'll be the death of me. Really you will. You'll marry me, indeed. What about me? Am I not to be considered? What if I don't want to marry you?'

'But—'

'But nothing. I've lived very comfortably without you for more than twenty years, thank you very much.'

'Had I known . . .' And Faro remembered his youthful flight from Orkney. Longing to be free, his ambition had made him luke-warm in his proposal that Inga might come with him. He had added, 'Eventually, when I am properly settled.'

Instead, she had passed out of his life and he had met Lizzie, with her young son Vince. And he had married her.

'To propose marriage to legitimise a child is, I consider, almost the greatest insult you could offer.'

So she had not known the details of Lachlan's Scots marriage?

Overwhelmed, confused, reduced again to stammering boyhood, all he could say was, 'I didn't mean—'

'I realise you didn't mean to be insulting. You thought you were being kind. And proper. Edinburgh manners have got through to you, Jeremy Faro,' she added bitterly.

Then suddenly she laughed again, laid an imploring hand on his arm. 'Let's not talk of it any more,' she said gently. 'It's past. Dead and buried with all the pain of long ago.'

They walked in silence the few yards towards the hotel Vince and Lachlan had indicated.

At the door, Faro said, 'I don't want to go in there yet. Come, let's walk round the square.' She made no resistance and he went on, 'You haven't answered my question yet, Inga.'

'Oh, I thought I had politely declined your proposal.'

Stopping, Faro seized her arm. 'Don't be evasive. Damn you, Inga. I want the truth. Is Lachlan my son?' And at her stubborn expression, 'I can count perfectly well, you know. I can ask him—'

'Don't you dare, Jeremy Faro. That would be unforgivable. How could you even consider such a thing?'

'That story about a father killed before he could marry you—'

'You have got it wrong, as usual. I was much more imaginative than that. When he was young I told him I was friends with his mother who lived in Aberdeen. She died when he was born. I was with her at the time so I brought him here to grow up with the Brown family—'

'And he believed you?'

She shook her head. 'Not entirely. Not after we once stood by a mirror and looked at our reflections together. That told all. He was about fourteen. He gave a sob. Took me in his arms and said, "Mother, Mother. I've always known you were my mother. Why did you tell me you weren't? Do you think there was anything in this whole world I would not be able to forgive you?" '

She paused to wave to the two young men who had reached the hotel door and hovered indecisively.

'Coming,' Faro called.

'We were very close, Jeremy. Like you and your stepson.'

That was the moment when Faro guessed why Inga St Ola had never liked Vince when they had met in Orkney. It was quite understandable, for the love Faro lavished on his stepson could, by a single word, have been transferred to Lachlan.

As they made their way slowly across to the hotel, Faro said, 'Eating, at this moment, is an activity I can well do without. I hope you are hungry.'

'Oh, I am. Deeside gives me an enormous appetite. You can always take a dram and watch us eat,' she added mercilessly.

'Look. We must talk.'

But now, bleakly indifferent, she said, 'I don't see what else we have to say to one another. Really I don't.'

Watching the two young men with their hearty appetites and Inga not far behind them, Faro did his best to carry on a normal conversation.

It was not easy, especially with Vince's anxious 'What's wrong, Stepfather? Come, you must eat something. Is your stomach playing you up again?'

With his lack of appetite the centre of attention, Faro snapped angrily. 'Oh, do stop fussing. Keep your doctoring for the hospital, if you please.'

Vince's eyebrows went up a little. Eying his stepfather narrowly, he refilled Inga's wine glass. 'Very well, very well. Only asking, you know.'

Having been so ungracious, Faro insisted on paying the bill.

'Will you be all right?' Lachlan asked Inga anxiously. He had observed that she had been somewhat reckless in her consumption of wine. 'I am on duty shortly. The Queen's picnic.'

Faro took Inga's arm firmly. 'I shall see her safe back to her lodgings.' Then to Vince, 'Get Lachlan to drop you off at Beagmill.'

And without waiting for their reactions he led her to the railway station. There the small boy left holding Steady and the pony-cart was agreeably surprised by the unusually large coin pressed into his hand for these services.

Once aboard, Inga gave directions and said, 'Thank you, Jeremy. I'm grateful, truly. I just wish we could have met under happier circumstances.'

In answer to his question, she sighed. 'I have no idea how long I'll stay. Lachlan is going to need me now. This terrible business. I can't believe it. Murder? That's something that happens to other people, not to one's own family.'

'Did you know Morag?'

'I met her on my last visit. Before she got involved with this other fellow at the Castle. I found it unbelievable; she was so utterly besotted with Lachlan. And who could blame her?' she added with a proud smile. 'First love and all that.'

She laughed softly, leaning towards him so that her head almost touched his shoulder. 'We know how that can hurt, don't we, Jeremy? Everyone else sees the holes and crevasses, the yawning pit of disillusion, but we go on our happy blinkered way. Just like Steady here—'

'What did you think of the girl?'

'Very pretty, very flighty. A tease. But such a horrible end. And yet although I was shocked, when I thought about it, I found I was not completely surprised. Girls like that, who entice men, often end up disastrously.' With a shrug she added, 'And I do get instincts, feelings about people.'

She looked at him. 'You know how it is. The witch in me, Jeremy. It's still active. Something from that first instant of meeting. I often see very clearly. Like looking down a long lane, with an uninterrupted view.'

' "Look well upon the face of the stranger . . ." '

She nodded. 'Yes, Jeremy. You have it too, I realise that. Perhaps it accounts for your survival all these years in your dangerous job.'

'Tell me, what did you feel about her?' Could Inga contribute something vital that he had missed, never having met Morag Brodie?

'I seemed to see deep inside her, behind her eyes. She was not what she pretended. It was as if she played a part and sometimes hesitated, trying to remember her lines, as if the rôle she had chosen was too hard for her. I realised that she had tremendous vulnerability. That men would love her for it and would use her too. This extraordinary appeal, but she wasn't clever enough to handle it. In that instant I almost pitied her—'

She held out her hands. 'I wanted to gather her in. Warn her. And then I knew it was useless, whatever lay ahead I could do nothing to prevent it happening. It was already written,' she added heavily.

'And I made a resolve. If she was what Lachlan wanted, then I would do all in my power to help them. But I didn't think it would come to that. I also knew it was very one-sided. Lachlan was not enamoured. So when he wrote me that they had been married by habit and repute, I was taken aback. Hurt, too, that I had not been invited even as a witness.'

'Did he give you any reason for the haste?'

'I presumed the worst. That she was carrying his child. When I heard of the tragedy, of course, I came at once. I was shocked to learn that she had left him immediately after the marriage, such as it was, and that he had never seen her again.'

Faro wondered if she knew the full story, of the £250 and

the mysterious benefactor, but she was asking the question he dreaded.

'I gather they have not found the murderer yet? Who do they suspect?'

Faro was saved an answer when she continued, smiling, 'I'm sorry, I suppose that is secret information. At least no one could suspect Lachlan, for which I must be thankful. And I gather he has been very helpful to the police.'

That was news, thought Faro cynically; obstructive would have been a better term.

On the outskirts of Ballater was a tiny private hotel, set among pretty gardens.

'This is where I leave you,' said Inga.

'When shall I see you again?'

Inga's face was in shadow. 'Do you really want to?'

'Of course I do.'

'Do you think that is wise?' A vestige of pain sounded in her voice this time.

He took her hand, held it tightly, not wanting to let her go. 'Wise or not, I would like to see you.'

'Very well. How about tea this afternoon?'

'Splendid,' he said, taken aback by her unexpected eagerness.

'Here, about four? Till then.' She smiled and he saw in the sudden dazzling radiance Lachlan's resemblance to her. Whatever Inga St Ola pretended, unless she had a twin sister, Lachlan was undeniably her flesh and blood.

And probably his.

Helping her down, wondering whether he ought to kiss her or not, he found the decision was spared him. Turning abruptly she hurried up the gravel path to the hotel door.

Watching her disappear inside, disappointed that she did not once look back, he climbed into the pony-cart.

His emotions in turmoil, he arrived back at the Crathie Inn. There his appointment with Inspector Purdie served to remind him that at four o'clock he could not take tea with Inga St Ola, for he would be on his way to Glen Muick and the Queen's picnic.

'Damn. And damn again,' he swore.

11 The Inspector was comfortably ensconced at a table by the window. As they shared a dram, Faro recounted the morning's events, how he had met Lachlan's mother.

'An old acquaintance of mine from Orkney days.'

Purdie's eyebrows lifted in faint surprise, especially as Faro after a little embarrassed throat-clearing drank up hastily, in the manner of one eager to change the subject.

Purdie's bespectacled eyes glinted in amusement. 'So you are hinting that the money was honestly come by.'

'I believe so. Willed to the boy by her former employer.'

Purdie nodded. 'So we have settled that mystery. Good. Incidentally, I have returned personally to Bush Farm the banknotes Craig – er, removed. I shall recover it from him later,' he added grimly.

'How did you explain it?'

'I left the envelope on the kitchen table. I did not even try to explain.'

Faro frowned. 'Will that not leave young Brown with a poor impression of the police's integrity?'

'Transparent lies would be even less likely to impress him,' said Purdie. 'Besides I suspect that he is no stranger to fabrications. A Scots marriage, did you say? I have never heard such rubbish.'

'It happens to be true, sir.'

'It will never hold up in a court of law.'

'Except in Scotland,' Faro insisted, regarding him

thoughtfully. As so often happened, an English upbringing had sadly blunted the Scots 'lad o' pairts' to the manners and customs of his ancient heritage.

'Hrmmph.' Purdie scowled. 'And what's all this salmon leistering the Queen is so interested in? Why doesn't she leave the catching of fish to her menials?'

'I presume it is all part of her wish to share in the peasant life of her tenants. She sees Balmoral as her own rustic Arcady.'

Purdie laughed harshly. 'Without any of the hardships. I am sure it has not gone unnoticed by you, Faro, that this is the sort of thing that brought Marie Antoinette to the guillotine. I, for one, will be heartily glad when I see Her Majesty safely aboard the Royal train in Ballater. This whole exercise has been an absolute farce, a waste of precious time, don't you think?'

And without waiting for a reply, he went on, 'It must be plain to our assassin by now that he cannot succeed when everyone except the Queen seems to know his intentions and is healthily alert. Don't you agree?'

Faro didn't. Through twenty years of dealing with violent criminals he had developed an acute sense of danger. 'I imagine there are always at least a dozen corners where an assassin might lurk unnoticed in the Castle. And another dozen weak spots in security arrangements, that have been overlooked by everyone concerned.' He paused. 'Except the assassin, of course – who must manage to stay one step ahead.'

'You are forgetting someone else.'

'Am I?'

'Yourself, Faro. We have it on record that in dealing with crime, it is Detective Inspector Faro who has always been that one step ahead.' He laughed. 'Why else did you think I wanted your help on this case?' And stroking his beard thoughtfully, 'Tell me, what is the secret of your success? Luck, care, or intuition?'

Faro shrugged. 'A little of all three.'

'Let's hope for all our sakes that none of these attributes has deserted you. You are coming to Glen Muick?'

'I am. Perhaps you would care to share the pony-cart?'

'Thank you, no. I would offer you the carriage but I have various things to do, enquiries which may take some time.'

Purdie hesitated as if about to impart their nature, then shook his head, saying, 'I will see you there.'

Glen Muick was the Queen's favourite area. She loved its 'real severe Highland scenery', and the loch which could look noble or sinister according to the mood of the weather.

As Faro rode Steady along the narrow rough track by the loch, the glen whose name meant 'darkness' or 'sorrow' was living up to its name.

It could hardly have been less inviting. He had forgotten that visitors, expecting a deer forest to be a picturesque dense tree-covered expanse, found on closer acquaintance a sparse wood on the lower foothills and sides of burns. Above, the naked mountainside covered in huge boulders and wild heather stretched skywards.

He was thankful that his destination was not Altna-Guithasach, called somewhat inappropriately 'The Hut'. In the higher and more treacherous reaches of the mountain, the bothy had been built for the Queen and her beloved Prince Albert.

When he died it held too many memories for her to visit it. But she could not desert her dear loch, so seven years later she built the Glasalt Sheil by its shores, accessible by boat or road.

At last the house appeared against the distant hills. Across the heather the sound of guns reverberated. The afternoon shoot was still in progress.

Faro shaded his eyes against the light. Small puffs of smoke and birds rising into the sky indicated that the sportsmen had now reached the wilder stretches of the hillside.

Steady did not care for this distant activity. It made him nervous. In deference to his horse's distress, Faro decided to anchor the reins to a large boulder and strike out on foot across the heath towards 'The Widow's House'.

Keeping to windward so that he might circle the guns and approach by their rear meant hard going. He was no tracker and the gnarled burnt-out roots of heather clung to his ankles one moment, while the next he found himself slithering across a treacherous slope or ploughing through an oozing bog marsh.

Leaping across a tiny stream he missed his footing, tripped and fell headlong. The fall which winded him also saved his life.

As he hit the heather, the air above him whistled and he heard the unmistakable sound of a bullet slam against a boulder and ricochet into the water.

He raised his head timidly, expecting to see one of the Royal party hurtling towards him, angrily questioning his right to be there.

Preparing to give a good account of himself, he stood up and stared round indignantly.

There was no one in sight. He had the vast boulder-strewn landscape to himself but for a belt of stunted trees and a glacial rock of large proportions on the horizon.

Even as he considered that as the direction from which the gunfire had emanated, another shot rang out. Dropping like a stone into the heather, he lay still, no longer in any doubt that he was the target.

Around him all was silent as before and with a fast-beating heart, he considered his next move.

Suddenly he saw a movement, a head raised about twenty yards above him and hastily withdrawn. His assassin no doubt. And he cursed the fact of being unarmed and completely vulnerable to attack.

In a fist fight he was confident that he could hold his own, but he could do nothing against a man with a gun.

Except to escape by using guile and cunning.

The watcher had moved. Keeping out of sight, he heard the

footsteps of someone leaping through the heather. They were heading in his direction.

He thought fast, realised he had one chance – only one, and that was to lie perfectly still, play dead until his attacker was upon him.

Keeping his head well down, he listened to the thumping of his own heart. The footsteps were close now, he could hear his assailant breathing.

He braced himself against another bullet thudding into his flesh and when instead a hand touched his shoulder, he sprang into life, with the speed of a coiled spring suddenly released. In a second, the rôles were reversed. He had his man, arms twisted behind him, face down in the heather, cursing and threatening.

Turning him over, he discovered the startled countenance of Peter Noble looking up at him.

'Mr Faro. For God's sake, let me go. What the devil has got into you? You're breaking my arms.'

Faro relaxed his grip enough to allow him to struggle into a sitting position.

Noble stared at him ruefully. 'I thought you were dead.'

'Then I am sorry to disappoint you.'

'Disappoint? What are you talking about, sir? I was watching you come up the hill when someone back there took a pot shot at me. At least I thought it was me. Then I saw you fall.'

As Noble spoke Faro saw he carried no gun. He did a quick calculation. If the footman had intended to kill him out here on the hill, he would not have approached empty-handed. In case his quarry was only wounded he would have come prepared to make certain, to give him the *coup de grâce*.

Noble looked round nervously, shaded his eyes against the horizon. 'This really is too much.' And taking Faro's arm, 'Hurry, sir. We're obviously in someone's line of fire. They shouldn't be allowed, such rotten shots. No regard for people's safety.'

Following Noble through the heather, Faro asked, 'What were you doing up here? Why weren't you with the guns?'

'I was sketching, sir.'

'Sketching in the middle of a shooting party?'

'I dabble, sir. Her Majesty is very encouraging. Come. I'll show you.'

He led the way up to the large rock, behind which were spread out his materials and easel. He pointed to the half-finished painting.

'It's a fine sheltered spot. As you see, quite safe from the guns. And a splendid view of Glasalt. At Her Majesty's request,' he added proudly.

'It's very good.' And it was. What was more, whether Noble lied or not the colour was still wet and to Faro's inexperienced eye, the composition represented several hours' work.

Noble's chosen site was also invisible from where he had been walking up the hill. On the road far below, Steady was happily cropping the grass where he had left him.

Now from over the hill another man appeared at the run. It was Purdie this time. Cupping his hands he was shouting, 'Faro – Faro.'

Faro came out from behind the boulder, waved vigorously.

Purdie stumbled over the heather breathing hard. 'I heard shots from this direction. There were no guns. I feared the worst.'

'I seem to have got myself in the wrong place.'

'You look a bit white about the gills.'

'Someone took a pot shot at Mr Faro, Inspector,' said Noble excitedly. 'Perhaps even two shots.'

Purdie's face as he looked at Noble registered disbelief. 'I was over at Glasalt.' He patted the telescope in his pocket. 'Keeping an eye on things. As I was scanning the terrain, I saw you leave the horse. I fancied you might be heading in the way of the guns so I sent Craig to direct you. Where is he, anyway?'

The three looked round. Of Craig there was no sign.

Ignoring Noble, Purdie took Faro's arm firmly, led him out of earshot. Staring across at the footman who was regarding his painting indecisively, he asked, 'Tell me, what exactly did happen?' He sounded worried.

'A bullet whizzed over my head, ricocheted. There was a second shot which, according to Noble, he thought was meant for him—'

'According to Noble,' repeated Purdie heavily.

'It could have been a mistake, sir. The Royal party are notorious bad shots—'

'Look again, Faro, see the direction the wind is blowing the smoke. There are no guns firing over this area.'

Again Purdie glanced back at Noble who seemed to have lost interest in the proceedings. Paint brush in hand, he was concentrating his efforts on Glasalt Sheil.

'There was no one else here, Faro. Except him.'

'True. But I didn't see any evidence of guns among his equipment.'

Purdie dismissed his theory about Noble's lack of a gun.

'He could have concealed it just a few steps away in the heather. If you were merely wounded, then he had only to snatch it up. God, man, you were unarmed.' And looking round, 'The heather is the perfect place for hiding spent bullets too.'

Purdie sighed. 'I think you are taking this far too lightly, Faro. I regard what has happened as a serious attempt on your life. All the evidence seems to point in that direction.'

'In the circumstances I'm afraid I have to agree with you, sir,' said Faro glumly.

'It's what I've been expecting. That we were to be the targets.'

'We, sir?'

Purdie smiled grimly. 'Indeed, yes. The second bullet wasn't for Noble. It was for me. I was in full view dashing across the heather towards you. I don't need to impress upon you the gravity of the situation, Faro. Our murderer is getting desperate. He is running out of time. He knows that we are on to him and that we are both too dangerous to live!'

Raising the telescope, he scanned the horizon, handed it to

Faro. On the hillside, the tiny figures of the shooting party, so clear he could see their heads moving as they chatted, were making their way slowly down in the direction of Glasalt.

'We might as well do likewise,' said Purdie. 'Let me have another look. No. Absolutely no sign of Craig.'

'Where can he have got to?'

'He might have missed us, got lost and tagged on to the beaters. Yes, I imagine that's what has happened.'

As they walked downhill, Faro turned. Now far above them Noble had emerged from the boulder and was making a cautious descent with easel and painting materials.

The afternoon was still warm and the heather was filled with the steady drone of insects. Faro signalled a young beater to fetch Steady.

As Purdie yelled 'Drat them!' striking out ineffectually at the cloud of midges, Faro realised he had been too preoccupied with a different kind of attack to notice their very painful presence.

On the sloping lawn beside the Widow's House, where already the party had formed into groups, the picnic was being unpacked by the ghillies.

Brown solemnly withdrew a whisky bottle from the carriage. He held it high to the accompaniment of cries of delight.

'Just in case of need, ye ken,' he said straight-faced.

'Will it help my midge-bites, Brown?' called one of the ladies.

'Aye, if ye drink it down, it will help ye to forget them.'

Faro looked round the assembled throng. The Queen was there with her pretty young daughter, Princess Beatrice, and their ladies-in-waiting; the two Captains Tweedie and Dumleigh, General Ponsonby, Mr Gladstone; the ghillies, Grant and Lachlan Brown; the beaters, young lads in rough tweeds, bonnets and shabby brogues.

Servants appeared from inside the house to dispense tea, scones and Dundee cake, all of which Faro thought fell far short of Aunt Bella's standards.

A party from Invercauld House made up the numbers. They were chiefly notable for their piercingly shrill English accents as Mr Gladstone regaled them with stories of his remarkable feats of hill-walking:

'. . . a mere bagatelle. Nineteen miles up Lochnagar. Came back fresh as a lark.' And patting his puffed-out chest, he surveyed them proudly. 'Sound as a bell. Not bad for a man past sixty, you'll agree.'

A burst of applause and delighted cries of 'Well done, Prime Minister,' brought a dour glance from the sovereign he tried so hard to impress.

Pausing in her conversation with Princess Beatrice she darted a glance, so frankly murderous, in Mr Gladstone's direction that Faro had to restrain himself from laughing out loud.

His eyes searched the little group. While their menfolk had indulged themselves with bringing down game birds on the hill, the ladies had prudently remained at Glasalt. Now they sat with their crinolines spread around them, a circle of pretty, gaily coloured flowers on the grass, their faces protected from the insects' attacks by wide-brimmed hats and the dextrous use of fans.

The men, more soberly attired, lolled beside them, some daring Royal displeasure by lighting pipes and cigars. For once this activity failed to arouse the Queen's disapproval. Turning a blind eye on the wreaths of smoke ascending, she was prepared to be indulgent, persuaded by Brown that this kept the midges at bay.

Today she too abandoned formality to the extent of sitting in a comfortable chair at a little distance and a little higher up the slope. She had chosen a position of vantage in keeping with her Royal image, from which she could look down approvingly upon the activities of her loyal subjects at play.

'It does make her look just a little like one of her many statues on a plinth,' murmured Purdie. And taking out a cigar, 'We might as well join the gentlemen. Care to?'

'Thank you, no.'

'Not even with a Royal dispensation?' Purdie smiled and then, noticing the two Captains, went on, 'If you will excuse me, Faro. I must have a word.'

A few moments later Faro observed him talking earnestly and found all three men staring fixedly in his direction.

Was Purdie telling them of his 'accident', warning them of the dangers now close at hand?

And scrutinising the faces in that merry carefree throng, were they what they seemed? Was this to be their only blood-letting, the massacre of game birds, their trophies spread out proudly before them on the grass?

And what troubled Faro most, where was Craig who up to now had been the shadow of the man from Scotland Yard? Why wasn't he here? Why hadn't he arrived to deliver Purdie's warning?

Who else was missing? He looked around. Noble. Where was he?

Somewhat unnerved still by his narrow escape, he would have enjoyed a pipe but decided instead to try out the cigars he had bought at the Crathie Inn. Taking Uncle Ben's silver case from the top pocket of his tweed jacket, he had just opened it when two footmen in liveried jackets but without wigs emerged from the house carrying drams on silver trays.

One was Peter Noble. As he approached Faro was about to ask him for a light when the footman whispered:

'If you would be so good, sir.'

And turning, Faro observed the ponderous face of the Prime Minister staring fixedly in his direction, his imperious beckoning action indicating that Inspector Faro was to advance rapidly to where Her Majesty now engaged him in conversation.

Guiltily Faro snapped shut the cigar case, made his way up the slope and bowed to his sovereign. He had rather hoped his presence might not be noticed by the Queen on this occasion, for he was well aware that ahead now lay the interview he most dreaded.

He was right. The Prime Minister was dismissed with a chilly 'You may leave us.'

Mr Gladstone left dejectedly and the Queen gave Faro her full attention. 'And what have you to report to us? Have you been successful in your quest?'

'I am afraid not, ma'am. One can only conclude that Your Majesty's dogs were the victims of some person out shooting – rabbits,' he added lamely.

'We presume you have explored every avenue with your usual expertise, Inspector?'

'That is so, ma'am.'

'Then we are very disappointed, very. As you are aware, we are about to leave Balmoral. And we are not pleased that we must do so without the guilty man being apprehended and severely punished. Very severely indeed.' A thin smile, as she added, 'We have been led to understand that Inspector Faro is quite infallible. And indeed, so it has seemed. You have always been quite reliable in our service at Holyrood.' Her accompanying glance showed more of sorrow than of anger.

'Forgive me, ma'am, but the task was unusual and the animals—'

'Dash and Flash,' she provided sternly.

'Indeed, ma'am, as Dash and Flash had, er – passed on – some time before my arrival, I am afraid that whatever trail and clues might have existed, they had gone quite cold.'

Suddenly the Queen smiled, patted his hand. 'We forgive you, Inspector. Brown has explained to us the difficulties involved.'

'Thank you, ma'am.'

'After all, Brown has given us to understand that this search for clues is quite a different matter to the work usually undertaken by detectives.'

Faro, grateful to Brown for his intercession, bowed. He refrained from adding that the Royal task was, in actual fact, just one stage removed from rescuing old ladies' cats stranded in the top branches of trees. A humble duty that was most often the unhappy lot of the junior police constable.

A shadow fell across the path. It was General Ponsonby.

'Ma'am, it is now time for the salmon leistering to begin.'

The Queen clapped her plump hands delightedly, her giggle of pleasure transforming reigning monarch momentarily into serving wench.

'We trust you will join us, Inspector.'

'I shall be honoured, ma'am.'

The assembled company rose, bowing as the Queen went into the house followed by her ladies to attend to their toilette.

As soon as they disappeared, an undignified scramble ensued among the men. Drams had been lavishly refreshed throughout the picnic and although half of the day's activity lay ahead, Faro could see that the whisky flasks much in evidence during every shoot 'to keep the cold out' had also been replenished. Now every half-empty whisky bottle was seized upon.

Several of the party including one or two of the ladies were in higher spirits than was reasonable for the time of day, already in that condition the Queen was pleased to describe as 'bashful'.

Faro guessed that once the sun sank behind the mountains and the leistering began not only the salmon would be ready to succumb. As the men with bursting bladders hastily sought relief in the little wood nearby, some had to be supported by their comrades.

Watching the exuberant groups emerge again, he wondered, was there hidden in their midst a murderer who behind a smiling mask coldly awaited his opportunity to kill the Queen?

And himself.

12 The salmon leistering was traditionally an autumn activity when the salmon were red and almost unfit for eating, or so Faro remembered from reading Sir Walter Scott's account in *Guy Mannering*.

At the Linn of Muick, a crowd had already gathered to greet the Queen and her party in their conveyances.

Riding Steady alongside the fast-flowing river, Faro saw that the floor of the glen was in deep gloom, the sun dipping behind the tops of the mountains. The air was suddenly chilly.

Cheers rose from the tenants drawn either by the activity ahead or by the proximity of the Queen. They lined the banks, the men bowing, removing bonnets, the women curtsying as the Queen rode past, her daughter at her side in her favourite open carriage, the 'sociable', with Brown on the box.

When she had descended, a hand on his arm, he led her to a vantage point from which she could have an uninterrupted view of the proceedings.

The fishermen were already positioned awaiting the signal.

The shout went up: 'Let the leistering begin.'

The word was passed along the river bank. The assembled tenants and fishermen waded into the water, poking under the stones to dislodge lurking salmon, while others waved torches back and forth to attract the fish to the surface.

As they leaped, the men struck out with the leister, a three-pronged implement reminiscent of Neptune's trident.

A flash of silver, a flash of iron and the salmon struggled once and was laid on the bank. Soon they were piled high, for those who escaped the tridents swam into a net.

Faro had positioned himself near the Queen. As the fever of the chase took over, he heard her deep laugh and once again remembered her taste for circus displays and wild animals.

In the gloaming, the weird long-lasting twilight of the Highlands, he dimly recognised Brown, Grant and Lachlan. Kilts tucked between their legs, they were walking the river, leisters upraised.

Perhaps encouraged by Her Majesty's cries, 'Oh, excellent. Well done,' some of the guests had joined them; rolling up trouser legs, they plunged laughing into the water. The sudden icy chill had its effect. Some were quickly sobered, while others, less steady, toppled from stones, took a drenching for their pains and came out shivering, much to their comrades' amusement.

Faro, seeing that Mr Gladstone and the two Captains had stationed themselves at the Queen's side, rushed down to lend a hand hauling out the inebriates.

And then tragedy threatened.

Further up water where the nets prevented the salmon leaping on to the higher reaches, the river became a rushing boulder-strewn tumult.

A small girl hovering on a rock, in her excitement, slipped and fell. Her screams were echoed by her mother. Hands were outstretched but, small and light, her clothes drenched, she was swept down towards the falls where she must be hideously broken and drowned.

Faro was never conscious of doing anything heroic. Acting instinctively, he threw off his jacket and leaped into the water.

As the child hurtled past him to the very edge of the falls, he managed to seize her skirts. A moment later, realising from her

screams that she was terrified but otherwise unhurt, he handed
her over to hands reaching out from the bank.

With danger over and everyone's attention diverted to the
child now safely restored to her sobbing mother's arms, Faro was
wading out of the shallows when something struck him hard in
the small of his back.

The sudden pain shocked him, knocking the breath out of his
body. He staggered backwards, backwards into the river where
the raging waters, swiftly descending, seized him. His lungs full
of water, blinded, he caught at an overhanging branch of a tree
and clung on grimly. Shaking the water out of his eyes, he looked
up, saw shocked faces above him.

The branch snapped and swirled towards the edge carrying
him helpless with it. Faces mouthing words of warning lost in
the deafening roar looked down at him.

Lachlan, Noble stretching out hands to him – but Purdie,
older and stronger, was nearest. Faro held out his free hand
desperately. Purdie had thrown himself face down, Faro grasped
at his hand, missed, reached out again. This time he encountered
two hands. Strong and firm, they held him.

Others followed and a moment later he was hauled on to the
bank, panting, half-drowned.

Purdie bent over him. 'That was a near thing.'

'Too near, sir. You saved my life. Thank you.' Faro looked
down at the boiling torrent. Another minute and if he hadn't
drowned he would have been dashed to pieces on the rocks
below.

'Think nothing of it,' said Purdie. 'But we had better get you
home. I didn't save you from drowning to have you die of a
fever.'

John Brown came running over with a blanket in Balmoral
tartan. 'From the Queen, sir. Put it around you.'

Faro took it gratefully.

'Lachlan's away for your horse.'

As he waited whisky flasks were proffered, but he was already shaking like a man with an ague when Lachlan handed over the reins of Steady to him.

'Would you not rather have the carriage?' asked Purdie.

'No. No.'

'Are you sure?'

'I will be fine. I'm just cold. And one of us must stay with the Queen.'

By the time Steady had trotted briskly into Easter Balmoral and, unsaddled, was bedded down for the night, Faro was chilled to the bone.

But inside the cottage, the best sight in the world awaited him. Vince had called in only to find that Bella and Tibbie were out visiting neighbours.

Vince took one look at him, brought out the hip-bath, put it before the glowing peat fire, and while he boiled buckets and kettles of water, Faro gasped out the details of the child's rescue.

'And completely forgetting, of course, that you cannot swim.'

'It never occurred to me, lad. It didn't seem important.'

'You make me furious, sometimes,' said Vince angrily 'Never did a man take less regard of his own skin. It's a mercy you weren't both drowned. Even a good swimmer would have been weighed down by the weight of those tweed trousers. And boots.'

He looked at the sodden heap, steaming by the fire.

'I'm afraid they'll never be the same again. But we hope you will.' Then he smiled, pouring another pan of boiling water into the hip-bath. 'A charmed life, that's what they say you have. I'm beginning to believe it.'

Half an hour later Faro, restored from his ordeal, was grimacing over a hot, strictly medicinal toddy as he related the events at Glen Muick. For Vince's benefit, he carefully omitted any sinister implications.

But Vince was not to be put off. 'How did you come by that very nasty bruise on your back?'

Vince had noticed it while he was sitting in the bath.

'When I fell down in the heather, I expect.'

'I thought you fell face forward?'

And when he didn't reply Vince continued with a look of triumph, 'Someone tried to kill you, Stepfather. Am I right?'

When Faro described what had happened, Vince said, 'Don't you think this has gone far enough? A daring rescue for a man who cannot swim is one hazard too many, when he has narrowly escaped death by walking in front of a shooting party.'

Vince shook his head. 'You are getting either very careless or remarkably absent-minded, neither of which are luxuries you can afford in your profession.'

It was scant consolation to realise that Inspector Purdie was not alone in failing to pick up obvious clues.

'Very well, but as you know, lad, I am the last to call "Wolf". There were a great many people milling about. Something hit me in the back, but it was over in an instant. I doubt if anyone noticed, all attention was on the wee lass. Besides, the gloaming can play tricks. Makes it damned difficult to see anything distinctly.'

'Sergeant Craig wasn't in the vicinity?'

'I didn't see him. I realise what you're thinking, but surely it cannot be Craig. After all, he is Purdie's right-hand man. He must have had an arm's length of references to be trusted by the Yard.'

'And yet he did succumb to the money from Lachlan's bothy. Now that I would call irredeemable misconduct in a police officer. At the moment, Stepfather, I'd be prepared to lay even odds on Craig and Lachlan, as prime suspects.'

Faro, beginning to feel the effects of the day's travail, grew weary of the conversation, the cut and thurst of speculation. Normally relishing such discussion he now saw it as a great tide that led nowhere, sweeping him helplessly along unable to divert the disaster awaiting in the wings.

There was one direction he did not want it to lead. To Lachlan Brown.

'What do you think of Lachlan, by the way?' he asked trying to sound casual.

'Pleasant enough. Yes, very pleasant when he chooses to be so, I imagine.' Vince shrugged. 'I did not feel that we had a great deal in common. Except, of course, for fathers who had abandoned our mothers,' he added bitterly.

Faro suppressed a groan. Little did Vince know that the link of illegitimacy they shared was more intimate than he could ever have imagined. That there might exist an even stronger reason for Lachlan's resenting Vince, who had usurped his rightful position by becoming Jeremy Faro's son in every way but the accident of birth.

Faro closed his eyes before the awful prospect looming ahead of him. Vince's bitterness and hatred were unrelenting towards the unknown man who had fathered him. How would he react to the knowledge that his stepfather had similarly abandoned Inga St Ola and left her shamed in her Orkney home, forced to have their child fostered?

If the lad ever found out, whatever excuses he made, Vince would never really forgive him. Their whole future relationship could be blighted, put in jeopardy by a truth coming home to roost after more than twenty years.

Bella's clock melodiously struck nine, reminding him that he was to have had tea with Inga five hours ago – a momentous five hours in which he had twice escaped death.

He swore with some feeling.

'What's wrong, Stepfather?'

'I had an engagement with a lady this afternoon. I forgot.'

'Inga?'

'The same. I had to go to Glen Muick instead, urgently. And it was too late to get a message to her.'

'Never mind, I suppose the Queen has precedence over all other ladies, including Inga St Ola.'

At Faro's faint smile, Vince said, 'How curious that she should come back into your life again. I mean, this connection with Lachlan Brown and so forth.'

'A strange coincidence indeed.'

'Do you know what I think, Stepfather?'

Although Faro knew perfectly well the pronouncement Vince was about to make, he shook his head obligingly.

'I think Inga and Lachlan are in this together.'

'Indeed. What evidence have you for that?'

'The evidence of my two eyes. You just have to look at them. Thick as thieves, they are.' He paused. 'I'm disappointed in you, Stepfather.'

'In what way?' Faro felt panic rising.

'Candidly, where are your powers of observation? They seem to be failing you badly of late.'

When Faro made no protest, Vince said, 'Obviously he wasn't born in Orkney or you would have heard all about him from Grandma. So it follows that the birth was kept secret. That some wretched man seduced her and left her. Just like my poor mother. But poor Inga did not have you—'

The wretched man in question wriggled uncomfortably, bit his lip. Listening to Vince's tirade, wanting to protest, No, it wasn't like that at all. He had not seduced Inga, although he was too much of a gentleman to say that it might well have been the other way round. Inga had loved him and his first experience of sex had not warned him of the consequences that might follow.

He wanted to protest that he never knew she was pregnant. If so, he would have married her.

Dammit, he had offered to do so.

'You knew her in those days, Stepfather.' Vince on the track of truth was relentless. 'You were a friend of hers, a cousin—'

'Much removed,' Faro interposed hastily.

'Could you not have advised her?'

'Vince, I was nineteen years old when I – when I knew her. She was twenty-one. Hardly the sort of thing she would seek to confide in me.'

'Did she never give any hint, I mean, about the man?'

'No,' said Faro shortly.

'Yet it must have been about the time you left for Edinburgh.' Vince's earnest pursuit of right made him wince. 'Wait a minute, lad, here we are gossiping like a pair of old fishwives, tearing apart a lady's reputation when her story might be true.'

But Vince was not prepared to let go. 'You can't mean that Lachlan was fostered by her, really the son of a friend who died.' Pausing he gave a bark of laughter. 'Stepfather, you surely don't believe that. How can you be so simple? Why, that's the thinnest story I've ever heard.' And shaking his head sadly, 'I'm disappointed in you, really I am. Here you are, a master of deduction, unable to see through an obvious tissue of lies. Unless—'

'Unless what?' Faro demanded sharply.

Vince regarded him narrowly. 'Unless you don't want to solve this one,' he said softly.

And at that moment Faro suspected that in a flash of enlightenment Vince had solved the case for himself, the implication being that Lachlan was guilty of Morag's murder. Even as the monstrous thought took root, the scene at the river flashed vividly before him, touching a deeper, stranger chord of memory.

What was it? Something Vince had said earlier? But he was too tired to think and determined to be in bed before his aunt and Tibbie returned and subjected him to the inevitable ordeal of retelling the rescue story for their benefit, he bid Vince goodnight rather sharply.

He slept badly, nightmare scenes engulfing him. Over and over he was drowning with hands outstretched in front of him. But as he seized them, the fingers came away like sticks in his hands and he hurtled backwards into the falls.

Next morning, hoping to escape with a light-hearted explanation for sodden garments left to dry by the fire, he found them all neatly pressed by Tibbie. As he related how he had slipped and fallen, how Inspector Purdie had rescued him, he remembered how strong his hands had been and the nightmare returned.

'You can overcome anything, if you will it.'

Anything but shrunken socks, it seemed, which he had placed on top of the hot oven.

But Bella, as always, had a solution close at hand.

From a drawer she took out a linen roll and withdrew a pair of kilt hose.

'This was the last pair I ever made for your uncle. Finished them the day he died and never had the heart to give them away. At my age, it's gey daft to hang on to things. It'll no' be long now afore we're t'gither again, an he'll say to me, "Bella, ye daft besom, ye always were a hoarder. Whatever came ower ye." So take them, Jeremy lad.' And burrowing further, 'This too, his skean-dhu. Ye should have had it long since.'

Holding it, he remembered in an instant how his Uncle Ben had taught him to spin his bonnet on to the peg by the door. And by the same flick of the wrist, he had demonstrated how the skean-dhu had been used in past ages with deadlier effect, to kill an enemy.

And Faro, saddling up Steady, was surprised to discover he had lost none of his expertise. He could still score a bull's-eye on the old beam above the door. But he expected less dazzling results with the excuses he had on hand to offer Inga St Ola.

On the way to her hotel he prepared himself for a very cool reception. Instead, Inga ran down the steps to meet him, grasped his hands.

Ready with his apologies he saw her expression was one of relief rather than anger.

'I am so sorry about yesterday—'

'It doesn't matter—'

'It is my own fault. I entirely forgot that I was to go out to Glen Muick—'

She shook her head. 'When you didn't arrive I realised that something had happened.'

Leading him to a garden seat, she sat down, spread her skirts and looked intently up into his face. 'I told myself that detectives are notoriously unreliable when they are engaged in the pursuit of criminals. And unexpected delays are the order of the day.'

At his startled expression, she continued, 'That's why you are here, is it not?'

Faro smiled wryly. 'I thought I was here for Aunt Bella's birthday and a fishing holiday. That, I assure you, was my intention.'

Inga laughed. 'Jeremy Faro, you'll be the death of me.'

'I'm glad you find me an object of mirth,' he said stiffly.

'I don't, I promise you.' And suddenly she was solemn. 'I don't. Anything but that. But I can guess that whatever you are supposed to be doing, the real reason is something very serious.'

A leaf fluttered down on to her lap and, picking it up, she smoothed it out tenderly. 'I know you scorn this sort of thing, Jeremy, but I knew you wouldn't come.'

'Is that so? I assure you I do try to keep my word—'

'You don't understand. I don't mean it like that at all. Listen, I was looking forward to your visit. It was a lovely afternoon and then, quite suddenly, it was all changed. Different. As if a giant shadow came across, between me and the sun.'

She looked around as if hoping to find some measure to fit the description. Then turning to him, she said, 'I knew you were in terrible danger. That your life at that moment hung by a thread. And there was nothing I could do – no warning I could give. So I concentrated hard, prayed, "Deliver him from evil." '

'What time was this, Inga?'

'Three o'clock had just struck on the hall clock.'

Faro looked away. He had checked his watch when he arrived

in Glen Muick. Two thirty. He must have been walking for half an hour when he had fallen in the heather, the assassin's bullet cutting the air where a second before his head had been.

Mistaking his preoccupation, Inga sighed. 'I know it's silly and you disapprove, Jeremy. But I can't help it, I just know things. I don't want to but I do.' Smoothing out the leaf again, she shook her head miserably. 'I don't want to be a witch, but that's what I am.'

He took her hands, said softly, 'Your prayer worked, Inga. I nearly had a very nasty accident.'

'What happened?'

'Oh, I got in the way of the stalkers' guns—'

'Dear God, how awful—'

'My own stupid fault,' he said lightly, knowing he must not worry her further.

At that moment a bell sounded within the hotel. 'Would you care to stay for lunch with me?'

'I would love that.'

As they took their seats at a table overlooking the garden, he said, 'You were right. I am here on a case.'

'Can you talk about it?'

'I think so. It will make you smile to see how far is the mighty detective fallen.' He told her about the Queen's dogs and was grateful that she did not find it amusing. An animal lover, she considered it a serious matter, and worthy of his skill in detection.

'The Queen leaves tomorrow or the next day and I still haven't solved her mystery or produced her criminal.'

'Don't you think it was most likely an irate farmer?'

'I'm not sure. Perhaps you could use your second sight on that one?' And he laughed suddenly, placing his hand over hers on the table. 'What a team we would have made, Inga. Think of it. With your psychic powers and my practical ones. Quite unbeatable. Don't you agreed?'

But his laughter died at the pain on her face. Contrite, he longed to say, Oh, Inga, what did I – or Fate – between us do to you? All these wasted years, so empty and barren for you, taking care of Saul Hoy whom you didn't love. And parted from Lachlan, whom you did.

He thought of the years they might have shared as husband and wife, and his mind raced ahead toying with the fleeting ghosts of other children they might have had. Instead he had Lizzie and Rose and Emily. And Vince, Lizzie's son – the lad dearer to him, he had told himself, than even his own son could have been.

As they were silent tackling the game soup which was steaming hot, he thought about the future.

After the Queen left Balmoral with danger and a national catastrophe averted, he would return to Edinburgh and to the less sensational everyday crimes that were the legacy of a great city. And in his own home, the pressing domestic problem posed by his housekeeper Mrs Brook and the care of her invalid sister.

As for the murder of Morag Brodie which had begun it all, that was Inspector Purdie's to solve. And he was thankful for once, that this was not his province.

He looked across at Inga. What on earth was he thinking about? Dear God, how could he go and leave her son, even if he wasn't his, to the mercy of the law? Especially if the lad was innocent. For he suspected a certain ruthlessness in the Inspector from Scotland Yard.

Purdie had a reputation to uphold and Faro guessed that he had already made up his mind that Lachlan, in the absence of any other suspect, must be guilty. In the Inspector's eyes, a suspect would be guilty until he was proved innocent.

There was no way to convince him unless, within the next thirty-six hours, Faro could produce the real criminal.

The maid interrupted his reverie, removing the soup plates and bringing in poached salmon. Inga smiled across at him.

'How long are you staying?'

'I shall be leaving on Saturday, in all probability. And you, Inga? What are your future plans?'

'I have applied for a situation of housekeeper. There are two possibilities in the area. Big houses, that sort of thing. And one with a professor in Aberdeen.'

'This is a big change for you.'

She shrugged. 'Without Saul, I have no desire to stay on Balfray. Besides, I want to be near Lachlan. It is all so different from the plan I made for this visit. I had thought to see him with a wife, a life of his own.'

'I thought you couldn't bear to leave Orkney.'

'Did I say that? It seems I did feel that way a long time ago. Now time seems to be running away from me, the old man with the scythe. The death of someone close always makes you aware that time is the enemy—'

He looked at her and thought how young she seemed; indestructible, this woman who was fast approaching middle age. Her black hair was still unstreaked with grey, eyes unlined, deep as bluebells, skin still satin-smooth.

'If Vince stays at the hospital, then who knows, we might all meet up again?'

With the turmoil she aroused in his heart, he wasn't sure that it was such a good idea.

As they prepared to leave, he apologised once again. 'I am sorry about yesterday. Truly.'

She shook her head, studying his face as if trying to remember every feature. 'It doesn't matter. As long as you are safe.'

Beyond the garden the distant river glittered silver. As he prepared to mount Steady, she watched him nervously, intently, smoothing on her gloves. Those gloves – another gesture he remembered.

His chaste goodbye kiss upon her cheek, she said, 'Be careful, Jeremy. That shadow, it's still over you, you know.'

The bright smooth lawn had been tranquil in sunlight. Suddenly the peace and stillness of that perfect autumn afternoon was invaded by a startled rookery, their raucous cries and ragged wings swirling overhead.

And he saw the sudden fear on her face as she glanced skywards.

Fear that neither would put into words.

Corbies. Those traditional birds of ill-omen.

Inga was watching them too. Closing her eyes, she was still as if for a moment she no longer occupied her body, still so shapely and comely, like that of a young girl.

'You're not out of the wood yet, Jeremy. There's danger, evil everywhere. All around you. And in the least expected places. Take care, dear friend, take care.'

13 Faro's route took him past the Crathie Inn to discover that Inspector Purdie had already left.

There was a message for him. He tore open the envelope.

'Plans are all changed. The Queen has announced her intention of remaining at Glasalt until her time of departure. I need not dwell upon the opportunities offered by a house so remote and virtually unguarded. *Come at once.*'

The last line was heavily underscored. Faro could imagine the chaos at the Castle, with frantic servants and only John Brown pleased since at Glasalt he enjoyed the full limelight of the Queen's informality.

In the light of his most recent deductions Faro had relived over and over in minute detail those desperate hours in Glen Muick. He had not the least doubt that Purdie was right.

The murder attempt would be made at the Widow's House.

The only hope of saving the Queen was in keeping one step ahead and in passing on certain vital information to Vince. But at Beagmill he was again thwarted. The two doctors had been called out to an accident case at a sawmill some ten miles distant.

Leaving an urgent message and praying that Vince returned in time, he set off for Ballater where he had some considerable difficulty in convincing Sergeant Whyte that he was in deadly earnest.

Following the bewildered policeman to the telegraph office, he stressed the urgency and hoped his two messages would be taken seriously by the startled clerk and not regarded as a hoax at their destinations.

Riding towards Glen Muick he decided that it was unlikely any attempt on the Queen's life would be made during the hours of daylight. At least such an attempt would not be made by one man acting alone, who would prefer to have the situation under his command with as few witnesses as possible.

In Glasalt he was interested to see the original numbers much depleted. Princess Beatrice and her lady-in-waiting had returned to Balmoral, for which he was grateful.

The young princess did not share her mother's enthusiasm for the great outdoors and on the excuse of a mildly sore throat had returned to the Castle. The excuse, flimsy as it might seem, was enough to alarm the Queen thoroughly, for her over-protection of 'Baby' included excessive worries about her health.

At the Queen's insistence, Mr Gladstone had also been returned to the Castle. He took a dour view of being deprived of the opportunity for another of his twenty-mile walks through the hills.

A more willing member of the princess's escort was General Ponsonby, a worried man with much to arrange in the light of the Queen's changed plans. Captains Tweedledum and Tweedledee were firm in their resolve to remain. The Queen had somewhat ungraciously agreed.

To Brown in his rôle as temporary master of the household was given the task of allocating bedrooms. Built with an eye to accommodating guests, the main house contained several spare rooms and there were others in the so-called barn and stables outside.

In addition to the security guards, the party at Glasalt was now composed of the Queen, Lady Churchill, John Brown, and Inspectors Purdie and Faro. As for servants, Lachlan Brown would take care of the horses and Peter Noble, a man of many accomplishments, would put aside his paint brushes and be in charge of supper.

Ponsonby left with a request for roast partridges, some salmon, chicken, Scotch trifle and Dundee cake: 'A simple picnic hamper plus two kitchen maids would be adequate.' The Queen had stressed also the need for lots of good wine.

She was less than delighted when they arrived under the personal supervision of her Prime Minister, who was determined not to let his sovereign out of his sight.

The Queen received his return with ill-concealed exasperation, almost rudely turning her back upon him as he bowed. Only Mr Gladstone was unaware of her petulant sigh of disapproval.

Faro had witnessed exchanges like this before and decided that Mr Gladstone was either deaf or insensitive, or conveniently, a little of both.

The Queen announced that all were here to indulge in pleasant relaxation and joyful activities. She would spend the afternoon sketching the view across the Loch of Darkness and Sorrow.

It now transpired that this was her urgent reason for remaining at Glasalt. The water-colour begun on her last visit was to be an anniversary present for Princess Vicky and her husband who were romantically inclined towards Deeside. For it was here that Prince Frederick had proposed. And while she painted, her lady-in-waiting, Lady Churchill, would read to her and Brown would remain in attendance.

Accordingly the visitors dispersed. The Captains elected for fishing, and Faro's sharp eyes detected a couple of rifles, hard to conceal, as unlikely fishing rods among their equipment.

'Have you any plans, Faro?' Purdie asked.

Faro decided to keep these to himself. He spoke vaguely of riding along the shore of the loch.

'You wouldn't care to accompany me?' Purdie enquired. 'I thought I might go in search of our missing policeman. A good walk would do us both good.'

Unfortunately this was overheard by Mr Gladstone and nothing short of a deliberate insult could dissuade him from accompanying the Inspector, who gave Faro a despairing gesture.

Noble left the house with them, carrying his easel, determined to complete his painting of Glasalt unless light and weather failed him.

Faro had his own reasons for a careful search of the hill where his life had been threatened. Brown's two collie dogs watched wistful-eyed the guests assembled in the yard. He was calling them to heel when Faro asked:

'Would they come with me?'

'Aye. They would that.'

'Very well. Come!'

'Are you sure you wouldn't care to join us, Faro?' said Purdie, viewing dogs and horse with curiosity.

Gladstone, whose speech on the splendid qualities of hill-walking and his own indomitable prowess were in full flood, viewed this interruption with disfavour. Faro watched the two men depart with some amusement, even the younger, taller Inspector having problems matching his stride to the elder man. At last Gladstone's voice faded and the two disappeared.

Faro rode up the hill and stopped to take out the field glasses which were always accessible at Glasalt. Noble was approaching the boulder where they had met the previous day, while Tweedie and Dumleigh were heading downwards to the loch.

Faro took stock of his surroundings. He was going to need a great deal of luck to find what he sought on that wild desolate hillside where Craig had disappeared so mysteriously.

He found that stalking was in fact a great deal easier in the heather than in the streets and wynds of Edinburgh, especially with a couple of borrowed dogs.

His search was rewarded, alas, and it was a sadder if considerably more enlightened Faro who started back for Glasalt. The fact that his theory about the second shot had proved correct did nothing to alleviate his distress as a chill mist rose from the loch and embraced him.

There were few things which struck naked terror into his heart, but fog – heavy blanketing fog, silent and unrelenting – was one of them. For years he had been unable to find one good sound reason to account for such a nonsensical fear in a grown man.

In Edinburgh, when Arthur's Seat disappeared from his window for several days at a time, when the top storeys of the tall High Street 'lands' vanished into swirling mist and day folded imperceptibly into night, he was consumed by supernatural fears. As the streets filled with the ghostly echoes of horses and riders looming out of nowhere to be immediately lost again, he was gripped by a primeval horror of the unknown which defied all his powers of rationalisation.

It was Vince who found the solitary clue to his stepfather's strange phobia which he would have been ashamed to admit to any of his colleagues. Vince believed that it belonged to the time when his father, Constable Magnus Faro, was run down by a carriage in heavy fog on the High Street. Faro was four years old.

An understanding of the origins of his fear did nothing to comfort him in his now certain knowledge of what lay in wait at Glasalt Sheil. He realised the importance of keeping his discovery to himself. His only hope of outwitting his adversary was to play for time and pray that his messages had been believed.

The Queen's life was at stake and there were few at hand to defend her. Should any premature move or alarm be made, he had no doubt that the assassin would strike fast and a bloody end ensue.

Despite his urgency, the man whose inbuilt sense of direction was a legend in the Edinburgh City Police failed dismally in the face of rapidly descending fog. He proceeded to get himself well and truly lost. Taking the wrong track, twice he landed up on what he thought were the shores of Glen Muick only to find that between himself and the path to Glasalt were sixty yards of bog-marsh.

Steady, it seemed, shared his unease. The dogs meanwhile had disappeared. He whistled in vain; presumably they were near enough home to have deserted him for the warmth of the stables, while the other guests at the first signs of the descending mist had wisely reassembled at Glasalt.

An hour later Faro's non-arrival was the signal for alarm. The Prime Minister was organising a search party when horse and rider appeared through the gloomy murk of the stable yard.

Gladstone seemed a little put out by Faro's return. He had rather liked the idea of being on the trail of a detective inspector, whose methods of detection he would claim he found difficult to assess. The policeman had been unable even to find the simple solution to who had killed the Queen's dogs.

Although Glasalt supposedly signified informal living, some of the proprieties were to be observed. Accordingly they all stood by their chairs round the table in the little sitting-room, until a bell rang and the Queen appeared.

Faro wondered if half an hour would be the statutory allow-ance for this so-called leisurely meal, as he understood was the rule in Balmoral.

That soon appeared to be the case. All was silent but for the clash of cutlery, the pouring of wine, and the scraping of plates. The other diners refused all his attempts to engage in polite conversation. They had been here before, he soon realised from their warning glances in the direction of the Queen, who gobbled her food at an alarming rate.

The Royal Scotch broth plate was emptied, bread demolished before it seemed the other diners had taken more than two spoonfuls.

At Faro's side, Captain Dumleigh belched quietly and refused the fish course. 'My indigestion,' he whispered. 'It is hell. Now you understand why.'

'I wanted to tell you—'

'Don't waste time,' said Captain Tweedie, timing his actions to coincide with the Queen's next course, 'I beg of you. Just keep eating, or you'll be starving by morning.'

Faro managed only half his salmon before the plate was whipped away. Resentfully he glanced towards the Queen, who was drumming her fingers on the tablecloth, impatiently awaiting the next course.

With warning, he did better by the chicken, and by refusing the Scotch trifle kept well abreast of the field of diners. Realising, however, that his stomach was never his strong point, he knew he would be exceedingly fortunate not to end the day with a severe bout of indigestion.

If he was still alive.

Half-past eight struck. The Queen rose and went over to the piano. Accompanying herself she sang a Schubert *Lied* in German. The words meant nothing to Faro, but he could tell by her expression that it was a sad, sad song.

She was loudly applauded and smiling, wiped away a tear.

'Most affecting,' whispered Gladstone. 'One of Prince Albert's favourites. They used to sing it together.'

With the mist swirling at windows already streaked with fine rain, a cheerful fire proportionally larger than those which warmed Balmoral Castle did little to dispel Faro's fear.

The Queen was waxing poetic about Scotland, saying how sorry she was to leave Balmoral and claiming this was because of her descent from the ill-fated Queen Mary. Touching Brown's arm, she whispered. He nodded and went out to return with Lachlan.

The Queen smiled. Indicating the piano she said:

'Come, Lachlan, you shall be our Rizzio.'

Faro felt his throat constrict. This was indeed a most unfortunate simile, he thought, remembering that other ill-fated supper room in Holyrood where more than three hundred years ago a

Queen had been entertained by her secretary who had died minutes later clinging to her skirts with thirty-seven stab wounds in his body. That supper room still retained for Faro something of that terrible atmosphere as if the scene had frozen into the walls. For Rizzio's death had set the pattern for a series of catastrophes from which, those with Jacobite inclinations would claim, Scotland had never recovered.

A moment later, listening to Lachlan's playing, Faro realised that the lad was a gifted performer. A music lover himself, his favourite activity was going to concerts at Edinburgh's Assembly Hall. He had heard the finest in the realm and recognised with awe that he was in the presence of a born musician.

The Queen, however, seemed quite indifferent. She chattered to Lady Churchill and prevailed upon her to play dummy whist. Lachlan's playing of a Mendelssohn concerto failed to interrupt the slap of cards on the table and the Queen's joyous triumph over her lady-in-waiting.

Meanwhile the rain on the window intensified. Where was Vince? Why hadn't help arrived? Faro, feeling trapped, was conscious of the enormity of what was about to happen.

Purdie obviously was also uneasy. Lachlan ceased playing and to applause conducted by Faro, bowed and left the room.

Purdie, catching Faro's eye, led him to a far corner of the room and whispered, 'We must talk. We must make some sort of plan. I have told Brown of our fears. He found them amusing. Amusing! Can you credit that? I told him we intend to remain in the house tonight and if necessary we will sleep outside the Queen's bedroom door.'

Producing a roughly drawn plan of the house, he said, 'Any attack will be made during the hours of the night. Here is the Queen's bedroom and next door Lady Churchill's. On the floor above, John Brown. The Captains have been allocated rooms next door to her. Servants in the stables—'

Purdie paused, held up his hand. 'Listen. Did you hear that?'

Faro looked towards the fire with its crackling logs.

'No.' Purdie interpreted his gaze. 'A shot. From outside.'

Springing to his feet, bowing briefly towards the Queen, who was oblivious to everything but the fact that she held a hand with several trump cards, he said to Faro, 'You stay here.'

'I'm coming with you.' Faro was about to follow him when his way was blocked by Mr Gladstone, who wanted a full account of how a detective inspector had managed to lose himself on the hill that afternoon.

Trying to withdraw with speed and tact was an impossibility. A minute later, no longer caring for politeness, he shouted, 'You must excuse me, Prime Minister,' and bolted.

Purdie had disappeared. Faro called several times, his voice swallowed by the thick mist. The only sounds were of the trees dripping mournfully, while somewhere close at hand a sheep lamented.

Closing the front door behind him, he walked round the house carefully, but there was no sign of a lurking intruder or of Purdie. Entering by way of the kitchen door he found Captain Tweedie vigorously stirring powder into a glass. 'Bicarbonate of soda. Dumleigh is suffering agonies of indigestion. We've made our excuses to Her Majesty.' And suppressing a yawn he added, 'If we are to be fit for this night vigil, we had better get Dumleigh on his feet again.'

'Is there anything I can do?'

'Not a thing. All Dumleigh needs is to lie low and let this take effect. Noble is bringing us a hot toddy, just to make sure.'

Faro went up to the room he was to share with Purdie but as he had expected it was ominously empty. He was overcome by a sudden feeling of helplessness and despair that the situation was running away from him, that in this case he was no longer in control and too much had already been lost.

Taking from his valise the gun he had acquired in Ballater and his uncle's skean-dhu for good measure, he ran downstairs. The corridor leading to the sitting room was dimly lit and intensely cold, the domestic scene heart-warmingly normal as Faro opened the door.

The party had broken up with the departure of the two Captains. Mr Gladstone, lacking an audience, greeted his arrival with delight.

Of Brown there was no sign. And where was Purdie?

The Royal game of dummy whist continued with the slap of cards on the table. The Queen, either by luck or design, was winning as usual.

'My trick, I think,' she said. 'And another – and another. For goodness' sake, my dear, why did you not play your trumps?'

Lady Churchill wisely pretended not to hear.

This time there was no escape from Mr Gladstone, who put down his *Lives of the Saints* with some eagerness. Advancing upon Faro, he picked up the threads of their broken conversation as if in fact Faro had not retreated in mid-sentence.

The clock struck nine. It had been a long evening which would soon end with the welcome sight of hot toddies all round. 'To keep out the cold', as Brown put it.

As the minutes ticked by, the ponderous question and answer game with the Prime Minister had been transformed into a monologue on the benefits of hill-walking to one's health and moral fibre.

Faro's mild protest about the weather brought forth the stern rejoinder, 'God made the elements, sir. They all have their place in His universe. It is not our place to question His will.'

The Prime Minister now switched from the perfection of healthy exercise to the imperfections of the criminal mind. Despairingly, Faro hardly heard Mr Gladstone's theories, his mind on Purdie's disappearance. Suddenly he realised that the Prime Minister nursed secret longings to be a detective.

His discourse was momentarily interrupted as the footman slid a tray of hot toddies on to the sideboard just inside the door.

The Queen's frugality in the matter of candles was firmly adhered to in the Widow's House, where all the illumination was centred on the fireside and an oil lamp provided for card players.

With his back to them, Noble added glasses to the jug on the tray. His livery now included his white wig, although such spruceness could hardly matter in this informal atmosphere, thought Faro, as he was not required to serve them individually.

As the door closed behind the footman, Mr Gladstone frowned at this new diversion. 'It appears that we are to help ourselves.'

Faro sprang to his feet. 'Allow me, sir.'

'Not Her Majesty,' warned Gladstone. 'She, er, makes her own arrangements with Brown.'

At Faro's questioning look, he added, 'It is traditional. They share a last dram together, after everyone else has retired. Including Lady Churchill. Her Majesty dismisses her last of all. The poor lady sleeps badly and is allowed to take a sleeping draught,' he said with a disapproving shake of the head.

At the door Faro noticed that Noble's spruce appearance had not extended to wiping his boots which had carried a great deal of mud into the room.

He offered the tray to Lady Churchill, who declined sharply. 'I never do, thank you.'

The Queen, intent on her game, slapped down another fan of cards. 'Our game, I think. We have won again,' she cried delightedly.

As Faro hovered indecisively, Lady Churchill whispered, 'Brown serves Her Majesty.'

Prim but eager, Mr Gladstone took the glass, stared at the contents and with an apologetic 'Just to keep the cold out. I am a poor sleeper you know,' drank the contents at one gulp.

Faro took one sip and hurriedly replaced the glass on the tray. He was a purist where whisky was concerned and disliked the addition of sugar and hot water. That for him savoured too much of Vince's 'medicinal purposes', his constant remedy for his stepfather's upset stomach.

As he returned the tray to the sideboard, the door opened to admit Brown, who took it from him. 'Let me do that, Inspector.'

And noticing the muddy footprints, Brown shook his head and whispered, 'I'll need to get one of the servants on to that. The Queen's a stickler for clean floors. Have you no' had your toddy, Inspector?'

'I prefer mine undiluted.'

'Aye, that's the way of it for me too. But we have to humour the Queen,' he added pouring some of the jug's contents into a glass. 'Shame to desecrate good usquebaugh, the water of life.'

And taking a large sip, he paused to grimace. 'This is awfa' stuff, right enough. Too spiced, half cold. I have my own secret receipt for the Queen's toddy.'

Faro glanced sideways at the Prime Minister, who seemed to have subsided into his chair. Brown's entrance had mercifully doused his monologue on the peculiarities of the Scottish law verdict 'Not Proven'.

Perhaps, Faro decided uncharitably, disliking the Queen's faithful servant, he had relinquished any part of a conversation which did not allow him the full share of the limelight.

With a glance over his shoulder towards the card players, Brown said: 'Ken how I got Her Majesty to take tea? Never cared for it as a lass and made outdoors with tepid water, even with the Prince's patent stove which never worked ...' His shudder was expressive. 'One day, ye ken, she asked what blend it was and so forth, said it was the best cup o' tea she had ever tasted. Do ye ken what I tellt her?'

Faro shook his head. 'Well, I said to her, So it should be, ma'am. I put a grand nip o' whisky in it,' Brown added, slapping his thigh.

As Brown was refilling his glass, Faro noticed that he was not quite steady on his feet. The reason for his absence now obvious, wondering how long he had been imbibing, Faro narrowly averted disaster to a small table bearing a collection of priceless Meissen china.

The Queen, alerted, said sharply, 'Brown, isn't it rather early in the evening for that?' and returned to her game.

Brown bowed, apologised and sat down in the chair rather heavily. He yawned. 'Dinna ken what's come over me, Inspector.' And yawning deeply again, 'I'm that sleepy, all of a sudden.'

As Brown's head dropped on to his chest, Faro turned his attention to Mr Gladstone, now slumped back into his chair and breathing heavily.

He was fast asleep. And snoring loud enough to alert the Queen. He would never forgive himself. He would be convulsed with embarrassment if his behaviour was noticed.

Faro leaned forward. 'Prime Minister, you were saying?'

There was no movement.

The Queen turned, frowning.

'The Prime Minister seems to have dropped off, ma'am.'

'So we hear, Inspector. So we hear.'

'Shall I waken him?'

A Royal gesture of dismissal. 'By no means, Inspector. All this healthy air, all these interminable walks have taken their toll. Let sleeping ministers be.'

Her eyes slid over Brown in the chair opposite. 'The drink makes him bashful.'

'He will sleep it off, ma'am,' said Lady Churchill wearily. 'He usually does.'

The Queen smiled at Faro. 'Silence is such a relief, do you not agree?'

And mercifully not awaiting an answer, she turned back to dealing the cards while Faro contemplated the sleeping Prime Minister with an ominous sense of dread.

He took up the glass again, sniffed it. Another tentative sip told him the truth. The hot toddies were drugged.

He walked to the window, stared through the curtains. The small astragals made it safe against breakage or intruders.

The card players were also out of range. Bowing himself out of the room, he glanced into the empty kitchen on his way upstairs to alert the two Captains.

There was no answer to his tapping on the door. Thankfully finding it unlocked he went inside. A candle burned between the two beds. Sprawled on one was the inert shape of Captain Dumleigh; on the other lay Tweedie.

Dumleigh was more heavily asleep than could be accounted for by the empty glass of bicarbonate of soda. The toddy glass on the bedside table accounted for the other Captain.

Faro ran downstairs. Where was Noble? And most of all what had happened to Inspector Purdie?

As he stood indecisively in the kitchen, he realised that the two maids must have retired, leaving a scene of disorder.

Lachlan Brown too. Where was he?

At that moment he heard a scuffling from one of the large pantry cupboards.

Mice? Rats?

A faint voice, female, from inside. 'Help – please help.'

The door was locked.

'All right. All right. I'll get you out.' Faro looked round for the key. There was one on the windowsill. Would it fit?

As it turned in the lock and he threw open the door, the two maids who had been expertly tied up and gagged, stared sobbing up at him.

He unfastened the ropes that bound them, and removed the elder maid's gag first. She gasped, 'Oh sir. The Lord be thanked. We thought you might be him again.'

'Him? Who did this to you?'

'Lessing. It was Lessing, sir.'

'Lessing – the footman?'

'Yes, sir.' The two were gibbering with fear.

'It was his ghost, sir. He came into the kitchen—'

'Back from the dead,' shrieked the other servant. Her voice

rising to a horror-stricken scream, she pointed over Faro's shoulder.

'There – there.'

Faro turned to see the bewigged footman standing in the doorway.

'It's me you want, Faro. I'm waiting for you. I've been waiting a long time.'

The face was half-hidden but he recognised the voice.

The two servants screamed again, but Faro had no time to attend to them.

'That's no ghost. And he intends to kill the Queen.'

With no further explanation, Faro plunged out into the mist after Lessing. Other footsteps passed nearby and he seized the man who was rushing towards him.

It was Lachlan Brown.

'I think I've just seen a ghost,' Lachlan panted. 'Lessing, the footman. Came at me like a bat out of hell. I thought he was dead—' **14**

'He is very much alive, alas. Have you a gun?'

'Yes, but not here.'

'Take this, then.' As Faro handed him the gun, he looked at it doubtfully. 'Can you use one of these?'

'I think so.'

'For God's sake, lad, don't just think. The Queen is in deadly danger and I'm going after Lessing.'

'Where's Johnnie?'

'He's been drugged.'

'Drugged Johnnie?'

'And the Captains and Mr Gladstone. In the hot toddies.' And cutting short Lachlan's bewildered questions, 'Where's Noble?'

'He took your horse. Said he had an errand. I thought you had sent him—'

Taking Lachlan by the arm Faro ran towards the sitting room. Opening it cautiously, he was relieved to hear the Queen's voice and Lady Churchill's. Heavy breathing continued to emanate from the slumped figures of Brown and the Prime Minister.

As he had expected there was no key in the lock.

Lachlan watched him as if he had taken leave of his senses.

'Listen. You're to stand guard here. Outside the sitting

room. And do not leave your post. Whatever happens. Do you understand?'

'I wish I did—'

'The Queen is in deadly danger. If Lessing tries to get into that room: shoot him.'

As he rushed outside, the fog enveloped Faro like a shroud. An unhappy simile, he thought shuddering. Perhaps that was the reason he had hated and feared the fog, that somewhere out there lay his death.

Angry with himself he switched from fear to practicality. How could he find anyone in this murk? He could not stray from the house but it was imperative that he should intercept Lessing, disarm him before he could get back inside. If he failed then only Lachlan stood between the Queen and murder.

He realised with growing horror that he was not ready for this, had never been ready for it. The momentum of events had taken him by surprise. Lessing's plan was brilliantly calculated to seize full advantage of the weather and the Queen's unexpected isolation.

He should have taken into account the cunning of his adversary. He should have stayed one step ahead but even visibility now ended at the garden wall and with it all hopes of taking the murderer by surprise.

From out of the mist every faint sound alerted him that the positions were reversed. Hunter into hunted, pursuer into pursued.

Lessing. The letters jumbled together in his head. Lord Nob's aliases were all anagrams of 'Noblesse oblige', the enigmatic clues to his real identity.

For once Faro had been blinded by his own deduction. By taking coincidence as fact, he had committed the worst transgression of a detective. He had underestimated the power of his adversary.

He was still considering his next move when he heard Purdie's voice.

'Faro. Faro, I'm over here. Where the devil are you?'

Turning, Faro saw through the gloom the kitchen door open and close. As he raced towards it, expecting to find it bolted against him, it flew open and the muffled cries from inside the pantry indicated that the maids had been locked up again.

His back towards him, Lessing was bending over a huddled form on the floor. Lachlan Brown.

'Did you need to do that?'

Lessing turned round. Without the wig and livery jacket, Faro still had difficulty in recognising him as his old adversary from the Case of the Killing Cousins. A man with a hundred faces, the chameleon features of the born actor.

But when he spoke it was in Purdie's voice.

'So we meet again. Hand over your gun, if you please.'

And waving a gun towards the still figure of Lachlan Brown he urged, 'Come along, Faro. If you tarry, I'll be forced to put a bullet through his head.'

'I am unarmed. I gave him my gun.'

'So that's where it came from. I'm much obliged to you. I need your help—'

'You'll get no help from me—'

Lessing ignored the outburst. 'But you are the key figure in my drama,' he said reproachfully.

Ignoring that, Faro asked, 'Who is buried in Lessing's grave?'

'Sit down. Do as I say. That's better. How should I know who they buried? Drowning fitted my plan excellently. Craig had already been recruited by our friends and sent here to await "Inspector Purdie's" arrival. A gossip in the local inn was all he needed to find out Purdie's childhood associations with the area, while he kept a sharp lookout for a likely candidate to double as Lessing's poor drowned corpse. The tinkers' arrival for the Ghillies' Ball would doubtless provide a conveniently drunken vagrant roughly my height and size. Unless we were very unfortunate.'

He shrugged. 'The rest was easy. Our last encounter on a clifftop in Orkney has, I am sure, convinced you that I am a swimmer of considerable ability, with a talent for survival. Indeed, I was once awarded a medal for life-saving.'

His laugh was without humour. 'Life-saving, Faro. Is that not capital, considering your present circumstance? But I digress. Craig had dry clothes ready and a corpse awaiting my swim downstream. When Morag saw her ring on his finger, she was certain to reel from closer examination of features battered beyond recognition. Meanwhile Craig kept me conveniently hidden in an empty cottage until it was time for Morag to leave us.'

'Did you have to kill the girl too?'

'I am afraid so. She was becoming burdensome. I did not much like being followed or the prospect of being father to her child. The idea of luring her to the mill and transporting her body on to Brown's doorstep, as it were, appealed to me.

'Surely you get the picture, Faro. That it was absolutely essential for someone at Balmoral to be murdered so there would be a police investigation requiring the skills of the bogus Inspector. We had to have a murder suspect and we both know how eagerly the local police would seize upon Lachlan Brown. Especially when that ridiculous custom of Scots marriage and the anonymous and highly suspicious annuity, which we had so generously arranged, became known. The Prince's Party leave nothing to chance and their forged papers are a credit to them. We even killed the Queen's spaniels in case they raised the alarm about the bogus footman.'

'Who *are* these people?' Faro interrupted.

'That, I am not at liberty to disclose. Not even to you, Faro, as your dying wish—'

'Is the Prince involved?'

'Bless your innocence, Faro. Can you see the future King of England condoning regicide – not to mention matricide. After all, this is the nineteenth century, we are supposed to be civilised.'

Again the laugh that accompanied his statement chilled Faro's blood.

'As far as His Royal Highness knows, we are a bunch of harmless fanatics, worshipping at the shrine of his popularity.'

'And the real Inspector Purdie?' asked Faro, eager to keep him talking, aware that his one forlorn hope lay in playing for time. And that Lord Nob's vanity and pride in his own cunning were his only weaknesses. He could never resist telling his victims how he had outwitted them.

Before he killed them.

'Our information from a source at Scotland Yard was that the Inspector was to be on a fishing holiday in the north of Scotland. Beard and spectacles were always a problem. I realised that this was a rôle I could not sustain indefinitely or indeed for more than a few days. And that if you saw me as Lessing, as I appeared to Nessie Brodie as her last visitor, then the game would be up. But see how beautifully it has all fallen into shape. Even Her Majesty has obliged us by her change of plans. I can tell you, it was going to be deuced difficult at Balmoral. But this, my dear Faro, is a walkover. Almost too easy.'

'What about Craig?'

'He had to be disposed of, alas.'

'I know. I found him.'

'You did? When?' A faint shadow crossed Lessing's face.

'This afternoon. The dogs nosed him out in a crevasse on the hill. Where you had shot him. I'd like to know why.'

'He failed to fulfil his early promise and there is no room for mistakes in our organisation. He was supposed to kill you on the hill, make it look like an accident. Instead he fell victim to the second shot. Craig had no finesse. Very useful for stealing things like drugs from the hospital while I kept the good doctors occupied. But behaving like the small-time criminal, stealing money from the main suspect – such behaviour threw our whole operation into hazard.'

He paused, smiling. 'As did your survival of the shooting accident. I decided on a brilliant new rôle for you, one I had in mind for John Brown originally. For when the Queen is found dead, you will have shot her. And then, alas, taken your own life. Is that not a neat twist? And such a scandal. A pity you won't be able to read about it in all the newspapers.'

'What have you done with Noble?'

Lessing smiled. 'When I rushed out to destroy all evidence of Purdie, I told him the Queen was in danger. He was to go to Ballater for help. He obligingly threw off his wig and livery jacket which were essential for me to play the footman. Poor Noble hates horses. I shouldn't be surprised if he doesn't come to an unhappy end in this weather—'

A clock struck the hour. Lessing looked round uneasily.

'How did—' Faro began.

'No more questions, Faro. I have no more time to give you. Much as I always enjoy pitting my wits against yours, this will be our last meeting. I must confess I'm disappointed in you, Faro. You haven't been very clever this time and now you have to pay the price of bunglers.'

Even as Lessing pointed the gun, Faro had one final chance. Seizing the skean-dhu from his sock, he hurled it.

Lessing staggered, fell. But Faro saw, too late, that the knife had struck his shoulder. He was only superficially wounded. As Faro leaped towards him, Lessing raised the gun, fired once.

The whole world exploded in pain. And as Faro slid slowly to the floor, he saw his own blood oozing from his chest.

So it was all over. All that remained now of the long career of Detective Inspector Jeremy Faro was the trivial business of dying.

Far away he seemed to hear the drum of hoofbeats, voices and a door opening. The Queen's voice raised in a shrill scream.

As his eyes closed he had one last wish: that he had been able to discover if Lachlan Brown was truly his own son.

It was one mystery he would never solve, an answer thrown to the winds of time.

*

For a long while the darkness enveloped him, but when he once more opened his eyes, it was to a small white world bounded by sheets, pillowcases, white walls.

He was in hospital in Beagmill, with Vince bending over him.

'That was a near thing, Stepfather. We thought we were too late—'

'The Queen?' Faro whispered.

'She's in London. Safe and sound.'

'Lessing?'

'Awaiting trial.'

The leaves outside the window were golden.

'How long have I been here?'

'A week.' Vince held up a cigar case, with a neat bullet hole plugged into it. 'If it hadn't been for this, nothing, no one could have saved you.'

And little by little, Vince pieced the story together for him. His messages had reached Aberdeen City Police, who had quickly telegraphed Scotland Yard to find the real Inspector Purdie returned from holiday due to a family bereavement. The police had immediately summoned the Gordon Highlanders regiment from the Bridge of Don barracks and it was a small army, hampered by the swirling mist, that Noble met riding towards Glen Muick with Dr Elgin and Vince in their midst.

'We had just returned to the hospital. There'd been a bad accident at a sawmill. We had to do some amputations on the spot. And then that damned mist. Then we got your message.

'I shall never forget the scene at Glasalt, Stepfather. Never. Like the last act of *Hamlet* with a touch of Sleeping Beauty's Palace. Lessing was taken prisoner. He's awaiting trial. It will be a sensation—'

'Lachlan Brown?'

'Nothing but a dunt on his head. Seems he put up a good fight though. He's gone to London with John Brown. Using Saul Hoy's legacy to study music.'

Faro nodded. He was unlikely to meet the lad again. It was just as well. But the boy's mother hadn't quite finished with him.

Vince was telling him, 'Inga has been in regularly each day to see you and so have Great-aunt and Tibbie. All the flowers are theirs.'

'I expect Aunt Bella was very upset about Uncle Ben's cigarette case?'

'On the contrary, she's delighted. You can imagine the story she's making of that. And his skean-dhu. How Uncle Ben reached out from the grave to save his favourite nephew.'

'Why is Inga still here?'

'She wanted to see you well again. And she's still hoping for a housekeeper's situation. She'll be back later this evening.'

Vince paused reflectively. 'I was just thinking. The problem with our Mrs Brook and her ailing sister. We could solve it by having Inga as our housekeeper—'

'We could, lad. But I think we won't.'

Vince looked at him intently. 'Then I will refrain from asking why not, Stepfather. Because if I tried very hard I might really guess your private reasons for such a decision.'

Faro was grateful for the sudden change of subject when Vince said, 'Tell me, how did you get on to Lessing being Purdie?'

'I almost didn't. Until too late. I should have seen it earlier. Purdie who had grandparents in the area and had stayed here as a child but was ignorant about the skean-dhu and Scots marriage customs. But I was blinded by working with a distinguished Scotland Yard detective and by the damnable coincidence that the name "Noble" fitted "Noblesse oblige" to perfection.

'It was Aunt Bella's story of the real Purdie's missing fingers that gave me the clue. A boy who loses fingers in childhood from his right hand will almost certainly begin to use his left. But Lessing was instinctively right-handed.

'But it wasn't until after he rescued me from the water that night that I realised that, without his gloves, he had two whole, strong hands. It must have irked him not to let me go, but in front of so many witnesses . . .'

'I imagine he saw that making you feel beholden to him was a marvellous move,' said Vince. 'How could you then ever suspect the truth?'

In the post came a letter from Buckingham Palace. It was from the Queen herself commending Inspector Faro's bravery.

'It appears I am to be presented with a medal,' he told Vince and putting aside the letter, he began to laugh, choking, helpless.

'What is it, Stepfather?' Vince demanded in alarm.

Faro was remembering the last thing he had heard before he lost consciousness in Glasalt.

Brown, with a stronger head than most, had been groggily awakened by the sound of a shot. The Queen, her card-playing disturbed by the ensuing uproar, had stamped out into the corridor, observed her favourite ghillie swaying into the kitchen and was shrilly demanding:

'Brown, are you bashful again?'

The Evil That Men Do

For
Ernest Kirkby

Detective Inspector Faro was a contented man. Life was good and not even the approach of his forty-third birthday could detract from the pleasurable anticipation of the next few months.

He didn't feel middle-aged. As he buttoned his dress shirt in his bedroom in Sheridan Place, he would, had he been a vain man, have accepted the evidence of his own eyes and the admiring glances of those of his acquaintance. True, the once fair hair was thinly streaked with grey, but this enhanced rather than diminished the powerful Viking image of a born leader, a king among men.

Now, as he tied his cravat, he whistled under his breath. Yes, life was good indeed and he had a strange feeling that lately things were getting better not worse in the Edinburgh City Police. It was six months since he had dealt with a murder case and he was almost persuaded that human nature had taken a turn for the better.

He smiled wryly at such an idea. If things continued like this he would be out of a job.

But his sense of satisfaction was more personal. Next week would see the end of his long separation from the elder of his two daughters. Fifteen-year-old Rose was to enrol at the Grange Academy for Young Ladies, with special instruction in Languages of All Kinds; Emily, who was two years younger, would remain in Orkney meantime.

Faro sighed. With Rose at home, he would be a family man again without the last desperate measure of taking a wife. For he could never rid himself of the guilty awareness that policemen made poor husbands and that his neglect had contributed in no small measure to his dear Lizzie's death.

Had his powers of observation and deduction encompassed his own four walls he might have realised that her health was too frail for the pregnancy that killed her – and took to the grave with her the son he had craved.

But Lizzie had left him a stepson and no father could wish for a better son than Dr Vincent Beaumarcher Laurie – a son who also fulfilled the role of companion and colleague.

In the spring one of Faro's long-cherished dreams would come true when Vince married Grace, niece of Theodore Langweil of Priorsfield House, his present destination. It was also the home of his own secret love. Ridiculous at my age, he told himself, blushing like a schoolboy . . .

As he closed his front door in Sheridan Place he recalled with gratification Grace's indignation at the merest hint that Vince's stepfather should move into a separate establishment.

'We will try it out for a year or two,' she said with a shy look at Vince, 'and if – if we need nurseries and so forth, then we will move into a larger house.' And taking his hand, 'But you will come with us. No, sir, I will have none of your arguments.'

Faro knew that they were useless in any case since Grace was a strong-willed modern young lady with a mind of her own.

The Langweils continued the old-fashioned custom of dining at four o'clock. As he walked the familiar mile from Newington to Wester Duggingston, he thought of the many less happy occasions when he had travelled this road in urgent pursuit of criminals. Rarely had he leisure to admire the gloaming, that curious stillness when the trees and buildings are sharply outlined against an azure sky and the very earth stands still.

Now the magic of a winter afternoon was enhanced by a rising moon, and from the loch three swans took flight, the sound of their wings audible, birds from an ancient legend come to life.

Then, silence restored, his ringing footsteps were the only sound in the wine-clear air as he thrust open the iron gates leading into the drive of Priorsfield House.

Birthplace of Langweil Ales Limited, the simple tower-house of centuries past had been enlarged in the eighteenth century. Overlooking the loch, tradition (which the Langweils were anxious to perpetuate) claimed that it had all begun with a humble medieval alehouse patronised by the kings of Scotland out hunting in the dense forest on the slopes of Arthur's Seat.

Perhaps this romantic and colourful notion had some roots in history, for the name Langweil had drifted in and out of local records. But whether Mary Queen of Scots had stayed there benighted by a snowstorm on her way to Craigmillar Castle and whether Bonnie Prince Charlie had supped there in a secret rendezvous awaiting the arrival of French gold to support his cause were matters for conjecture only.

What was undeniable, however, was that the Langweil fortunes had dwindled until Grandfather Langweil discovered an old recipe for ecclesiastical ale, reputedly served by the monks of Kelso who had owned the lands of Duggingston in the twelfth century.

Grandfather Theodore's recipe flourished. He bought a disused mill on the Water of Leith, whereupon Langweil Ales became a redolent part of the western approaches to the city and Priorsfield Inn became Priorsfield House as successful ventures into port wine and claret swiftly followed.

The Langweils bore an unsmirched reputation, not least as philanthropists whose names appeared on all the distinguished guest lists and charitable societies; and their loyalty to past Scottish monarchs was acknowledged by the coat of arms of HRH Albert, Prince of Wales, who was partial not only to Langweil

Ales, but to the liqueur, their latest production, which he had graciously endorsed.

Grandfather Theodore was less successful in a recipe for raising children. His one surviving son produced four sons and a daughter. The eldest, Justin, a sickly infant and invalidish child, was followed two years later by Theodore, then Cedric. A decade of stillbirths followed before the safe arrival of Adrian.

As an adult Justin's deteriorating health meant that survival depended on living far from Edinburgh's cruel climate. In the 1850s he departed for North America, where he promptly severed all connection with the family.

'In fact,' Vince had said, 'they don't know whether Justin is alive or dead, which might make complications in the matter of inheritance. I mean, suppose a son or daughter walked in some day and claimed the Langweil fortune,' he added anxiously.

Faro had smiled wryly. Theodore's first wife had died in childbirth long ago. If his second marriage and Adrian's first were without issue then Grace would inherit the Langweil fortune, including two breweries and two very large houses.

'I shouldn't bank on your future wife's expectations,' Faro warned him good-humouredly. 'Theodore's young wife looks healthy enough and so does Adrian's.'

'Barbara is touching thirty and they have been married for twelve years,' Vince reminded him. 'Offspring don't sound very likely.'

'I imagine Adrian and Freda might yet produce a quiver of bairns to carry on the Langweil name.'

'After six years? Do you really think so?'

Faro pondered. Six years *was* a long time for a couple who allegedly wanted a family.

'Besides I sometimes think Adrian's ruling passion for the golf courses leaves him little time or energy for the more important things in life,' said Vince.

'Be careful that ruling passion, as you call it, doesn't also becomes yours,' Faro warned the newest victim of golfing fever.

Vince grinned sheepishly. Hitherto a reluctant morning riser, he now dashed off to play nine holes with Dr Adrian before their first patients arrived at the surgery. In his role as Cupid in Vince's romance, Adrian's word was sacrosanct.

The two doctors had met at a colleague's wedding in Aberdeen where Adrian was in general practice. Returning to Edinburgh for family reasons last year, Adrian had promptly invited Vince to set up his brass plate alongside his own.

The wheel of fortune that was to change all their lives having been thus set in motion, it was no time at all before Vince, invited to Priorsfield, sat next to Cedric's daughter Grace, and fell in love. This was in no way a remarkable or unusual event since Vince was particularly susceptible to pretty girls. Except that this time fate took a hand.

The lady in question was equally entranced by the handsome young doctor and the rejoicing from both their families was mutual and spontaneous. The Langweils were known for their lack of side; 'a man's a man for a' that' could have been their motto on their coat of arms, if they had chosen such niceties. Although Vince was illegitimate, and his stepfather a 'common policeman' who had risen through the ranks to become detective inspector, such social limitations aroused no feelings of resentment. After all, the liberal-minded Langweils were proud to claim descent from an alehouse keeper.

As Faro climbed the front steps of Priorsfield he looked back towards Edinburgh. The twilight sky was dominated by the silhouettes of Salisbury Crags on one side and the Pentland Hills on the other. Not lacking in imagination, he still found it difficult to realise that Duddingston, now so accessible to the new villas on the rapidly developing south side of the city, had, according to the historians, once been covered by the dense Caledonian forest now as extinct as the volcanic origins of Arthur's Seat. There, legend claimed, in a hidden cave the valiant king whose name it bore slept with his true knights, awaiting the clarion call that never came.

The Romans had marched here, and with the Christian era came the priory lands. In relatively modern times, the armies of King Edward of England, of Cromwell, and of Bonnie Prince Charlie had stumbled along the once inaccessible cart tracks now transformed into Queen's Drive, a handsome carriage road from the royal residence of Holyrood Palace where it frequently bore illustrious guests to dine with the Langweils.

The imposing mansion was considerably more ancient than the Gothic towers and turrets which had been added fifty years ago. In the fast fading light the sky was bright with a thousand stars and a pale moon touched the ancient central block and throwing into sharp relief corbie stepped gables and gun loops, a grim reminder that Priorsfield had survived dangerous times when this part of Edinburgh was a wilderness threatened by wild beasts and wilder men. After the Jacobite forces' defeat at Culloden, rumour had it, the Langweils had 'bought their way' into the favours of King George II and had so remained intact while other royalists, dispossessed, saw their men ride into exile or execution in Edinburgh's Grassmarket.

As Faro waited for the door bell to be answered, he remembered something Vince had said only recently. 'As you told me long ago, Stepfather, and as you've never allowed me to forget, history is written by the victors.'

'Or rewritten, if they're clever enough to destroy the original records,' had been his laconic response. But he little knew how he would have cause to remember his words.

Now he heard footsteps and returned his thoughts to the present, and to a living example of this very situation. The door was opened by Gimmond, the butler, who greeted Faro politely and removed his cape and top hat. Only the merest flicker of an eyebrow would have revealed to the observant that the two men were old acquaintances. Gimmond, or 'Jim Gim' as he was better known, had been involved in shady dealings, and his common-law wife, a known prostitute, had died in mysterious circumstances. He was saved from the hangman's rope by Faro's evidence and the Scottish verdict of 'Not Proven'. A verdict which those concerned with justice wryly dismissed as 'We know you did it, go away and don't do it again.' Five years had passed and Faro, on his first visit to Priorsfield, had recognised Gimmond who, with his second wife, was now respectably established as butler and housekeeper. Gimmond's relief had been considerable when he realised that Faro was not going to 'shop' him with 'the boss'. Faro's philosophy, unlike many of his colleagues, did not subscribe to 'once a murderer, always a murderer'. He considered in the case of the *crime passionnel* that this was unlikely to recur and believed profoundly that men and women can be reshaped for better as well as worse by bitter experience.

Now he followed Gimmond across the vast panelled hall and up a great winged oak staircase, its landing adorned with ancient tattered flags and rusted armour, proud mementoes of battles long ago. Alongside were portraits of generations of past Langweils and a fine rare painting of Bonnie Prince Charlie, his modern-day royal successors represented by an imposing array of signed photographic portraits. Such displays, Vince informed him, were essential for any well-off family who were going anywhere and had pretensions towards aristocratic connections.

As Faro approached the drawing room, voices raised in heated but friendly argument were hastily hushed as Gimmond announced him.

Grace, with a beaming Vince at her side, rushed forward to introduce a middle-aged man wearing a clerical collar.

'Meet our second cousin, Stephen Aynsley.' And as the two men shook hands, 'Stephen has just arrived from America.'

'Not quite, my dear. I have been in Scotland several months now. In St Andrews, where I recently took holy orders,' Stephen explained with a shy fond smile in Grace's direction. 'I have only recently had the pleasure of making the acquaintance of my charming family.'

All this information surprised Faro since Aynsley looked considerably more mature than the usual run of students nearer Theodore in age than Adrian. Stoop-shouldered, presumably from carrying the cares of the world, with the skeletal thinness of the aesthete, Stephen, he was informed, was son of Grandfather Langweil's only sister Eveline.

Little of the Langweil good looks had descended by the distaff side, Faro decided. Learning that Aynsley was shortly to leave for missionary work in the unexplored regions of Africa, he realised that a superabundance of the Langweil famed zeal and enterprise more than compensated for this deficiency.

The second stranger was Piers Strong. Introduced as an architect, Faro suspected that his agitated manner and heated complexion concerned the yellowish documents he clutched so anxiously and were possibly the cause of the argument he had interrupted.

'Congratulations, Stepfather,' muttered Vince. 'You arrived just in time.'

'Nonsense, Vince. Blood hasn't been spilt yet,' said Theodore. And to Faro, 'We are merely trying to sort out whether to have or to have not some new alterations and additions to the house. Vince has given me to understand that you are a traditionalist, so I am relying on you to take our side.'

Traditionalist, eh? Vince's quick glance in his stepfather's direction pronounced that word as a rather less flattering 'old-fashioned'.

'My dear sister-in-law here' – with a gesture in the direction of Grace's mother Maud, Theodore continued – 'has succeeded in tearing the town house apart and now, aided and abetted by young Adrian and Freda, with their infernal notions about hygiene, they are directing their missionary zeal – beg pardon, Stephen – towards Priorsfield. All I say is what was good enough for my grandfather – and his grandfather – is good enough for me.'

'Rubbish, brother. Rubbish,' said Adrian. 'Bathrooms and water closets are an absolute necessity if we are to stay healthy. I'm sure Barbara as a modern young woman will agree.'

Barbara. Where was she?

Faro had known on first entering the room that she was not there. Now at the sound of her light step outside the door he turned and once again felt as if he had been thumped hard in the chest by a sledge hammer.

She came straight to him, took his hand. 'Welcome, Mr Faro, it is good to see you again. I trust you are well.'

Faro stammered something appropriate in reply, conscious that he was blushing like a lovesick lad. Then she was gone.

'I have spoken to Mrs Gimmond as you suggested, Theo.' And to Adrian: 'And what is this I am to agree about?'

Feasting his eyes, his whole being upon her as Adrian reiterated the argument, Faro was amazed that the rest of the company were oblivious to her effect upon him. She was so strikingly lovely. Quite the most beautiful woman he had ever seen. Not only in the composition of her looks, but the essence of womanhood without which, he knew, good looks are as dead as the portraits that stared down from the walls.

Again he found it difficult to realise that she was touching thirty. She could have passed for eighteen. Here was a woman who would grow more beautiful with time's passing. Like Shakespeare's Cleopatra whom 'age cannot wither, nor custom stale her infinite variety'.

He suppressed a sigh. She was not for him, could never be for him. But every man has his own fantasy, his own goddess, and Barbara Langweil was his.

Drawn once again into the round of domesticity, the argument resumed over the merits of a bathroom, Faro observed that Barbara's smile contained a nervous glance at Theodore.

'Oh, come now, I'm sure you'd appreciate more than one bath a week,' said Adrian.

'Well, I do manage that—'

'I dare say you do, with the maids carrying pails of hot water upstairs.'

'Um – yes.'

'That was good enough for most folk,' Theodore repeated.

'Not that old story again, Theo, for heaven's sake. Come on, Cedric, you haven't contributed much to this argument. Aren't you going to support me?'

All eyes turned in Cedric's direction. But the enthusiasm of the converted was strangely lacking. Sighing, almost wearily, he said: 'You had better ask Maud. I leave matters involving the household to her. And I stay quietly out of sight when the builders move in.'

Maud laughed. 'But you did approve of the results, didn't you, dear? Be fair, now. You spend more time in the bathroom than any of us.'

Cedric shrugged. 'Yes, I have to be honest. I approved of the result. Once the dust cleared.'

'There, you've admitted it, Cedric,' Adrian said triumphantly.

Vince had complained to Faro that the serenity of the fifty-year-old town house in Charlotte Square had lately been shattered by a tide of architects and builders. One of the fine houses built by Robert Adam, it fell short only in lacking one of the indoor bathrooms now *de rigueur* for well-off families.

The Georgians had been content to deal with the natural functions by a commode behind the screen in the dining room and one under the bed for more intimate occasions, but those who could afford to be health conscious in modern Edinburgh now produced written evidence to add to their arguments.

'The spread of disease,' they claimed, 'undoubtedly begins in the home, where matters of hygiene can no longer be ignored.'

'Dammit, Cedric,' Adrian persisted, 'you told me that life had never been so good. So why don't you convince our stubborn brother here?'

'Priorsfield is his business, not mine.'

Adrian sighed warily and turned again to Theodore. 'Think of the advantages. You have more rooms than you know what to do with. What about HRH's ablutions when he visits? He's a heavy drinker, after all.'

'I get your meaning, but we do have a water closet, you know that perfectly well,' said Theodore stiffly.

'One wc. In a house this size,' said Adrian. 'And what does our architect think about that?'

Piers looked anxiously at Theodore. 'As Dr Langweil has pointed out, sir, this is not just a matter of vain extravagance. This ever-growing city of ours desperately needs up-to-date sanitation.' Having begun nervously, the architect now gathered the strength of conviction. 'And healthy citizens need more than efficient drains in the streets—'

'They do indeed,' said Adrian. 'We don't want any more out-breaks of cholera and typhoid. Isn't that right, Vince?'

Faro felt that his stepson would rather have been left out of this domestic argument, torn between pleasing his senior partner and displeasing Grace's uncle, as well as his future father-in-law.

'There are problems, quite serious ones, sir,' Vince said to Theodore. 'Ones I know you are fully aware of. All this new build-ing on the south side, the villas in Duddingston' – he pointed vaguely – 'have created new problems. For Priorsfield too.'

When Theodore did not respond, Vince went on. 'The rats which haunted the old Nor Loch have now taken refuge in newer buildings. A regular plague of them, which the city fathers are anxious to conceal, especially since the building of the railway station.'

'And with the rats go our worst diseases, we are sure of that,' said Adrian.

Turning his back on his brother, Theodore indicated Piers Strong, who having raised his hornets' nest, now shuffled miser-ably from foot to foot.

'Can't we leave this discussion until later, Adrian? Hardly fair to our guest—'

Piers regarded him gratefully.

'Or to Mr Faro—'

At that moment the dinner gong sounded.

'Splendid,' said Theodore, in tones of relief. 'Saved by the bell. Shall we proceed?'

As the family, now chattering happily, made their way in the direction of the dining room, Faro, hoping to escort Barbara, found she was claimed by Stephen, and offered his arm to Grace's mother. Half-way downstairs, Maud exclaimed: 'Oh, I have left my fan upstairs. Bother. Oh, would you, please? Bless you.'

As Faro ran lightly upstairs, the drawing-room door was open. Theodore was leaning forward, his hand gripping Cedric's shoulder.

'Look, I only invited the fellow here because you said he wanted to see over the house. Nothing more,' he added heavily. Suddenly aware of Faro's presence, he swung round and with a startled look almost guiltily released his hold of Cedric. 'Just telling him that what I do in my own house is my business. Don't you agree?'

Faro smiled. 'It's a gentleman's privilege after all.'

Following the two brothers downstairs, the scene he had witnessed, with its air of urgency, their strained faces, had a menacing quality which stubbornly remained, filling him with strange uneasiness.

Uneasiness very soon to be justified.

In the dining room, the candle-lit table could not be faulted. Silver and crystal gleamed, mahogany shone, there were skilfully arranged exotic flowers from the greenhouses on which Theodore prided himself.

Not only was the table exquisite but so too were the Langweil family. Almost, thought Faro, as if they had been chosen especially to grace the setting. Such a gathering gave him a vicarious sense of family pride, for as an only son, left fatherless in infancy, close kin was a commodity he had in very short supply.

The two brothers Theodore and Cedric had the perfection of features commonly associated with Greek gods, Cedric's unusual pallor accentuating the likeness to alabaster statues.

Of that handsome trio, Adrian's looks were most outstanding. Despite his intensive personal research into the effects of chloroform and dangerous excursions into new methods of alleviating human suffering, his complexion was radiant. Doubtless those hours on the golf course were responsible.

Looking across the table at Freda, his plump and pretty young wife, Faro realised that the strongest likelihood was that Adrian's branch of the family would eventually succeed if, as seemed likely, Theodore and Barbara remained childless.

Barbara. Faro found his gaze drifting back to her constantly, unable to linger, sure that he carried his heart in his eyes for this woman with all the ethereal beauty of an angel from a Botticelli painting. He found himself wondering uncharitably if Theodore had chosen her with the same meticulous care as he had collected the other adornments of his house.

Looking round the table he saw that he was not alone in his admiration. Each time she spoke, every male head turned eagerly in her direction. Her voice, with its slight American accent, was beautiful and unusual. Although she spoke rarely and only a little above a whisper, that was enough to still all other conversation.

Theodore obviously adored her. He had brought her home – 'captured her' as he called it – from one of his rare visits to New York. A fortunate man indeed. And Faro sighed at the game of chance that was life itself.

If Theodore had chosen for outstanding beauty, the same could not be said of Cedric. If Barbara's looks suggested the purity of a painted angel, Maud's finely boned features merely suggested a washed-out water colour abandoned by an indifferent artist.

He saw Vince glancing in her direction and wondered if the same thoughts were going through his stepson's mind. For this was an oft-discussed topic between them: why many handsome men chose plain wives. Vince called it the 'peacock syndrome', a kind of vanity whereby a man's own good looks were enhanced by a plain mate.

At his side, Grace was smiling across into Vince's eyes. A well-matched couple who gave the lie to Vince's theory, thought Faro with some satisfaction. Grace had inherited her father's exotic Langweil looks.

Piers Strong sat next to Vince and having discovered a sympathetic ear was waxing eloquent on the latest development in domestic sanitation and the city sewage systems.

Faro listened with some amusement to a monologue not entirely suitable for the dining table, but delivered with the same missionary zeal that Stephen Aynsley was expounding to Maud on heathen Africans.

'He has worked wonders with our house,' whispered Grace. At Faro's startled glance, she giggled.

'Not Stephen, Piers, I mean. Even Uncle Theodore was impressed with our two bathrooms. I can't imagine why he's so stubborn about making changes here.'

Faro smiled. Vince had told him that as a subject of admiration, visiting guests to Cedric's home were now taken directly upstairs to view and acclaim these new masterpieces of elegant plumbing.

'A little more wine, sir.'

Allowing Gimmond to refill his glass, Faro sat back in his chair. Listening to the gentle arguments, the laughter and teasing, the family jokes, he felt extremely well blessed.

Vince had done well, very well indeed. Much better than his earlier less fortunate ventures into prospective matrimony had suggested, and Faro thrust from his thoughts the disastrous choices that had blighted Vince in the past. As for his own fears that a young wife might have objections to a stepfather sharing their establishment, Grace could not have made it clearer that instead of losing a stepson he was gaining a stepdaughter.

Game soup and salmon had been followed by roast goose and a dessert of plum pudding. An excellent meal prepared and served with the meticulous attention to individual taste that made dining at Priorsfield House a gastronomic delight.

Only one apparently meaningless incident threw a faint shadow on that evening. Cedric twice retired hastily from the table in the middle of the meat and the dessert courses. Looks were exchanged but the company was too polite to do more than acknowledge his return.

To a whispered question from Maud, he said: 'Yes, of course, I'm all right, m'dear.' And leaning over he patted his daughter's hand. 'I've been celebrating rather too well before we sat down to dinner.'

Faro glanced round the table and caught a long look exchanged between Theodore and Adrian while Barbara studied her plate rather too intently, he thought, than the situation merited. Then without any further glance in Cedric's direction, hastily the brothers resumed the general conversation. This deliberate ignoring of Cedric struck a false note somehow. As if they were all too well aware of the cause of his withdrawal.

And Faro, well used to interpreting his own observations, felt uneasily that there was perhaps more in that moment of shared anxiety than could be justified by mere overindulgence in the Langweil cellars.

At last Barbara stood up. 'Shall we adjourn for coffee?'

This was a new innovation which had Faro's full approval. The Langweils on all but the most formal occasions had dispensed with the custom of gentlemen remaining to enjoy their port and cigars apart from the ladies.

The company followed into the upstairs parlour, a welcoming withdrawing room with rose velvet curtains and a glowing fire. Here the family visitors usually spent their evenings together, reading and listening to Barbara play the piano.

At Faro's side, Piers said: 'We are now in the oldest part of the house. This is the central block, the old tower-house.' And tapping his foot on the floor, 'Below us are the foundations of the original alehouse.' To Theodore he added: 'I suppose you realise, sir, that according to the original plans and the Session Records, this room was once considerably larger than it is now.'

The position of the fireplace, set two-thirds of the way along the wall, instead of centrally as was customary, was out of symmetry: a curiosity which had often jarred on Faro's earlier visits.

'One of Grandfather's alterations last century,' said Theodore.

'I don't think so, sir. Pardon me if I disagree but it is much more recent. When I was last here with Mrs Langweil and Mr Cedric—'

'While I was absent in Glasgow, of course,' said Theodore shortly with a veiled glance in his wife's direction.

'My dear, it was merely—' Barbara began.

As usual she was not allowed to complete the sentence.

Theodore patted her arm. 'I'm not blaming you, my dear, of course I'm not,' he added, with a gentle smile at her anxious expression.

'I merely thought, sir,' Piers put in, 'that this room, adjoining the drawing room, would have been in the old days the laird's study, or the master bedroom. However, there is something not quite right.' And tapping his foot on the floor, 'There's a ten-foot discrepancy in the original plans which I've had access to. You may be interested in seeing them—'

'No need,' said Theodore shortly. 'I'm fully aware that the room has been altered at some earlier stage. You know what it's like in these old houses, full of odd twists and turns. I'm sure you'll find some cupboards on a later plan that have been dismantled to enlarge the rooms.'

Piers was not to be put off. He continued eagerly: 'I believe you were born here, sir.'

'Indeed, as were all the family.'

'Then these changes must have been quite recent. In your childhood even. Perhaps you've forgotten?'

'No. I have already told you,' Theodore said coldly. 'There has been nothing done to this room.' And with a gesture, 'Not even decoration that I can recall.'

Piers turned hopefully towards Cedric, who shook his head.

'My brother is younger than I am,' said Theodore.

Cedric smiled. 'I expect it was in our Papa's day.'

'But that isn't possible, sir. The wallpaper—'

'Ah, here's the coffee. At last,' said Theodore, his relieved tone indicating boredom with the architect and his intensity.

The evening over, Faro and Vince declined the offer of a carriage in favour of walking the short distance home to Sheridan Place.

'We are thinking of a honeymoon in Paris,' said Vince. 'Are you pleased?'

'I am indeed, lad. It's great news. Hey, slow down. You're walking too fast.'

'You're out of condition, Stepfather. Have to get you out on the golf course. Nine holes before breakfast. That'll get you in perfect trim in no time.'

'I get enough exercise,' grumbled Faro, 'without chasing a blasted ball around a green.'

'You don't know what you're missing. Marvellous for the digestive system. A necessity after dining at Priorsfield.'

'Indeed, another memorable meal, but a little too rich for your future father-in-law. I can sympathise with him.'

'I didn't think he looked at all well,' said Vince.

'True. Very pale, I thought earlier in the evening.'

'You noticed that too.'

'I think you should recommend a few rounds of your golf to put some colour back in his cheeks.'

'As a matter of fact I am rather worried about him.'

'My dear lad, I've seen you just as bad – worse even – after a night out at Rutherford's—'

'It's more than that, Stepfather. This isn't the first time he's had to leave the table hurriedly during dinner. A weak digestion, he calls it.'

'And what does Adrian call it?'

'Oh, he gives him a bottle to help and grumbles that families with doctors never want to listen to their advice.'

Faro's own digestive system was not his strong point and he could understand Cedric's impatience. Especially as Vince's attempts to coddle him, as he called it, drove him to distraction.

'You know what he's talking about,' Vince added with a grin.

'I do indeed, but I don't usually have to take flight from the dining table in the middle of a meal.' Faro had long ago diagnosed his stomach upsets as due to the stress of a detective's life, with hasty, infrequent, and often inedible meals. Doubtless, Langweil Ales had their anxious business moments too.

But that look he had interpreted between Theodore and Cedric, as if they shared some secret awareness, continued to haunt him. It came to mind vividly when next day a constable brought into the Central Office a note from Vince.

Stepfather. Prepare yourself for a shock. Cedric died during the night. I am going to Priorsfield.

Faro carried the news into Superintendent McIntosh's office. 'Can't believe it, Faro. Saw him only yesterday morning. Seemed perfectly fine in wind and limb.'

When Faro told him about the dinner party, McIntosh shrugged.

'No one dies of indigestion. Doubtless his doctor brother will know the real cause.'

As they left together, the newsboys on the High Street were calling: 'Sudden Death of Cedric Langweil. Read all about it.'

Buying a paper, with McIntosh staring over his shoulder, Faro was somewhat frustrated to find only a heavily black-edged paragraph giving Cedric's age and brief biographical details.

'That's how they sell newspapers,' grumbled McIntosh.

As they parted and Faro headed home towards Sheridan Place, a series of melancholy pictures filled his thoughts. There would be a funeral, followed by six months' deep mourning for the family, before the marriage of Grace to Vince Laurie could now take place.

Suddenly the world of happy families he had pictured to himself only yesterday was no longer a reality. Ominously he felt it was in danger of collapsing like a house of cards.

*

Anxious for news he waited up until midnight, but Vince did not return until breakfast the following morning.

'Grace is inconsolable. As for her poor mother – the whole family are absolutely shocked. It seems quite unbelievable. None of them could have imagined such a catastrophe.'

Faro agreed sadly. In the tragedy of personal grief, Vince the doctor had been obliterated by Vince the lover, momentarily refusing to accept that the symptoms of indigestion could be also those of heart failure.

'Men do drop dead in the street every day, in what seems like healthy middle age,' Faro reminded him gently. 'And women too. I thought you might be used by now to sudden deaths, lad. It's only when it comes close to home, it's so very hard to bear—'

'If only you were right, Stepfather,' Vince groaned. 'But it's worse, much worse than you imagined.'

'In what way, worse? Sit down, lad. Come along now, have some breakfast.'

Vince went instead to the sideboard and poured himself a whisky.

'No. I need this more,' he said and huddled exhausted over the fire. 'I was expected to sign the death certificate.'

'He was a patient of yours? Not Adrian's?'

'A member of the family cannot sign the death certificate, you know that. Anyway, Adrian asked me to attend the whole family, for purely minor ailments, since they refused to take him seriously. You know how it is. They all seemed exceedingly healthy and I never had more than a cough bottle to make up for any of them. As for Cedric, he was adamant that he never saw doctors, especially siblings or their partners. All he has ever asked for was a prescription for his indigestion.'

'Which you dispensed?'

'No. Adrian always made it up.' Vince drained his glass and stared miserably at him. 'I did the routine death examination while Theodore stood at my elbow. I knew that he found it painful and he was very anxious that I sign the certificate and get it over with.'

Pausing, he shook his head. 'Then I knew I couldn't do it. There was something wrong.'

'Wrong?'

Vince nodded. 'Very wrong. You see, I was quite certain that I wasn't looking at a man who had died of a sudden heart attack.'

'Then what—'

Vince shook his head. 'Nor did he die of a massive dose of indigestion. As I examined him I had an uneasy suspicion that I was looking at a man who had died of poisoning. I've seen it all too often, those discoloured and inflamed patches on his skin, particularly over his abdomen. And I learned from Maud that what he politely called indigestion for the family's sake, was in fact chronic and persistent vomiting and diarrhoea.'

With a sigh he added, 'I hardly need to have the Marsh Test done on this one, Stepfather. The symptoms are unmistakable. Cedric died of arsenic poisoning.'

3 'I'm notifying the Procurator Fiscal,' said Vince, 'there will have to be a post-mortem. You can imagine all the trouble that is going to get me into, hinting that my future father-in-law's death was not due to natural causes.'

If this was to be a murder enquiry, which Faro also dreaded, for inevitably the investigation would land on his desk, then he had better save time by getting certain facts in the right order.

'You said Theodore was standing at your elbow. Surely you mean Adrian?'

'No. Adrian was away at Musselburgh at the crack of dawn. He's practising for a club championship, and of course that—'

'Wait a moment. You said, at the crack of dawn. Hold on, lad. Let's get back to the beginning. When did Cedric die?'

'During the night. They stayed at Priorsfield, as you know.'

'Was that unusual?'

'Not at all. They frequently do so after a dinner party.'

'And so Maud made the unfortunate discovery this morning, after Adrian had left for the golf course. How very distressing for her.'

'No, no. Early morning ritual is that the maid leaves trays outside the bedroom doors at seven o'clock and Maud noticed Cedric's was still there on her way down to breakfast at nine—'

'Wait a moment. Are you implying that Maud was not sleeping with Cedric that night?'

'Exactly. She was sharing with Grace. You see, Grace refuses to sleep alone at Priorsfield. When she was a little girl she had, well, rather a scaring experience.'

Vince seemed reluctant to continue and Faro prompted him: 'What happened?'

'She – thought – she saw a ghost. It wasn't just a dream because it happened more than once,' he added hastily. 'Everyone knows that small children often fancy they see things. I know it sounds ridiculous—'

'Not to me, it doesn't.'

Vince smiled. 'Of course, you're sympathetic, aren't you. Well, this will interest you. She always described his white bagwig and old-fashioned knee breeches – and how he walked straight through the wall.'

'And who was this spectre supposed to be? Any ideas?'

'From his dress, I should say the French officer who came to deliver the gold to Prince Charlie while he was preparing for the Battle of Prestonpans. The gold that might have changed the face of Scottish history.'

'One of many similar legends, I should say, of gold hidden and lost for ever.'

'Rather different in this case. The French count's ship came too late, pursued by ill luck, an English frigate, and then a storm. He arrived in Leith after Charles Edward had departed. Then rumour takes over. The alehouse keeper at their rendezvous, the original Langweil, if truth be told, got rid of him as he slept. Poisoned him and when things went against the Jacobites used the gold to bribe himself into Butcher Cumberland's favour.

'I don't think people give much credence to such rumours. But the whole thing was revived, Cedric told me, much to his family's distress when a skeleton was dug up in the grounds during the last century with a knife blade between its ribs.'

'Probably one of the Prince's gallant soldiers who had fallen foul of a drinking companion. People have very romantic imaginations, especially when it comes to historical misdeeds. No doubt Cedric had told Grace the story when she was quite small and she had dreamed the rest.'

'I agree. I think that is most likely the reason. Anyway it made quite an impression on her. Now she insists that her mother share her room.' Vince looked at Faro. 'You know, I was quite surprised when she told me she thought Priorsfield was haunted. Especially as Grace is such a sensible, practical sort of girl.' He sighed. 'How did I get on to all this?'

'You were telling me that Maud noticed the untouched tray outside Cedric's room as she went down to breakfast at nine.' Faro thought for a moment. 'But she didn't look into the room. Wasn't she curious?'

'Not at all. Theodore and Cedric boasted that they needed little sleep and they rarely retired before three. As on this occasion when they decided to polish off another bottle of Langweil claret as a nightcap.'

'Did they indeed?' said Faro significantly.

'No, no, Stepfather. It couldn't have been in the claret otherwise Theodore would have been poisoned too—'

'Unless the arsenic was added to Cedric's glass only.'

Vince registered astonishment. 'But that would mean – Theodore—'

Faro said nothing. But a demon in his brain said only one thing. If Theodore had murdered his brother for cause or causes still unknown, then he would hang.

And Barbara – Barbara will be free—

'You are wrong, Stepfather.' Vince interrupted his giddy tide of fantasy. 'It cannot be Theodore. I'll never believe that—'

'We won't know whether I'm right or wrong until we get all the facts together in their right order and see what we have left over. So at what time did Maud finally go into Cedric's bedroom?'

'About eleven o'clock. They had an engagement in Edinburgh

for lunch. Of course, she was in a terrible state of shock and Theodore raised the alarm immediately. The coachman was sent for me and when I arrived nearly an hour later I knew from the state of his body – rigor mortis had set in – that he had already been dead for several hours.'

'So the breakfast tray couldn't have been tampered with. Therefore his brother had been the last to see him alive – after they'd finished off that bottle together.'

'Surely you can't believe that? Why, they are devoted to each other—'

Faro cut short his protests. 'I'm trying to concentrate only on the facts. What you found when you got to Priorsfield. Namely, Cedric was dead and his brother anxious for you to sign the death certificate—'

He had hardly finished when the doorbell rang. The two men exchanged glances and, looking out of the window, Faro saw that the caller was Grace Langweil.

Mrs Brook ushered her into the drawing room. Throwing down her gloves, ignoring Faro, she rushed across to Vince.

'What is all this about? Uncle Adrian tells me that – that you made a great fuss over the – the – certificate for poor dear Papa. And that you refused to sign it. Refused,' she repeated, eyes wide in astonishment. 'Now they tell me that you are insisting that there must be a post-mortem. Vince – Vince, what in God's name has got into you? Are you mad or something?'

Suddenly she broke down sobbing and Vince took her into his arms. But she refused to be comforted and pulling away from him demanded: 'How could you be so cruel. How could you do this to Mama and me? And to our family who have always treated you with such kindness?'

'It has to be done, Grace.' Vince's voice sounded hollow.

'Has to? I don't understand "has too". I know about post-mortems. Surely you could permit my father' – she emphasised the words – '*my father* to go to his grave without carving up his poor body. Surely you owe us that much.'

Over his shoulder Vince gave a despairing glance at Faro who quietly left the unhappy pair. He saw them leave the house together, unspeaking, their faces pale, stony.

Shortly afterwards he departed on the train to investigate a fraud case near Musselburgh. Its intricacies kept his mind and energies away from the scene he had left at Sheridan Place and when he returned home late that evening, Vince was still absent.

At midnight his eyes drooped with weariness. It had been a long and gruelling day and he was glad to retire. Sleep was not to be his, however; he was alert at every sound, every footstep or carriage outside the house that might indicate Vince's return.

One thought refused to leave his mind. If Theodore was innocent, who then in that apparently devoted family should wish to poison Cedric Langweil? All evidence must incriminate the last person who had poured him a glass of wine, who was apparently the last one to see him alive.

Faro found himself hoping for a miracle, that the post-mortem would prove Vince's misgivings were wrong, for he knew his stepson too well not to understand the anguish this decision had given him. To go against the whole assembled family of the girl he was to marry and declare that her father and their beloved brother had not died of natural causes.

Dawn was breaking, the first birds cheeping in the garden, when at last he drifted off into an uneasy slumber.

At the breakfast table Mrs Brook had a message for him. 'A lad has just handed in this note from Mr Vince, sir.'

Detained on a confinement case. Theodore would like us both to present ourselves at Priorsfield at four o'clock this afternoon.

In happier circumstances Faro would have enjoyed the walk to Wester Duddingston. There were swans gliding on the loch's mirrored surface and in the pale muted sunshine he stopped at a vantage point to gaze back at where a dwarfed castle crouched like a heraldic beast on a horizon misted with the approach of day's end. This was his favourite hour, his favourite aspect of Edinburgh.

A city of dreams and a city of nightmares where the past walked close to the present. Close your eyes and you could sense that the past was alive and that history was still happening.

As he approached the gates of Priorsfield with its lawns rolling down to meet the rushes of Duddingston Loch, a skein of geese moved overhead, their faint cries filling the still air with a melancholy sweetness as they circled to feed on the rich sandbanks of the River Forth.

To think that mere hours ago he had approached this house with such hopes and optimism for the future. Already it seemed like part of another happier world, and, filled with sudden ominous dread for what lay ahead, he wondered as he walked up the front steps whether any of them would again be so happy and carefree as that last fateful dinner party, with no greater problem than whether or not to install a new bathroom.

Vince had already arrived. And taking him by the arm, he said:

'They're upstairs, in the drawing room.'

The family were assembled, waiting; silent, subdued under the curious numbness of sudden and unexpected bereavement. Their funereal blacks contrasted strangely with the garden glowing under the approach of sunset. In the shrubbery a robin added his plaintive winter song and a blackbird's warning cry was lost in the strident screech of one of the Priorsfield peacocks.

With a slight bow in Faro's direction Theodore stood up and with his back to the fire addressed them, his manner little different from that used to point out some approaching crisis to the shareholders of Langweil Ales.

'Since Dr Laurie has cast doubt on the probable cause of my

brother's unfortunate death, as head of the family I have asked you to be present on this occasion to put on record that we are all in agreement that a post-mortem, however regrettable and distasteful to us, must be carried out. Before the matter proceeds any further there are certain other matters involved.' Pausing he looked directly at Faro. 'You get my meaning, Inspector.'

The formal address left no doubt whatever in Faro's mind as Theodore continued: 'I mean, of course, that following notification to the Procurator Fiscal, a police investigation might ensue into the possible cause of Cedric's death.'

A shocked silence followed an outbreak of whispered comments. Anxious looks were exchanged and angrier hurt looks directed towards Faro.

A moment later Theodore continued: 'I think we should make it plain to the Inspector that all of us, with the exception of Grace here' – he looked across with gentle compassion to where she huddled close to her mother's side, clutching her hand for comfort – 'all of us present can verify that Cedric's death was not in the least unexpected.'

Heads were nodded in agreement as he turned again towards Faro. 'My brother was in fact gravely ill. Dying. We have all been sadly aware that for the past six months he was suffering from an incurable brain disease and that his days were numbered.'

'Oh, no, no.' The cry was from Grace and Maud put her arms around her. 'Hush, darling. Hush.'

'No, Mama, it can't be—'

'My darling, I assure you it was. But your happiness was his main concern, we were to keep it from you—' Maud's voice failed and as she sobbed quietly Theodore went over and took Grace's hands.

'Dearest child. It was your papa's earnest wish to spare you, his only child, so that you would prepare in joy for your wedding, and even that he would still be with us and well enough to lead you down the aisle.'

'Oh, Papa, dear Papa,' Grace sobbed. Now it was Vince's turn to reach out for her, but turning from him she clung to her mother.

'Naturally this secrecy he imposed upon us all has been a great strain,' said Theodore. 'Especially Adrian—'

Faro and Vince looked quickly at Adrian, who nodded slowly as Theodore went on: 'He did not wish to involve his own brother, I'm sure the reasons are only too obvious and painful to need any further explanation.'

'He asked me to recommend another physician,' said Adrian. 'I suggested he consult Wiseman in Heriot Row.'

'Who will confirm all I have told you,' said Theodore to Faro. 'I am sure this will put your mind at rest when Wiseman gives you details of the magnitude of my brother's illness.' Then, to Vince: 'Although we can heartily commend Dr Laurie's integrity and need for absolute truth and scrupulous accuracy, the result was unfortunately a little ill timed without being in full possession of the true facts leading to my brother's death.'

His thin-lipped smile and slight bow in Vince's direction contained, Faro thought, not a little barely concealed resentment.

'Since Mr Cedric was consulting Dr Wiseman, why was he not called upon to sign the death certificate?' Vince demanded sharply.

Theodore sighed. 'He was. But unfortunately for us, as he was at a family wedding in Ireland and neither available nor immediately accessible, it seemed the most natural thing in the world that Dr Laurie, as our family physician, should perform this merely routine task—'

'If you had thought to inform me, sir—' Vince began desperately, and turning to his partner, 'Or you, Adrian,' he added accusingly.

Theodore spread his hands wide. 'Gentlemen, gentlemen. What's done is done. No one is to blame.'

Pausing he glanced at the clock significantly and then

addressed Vince and Faro. 'There is much to do. I am sure you will both appreciate that this is a difficult time for us.'

As they rose to leave, accompanied by Adrian, Theodore added: 'I'm sure we can rely on your discretion not to make the unhappy circumstances of my brother's death more painful for us than is absolutely necessary. And now we have important family business matters to discuss. Our lawyer Mr Moulton will be arriving shortly. Perhaps you will excuse us?'

In the hall an elderly man, white haired, bearded, his slightly built frame exuding an air of authority, was handing his cape and tall hat to Gimmond. Faro's first thought was that he was an undertaker by the solemnity of his attire.

'Good day to you, Dr Langweil,' he addressed Adrian. 'Permit me to take this opportunity to express the sincere condolences of our establishment on the sad loss of your brother, and indeed to all the family. Such empty places—'

Adrian cut short the threatened eulogy, which promised to be lengthy, with a bow. 'Thank you, Mr Moulton. I believe Theodore is awaiting you in the drawing room.'

The lawyer's manner seemed to crumple. 'Oh, indeed,' he said nervously. 'If you will excuse me, gentlemen,' he added and walked quickly upstairs.

'What a bore the man is,' whispered Adrian, catching up with Faro and Vince who had reached the front door. 'We used to call him Old Mouldy when we were children. His documents are even wordier than he is.' Then taking Vince's arm, he said: 'If only you'd mentioned your suspicions to me, I could have cleared up all this unfortunate business at once.'

'I doubt that,' was Vince's sharp reply.

'For heaven's sake, I had no idea that was what was in your mind when you wouldn't sign the death certificate. I thought, fool that I was, that it was because you regarded it as not right and proper – since you were – almost – one of the family—'

*

And so Cedric Langweil's body was interred in the family vault at Greyfriars Kirk with all the pomp and splendour attributable to a high-ranking citizen. It was one of the largest funerals Edinburgh had ever witnessed and brought crowds of sightseers into the High Street. St Giles was tightly packed and the funeral oration, conducted by Reverend Stephen Aynsley, as cousin of the deceased, told of 'a grave illness courageously borne and kept secret from all but the members of his own family'.

While all this was happening in the public eye, Cedric Langweil's main organs were being subjected to the Marsh Test for arsenic, carried out in the police laboratory at Surgeons' Hall.

Vince awaited the results with some apprehension, finding himself in a now totally unenviable position, made to feel by his future wife's family that he had let them down badly.

'They've done so much for me, and now the way they look at me, the coldness in their attitudes, makes me feel as if I've betrayed them. The hint is that I have brought their good name into disrepute and have also heartlessly besmirched the reputation of a dying man.'

'Surely Grace believes in your good intentions,' said Faro.

'Of course. The dear girl is loyal to me, but she is naturally torn by the deep-rooted image of her devoted family. Then of course, there is her poor mother's anguish. It's worse for her than any of them. Damn it, if only I had signed the wretched certificate and let it go at that. If only Adrian had told me that Cedric was dying anyway, I could have accepted that he had taken his own life.'

Faro looked at his stepson in shocked surprise. 'Vince, lad, you couldn't do that. It's against everything you've ever believed in. Sign a declaration that might be false—'

'I know, I know. But now there is so much at stake. My own personal happiness and Grace's. We love each other, but now I see this scandal of her father's death will always be between us. A dark shadow.'

'A shadow that time will erase, when two people love each other,' said Faro soothingly, aware that his voice carried little personal conviction.

Twenty-four hours later his suspicions were proved right. Vince returned to Sheridan Place and threw down the report of the post-mortem on the table in front of him. 'Well, Stepfather, it seems I was right to trust my instincts and observations, scant good that they will do me. There was no trace of a brain disease or any other evidence of ill-health. His heart and lungs were sound. In fact, whatever the Langweils' claim, Cedric was a healthy man in the prime of life who might reasonably have expected to live for another thirty years.' Vince sighed. 'I had actually been hoping that he had some incurable illness and had taken his own life. But not now. Someone is lying,' he added heavily.

The same thought had been running through Faro's mind.

Now, putting his hand on the report, Vince regarded him solemnly. 'According to this, the stomach contents revealed that Cedric Langweil died of arsenic poisoning. He had in fact six times the normal fatal dose.'

So their worst fears were realised.

'I dread to think how this will affect me. And Grace. As for you, Stepfather, it looks as if you might well have a murder investigation on your hands.'

This was a situation Faro knew only too well. After the post-mortem, the verdict of cause of death; and then all the heavy machinery of criminal investigation by the Edinburgh City Police would go into immediate action, as personified by Detective Inspector Faro.

Someone had poisoned Cedric Langweil. Faro had no doubt that whoever spread the rumour that Cedric was dying was also his murderer. In the present case, clues to the identity of the killer were painfully easy to follow. And sooner rather than later the guilty person must be run to earth, charged, brought to trial. And hanged by the neck.

No other way, no way of escaping or forestalling the law's mechanism existed. And it was no consolation to Faro to recognise that in the particular province of murder detection lay his greatest skills. Skills which he must exercise to the full extent of his powers regardless of the fact that he and his stepson were both intimately concerned not only with the guilty but also with the innocent members of the murdered man's family.

He had not the least doubt, nor he guessed had Vince, that Cedric Langweil's killer would be unmasked with a minimum of effort, found where poisoners were almost always found, in the bosom of that apparently devoted family circle.

There was no pride in knowing that there was only one prime suspect to follow. When he was brought to trial the sufferings of the other Langweils would be intense as their emotions and motives were laid bare and subjected to enquiry and careful scrutiny. For the guilty man's motive, he did not doubt, would not have changed since Cain had killed his brother, Abel. Gain, or jealousy or secret resentment that had festered over many years.

What secrets were they about to unlock? Faro wondered. And how would their revelation affect, distort, or change for ever the hopes of marriage between Vince and Grace?

Knowing that in his hands lay the outcome of an investigation calculated to destroy all hopes of two young people's happiness, Detective Inspector Jeremy Faro was a profoundly unhappy man.

4 On being informed that Dr Wiseman was expected back in Edinburgh later that day, Vince and Faro set off to call upon Theodore Langweil.

'If only we could have seen Wiseman first,' said Vince. 'This is most unfortunate.'

The visit to Priorsfield at least promised to be both painful and brief.

Faro observed Theodore Langweil narrowly as he read the post-mortem report on his brother. His expression remained impassive. Although his hands shook as he laid it aside, such reaction was understandable, and his lips moved silently, as if repeating the monstrous conclusions of the report.

A beloved brother murdered.

Bewildered he gazed helplessly from Faro to Vince and back again. Then he shook his head several times like a man awakening from a dreadful nightmare as he searched for some explanation.

'I cannot understand this at all. It is as I told you,' he said dully. 'We all knew that Cedric had been seriously ill, fatally ill, for the last six months. Wiseman will confirm that, whatever this wretched piece of paper says. Why don't you ask him?'

Vince said: 'There is one possible explanation, sir. Knowing that he was dying, could he not have taken his own life?'

'Impossible. I could never entertain such a thought,

not for one moment. He was a courageous man. And he would never have done such a thing. He loved life.' Silent for a moment, he looked towards the window with its darkening clouds.

'The fact that it was to be short made it even more precious. He was determined to live it to the utmost. "Every minute of every hour of every day, Theo." Those were his very words to me, here in this room.'

'What about pain, sir?' asked Vince gently. 'Was he not afraid that he might suffer a great deal?'

'He had learned to live with blinding headaches. He told us the consultant had assured him that with the help of a little morphine – near the end – the end would be speedy, total collapse, a coma, days only. But you are no doubt aware of all this, surely, Dr Laurie,' he added irritably.

Vince nodded. 'It rather depends upon the exact location of the tumour.'

With a sigh Theodore continued, 'I know of one very good reason why Cedric would not have taken his own life. There was a very large insurance taken out at the time of Grace's birth and this, as you know, would be forfeit if he had taken his own life.'

Looking at their faces, he said, 'I see you are not convinced, but I have one other reason for believing that he did not intend to die. There were important documents awaiting his signature.' He tapped a drawer. 'They are still here in my desk.'

'May I ask what was the nature of these documents?' Faro asked.

'Transfer of business shares. Oh, nothing serious. We were merely selling some properties. I can assure you that we are not in danger of bankruptcy.' Staring again towards the window, he frowned. 'He also talked of revising his will.'

'In what way revising?' said Faro sharply. In his experience changed wills were frequently the cause of mysterious and totally unexpected family fatalities.

'I am not at liberty to discuss such matters at present,' was the scornful reply. 'But I can tell you that the clauses under discussion related to the family business concerns only. I hope all this information satisfies you.'

It did not satisfy Faro at all, but presumably Theodore was now aware that in the event of a murder enquiry – should he, as the prime suspect, be accused of his brother's murder – then such information and more, much more, painful information must be laid bare.

Theodore left his desk and indicating that the interview was over, held open the door for them. 'I leave to your imagination the embarrassment to say nothing of the distress your somewhat over-conscientious behaviour has caused this family in their time of sorrow and bereavement.'

Oh, Barbara, Faro thought. If only I could spare you the humiliation, the grief of all that is to follow. Not only Barbara, but Grace too. And Vince.

For although Theodore's remark applied to both men, his resentful glance sliding off Vince held this impulsive young doctor his niece was to marry directly responsible for this dread blight on the Langweil name.

'There are a lot of things that require explanation,' said Faro as they walked homewards, breaking the long silence between them, for Vince wrapped in his own despair had not yet given thought to the shortcomings in Theodore's statement.

'First of all, what I still fail to understand is why Adrian did not warn you of Cedric's condition.'

'Loyalty to the family and all that, I suppose. You must remember, Stepfather, that he wasn't expecting Cedric's end to be by poisoning either.'

'What about this prescription Adrian gave him?'

'For indigestion, you mean?'

'Yes, how often would he take a dose of it?'

'Whenever he had an attack. I imagine. Or if attacks were persistent, then last thing at night.'

'Then doubtless he took at least one dose during or after the dinner party.'

'I should imagine he would have done that, yes. Hold on, Stepfather,' Vince laughed uneasily. 'You're not suggesting that Adrian's simple mixture—'

'I'm only suggesting from the facts known to us that the poison was administered sometime before Cedric retired at three o'clock. Either in a glass of wine or in a spoonful of medicine.'

'Meaning that the chief suspects are now Theodore and Adrian. Is that what you are suggesting?'

'Or Maud. Or one of the staff. Oh, I don't know, lad. All I'm indicating is that we are only at the beginning and we need to know a lot more about those critical last hours Cedric spent at Priorsfield. Did he really believe he was dying, or did someone persuade him that he was a doomed man?'

'Our only hope is Dr Wiseman. We've met on the golf course. Let's hope he'll be able to throw some light on this wretched business.'

Outside his house, Dr Wiseman was paying off the carriage which had brought him and his travelling bag from the railway station.

Faro's first impression was of a younger man than the affluent middle-aged consultant he had expected to meet. Or perhaps, he thought wryly, like policemen, doctors gave the illusion that as one got older, they got younger.

His confidence in the interview was also blighted by realisation that their arrival was most inopportune. Wiseman appeared very put out and agitated, especially when he learned the nature of Dr Laurie's visit and that he was accompanied by a police detective.

'Yes, indeed, I read about Mr Cedric Langweil's death in the London newspapers when I got back from Ireland.'

When they showed no signs of departing he invited them into the house with certain reluctance, watching the maid carrying his luggage upstairs. Finally he ushered them into what appeared as a bleak and inhospitable consulting room.

'Please take a seat, gentlemen. What can I do for you?'

'We need some information about your patient, Doctor,' said Faro.

Dr Wiseman was trying hard not to tremble. 'What kind of information?'

'Dr Langweil has given us to understand that his brother consulted you.'

Dr Wiseman frowned. 'Yes, I believe so,' he said vaguely.

'Then perhaps you knew something of his case history.'

'Case history?' he repeated warily.

'We understand from the family that Cedric Langweil was incurably ill, that he had a disease of the brain,' said Vince, 'and that he had only a short while to live.'

Dr Wiseman's bewildered glance went from Vince to Faro and back again. 'I'm sorry to hear that, gentlemen. Very sorry indeed.' And shaking his head, 'What you say may be true, but it is new to me. I assure you he never consulted me about any such condition. Your informant is mistaken. It must have been some other physician.'

'Are you sure?' demanded Vince.

'I am indeed. As I am personally acquainted with Dr Adrian and have had the honour of attending various members of the family, it is unlikely that I would not have remembered such an illustrious patient as Cedric Langweil.'

Dr Wiseman smiled and in his expression Faro detected relief. Somehow this was not what he had been expecting.

'I do apologise for having seemed so vague when you asked me about him. You see, I think I only saw Cedric professionally once and that was when he had a festered thumb. I have attended Miss Langweil and her mother on one or two trivial medical matters.'

'You don't know then who he might have consulted?'

'I'm sorry. I haven't the least idea. But surely Mrs Langweil would be the one to ask.'

A now very cheerful Dr Wiseman saw them to the door, his parting remarks about the coming golf championship and comforting words on the present state of Vince's handicap. With an early meeting proposed between two doctors, they shook hands and parted most cordially.

As they headed towards Princes Street, Vince said: 'I don't know about you, Stepfather, but I'm completely baffled. Why on earth did Cedric lie to his family about Wiseman? A complete waste of time, and very embarrassing for a colleague, I can tell you. And we're not one whit wiser now than we were before.'

But Faro, remembering Wiseman's anxiety, had his own thoughts on the matter. 'I wonder who is lying. You realise, lad, that in the circumstances, with no evidence apart from his family's insistence that Cedric was a dying man, we now have no other option than to treat this as a murder case.'

At the Central Office, Superintendent McIntosh wasn't at all pleased by this turn of events as he threw down the post-mortem report on to his desk and regarded Faro darkly across the table.

'This is your province, Faro, and frankly not one I envy you. Dashed difficult I know, with your stepson almost a member of the family. And the Langweils respected pillars of society. I'm afraid this is going to create one hell of a scandal.'

McIntosh's feelings were understandable, since he too had enjoyed the Langweil hospitality at Priorsfield over a number of years.

'If only we hadn't brought in the Fiscal,' he sighed. 'I suppose we could have ignored it. Presumed that the poor chap had taken his own life. Not unusual in the circumstances for a dying man to be unable to face up to the last weeks—'

'Look here, sir,' Faro interrupted, 'you know as well as I do that if Langweil was poisoned, for some motive as yet unknown to us, then the possibility exists that the murderer will strike again.'

'He or she,' McIntosh reminded him, 'especially as the first place you'll need to look is in the victim's family circle.' He shrugged. 'Devoted family like that too.'

Faro regarded him cynically. The words were beginning to have a familiarly hollow ring. As for his superior, McIntosh could display almost childlike credulity at times, quite at odds with a tough exterior and more than thirty years' experience of violent crimes and criminals.

His own thoughts at that moment were concentrated not only on who had given Cedric Langweil an overdose of arsenic, but also on why? To kill a man known to be dying imminently called for an exceptional motive. If he could find it, then he was half-way to success.

His compassion lay with the murdered man's daughter Grace and the inevitable repercussions on her relationship with Vince when his detective stepfather metaphorically tightened the noose around the neck of one of her so-called 'devoted family'.

Walking slowly homeward through the moonlight, the cold and pitiless beauty of a frosty evening with the stars bright above Salisbury Crags, Faro thought sadly how so much beauty wears a mask of cruelty. And he remembered his own thoughts of a week ago, how he had been congratulating himself on how well their lives were going.

'Tempting the gods,' he said out loud. 'I should have known better.' That's what always happens. Measure happiness, feel secure, and it all vanishes like fairy gold.

His next call must be upon Cedric's widow, Maud. Fully aware of the nature of questions to be asked, such poking and prying into her distressed and shocked condition filled him with a natural disgust.

Could he take the coward's way out and ask if the enquiry

could be delegated to someone else? He was sorely tempted. Knowing Vince's personal involvement with the Langweils, McIntosh would understand.

The more he thought of it the greater temptation became, but even more clearly came realisation that he could not abandon Vince and the Langweils. The fact that his stepson was involved made it even more imperative that he personally solve the case. He could not take a chance on some other less experienced detective, working on a case where the evidence of one suspect was so inviting, reaching a false and fatal conclusion.

Distasteful as it was, he had no alternative but to proceed along the given lines. He needed a helper, someone strong, steady, and reliable, and the face of Danny McQuinn passed uneasily before his eyes. Once his old enemy, Sergeant McQuinn had recently returned enriched by his experience working with the Glasgow City Police. Whatever his personal feelings, Faro knew McQuinn would be a good man to have at his side.

Although his methods were a little too ruthless and tactless for the genteel drawing rooms of middle-class Edinburgh, McQuinn's easy manner and common touch were particularly expert in extracting confidences from the servants' hall. He had a natural charm with the female sex, which Faro had secretly envied when on more than one occasion such information had helped to solve a baffling case.

Black-haired, blue-eyed, with an abundance of Irish charm and good looks, the sergeant listened intently when Faro put the facts of the case before him. 'Superintendent McIntosh wants this conducted with the utmost discretion.'

'You can rely on me for that, sir. I suggest the kitchens at Priorsfield would be a good place to begin.'

As they parted, McQuinn saluted him gravely and then with a cheeky grin. 'Good to work with you again, sir. You'll be pleased to know that Glasgow has sharpened my wits.'

Not that they needed much sharpening, was the rejoinder

Faro might have made in the past but now bit back in the interests of diplomacy.

Before leaving the Central Office, he learned that arson was now added to the perplexing fraud case near Musselburgh. He set off on the train once more, deciding that if the poisoner of Cedric Langweil lurked, as he suspected, within the family circle, it did no harm to allow a couple of days for the shock of possible exposure to take its toll of already frayed nerves.

As the train carried him towards his destination Faro considered the motives of his two chief suspects in the Langweil case. Theodore, who had shared the last bottle of wine with Cedric, and could so easily have tampered with the final glass. Was there some information about the family business that had decided him to speed on his brother's end, before new documents could be drawn up or an existing will revised?

Then there was Adrian, Vince's friend and partner. Adrian, who had personally dispensed the powder for his brother's indigestion.

Perhaps Adrian had the best motive of all. Inheritance. Cedric's death drew him one step nearer the Langweil fortune. Yet that didn't make sense either, if he believed that his elder brother was doomed anyway.

Of the two, Faro favoured Theodore. And he knew the reason why. Barbara. But even if she were free, did goddesses ever marry policemen?

Turning his thoughts away from such folly he was conscious of something at the back of his mind which was of vital importance. A shadowy something he had seen, or heard, that suggested he might, unlike this train, be on the wrong track completely when on Monday morning those other wheels of the law went into motion.

The opening of the official enquiry, police interviews with the

Langweils, and the inevitable unpleasantness of muddied waters vigorously stirred, signalled the investigation he knew he had least wanted in his whole career.

Before that the weekend lay before him, two whole days with his daughter Rose, a small oasis in a desert of despair.

5 Faro watched while the Orkney boat docked at Leith, his spirits downcast by the icy wind blowing across the River Forth.

Vince and Grace had insisted on accompanying him. Leaving them in the carriage, both pretending that nothing in their lives had changed, he wished more than ever that he could have delayed or postponed Rose's arrival.

He had an ominous feeling whatever the outcome of the official enquiry into the circumstances of Cedric's death this domestic tragedy must inevitably touch and indeed even engulf his own household.

His mind was so absorbed by his misgivings that he failed to recognise immediately the young woman who was waving to him so frantically from the boat rail.

It took him several seconds to realise that this was his daughter Rose. A new Rose in a fashionable blue velvet cape and bonnet. As she ran lightly down the gangway and he clasped her in his arms, he realised that his little lass had vanished for ever.

Their embrace told him that this Rose was already rounded in early womanhood. It came as a considerable shock that the six months that had elapsed since their last meeting could have brought about such changes, giving much and, alas, taking much away.

As she kissed him, and clinging to his arm hurried towards the waiting carriage, he had only time to warn her that Grace had lost her father before the two leaped from the carriage to greet them.

And now Faro saw his own astonishment mirrored in Vince's eyes. Having hugged her stepbrother, Rose was shyly greeting Grace. Watching the two girls, Faro and Vince exchanged glances, delight on Vince's face, bewilderment, even a little resentment on Faro's, for to the casual observer, Rose, well-rounded, and Grace, slightly built, seemed little different in age.

And Faro saw too with a pang of loss that Rose was going to be as curvaceous and bonny as her mother his dear Lizzie had been, except that she was taller, and her resemblance to Vince, the same blond curls and bright eyes, was steadily increasing with the years.

As they headed for Sheridan Place, Rose spoke gently to Grace, offering her condolences. Grace's eyes filled with tears while Vince and Faro too felt the echoes of that anguish, the full depths of the tragedy which had robbed her of a beloved papa and had stricken that happy carefree family to the heart.

Grace looked across at Vince and said sadly, 'Our wedding, alas, has had to be postponed'

But Grace was too sensible and practical a young person to let her own deep sorrow cloud over Rose's arrival in Edinburgh. Straightening her shoulders, she dabbed at her eyes and tried a brave smile. 'You know, of course, that I was once a pupil at the Grange Academy for Young Ladies. In fact, it was on my recommendation that Vince chose it for you. They have an excellent reputation in the department of foreign languages.'

She spoke enthusiastically about the teachers and the rules. But like all schoolgirls, it was the uniform that concerned Rose most of all. 'Is it becoming?' she asked anxiously.

'My dear, I would never have recommended it otherwise.'

Rose smiled gratefully at Vince. But such trivialities had not been the reason for his choice. Certain that marriage into the Langweil family would open up all manner of splendid

matrimonial chances for his pretty stepsister, Vince felt the acquisition of a little extra culture and learning would not come amiss
in the circles in which they would move.

Rose's reasons were quite different, her ambitions more
modest than those of her stepbrother. Her heart long set on
becoming a governess, she fancied this was the way for a young
lady to enjoy foreign travel. And the acquisition of French and
German would be to her advantage.

'The Queen has made Scotch governesses very popular among
European royalty,' said Grace encouragingly. 'Especially when so
many of them are related to her. And we have lots of very
distinguished contacts in foreign embassies, have we not, Vince?'

Grace, smiling, tried to include him in the conversation, while
Rose listened wide-eyed to the prospects opening before her.

When at last Rose and her father were deposited at Sheridan
Place, Grace declined the invitation to join them for tea.

'I do not care to leave Mama on her own just at present,' she
said apologetically. 'But very soon you shall come to tea with
your father and I will take you to all the best shops in Princes
Street.'

Delighted with such a promise, hugs were exchanged under
the approving eye of Vince. Then the door of 9 Sheridan Place
opened and Rose was delivered into the welcoming arms of the
housekeeper Mrs Brook. Her 'bairn' was home again.

'Let me look at you, Miss Rose. My, you are a young lady
now. How you've grown. I'd never have recognised you, not even
if we had passed one another in Princes Street. Isn't she lovely,
Inspector? Aren't you proud of your little girl. And you, Dr
Vince, what have you to say?'

The two men murmured the replies expected of them as Rose,
sparkling-eyed, was swept upstairs to her room by Mrs Brook.
'Now tell me all about Miss Emily—'

*

As they sat down to dinner that evening, Faro too wished for news of his younger daughter, feeling guilty that she had not accompanied her sister.

Rose shook her head. 'Emily does not mind in the least. She is happy and content in Kirkwall. She is clever with her hands, not like me; she thrives on cold winds and stormy days,' she added with a shudder. 'Edinburgh frightens little Emily, Papa. She loathes sea voyages and besides, she says she would hate to live in a great city. I think she will be quite content to settle down with an Orkney farmer some day. And she shouldn't have much trouble finding a husband. Already the young men have an eye on her, much to Grandmama's distress.'

Leaning across the table, she smiled at him. 'We aren't a bit alike really. I take after you, Papa. You've always said that. And now I see it's true. I'm eternally curious, I want to know everything about everything . . .'

Faro was inordinately proud of Rose, as they walked arm in arm along the Princes Street Gardens after church on Sunday, aware of admiring glances in her direction and delighted to introduce her to several acquaintances who were more ardent churchgoers than himself.

Conscious that religion played a very small part in his own life, Faro felt that like marriage it seemed too complicated for a policeman to handle successfully. But shy of admitting such a fact to his daughter, he had accompanied her to St Giles where – it seemed only a few years ago – she had been christened.

Walking in the warm sunshine, his present anxieties about the Langweils retreated to a safe distance, banished by Rose's enthusiasm. Her energy limitless, she insisted on visiting all her favourite places again.

Calton Hill, the Castle, and Holyrood Park. From the top of Arthur's Seat they looked on Edinburgh spread out before them, the distant prospect of the Bass Rock, the East Lothian coastline.

Rose clapped her hands excitedly. 'Well, Papa, where now?'

'No more, I beg you,' Faro groaned. 'Unless you want to carry your poor father home.'

The promise of afternoon tea, with scones and cakes delectably prepared by Mrs Brook, was all the temptation a healthy young appetite needed.

As they ate together, and laughed and reminisced, he realised that his brief sojourn in the happy world of domesticity was almost over. Tomorrow loomed unpleasantly near. And tomorrow he would be Detective Inspector Faro again, with all that implied.

When, early on Monday morning, Faro entered Charlotte Square and walked up the front steps of the Langweil town house to talk to Cedric's widow, he was in time to encounter Dr Wiseman taking his departure.

The doctor greeted him nervously, eyeing him with some suspicion.

'I trust you are not here in an official capacity, Inspector. My patients are understandably shocked and upset.'

'Quite so, Doctor. This is just a routine matter.'

As he walked away, the doctor turned. 'For your information, Inspector, I cannot think of any reason why Cedric Langweil should have pretended to be seriously ill. He would never have needlessly distressed his family. Or anyone else. He was a kind father and husband.'

'Then who told him that he was a dying man? He must have consulted someone?'

'I haven't the least idea who he consulted. Except that it wasn't myself. You are the detective, sir. Perhaps if you could find the missing doctor, you might get more results than plaguing his unfortunate family.'

'I appreciate your sentiments, Doctor, but I am not conducting this enquiry for my own pleasure. My stepson and Miss Langweil are shortly to be married. They – and I – are intimately concerned in the outcome of this enquiry. I assure you we are all distressed by this unhappy turn of events—'

'Is that so?' Wiseman interrupted sharply. 'Then all I can say is that Dr Laurie might have handled the whole affair with more discretion.'

'By discretion, am I to presume you mean ignoring the obvious?'

Dr Wiseman smiled bitterly. 'I can assure you, Inspector, that what you call the obvious has been done by many in the medical profession before today, and I dare say will be done often again, and for no more sinister purpose than to spare the family.'

'Suppressing dangerous evidence, Doctor. Is that what you are implying?'

Wiseman shrugged. 'Surely it is not beyond the bounds of possibility even for you to imagine that a man who feared he was gravely ill might decide to take his own life.'

'Except that by suicide his family would forfeit any insurance claim.'

'I doubt that the matter of an insurance made forfeit would weigh very heavily upon the fortunes of the Langweils. As for Mrs Cedric Langweil, it is no secret that she is very well connected.'

Pausing to let that information sink in, he said: 'And I understand that Miss Langweil inherits a comfortable income on her twenty-first birthday. By which time she will be the wife of Dr Laurie. All going well in that direction, of course,' he added significantly. 'Good day to you, sir.'

For a physician who rarely attended the Langweils, Wiseman was particularly well informed about his patient's prospects, Faro thought as he waited in the extravagantly furnished hall with its marble statues, staircase, and lofty cupola.

Town houses in an expanding Edinburgh were no longer a necessity for the rich. With better roads Priorsfield House was easily accessible; the long and tortuous coach journey to Duddingston, liable to be snowbound in winter, was a distant memory. Considering the size of Priorsfield a separate establishment for the younger brother seemed excessive, especially at a time when all over Edinburgh less fortunate families shared one bedroom and the poor of the High Street tenements lived out their lives in one room.

Doubtless Cedric had his own reasons for not wishing to reside in one vast wing of the family home.

'Perhaps the reason that they have a close business relationship makes living apart desirable. Or possibly their wives wish to be independent,' Vince had told him. 'Grace tells me that her parents moved into Charlotte Square soon after Theodore remarried. Now don't you feel that is significant? The young wife with new young ideas. I fear Maud is a little conventional, rather rigid in her outlook.'

Alerted by footsteps above, it was Grace Langweil who stared down at him from the upper floor. Running lightly down the stairs to greet him, he fancied that she kissed his cheek with less enthusiasm than she had done hitherto.

'I was expecting Rose to be with you. I hoped to take her shopping with me. I presume it is Mama you wish to see.'

Faro was aware of a coolness about his future step-daughter-in-law that he regarded ominously. He had hoped that the pleasant interlude of Rose's arrival had put them back on their former easy footing. However, her manner said plainer than any words that he was already regarded as the one to blame, the instigator of the reign of terror her father's unfortunate demise had inflicted upon the family.

'Rose was still abed when I left the house. She will be arriving later.' And taking her hands in a determined manner, he asked: 'And how are you this morning, my dear?'

'None of us is sleeping well. That's hardly to be wondered at.' Her reply and slight withdrawal from him indicated that asking after her health was lacking in tact and sensitivity.

'You will need to return later if you wish to see Mama.

Dr Wiseman has prescribed a sedative. You must realise how terribly upset she is, by all this – this business,' she added reproachfully. 'Bad enough for her knowing how ill dear Papa was for months, without these ridiculous suggestions that he has been poisoned.'

Faro laid a hand on her arm. She was trembling. 'Grace, my dear, you must believe me, I feel deeply for you in all this. And Vince too, but the law must proceed whatever our personal feelings. And the law calls for an enquiry in such circumstances.'

'Surely with all your influence you could have spared us—' she began hotly.

'That I cannot do, much as I would wish to out of regard for your family, not if there is any possibility, however great or small, that death did not come about by natural causes.'

'Oh, this is intolerable,' she cut in. 'You mean you really do believe that someone in Priorsfield poisoned dear Papa. One of our servants, perhaps.' If you knew how devoted they were to him. The idea is so preposterous, only a policeman who did not know us could give that a second thought.'

Faro winced from the contempt in her voice, the anger in her gaze, but he said gently as he could, 'My dear, I have had second, third, and even fourth thoughts, believe me. Murder is an endless chain, once established with a link, it has an unhappy tendency to lead on and on—'

'Murder? In this family? You must be mad – or entirely wicked – to even imagine such a thing. If it wasn't so terrible, it would be laughable.'

Her face pink with anger, Faro regarded her with compassion. Poor innocent child, how would she ever cope with the even more monstrous truth: that the most probable explanation to which the scanty evidence thus far pointed was that for some reason as yet unknown, her father had been murdered not by a servant but by one of his, and her, close kin.

'You must believe me, my dear, what I am hoping to prove is not who is guilty, but who isn't.'

What else could he say? But his words had the required effect and Grace, mollified, shrugged.

'Very well. You can start with me. I adored my father. I have absolutely no motive for wishing him – him—' Her voice broke. 'Dead. I had not the slightest notion that he was dying. He had bouts of indigestion and suffered from bad headaches. And I used to, God help me, tease him, about drinking too much port. Tease him about – getting old. Oh – oh.'

And sobbing she steadied herself against the staircase and Faro took her into his arms, held her against his shoulder.

'There, there, my dear. There, there.'

Suddenly he was aware of Maud Langweil's face regarding them from the top landing. Slowly she descended the stairs, holding firmly to the banister. Deep mourning's black bombazine and flowing crêpe did not become her, its dramatic veils enveloped her, making a pale face and lips paler, light eyes lighter. It drained every shred of living colour from her countenance.

She took Grace from him. 'There, my darling, hush now. Don't distress yourself.'

'Mama, you should be resting. Remember what Dr Wiseman said,' she added with a reproachful look at Faro.

'I'm quite rested, darling. I gather Mr Faro is here to see me. We will talk in the sitting room.'

Grace regarded her mother's face anxiously. 'Are you sure, Mama?'

'Of course I'm sure. No, I don't need you, dearest. Go to the kitchen and get Molly to give you a nice soothing drink. Now, off you go, there's a good girl.'

As he followed her upstairs, she said: 'I am looking forward very much to meeting Rose. Grace tells me she is absolutely charming. I am sure they will be great friends. After all there is little difference in their ages – or so it seems to those of us who are middle-aged.'

In the sitting room, the door firmly closed, Maud said, 'Please be seated, Mr Faro. I am most anxious to give you all the help I can to clear up this unfortunate misunderstanding regarding my late husband. I do realise that this is no ordinary enquiry for you either, and it is as painful and as difficult for you as for any of the family. As you know Vince is already like a son to me, the son I never had.'

She paused to smile at him sadly. 'That I gather we have in common, for you also lost a son long ago. You must try not to think of us now as your enemies, your suspects, Mr Faro. We are indeed your friends and Vince's. And if my late husband did not die from the disease we believed was killing him, then we are as eager to co-operate with the law and find whatever, or whoever, ended his life.'

Up to now Maud had made no impression upon him. At their few meetings, she had seemed something of a nonentity among the bright and shining Langweils. Obedient to her husband's commands in public, the dutiful hostess, the devoted mother but with little conversation that was not merely a yes or no, an echo of her spouse's sentiments. A woman not encouraged to suffer original thoughts or express opinions of her own.

Now he looked at her with new admiration. This was not the widow he had dreaded meeting, devastated, distraught, eternally weeping. Maud Langweil it seemed was one of those admirable women dismissed as frail, spoilt by a lifetime of riches, that men expect to collapse under adversity and are constantly surprised, as he was, that instead they find new fortitude in facing up to life's tragedies.

'Will you take tea with me?'

Faro noticed that the tea tray had already been in service and presumably Dr Wiseman had accepted the invitation he now declined. If Mrs Langweil could have read his thoughts and his expression, she would have realised at that moment he would have greeted with enthusiasm something considerably stronger than the China tea on offer.

'Very well.' Maud sat in the high-backed chair, her face in shadow. 'What can I tell you, Mr Faro, that would be of help to you? I understand you believe my late husband was poisoned.'

Faro was taken aback by her directness. He suspected that she was mistress of the situation despite Grace's claim that her mother was too distressed to talk to him. He was also embarrassed, at a loss for the appropriate response. The kind of questions he was used to asking widows, whose husbands had died under very suspicious circumstances and arsenic poisoning, were suddenly quite shocking before this gentle woman whose daughter was to marry his stepson.

6

And yet – and yet. In the past had he not conducted just such interviews in just such elegant surroundings with an apparently inconsolable heart-broken widow? Invariably a young widow in the course of investigation revealed as a scheming murderess who had heartlessly watched an old husband die a slow and agonising death. To gain a fortune, or an insurance, or to free her for a waiting lover's fond embrace.

Barbara's face loomed before him in all its unattainable loveliness. The sudden thought appalled him.

Could there possibly have been a ghastly mistake? Had it been Theodore and not Cedric who was the intended victim?

Observing Maud Langweil closely as she attended to the tea ritual, her hands were quite steady, and Faro would have found it difficult to doubt that he was regarding an innocent woman.

He prided himself upon occasional flashes of intuition

and decided he would be surprised indeed to discover that Cedric's widow had secret reasons for wishing to rid herself of an unwanted husband. The whole idea seemed ludicrous, even indecent, to contemplate, especially as she was so eager to befriend his daughter.

Again he wished he had been able to postpone Rose's arrival for enrolment at the Academy. The thought of his daughter besmirched by association with the as yet undiscovered murderer in the Langweil household was sickening, intolerable.

As if interpreting his discomfiture, Maud asked: 'I suppose the question that is framing itself in your mind and that you are too polite to ask is the obvious one: were the relations between my late husband and myself quite amicable?'

Her casual tone took him aback, especially as she paused with the teacup half-way to her lips and said: 'Isn't that what you really are here to find out? If we were happy together?'

Faro took a deep breath: 'And were you?'

'Indeed we were. The best of friends and comrades as well as having a marriage as harmonious as most of our friends' after twenty years.'

When Faro frowned, she again interpreted his thoughts. 'Perhaps that answers the next question you are too much of a gentleman, outside your professional capacity, to ask: Did Cedric have a mistress?'

Looking towards the window, she smiled as if at a sudden vision. 'He may in the way of many gentlemen who belong to private clubs and societies have had access to ladies of a certain profession.' Her shrug was eloquent. 'I never enquired, nor had I any desire to know of such occasions. A man is a man, Mr Faro, and we women are brought up to realise that such small indiscretions are part of their nature but have naught to do with destroying the structure of an otherwise happy marriage.'

She shrugged. 'We are taught to tolerate such matters and ignore them. Lusts of the moment and nothing more, Mr Faro.

With as little lasting effect as the gratification of appetite. Which in fact, as a man, you must recognise is all that it is—'

Faro was saved the further embarrassment of a reply to this forthright condemnation of his sex's morals by a tap at the door.

'Mama?' Grace looked in anxiously. 'Are you able to see Madame Rich? Or shall I ask her to come back later?'

'No, my dear. Tell her I will see her. If Mr Faro will excuse us. Madame Rich is our dressmaker,' she explained. 'We have certain requirements for mourning attire – and orders that must now be postponed for Grace's spring wedding,' she added with a small sigh.

Faro held open the door for her, and she turned to him anxiously. 'I do apologise, Mr Faro, for I have not answered all of your questions.'

As they descended the stairs, she added: 'Do please come again if you think I can help you in any way.'

At the front door, she extended her hand. 'I can only assure you of one thing. That my husband loved me, and his daughter. A good father and husband, a splendid employer – everyone who met him and knew him will tell you that. I can think of no earthly reason why anyone should wish to murder him. Certainly not in this household.'

Since the time of Cedric's death pointed to the fatal dose of arsenic having been administered in Priorsfield, Faro was thankful that he did not have to interview the servants.

Walking briskly down Princes Street in the direction of the High Street and the Central Office, he heard rapid footsteps behind him.

It was Sergeant Danny McQuinn. 'Been interviewing the sorrowing widow, sir?'

McQuinn's words made Faro wince. Words that were all too often used mockingly in the Edinburgh City Police.

'I was in the servants' hall. Heard you leaving.'

'You didn't waste much time. Anything to report?'

McQuinn shook his head. 'Think she's guilty?' he asked

eagerly. 'Tricky situation for you, sir, going to be a relative by marriage and so forth. No doubt you have a reluctance—'

Faro ceased walking and regarded the young sergeant sternly. 'I have no reluctance, McQuinn. If she damned well poisoned her husband then she's as guilty as any common murderer. And she'll suffer the same fate if I can prove it,' he added angrily, and proceeded to walk faster than ever.

'Your stepson's future mother-in-law, Inspector?' McQuinn's long stride kept an easy pace with him. 'Now that would create a sensation in the police, wouldn't it now?'

McQuinn laughed, then, perhaps taking pity on Faro's agonised expression said: 'But you don't really think she's guilty, do you? Nice lady like that. If it consoles you, no one below stairs would believe it either. They think the world of her. And of the master, as they call him.'

'What else did you find out?'

McQuinn sighed. 'Not a lot, sir. On this visit, I thought it tactful to take refuge in a little subterfuge.'

'What kind of subterfuge?'

'Lies, Inspector,' McQuinn said cheerfully. 'But like all the best distortions of fact, based on a core of truth. As you know there are always burglaries in this area. Not too difficult to invent a cache of objects found near their basement. Worked a treat. All the maids were suitably impressed. No, there was nothing missing of that description from their establishment.'

Again McQuinn laughed. 'And I would have been the most surprised man on earth if there had been. However, there wasn't much point in prolonging the visit seeing it was Priorsfield where their master died.'

And taking out the handsome silver timepiece which McQuinn proudly boasted was 'a parting gift from my Glasgow colleagues', he added: 'Looks as if I have just enough time to present the robbery story to the servants there. With a bit of luck, I'll have more vital information from them. In fact, if I look sharpish, the Musselburgh train passes the gates.'

'Papa! Over here.'

Faro turned and there was Rose clutching her bonnet against the shrill wind blowing up the Waverley Steps, and thereby affording, in her descent from the horse-drawn omnibus, a glimpse of slender ankles.

One look at McQuinn's amused face told Faro that he was suitably impressed by this revelation as breathlessly Rose rushed to her father's side.

'I am meeting Grace.' And smiling at McQuinn, she held out her hand. 'Hello.'

'Aren't you going to introduce me, sir?' said McQuinn, smiling delightedly.

'Introduce yourself,' laughed Rose. 'We are old friends.'

'We are?' McQuinn, plainy embarrassed, looked quickly at Faro and then to Rose and back again.

'Don't you remember? You once rescued me from probable death or dishonour when a silly French maid had mislaid me on the way from the Castle. Emily and I never did discover whether we were about to be abducted,' she added with a shiver. 'And Grandmama had wicked thoughts about white slavers.'

Gradual enlightenment dawned on McQuinn. 'But you were – I mean, it was two little girls I found wandering—'

'It was also years ago, when Papa was investigating the case of the baby in the wall of Edinburgh Castle.'

'By all that's holy, Miss Faro,' said McQuinn. 'Sure and who would have thought you'd grow into such a blithe and bonny young lady.'

As Rose blushed under McQuinn's appraising gaze Faro decided this had gone far enough. Hailing a passing hiring carriage, he bundled Rose into it with directions to Charlotte Square.

'But, Papa,' Rose protested. 'I can walk there. This is nonsense.'

'It isn't nonsense. And I won't have you walking about Princes Street, a stranger unescorted.'

'But – Papa—'

'Do as you're told,' said Faro, nodding to the driver and slipping him a coin. 'Now, off you go.'

Watching them depart, he said coldly to McQuinn: 'Haven't you a train to catch?' And without waiting for a reply, he hurried across the road and over North Bridge, murmuring angrily to himself that the last thing he wanted in his life at the present time was a daughter who was going to need watching.

Rose was already abed asleep when he returned to Sheridan Place late that evening and found a very gloomy Vince awaiting him.

'We've drawn a complete blank. Adrian and I have spoken to all the leading consultants in Edinburgh whom Cedric might have visited. Wiseman put in an appearance at the surgery, by the way, most anxious to help us. He'd met you at Charlotte Square and was baffled and rather hurt too, I might add. Feels that as a long-standing friend of the family, Adrian and Cedric should have confided in him and not gone above his head to consult another doctor.'

Vince looked at him. 'I was going to suggest that you cross Adrian off your list of suspects, then something happened to change my mind.'

'And what was that?' Faro demanded eagerly.

'As you know he's a good friend of mine and I thought I was in his confidence. However, Wiseman let slip an important piece of information during his visit. Freda came into the hall as he was leaving and he said: "I believe we are to congratulate you, Mrs Langweil." Freda blushed and smiled shyly. "I hope so." Then Wiseman said: "I trust your husband is taking good care of you. After all this long time, we don't want any problems, do we?" '

'Well, there wasn't any doubt in my mind what he was talking about. Freda was pregnant. I'd noticed that she had put on rather a lot of weight recently, but fool that I was and because Adrian never said a word, its possible significance escaped me.

'When Adrian and I were alone, I added my own congratulations. He apologised for not telling me earlier and added somewhat hastily that as he hadn't told any of the family yet he would be grateful if I'd keep it to myself. Early days still, and as they'd had a few false alarms. They intended telling the family at Barbara's birthday party next week.'

Both men were silent, aware that if Adrian and Freda produced a son, he would inherit the Langweil fortune after Theodore's death. Only Cedric had stood in the way. And now Cedric was dead.

'So only Adrian and Wiseman knew. You say Wiseman is a long-standing friend of the family?'

'Oh yes. I rather guess from Adrian that the main attraction was Grace. Adrian suspected that he had hopes of her, even teased him a little about it.'

'Surely she was a little young for him.'

'Not really, although she must have been a mere schoolgirl when he first went to the house.'

I must be getting old, thought Faro. But doubtless that was why Wiseman seemed so embarrassed and discomforted by his presence. Knowing that Faro's stepson was to marry Grace, he was afraid that the Inspector might be aware of his infatuation for his young patient and that his behaviour towards her was under constant scrutiny, the subject of mocking comment.

Faro could sympathise, since he was self-conscious as a guilty schoolboy in Barbara Langweil's presence, certain everyone guessed his feelings for her.

'I presume Grace never gave him any encouragement.'

Vince laughed. 'She regards him as a benevolent uncle. That he had any amorous inclinations had never occurred to her, I can assure you.'

Realising they were slipping away from the vital subject once again, Faro said: 'As you've drawn a blank in Edinburgh with consultant physicians, I wonder if Cedric went elsewhere.'

'I suppose it's a possibility, Stepfather, but rather like searching for a needle in a haystack. You're thinking of London – somewhere like that?'

Vince frowned. 'I seem to remember he went to Aberdeen rather a lot. Something to do with the whisky business.'

'Then that is perhaps where we will find our missing consultant.'

'I'll put it to Adrian. See if he comes up with any names.'

'We have to clear this up, lad, make absolutely certain that he was not a dying man, before we can proceed with the possible enquiry into a murder.'

'My poor Grace,' whispered Vince with some feeling.

To which his stepfather added silently, my poor Vince. For whatever happened, if Inspector Faro succeeded in tracking down whoever poisoned Cedric Langweil, his triumph would shake the entire family to its very foundations and shatter the delicate fabric of Vince's forthcoming marriage to Grace Langweil.

'Vince has been called away to attend a sick child,' Rose told her father when they met at breakfast.

7

Faro was never at his best in the morning, especially when a murder case kept him awake half the night wrestling with theories, sifting through evidence, and discarding improbabilities. Since he was emotionally concerned with Cedric's death and the outcome, he had fallen into a deep and exhausted sleep at dawn.

Normally he always claimed he needed his first breaths of fresh air to sharpen his wits. Vince appreciated his stepfather's approach to each new morning and the two men were normally silent as each read his own mail and their comments were few and only where strictly necessary.

Rose, who saw her father rarely, was unaware that at breakfast time he was apt to be grumpy. She prattled at a great rate about her plans for the day. Grace was taking her to the shop where she could look at the school uniform and then they were to go on to the Botanic Gardens.

Faro listened, polite but vague and trying to smile a little, just to please her.

'You will enjoy that. I presume Grace will be calling for you in their carriage.'

Rose frowned. 'It is rather out of her way, Papa. I thought I would take the omnibus to Charlotte Square.' And clasping her hands delightedly, 'I do so enjoy public transport. We have nothing like that at home. It is quite thrilling—'

'Rose,' he interrupted. 'I must insist that you avail yourself of Grace's carriage, or if you wish to explore, then you take Mrs Brook with you.'

'Mrs Brook—'

'Yes, my dear. You see, it isn't quite right for a young girl who is a stranger to Edinburgh to wander round unescorted.'

'How am I to cease being a stranger if I can't search out places for myself? I like my own company. Besides, I am used to going about Kirkwall alone.'

'Kirkwall is not Edinburgh. There are dangers in a city that you would not encounter in Orkney.'

'I'm not a child any longer, Papa,' Rose said in wounded tones.

'I am quite aware of that,' he said coldly.

Then, her heightened colour warning him that she was upset by his remark, he put his arm around her, hugged her to him.

'I want you to be happy here, my precious. And safe. I realise your papa is a great fusspot, but do bear with me. Will you – please?'

Resting her head against his shoulder, her sunny smile restored, she said: 'Of course I will, dear Papa. I just love Edinburgh so much. I can hardly believe that I am to stay here soon – for always – with you. And I want to know everything about it.'

'And so you shall, love. Now – another piece of toast?'

Fondly he watched her pour out his second cup of tea. She was so lovely, this daughter of his. It was a dream come true, having her sit there across the table. They would soon get used to each other's ways.

As he was leaving for the Central Office, she helped him into his cape and, handing him his hat, smiled.

'Aren't you fortunate to have Sergeant McQuinn with you. Such a nice man, isn't he? He'll look well after you, I'm sure.'

Faro bit back an angry response at thus being entrusted to his sergeant's care, kissed her goodbye, and with the domestic harmony only slightly dinted by her innocent remarks walked more sharply than usual in the direction of the High Street and the Central Office.

There McQuinn awaited him, busily writing notes at his desk.

'Well, sir, I've been to Priorsfield. Mention of burglars in the district works wonders,' he added with a chuckle. 'I sternly demanded what security measures they had on hand and as one thing led to another I expressed an admiration for all those lovely exotic potted plants and was told they came from Mr Theodore's greenhouses.

' "How do you keep them so well?" I asked. "I hope if any of you are using poisonous chemicals you sign for them."

'And what did I discover? That the only poison used in that house was rat poison.'

'Rat poison?'

'Rat poison, the very same, Inspector. Arsenic, ordered and signed for by who but Mr Cedric himself.'

'Don't you mean Mr Theodore?'

'No, definitely Cedric. Like you I thought they had said the wrong name. But it seems that most of the Langweil business is conducted from Priorsfield. According to Mrs Gimmond, there were rats in all their malthouses. Everyone knew about that, but Mr Theodore also left domestic matters like vermin extermination to his brother.

'As you know there's been a plague of rats in the sewers for as long as folk can remember. In spite of all attempts to get rid of them, no sooner is one old rat-infested building pulled down than they spread like wildfire into the foundations of the other houses.'

Faro nodded. 'Including Priorsfield, McQuinn,' as he remembered Piers Strong's argument for hygiene, for an all-clean, rat-free Edinburgh. 'They're an infernal nuisance.'

'Right, sir. And I gather Mr Theodore wasn't aware of their presence until he found they had gnawed their way into his new library. Carried in with boxes of old books stored in the cellars they were nesting behind the shelving.

'The maids all shuddered and squealed, going on about how they went to light fires in the morning they could hear the rats scuttling about.'

'So there was arsenic in the house.'

'A plentiful supply, to all accounts. And in regular use,' was the reply.

'Did you get the impression that Cedric had any enemies on the staff?'

'No. From what Mrs Gimmond said, he was well liked. Seemed she was acquainted with the servants in Charlotte Square too. Said they were all shocked, that he had been a good master and would be sadly missed.' McQuinn frowned and shook his head. 'But you know, I got an odd impression that she didn't care for him personally.'

'Indeed? How so?'

McQuinn frowned. 'Nothing in what she said, but her face gave it away somehow.'

'What is she like, this Mrs Gimmond?'

'Handsome woman. Well spoken. Not quite the wife you'd expect Gimmond the butler to have. Odd that she'd marry a low-class chap like him.'

Faro looked at McQuinn. Gimmond's impeccable accent hadn't fooled his sergeant. 'What makes you think he's low class?' he asked.

McQuinn shrugged. 'You can always tell. Something in his manner gives him away. He's not quite the ticket, not confident enough. I've met a lot of butlers in my time and Gimmond is not quite easy in the part.' He shook his head. 'You know, sir, I wouldn't be at all surprised if he's had trouble with the police at some time. He has that nervousness, the sidelong shifty look that old lags display when a uniform shows up on the doorstep and their old sins begin to bother them.'

Faro remained silent. He was not at that moment prepared to take McQuinn into his confidence about Gimmond's past. But his sergeant's observations were worth noting.

'Did you get any useful information about upstairs?'

'Scandal, you mean?' grinned McQuinn. 'Not a whiff. As I said, all seemed to be blessed harmony, a devoted family. Not only working together but holidays too. Never seemed to tire of each other's company. As you know, I expect, the brothers were also keen golfers and their wives often accompanied them. That seemed to surprise Mrs Gimmond. Quite unusual for keen golfers to want their wives along, she said.'

Faro smiled. 'You've done very well, McQuinn.'

McQuinn laughed. 'And I've been invited to look in again. So I'll keep at it. Mrs Gimmond is a good cook too.'

'I would have expected that.'

'But then, Inspector, you're not a poor bachelor like me. You have good connections.'

Faro refused to rise to the bait even when McQuinn added with a grin: 'How's that pretty daughter of yours, sir? Staying long?'

'She is here to finish her education. Going to school.'

McQuinn whistled. 'School, is it? Well, well, you astonish me. I'd have thought she was more ready to be here to find a husband,' he added with a grin.

Faro seized the papers on his desk without further comment. He was determined to stick to his resolution to stay on cordial terms with McQuinn and not allow his sergeant's abrasive personality to threaten the efficient performance of their working relationship.

'Where next, Inspector?'

'Somehow, somewhere, we need to track down whoever attended Cedric Langweil and told him that he had a diseased brain which was going to kill him in six months.'

'Sounds like Dr Laurie's domain.'

It was, but all enquiries regarding the missing consultant seemed doomed to failure.

And then they had a piece of luck.

Faro found a note awaiting him from Maud Langweil. With it a letter of condolence from a Dr Henry Longfield who had just heard on his return from New York that Cedric had died.

'Perhaps he will be able to help you,' Maud wrote. 'He has been in America for the past six months. It is possible that Cedric saw him just before he left.'

When Vince read the letter, he looked almost happy for the first time in weeks. An enquiry at Surgeons' Hall confirmed that Longfield dealt with cancer patients at the Infirmary. He was also a consultant physician.

Considerably heartened by this information, Faro went to visit the doctor in his house in Moray Place.

Dr Longfield was not dismayed by the presence of a detective inspector. The police often called when sudden death required discreet enquiries.

'Cedric was a friend of mine, yes. We had known each other since student days and I was sorry to hear of his death.'

'Sorry but not surprised?'

The doctor frowned. 'Both, as it happened. Why do you ask?'

'Did he ever consult you professionally?'

'Only once, curiously enough, just before I left for America. He wanted me to give him a thorough examination. I did so and gave him a clean bill of health.'

'You mean there was no sign of illness?'

'None at all. He was strong and healthy, in excellent condition – a man in the prime of his life. It would not have surprised me had he lived to be ninety. And yet such things do happen. Massive heart attack, was it?'

'Not exactly. I will be frank with you, Doctor. Cedric Langweil's death is baffling. He told his family that he had a brain disease and was unlikely to live until the end of the year. Which prediction was in fact correct. But that was not how he died . . .'

And Faro proceeded to relate the facts as he knew them.

At the end, Longfield was silent for a moment. 'So that is the reason for this visit, Inspector. It does sound as if someone gave him a helping hand. Curious, because on several occasions he showed considerable interest in the workings of the human brain. Why we did certain things and so forth; a true Darwinian, he regarded man as just a little higher than the apes. Often he said it was only our superior thought processes that kept us above the laws of the jungle. Some of us, that is,' he added with a wry smile.

'In fact, now that I give it particular thought in the light of what you have told me, Cedric frequently asked me what were the first indications of disease of the brain. Most unfortunate,' he sighed, 'this morbid preoccupation must have preyed on his mind until he believed that he was suffering from some abnormal condition.'

He shrugged sadly. 'The result was that he took his own life, in a state of mental aberration and disturbance. And yet that does amaze me. You see, he did not strike me as a man who would entertain such notions. He loved and lived life to the full even as a student. He would never accept the second best and he worshipped beauty.'

The picture of Cedric greedy for life did not fit the picture of the desperate man who believing he was dying, panicked, thought Faro as he thanked the doctor for his help.

Returning to the Central Office Faro realised that the interview he most dreaded could no longer be delayed or avoided.

He must talk to Barbara Langweil, who had also been present in Priorsfield when her brother-in-law died.

Faro was more than usually nervous about the procedure, anxious not to upset that beautiful sensitive woman by any hint that she was responsible for Cedric's unfortunate demise under her roof. Or since the evidence pointed to his having been murdered that her hand might have been capable of administering the fatal dose of arsenic.

Gathering together the notes that he had written on the case so far, Faro leaned back in his chair, his back rigid as he closed his eyes and his mind tightly against such a thought.

That his goddess might also be capable of murder.

8

Walking rapidly in the direction of Duddingston, Faro was again aware of the historical drama of Scotland's past surrounding him.

To his left the sun glanced off the rolling fields outlining the parallel lines of the old runrig system of agriculture. Begun with the monks and discontinued long ago, its evidence was still visible also on the upper reaches of Arthur's Seat, whose towering mass overhung the road on which he walked.

Samson's Ribs, they called it. Out of sight lay Hunter's Bog, where once the Young Pretender had camped with his troops, certain of victory. Looming darkly on the horizon above Duddingston Loch, Craigmillar Castle. Within those now ruined and roofless walls the Prince's thrice-great-grandmother Mary Queen of Scots had, according to legend, let the besotted Earl of Bothwell whisper in her ear a plan to rid a wife of a loathsomely diseased and unwanted husband.

As Faro entered the iron gates of Priorsfield he was again aware that an air of mysteries unsolved, lost in time, clung to the great house before him. He would not have admitted to his colleagues in the Central Office, or to a great many other people, his belief that as well as bricks and mortar houses were built of the lives of the generations who have lived there, their memories of good and evil, their scenes of sadness and joy absorbed into the stones.

What then was the strand linking Prince Charles Edward Stuart's fortune with the humble alehouse that had been Priorsfield? And the mystery never to be solved of French gold that might have changed the destiny of the Stuart monarchy? And what of the skeleton dug up a century later with a knife in its ribs?

Sometime he must talk to Grace about her ghost. Children were sensitive to such things and for his money, Priorsfield, secret in its nest of trees, seemed haunted by more than raucous crows.

Out of sight, the peacocks screeched a warning.

He shuddered. He didn't like peacocks, they offended his sense of justice that an unfeeling Creator had crippled such beauty by a terrible voice.

Gimmond opened the door to him. As usual they exchanged a minimum of words.

'I will see if the mistress can see you.'

Waiting in the hall, Faro rehearsed his opening speech to Barbara with such elaborate anxiety he decided it would be a relief if she were unable to see him.

He was almost surprised when Gimmond returned. 'Will you come this way, sir. Mrs Langweil will receive you in the library.'

Barbara was seated by the window, overlooking the drive. She must have seen his approach and as always, at that first glance, her beauty took him by the throat, rendered him speechless.

Unlike her sister-in-law, deep mourning became her, the veils and jet adding vulnerability, enhancing the luminosity of her skin, the brightness of her eyes. Where grief blotched other faces, eyes reddened, here was a woman who cried and became even more beautiful.

More desirable. His eyes avoided the slightly heaving bosom, the tiny hand-spanned waist. He tried to glance at her sternly, painfully aware of the honey-coloured hair, of amber eyes that changed colour. Her hands were very white, with long tapered fingers. Her handshake was lingering, cool.

She dismissed his apologetic, stammering reasons for 'this unexpected visit' with a smile.

'It is necessary, I quite understand. In the distressing circumstances of my brother-in-law's death I realise you must interview all members of the family who were present in the house. You must do your duty, Inspector Faro, however unpleasant.'

Another smile, brilliant this time, revealed small exquisitely white teeth, lips very red against the ivory skin. 'Please go ahead, I am quite ready. I thought it was quite vital that you should see these, for instance.'

With the important air of a conjuror producing rabbits from a hat, she took from the side table cards on which were written the menus for that fatal evening's dinner party.

Faro was more interested in the list of the wines.

'Will they help in your enquiries?'

'A little.'

'How else can I assist you then? Please do not hesitate to ask – anything. And I will try to answer.'

She was very anxious to please, but the answers to his routine questions were valueless.

Did she know of any reason why someone should poison Cedric Langweil? No. Did he have any enemies? No.

And the more searching: 'Were the relations between your husband and his brother amicable?' And softening the blow, 'Any business troubles, perhaps?'

He thought that question brought a fleeting shadow, the merest hint of a frown. The instant later it was gone.

'I know of none. My husband told me you had asked him if Cedric had any enemies, if there was a family feud.'

She looked at him boldly. 'I can only confirm what he said to you, Mr Faro, add my assurance to his. You must believe us when we tell you that in this family we are all devoted to one another. And loyal too.'

Aye, and there's the rub, thought Faro. Loyal. That's the

insurmountable barrier all policemen stumble over, again and again, hampering any enquiries. Whatever the stratum of society, rich or poor. Family loyalty so fierce and protective that getting at the whole truth and nothing but the truth was an impossibility.

'Do you consider the absence of a suicide note significant?'

She looked thoughtful, a fleeting expression as if something had occurred to her. A moment later it was gone.

'Surely it would have saved the family a great deal of anxiety and such enquiries as this would have been quite unnecessary if such a note had been written,' Faro prompted her.

She looked away, shook her head. 'I suppose so.'

It wasn't the answer he had hoped for. And, again feeling she had not been completely honest with him, he handed back the menu, which was impeccable, its ingredients innocent of venom. They had all eaten the meal, shared the same dishes. As for the wines served at the meal, they were innocuous, otherwise more than her brother-in-law would be now lying in Greyfriars Kirk. The fatal dose had been administered during that last hour Cedric and Theodore spent together.

And in this room.

All the time he was thinking: She could have done it easily. Slipped into this shadowy room unobserved. The serving table conveniently placed just inside the door, in order that an unobtrusive butler could attend to decanters and glasses without disturbing the two men sitting on either side of the fire. The armchairs Faro noticed had high backs, too, concealing the occupants from draughts and intrusions.

He reconstructed the scene. A noise, a door opening quietly, and neither man would have made the effort to sit up and look round, dismissing the newcomer as a soft-footed servant—

No, that would not do. What if Theodore had picked up the wrong glass?

If indeed Cedric had been poisoned by the claret, then his murderer had to have an accomplice. And if this lovely woman before him was the guilty one, then she had to have someone who would make sure that Cedric got the right glass. Someone she could trust.

A servant. Gimmond? Unlikely.

Then it could only be her husband. And Theodore would lie and lie. As he, Faro, would have done had such a woman been his wife. He knew that, recognised it for his own weakness. That love – and loyalty – could be stronger than justice.

Switching from such uneasy thoughts, he asked: 'You must have known your brother-in-law very well. Granted that he thought he was incurably ill, did he ever show signs of mental disturbance? What I'm trying to say, did he ever hint that, let us say, if things got too bad, he might put an end to it all?'

'Never. No, never,' she replied quickly without the slightest hesitation, her eyes bright and shining, a slight smile playing about her lips intensifying that likeness to a Botticelli angel, as Faro had first seen her.

'When we – knew – what Cedric believed we were distraught. It was as if this death sentence had been passed on each one of us personally. There is nothing we would not do for each other, no sacrifice too great. We are that kind of family.'

In the silence that followed her words, for Faro could think of no rejoinder beyond a curt nod totally inadequate to the occasion, Barbara gazed up at the family portraits above the mantelpiece.

'That I think is the secret of how the Langweils have survived and prospered over so many centuries.'

When he declined the inevitable offer of tea, which seemed to be on hand at all hours in such houses, Faro recognised that it was also an indication that the interview was at an end.

About to take his leave, Barbara stood up saying she would accompany him.

Wrapping a shawl about her shoulders, she smiled. 'Just to the end of the drive. I would enjoy a little exercise. I get little chance these days. It is not the done thing for recently bereaved ladies to show their faces in public.'

Faro could think of nothing to say as they walked down the front steps. 'I understand you are from Orkney, Inspector. What brought you to Edinburgh?'

Faro told her, keeping his life story as brief as possible, certain that was not her reason for wishing to walk with him.

'That is very interesting,' she said. 'As for me, not even the wildest stretches of imagination could have prepared me for what my destiny held. My family were poor immigrants from Eastern Europe and we lived in direst poverty. I went to work as a waitress in a restaurant and it was there by the merest chance that Theodore Langweil, on a business visit to New York, and slumming it, you might say, came into my life. And stayed there.

'A fairy-tale story, is it not, Inspector? And yet so simple. Complete with happy ending. With Priorsfield – and all this – at the end of it. A happy devoted husband, and a loving family. What luck. Who could have imagined it?'

She turned and left him almost abruptly. He watched her go, walking lightly back towards the house.

Opening the gate of Priorsfield and shedding the enchanted spell of Barbara Langweil, he began to have his doubts.

There was something about so much loving, so much sweetness and light that he felt uneasily did not ring true to reality. It was the major obstacle in sniffing out murderers, rapists and petty criminals in a family circle. He thought again about loyalty. How even those who hated each other, screamed and railed and battered each other, or bore a lifetime's secret resentment, would lie and perjure rather than suffer the shame of seeing one of their kin sentenced to prison – and the noose.

If this was true of Edinburgh's poor, how much more so of the society where the good name was everything, the façade of a united family to be protected at all costs?

Squaring his shoulders with new determination he walked past

Duddingston Loch, for in his eyes Barbara Langweil's proclamations of her family's apparent innocence took on a new meaning.

Surely her past was one of the Langweil family's best kept secrets? Why then had she confided in him this story of poor girl into rich wife? A simple story that any detective worth his salt knew perfectly well was all too often a motive and incentive for murder.

9 Unpleasantly wrapped in his own gloomy thoughts, Faro had reached the outskirts of Holyrood Park when he was hailed from a passing carriage.

It was Vince, accompanied by Grace and Rose. 'We are going out to the Golf Hotel for tea.'

'Do come with us, Papa. Please,' cried Rose.

'I ought to get back—' said Faro doubtfully.

'Oh, please, Papa. Vince, you make him come,' Rose persisted, reinforced by Vince's insistence.

And as they made room for him his stepson continued sternly: 'Time you stopped being so conscientious. Gave a little more time to the lighter things in life. I suppose you've been to Priorsfield.' And without waiting for an answer, 'That's enough activity for one day, surely?'

Faro glanced at Grace, awaiting her reaction. There was none. She merely adjusted her parasol, serenely regarding Salisbury crags. 'These mild days are too good to miss.'

Her smile while a little lacking in her usual warmth was reasonably welcoming.

'We decided it was time we escaped from Edinburgh,' said Vince. 'It's my half-day off.' To which Grace glanced at Vince lovingly and tucked her arm into his, while Rose snuggled up close to her father and took his hand affectionately.

Sitting opposite the smiling couple in the carriage, Faro was both pleased and relieved by this return to the normal behaviour between them he had witnessed many times before Cedric's death. All was apparently well again between the two lovers.

At the hotel, Vince went to book in his guests with Rose skipping alongside. Grace, however, seemed glad of the opportunity to be alone with Faro.

'I'm so glad you came with us. I realise now how badly I have behaved and that it was quite silly to blame you – and my dear Vince – for doing what you thought was right.' She paused and looked towards the door where he had momentarily disappeared. 'I have always admired you for your integrity, you know that. And in similar circumstances I am sure I should have acted in exactly the same way myself.'

As Faro smiled down at her and took her hands she sighed. 'You see I do love Vince very much and I want to be his wife. Even if I do most earnestly hope – and believe – that you are mistaken and will find some perfectly innocent explanation of dear Papa's death.'

'We all hope that, my dear, I assure you.'

Grace looked at him gratefully and nodded. 'So Vince says. And you are so clever, he said we could rely on you to find out what really happened—'

As Vince reappeared with Rose, Grace took Faro's arm and, standing on tiptoe, kissed his cheek and whispered: 'I am still your devoted future daughter-in-law—'

'What's all this?' Vince said. 'Do I perceive a rival for my affections? Am I to call you out, sir?' he demanded mockingly. 'And you, madam, did I not observe you bestowing kisses on another man, and in public too?'

Grace prodded him in the ribs and seizing her he swung her off her feet, much to Rose's delight, while Faro observed this little pantomime with considerable relief. All was forgiven and he prepared to enjoy the afternoon tea, which was one of his weaknesses.

The hotel was famed for its Scotch pancakes, scones and Dundee cake. Their table in the large window overlooked the course's rolling greens occupied by a few enthusiastic players, now straggling towards the hotel as the sun dipped low over the Pentlands.

And Faro was suddenly content, glad to be with the two happy young people who at that moment appeared to have not a care in the world. As for his dear Rose's presence, that was for him a wistful return to the domestic life which was increasingly one of his fleeting and ever retreating dreams.

Wednesday was half-day closing in Edinburgh and around them were other families with young children, enjoying the kind of life other men accepted as normal that he had so briefly known with a loving wife and bairns. He thought of Emily, seen, with luck, perhaps twice a year. Soon she too would be grown up like her sister, two young women with their own lives and dreams wherein he would have no part.

On to the peaceful scene beyond the window a dark shadow hovered, and as Faro lifted his second scone to his mouth a sparrowhawk swooped and with a scream of triumph ascended with its own ending to a hungry day's hunting.

Faro shuddered. There had been something ominous about that picture of sudden death which his three companions had not witnessed.

'Hello, Faro. You're a stranger.'

The deep voice at his elbow materialised as the manager of the hotel, an ex-colleague from the Edinburgh City Police. Peter Lamont's wife had been cook at a big house and when he retired, a hotel had been their particular ambition.

Vince and Grace, after greeting him cordially, returned to their own quiet chat.

Introduced to Rose, Lamont chuckled. 'Your daughter, eh, Faro? I remember you well, lass. I used to dandle you on my knee when you were a wee one.' And to Faro: 'Like to have a look round? We've made some improvements since we moved here a few weeks ago,' he said proudly.

'May I come too?' asked Rose.

'Aye, lass. Dr Laurie and Miss Langweil know the house well from the previous owners. They've been constant visitors.'

They followed him up the wide staircase into a handsome drawing room where visiting guests took their ease and then into the dining room overlooking the estuary of the River Forth.

'So that's where you are.' Mrs Lamont appeared clutching an armful of rolled papers. Seeing Faro again she flattered him by saying that he hadn't changed one scrap since she last saw him five, or was it six, years ago. 'How do you keep so slim and so young, Jeremy?' she said, eyeing her husband's corpulent figure and thinning hair.

Looking curiously at Rose, her eyes opened wide with astonishment. 'This young lady is never your daughter, Jeremy. Surely? My goodness.'

'I was just telling him that he ought to do a few rounds of golf to keep fit,' said Peter.

'He doesn't look as if he needs that. Besides, dear, it hasn't done much for you.'

'It's not the golf,' Peter grinned, 'it's all the ale and the appetite I have for your good food, dear.'

Mrs Lamont smiled at Faro. 'That's a very bonny lass your young Vince has got hold of.'

'We haven't seen so much of him since they got engaged.'

'I expect you will in the future. He's marrying into a golfing family, I understand.'

'And he could do a lot worse. We were right sorry to hear about her poor father.'

'Aye,' said Mrs Lamont. 'We'll miss them. Grand customers they were. Mr and Mrs Theodore and Mr and Mrs Cedric stayed with us in Perth too.'

Glancing at Faro and Rose, she chuckled. 'And talking of

fathers too young-looking to have grown-up daughters, I really put my foot in it, thinking Mrs Cedric was far too young to have a lass the age of Miss Grace—'

'Then she realised that she must be her stepmother.' Peter's smiling interruption held a note of warning.

'Such a beautiful woman,' sighed Mrs Lamont.

No one could make that mistake. And Faro shook his head. 'I think you're confusing the two ladies. The young one is Mrs Theodore.'

'Oh – is she? Now that is interesting—'

Mrs Lamont looked quickly at her husband. 'That's even worse. Oh my goodness, how terribly embarrassing—'

'What was it you wanted, Betty?' Peter demanded rather sharply.

'Nothing, dear. I was just on my way to Room 37. I thought we might have enough of this paper' – she unrolled a length – 'to do that badly stained wall.'

'Let me see. Yes, I think that would do.'

'It was very expensive. Seems a shame to waste it.'

'May I see?' asked Faro. 'I recognise this one.'

'I expect you do, Jeremy. It was the rage in all the big houses about ten years ago. Fashions change and it's out of date now, of course, so we got a batch cheap when we moved into the hotel.'

Shaking hands with the manager and his wife, promises were exchanged to meet again soon. As they walked towards the staircase Faro asked Rose: 'Do we have that wallpaper in Sheridan Place?'

'No, Papa. I've never seen it before.'

'I have. And recently. Wish I could remember where.'

Rose chuckled. 'Dear Papa. Your much vaunted powers of observation and deduction never did reach the realm of ordinary things like clothes or decoration—'

'That, young lady, was a blow below the belt.'

She took his arm fondly. 'But you can't deny it. This is one case where you have to accept that you are guilty.'

From the landing they saw Vince helping Grace into her cloak. Setting off in the carriage once more they reached the outskirts of Edinburgh as a sunset glow touched the Pentlands with rose, echoing its majesty of crimson and gold on Arthur's Seat. A scene of tranquillity and harmony outside, laughter in the carriage as Vince and Grace held hands and talked about their wedding plans.

'Papa, Grace would like Emily and me to be bridesmaids.'

Faro looked at Grace.

'As I have no sisters or girl cousins, it would make me very happy to have Vince's sisters. As long as you approve—'

Faro leaned over and took her hand. 'An excellent idea. And a very thoughtful one too.'

Here was an unexpected end to a routine working happy day, thought Faro. Vince and Grace had made up their differences, he had been reinstated and forgiven. He had renewed acquaintance with the past, an elderly couple with their lifetime's dream fulfilled, and before him sat a young couple whose happy future beckoned only a few months away.

He should have been happy. But he remembered other dark shadows: a sparrowhawk making its kill unobserved by all but himself, reminding him ominously that in the midst of life there is always sudden death. Death striking, unexpected and violent.

There was other residue from that afternoon's pleasant interlude which troubled him more. Lingering at the back of his mind, it refused to be banished. A case of mistaken identity perhaps but with such monstrous implications he could not bear to bring it into the light and scrutinise it closely.

For what he could not fail to recognise was its overwhelming significance in the murder of Cedric Langweil.

Sitting in his study that evening, he made a series of notes regarding his second line of enquiry: three people who had been present at the Priorsfield dinner party that fatal evening. None were witnesses to Cedric's demise but one had slept in the house that night.

As for the other two, their association with the Langweils might have some fact of vital importance to contribute.

He knew from years of past experience that it was often the seemingly innocent observation, the frailest of threads that he had followed, which had led his way out of the labyrinth to a confrontation with a murderer.

First on his list was the Langweil cousin, Reverend Stephen Aynsley, who, Grace had told him, was now living with them until his plans were complete for going out to Africa.

Faro was relieved to find him at home in the town house, a visitor of sufficient importance to be allocated a handsome bedroom overlooking the Charlotte Square gardens.

When the maid announced Faro, Stephen Aynsley laid aside his Bible and received him graciously, not one whit put out when Faro said it was in connection with Cedric's death.

He nodded sadly. 'No need to apologise, Inspector. I am perfectly aware of police procedure in such matters. Of course you must talk to everyone who was in the house that night.' He smiled gently. 'For if my poor cousin was murdered, then we are all likely suspects, all capable of having criminal motives. None of us is safe.' Again he smiled. 'And it would not, I am sure, be the first time a clergyman has figured in your enquiries. All I can tell you is that I retired on the stroke of midnight. As I am a temperance man, my presence would have been an embarrassment long before Theo and Cedric began their serious drinking.'

Regarding Faro narrowly, he went on: 'Having said that, I have no witnesses for my departure except Theodore. I saw no one, rang for no hot milk. Nothing. Merely got into bed and was asleep, as is my wont, before my head touched the pillow. And you have only my word for that. After the servants retired, there was nothing to stop me from going quietly downstairs and slipping poison into Cedric's glass.'

Pausing, he gave Faro a triumphant look. 'As you will have observed the side table containing the decanters is very conveniently placed just inside the door. I could have done it easily. And so could – well, several other members of the household. Or a servant who had some mysterious reason, or some grudge, against his master. You look surprised, Inspector?'

Faro laughed. 'Only that I am wondering if you have chosen the right profession, sir.'

'Calling, Inspector. That's how we refer to it. We are called to the ministry.' He gave Faro a shrewd glance. 'There is one more vital question you have no doubt thought of? Surely the very first one that is in any policeman's mind. What have I to gain by my cousin's death?'

'I had thought of that, sir. That by nipping downstairs and putting poison in the wine you could have poisoned both Theodore and Cedric.'

'Ah yes. Now you are making sense. Although getting rid of poor Cedric would have availed me nothing. Polishing off both of them would have got me two steps closer to the Langweil fortune.'

He paused and then shrugged his shoulders. 'If I wanted it. Which I don't. You have to believe that. My destiny lies in Africa and although some money would undoubtedly have its uses in our mission work, I assure you it is not the kind that men murder for. Besides if we take this theory that I perhaps intended to murder both cousins, then it still does not make sense. I have not the least hope of inheritance unless the whole family is deceased. An impressive list, Inspector, including the expected new arrival in Adrian's household—'

At Faro's expression, he smiled. 'Adrian has just announced it. The family are delighted. And as I suspect this baby, if God wills it, to be the first of several, these are hardly the odds any sane man would take on, especially one with my modest expectations. One who believes in accordance with his mission, that poor as we are, if we have faith, then God will provide for our needs.'

Leaning across the table he said earnestly, 'I, for one, cannot believe the Langweils are capable of murder. The whole suggestion is too absurd even for outrage.' He laughed and shook his head. 'Of one thing I am absolutely sure, Inspector. Your investigations will prove only that they are innocent of Cedric's death.'

'What makes you so certain?'

Aynsley shrugged. 'You are much too clever a policeman not to have thought all that out for yourself. You have by now, I am sure, laid all the evidence in the case very neatly upon the table and examined it bit by bit and come to certain conclusions. Am I right?'

Faro regarded him thoughtfully. Surely a man of God should be more upset at the mortal sin of murder? Was his attitude not just a little too flippant for these serious allegations? Perhaps he would be wise to investigate the Reverend Stephen Aynsley a little more closely.

Aware of the other's smiling scrutiny, he shrugged. 'You are certainly very well informed for—'

'For a clergyman? Perhaps it seems a strange confession but I am particularly addicted to that form of literature. I am a great admirer of Poe, and Wilkie Collins and of course, even the late Mr Charles Dickens quite captivated me with his portrait of a detective, not unlike yourself, in *Bleak House*.'

'Inspector Bucket?'

'Ah, I see we share a similar taste in books, too.'

As they discussed the merits of Charles Dickens and Sir Walter Scott, Aynsley said: 'And there are the new scientific methods of detecting criminals. It must be extremely fortunate having a doctor at hand, especially one who I am given to understand served his apprenticeship with the police surgeon.'

As Faro prepared to leave, he asked: 'Have you any theories as to how your cousin died?'

Aynsley shrugged. 'Everything so far points to the possibility that Cedric took his own life. If so then there is one thing that does not make sense. Why did he leave no suicide note?'

'That has occurred to me.'

'I thought it would. Let me put to you, Inspector, that a man so devoted to his family would certainly have left some such evidence of his intention.' And shaking his head, 'Self-destruction is the most distressing exit from the world if one is a believer. In Cedric's case, the circumstances were understandable, but I find it difficult to believe or accept, knowing his deep family feeling, that he would not have left the simple explanation that would have saved any police investigation.'

When Faro walked down the steps of the Langweil house, he found himself the recipient of a handful of religious tracts and the distinct impression that Stephen Aynsley was labouring under the mistaken idea that Detective Inspector Faro had seen the light, bright as St Paul on the road to Damascus.

Not quite sure how he had found himself in such a situation or how the roles had been reversed, so that the detective-story reader Stephen Aynsley had asked the questions while he provided the answers, Faro had weakly left a handsome contribution to the Mission Fund with the certainty that if Aynsley could convert a man who hardly ever entered the doors of a church, then the heathens waiting in all their blissful ignorance in Africa were a walk-over.

As he staggered down the steps and pocketed his fistful of tracts, he shook his head sadly.

'I'm losing my grip, dammit,' he later told Vince, whose laughter at his stepfather's discomfiture was both long and hearty.

Next day, Faro walked down Albany Street to call on Piers Strong. He was received in an office where the architect was barely visible among the many and varied rolled-up plans which threatened every available inch of floor and desk space.

As the circumstances of Cedric's demise were still being kept secret, Faro had to choose his words carefully.

'I won't keep you, sir. There are some complications regarding Mr Langweil's sudden death.' At Piers' anxious expression he added hastily: 'Family business matters and so forth. It isn't all as straightforward as one might imagine.'

'Are you suggesting that it might be murder?'

'What makes you say that, sir?'

Piers shrugged. 'Why else would I be getting a visit from a detective inspector? Well, well. Pray continue.' And the architect sat back in his chair regarding him eagerly. Obviously he wasn't used to such drama among his clients.

Before Faro could say another word, Piers interposed: 'Mind you, I have to say, I find the idea a bit hard to believe. They all seemed happy and so at ease. A devoted family even if tempers were raised over the proposed alterations – the new bathroom business – that is perfectly natural. I can vouch for it among many of my clients. Hardly enough to commit murder for, surely.'

When Faro made no comment Piers laughed. 'Mind you, I have men who would murder their wives rather than suffer all the inconvenience of a disrupted household. But that's only in small houses. Alterations in a place the size of Priorsfield would hardly be noticed. That's what I can't understand about Theodore's attitude. You'd think he'd want to please that young wife of his by letting her have everything up to date. In fact, you'd think he'd give her anything she asked for. And a bathroom wouldn't cost nearly as much as any of those lovely jewels she was wearing that night, I can tell you.'

Again he laughed. 'Now if it had been Theodore, there might have been a motive. Barbara is an absolute stunner, I'm sure there's men who'd commit murder to possess a wife as lovely as his missus.'

Faro looked at him thoughtfully. There seemed no reason for

Cedric to have been murdered unless it was a desperate measure to prevent him changing his will.

Theodore's death made a lot more sense. And again he wondered, was he seriously on the wrong track? Had Cedric's death been a mistake? Had the poison been intended for his brother?

And if so, was the hand long and white, with exquisitely tapering fingers?

10 Faro's next call was on Mr Moulton, the Langweil lawyer. He felt that the old man received this visit with considerable caution and realised that getting him to part with any information concerning the family was not going to be easy.

The much-vaunted devotion and loyalty also extended to those they employed. A small, tight, impenetrable group.

Moulton's face remained expressionless as Faro repeated the reasons he had given Piers Strong for this enquiry.

'If it is about Mr Cedric's will, then I am afraid I cannot help you, Inspector,' he cut in sharply. 'We had only discussed the terms of the new will, it was in the process of being drawn up.' He spread his hands wide. 'The terms of the original will leaving his wife and daughter as benefactors now apply.'

'What were the terms of the new will?'

With a thin wintry smile, Moulton said: 'You have to realise, sir, that the lawyer is in much the same position as the priest in the confessional. And for your information I happen to be of the Roman Catholic persuasion.'

Realising that Moulton probably knew more about the internal politics of the Langweil regime than anyone else, Faro decided to take him into his confidence.

'I quite understand, sir, your reasons are most commendable, but surely you would reconsider if you thought that Mr Cedric had been poisoned. And you would wish for the family's sake to help us find out who had murdered him.'

The old man shuddered. 'Murder,' he whispered. 'Such an idea is incredible. You cannot be serious, Inspector. Who on earth suggested such a thing to you?' he asked indignantly. And without waiting for Faro's reply, 'You must take my word for it, Inspector, I would be prepared to swear on one thing. That Mr Cedric died by his own hand.'

'For what reason?'

'His reasons appear patently obvious – to everyone but yourself, it appears. He believed that he was incurably ill, a dying man. Such conditions often make men's behaviour irascible, wondering when the fatal hour is to strike.'

'And what if I told you that he had never consulted any doctor, any reliable authority, to our certain knowledge, who confirmed his fears that he was incurably ill?'

Moulton looked worried. 'The important thing is that he believed it. Perhaps he lied to his family because he was afraid to face the truth. We all know, and I am sure your stepson can confirm this, that many people are afraid of doctors confirming their own suspicions and, alas, die needlessly. We all have our Achilles' heel.'

'You say that Cedric was a caring man, sir. Then, in your own experience, do not most suicides leave a note of intent for their loved ones? Is it not curious that he omitted to do so?'

When the lawyer did not reply, Faro continued: 'You have known the family for many years.'

'I have indeed. I had the honour to serve Mr Theodore Langweil Senior.'

A new idea occurred to Faro. 'Perhaps then you know of the existence of something in the family's history that might have led Cedric to believe he was suffering from a brain tumour.'

A fleeting shadow touched the lawyer's face. 'I know of no such circumstances,' he said stiffly.

'What of the eldest son?'

'Justin, you mean? Gone long since,' Moulton replied sharply.

'You knew him then?'

'Of course I did. An unhappy young man. I hope he found his peace in America.'

His peace seemed a strange expression for the invalidish eldest son and heir of the Langweils.

Faro looked at Moulton quickly. His impression that the lawyer had not liked Justin Langweil was confirmed when the old man laughed harshly.

'Wilful and violent, perhaps such a nature fitted in better with the somewhat primitive conditions he sought in the wilds of California than with his respectable family background. You seem surprised, Inspector.'

'I am, a little, since such aspects of his character as you describe do not fit the description of the consumptive I have been given so far.'

'Who told you he was consumptive? He was – oh well,' Moulton shrugged, 'you had better get Mr Theodore to tell you all about Justin.'

'You make it sound very mysterious. And mysteries intrigue me, Mr Moulton.'

'I say no more, sir, than that he was not at all the sort of man the family would have been proud of. Quite different, thank God, to his brothers.' And eyeing Faro shrewdly, 'There's one in every pack, but young Justin was worse than the black sheep of the family. Much worse,' he added soberly.

'I can assure you of one thing, he left no broken hearts behind when he set sail for New York. As for not writing to them, that too was typical of the man. Thoughtless, uncaring, he had none of the sensitivity, the finer attributes, of the Langweils. From the day he walked out of Priorsfield, he literally shook its dust from his feet and has never communicated with any of them.'

A thought came into Faro's mind quite unbidden, a concept

that would make quite a story from the one he sought to untangle.

'Do you think there is a chance of him still being alive?'

Moulton frowned and then said quickly, 'Indeed, yes. Accidents and misinformation apart – as well as a hazardous mail service in that violent land – since he was just two years older than Theo I should think there is every chance.' Giving Faro a curious look, he added: 'What are you thinking, Inspector?'

'Nothing important, sir.' But he left the lawyer's office thinking that the Langweil fortune might well be worth re-crossing the Atlantic for.

'And killing for,' he added later when he retold the day's interview for Vince's benefit.

'Justin Langweil. The black sheep of the family,' Vince whistled. 'Of course I've heard about him, Stepfather. In suitably hushed tones.'

'And what have you heard?'

'Well, you know what it's like. The family aren't exactly proud of him, they prefer to draw a veil over his early life, bit of a hell-raiser, I gather. I didn't know of his existence for a long time, they like to give the impression publicly that there were only three sons and that the eldest had died in infancy. Then Grace told me that she gathered that he had gone to America long ago. Naturally she was very curious, got this romantic idea of a rakehell uncle who had thrown away his birthright for a life of adventure.'

Pausing, he grinned. 'Grace is very addicted to novelettes with heroes who rush off, endure terrible hardships, and return in time to save the family fortune – and marry a rich second cousin.'

He stopped, frowning at his stepfather's look of pre-occupation. 'Do I understand rightly that you are toying with some notion that Justin might be very much alive and lurking around Priorsfield waiting for the right moment to make a dramatic entrance? The prodigal son returned. But in this case, judging from what Moulton told you, I think the fatted calf could breathe easily. There wouldn't be much rejoicing.'

He was silent for a moment then said: 'There's only one flaw in this argument, Stepfather. If your assumption is right then Justin Langweil can walk in any day of the week and claim his inheritance. All he needs is to prove his identity. There is absolutely no reason for him to kill anyone or to poison Cedric – Theodore would make more sense if that was his intention – to repossess what any court will say is rightfully his. So why put his neck in danger?'

'There is one good valid reason for him returning incognito which we must not overlook.'

Vince thought for a moment. 'You mean that he might have a criminal record in America? Sounds just that sort of fellow from Moulton's description too. Could that have been what he meant by "misinformation"?'

Faro nodded and both men were silent considering this new aspect of the case.

At last Vince said: 'On the other hand, Moulton could be right about Cedric having done away with himself. Adrian is still very upset about the whole business, as you can well imagine. Cedric was his older brother, closer to him than Theodore. He's going to miss him. He shares Moulton's opinion, mine too, for what it's worth, despite the absence of any suicide note.

'Adrian was telling me that Cedric was morbidly interested in poisons, not just in a general way, he used to read books about poisoners and their methods.'

But it was Sergeant Danny McQuinn who unearthed a completely new motive in his conscientious interviewing of Maud Langweil's household. Getting his feet under the table, he called it, he was now on first-name terms with the housekeeper, Mrs Molly Bates.

'There I was, sir, sitting cosy by the fire, enjoying a rare cup of tea when the kitchen door opened and an ancient crone sidled in.

'Molly introduced us. This was her cousin Bess and Bess's proud boast was that she had been wet-nurse to Justin and Theodore. So between the two of them there was quite a bit of family gossip. Not particularly interesting to begin with: "D'ye mind the second cousin of old so-and-so – well, he's deid." That sort of thing. But I'm a good listener, Inspector. I believe in keeping my ears open, and I was rewarded. It wasn't until the old lass said how sorry she's been about poor Mr Cedric. And shaking her head, how history repeated itself.

'I sat up at that. The whisper had got round the servants that the master had done himself in.

' "Just like poor Mr Justin's young wife."

' "Say that again," says I. And she didn't take much persuasion to tell the whole story. I'll keep it nice and short for you, Inspector.

'Apparently when Mr Justin was about eighteen, he brought a lassie home, claimed they were wed, even produced the lines. But it was plain as plain, according to old Bess and the rest of the family, that she had trapped him. Wasn't in their class at all. Well, she didn't last long.

'The old biddy used to go in and do a bit of ironing for them and the lassie often came into the kitchen in floods of tears. Mr Justin used to use his fists on her. "He always was a bully, even as a wee laddie," says old Bess.

'Well, one day, she put an end to it all. Topped herself. The family hushed it up, of course, and Justin left for America. Heart-broken and full of remorse, they said.'

'Wait a minute, McQuinn. How could they hush it up? Surely there was an enquiry? When was this, anyway?'

'Hold on, sir, I'm coming to that. According to old Bess, everyone believed she had died of a fever.'

So they got a doctor more willing than Vince to sign a false death certificate, thought Faro grimly.

'You won't find anything,' McQuinn continued quickly. 'I've looked.'

'Strange I never heard about it. Never even heard it mentioned.'

'It was before your time. Year before you joined the force. Looked up the record and there's nothing. No enquiry, nothing. Money can buy such things, as you know, sir, for those in high places. But I thought you'd be interested.'

'I am indeed. Especially since I doubt whether even Vince knows that Justin had a wife who did away with herself. Thanks, McQuinn, this does change the picture.'

When Faro returned home that evening it was with almost a feeling of guilt that he had been in the house for some time going over his notes without asking where Rose was.

Matters were not improved when Mrs Brook brought in his supper.

'Miss Rose, sir? Why, she has gone to stay at Charlotte Square with Miss Grace overnight.'

Faro bit back his anger and disappointment. When Vince arrived he said: 'Of course I'm not objecting, but surely I should have been consulted first.'

'Not very easy, Stepfather, I took it on myself to give permission. Thought you wouldn't mind, seeing that you are so seldom at home.'

It was true. He had hardly seen Rose since the weekend they had spent together, a fact which did nothing to lessen his feelings of guilt. He had longed for his daughter's visit but realised he had seriously neglected her ever since.

'You seem to forget I am involved in a murder case.' The words were out before he realised how tactless and hurtful they

were, especially as that same case stemmed from within the house
where his daughter was staying.

Was that what troubled him most of all?

Vince put a hand on his shoulder. 'Any progress?'

Faro threw down his notes and sighed. 'Every new factor just
adds new complication. Did you know that Justin had a wife?'

'A wife? Heavens, no.'

'I thought Grace might have told you.'

'I'm sure she would have done so, if she'd known. She's always
given the impression that he was just a lad when he rushed off.'

'Even a lad of eighteen can take a wife.'

'This is news. Tell me about her.'

When Faro finished the story McQuinn had told him, Vince
whistled. 'I'm sure Grace doesn't know any of this. Not exactly
a piece of family history the Langweils would be proud of.'

'I think you might discover that a lot of things have been kept
from Grace, for her own good – they would say.'

In the silence that followed Vince stared at him. 'Do you think
Justin might still be alive then?'

'Not only alive but in Edinburgh. And a possible suspect.'

'You mean, you think he might have had something to do
with Cedric's death. But why and more important, how? I mean,
it just doesn't make sense, if he is alive then he is the legitimate
heir so why all the secrecy—'

'Necessary if, as we discussed earlier, he has a criminal record.'
And before Vince could interrupt, he went on: 'As a matter of
fact I was thinking along quite different lines. In the light
of McQuinn's discovery, we have a new motive for his return –
incognito.'

'I see what you mean. Revenge—'

'Aye, revenge. Something we'd never even thought of. An
execution sentence on the Langweils for the death of his young
wife who made her so unhappy she took her own life.'

'Wait a moment. Adrian couldn't be guilty, he was just a boy then. The only ones who could be blamed were Theodore – and Cedric. God save us.'

Pausing he looked across at Faro. 'I've heard of cases like this. If Justin was mad, or bad, enough— Do you know, Stepfather, nothing in this case has made sense so far, but now, maybe there is something in what you're suggesting.'

Faro lit a pipe and watched the smoke ascending. Poor Vince, he was pathetically eager to find a new scapegoat for Cedric's death. 'He had to gain access to the house. And, seeing that Theodore and Cedric might recognise him, even after twenty years, what would be his easiest way of entering the Langweil house?'

'As a servant?'

'Precisely. People like the Langweils never look twice at servants.'

'And once he was inside, the rest was easy – well, moderately easy. There's only one thing I don't understand, Stepfather. Poison was put into one glass only, when he could have just as easily used the opportunity to get rid of both of them.'

'Perhaps that was part of a diabolical plot, that he wanted to poison one brother and have the other blamed.'

Vince looked at him, shook his head. 'I just can't take any of this as a serious proposition. I'm sorry, Stepfather, it's too far-fetched for me.'

Faro knocked the ashes from his pipe. 'You're probably right, lad. What is it we say? Discard all the impossibles and what remains must be the truth.' He stood up wearily. 'All I know is that somehow we've got off the right track. We have to begin again, sift through the evidence, starting with the servants' hall at Priorsfield.'

Early next morning, Faro called on Theodore Langweil, and asked him for a list of their domestic servants, indoors and out.

'Is this to do with my brother's death?'

'Perhaps, sir.'

'Very well. Anything to get this accursed enquiry settled. However,' he added, drawing a ledger from his desk drawer, 'I can assure you that you won't find your murderer, if such a creature exists, in this household.'

Opening the pages he said: 'Where would you like to begin?'

'My sergeant, with your permission, will copy down the names and the lengths of time they have been in your service.'

'Is that all?' said Theodore heavily. 'And your sergeant—'

'McQuinn, sir. He will be arriving later today to talk to them. All I need from you are the long-term servants who need not be interviewed. Those who have been with you more than twenty years. Before your eldest brother went to America.'

'Oh, indeed.' Theodore was suddenly very still. Watchful, thought Faro. Suspicious. And he was sure that he had also turned a shade paler. 'What is all this about?' he rapped out sharply.

'Certain facts have come to our notice—'

'Facts? What kind of facts?' Theodore demanded.

'Concerning your brother Justin. Look, sir, we know that he had a young wife, who did away with herself.'

Theodore winced. 'That is not true. Her death was accidental.' But he looked frightened.

'How did she die?'

'I am not prepared to discuss this with you, Inspector. It has no connection with your enquiry. Let us just say she was a very disturbed and unhappy young woman. And leave it at that.'

'I must disagree with you, sir. It could have quite a lot to do with Cedric's death. If Justin is still alive.'

For the first time Theodore looked frightened. 'I assure you Justin is dead. Long since.'

Theodore had recovered his composure. His scornful laugh and his tone were emphatic. 'Before you go to any more ridiculous lengths of alarming my staff and the rest of my family, let me assure you, Justin is dead.'

'Have you proof of that, sir?'

'Only that the gold camp where he was prospecting was over-run by renegade Indians. The white men were tortured to death. And Justin was one of them.'

'How do you know all this? The story I heard was that your brother had disappeared and never communicated with you.'

Theodore smiled sadly. 'Nor did he. That was true. Cedric and I agreed not to distress the family by revealing the true facts regarding Justin's ending.' Unlocking a drawer in his desk, he handed Faro a folded paper, yellowed and dog-eared.

It was headed: 'A true copy of a letter from Messrs Mace and Mace, Bush Street, San Francisco', and dated February 1856:

Dear Sir—

Our exhaustive investigations on your behalf into the disappearance of your brother Justin Langweil have now revealed that he was murdered by Indians . . .

Faro skimmed the remaining paragraph, which was in essence what Theodore had told him.

He handed it back and shook his head. 'I'm sorry, sir.'

'No need for condolences, Inspector. Justin was no adornment to this family, but the search had to be made. In order that certain business matters be cleared.'

He paused, then added, 'If you wish for additional proof, then Moulton our lawyer has the original letter. In a sealed envelope marked private and confidential.'

'Moulton does not know the contents of this letter?'

Theodore shrugged. 'No, why should he? There are matters concerning the family which are no business of his.'

So Theodore didn't even trust the old family lawyer. What was it Moulton had called it: 'misinformation'? Did he suspect the truth. Or was Theodore lying? Again.

There was one way of finding out.

Eager to hear McQuinn's report on the Priorsfield servants, Faro returned to his office later that day. Expecting to find him alone he was surprised to hear feminine laughter as he opened the door. Throwing it open, the last person he expected to see there was leaning across his desk.

11

It was Rose. Rose, happy and animated, her face flushed with pleasure. Danny McQuinn wore an expression of wry amusement and it was some moments before the young sergeant became aware of Faro glowering in the background.

Springing to his feet, he saluted smartly. 'Morning, sir!'

Rose turned, smiled delightedly. 'Papa! I've been waiting for you.'

'What are you doing here?' Faro asked.

'I came to see you, of course.' Anyone but Rose would have detected a certain steely quality had crept into her father's voice. 'Sergeant McQuinn has been very hospitable.'

'Has he indeed?' And ignoring the unhappy-looking sergeant, Faro said: 'Well, I am here. What is it you want? I thought you were staying with Miss Langweil.'

'Just for one night, Papa. I decided as the carriage was passing close to your office that I would look in and see you. Just for a few moments. I'm usually in bed when you get home in the evenings.'

Although there was no reproach in Rose's statement, Faro was again guiltily aware that he had sorely neglected his daughter on this visit.

Looking round his office, each shelf stacked high with documents, she commented: 'It is years since the last time I was in here. It hasn't changed much, has it? They don't spend much on paint and paper, do they? And you still have the same books on the shelves, in exactly the same places. Do you ever open them?'

'Rose dear,' he interrupted, conscious of McQuinn's knowing smile, 'what was it you wanted? Are you short of cash?'

'No. Do I have to have a reason to look in and say hello to my Papa?'

Faro forced a smile. 'I appreciate your visit, Rose, but I do have rather a busy morning, a lot of matters—'

'To attend to,' she completed with a sigh. 'But then you always have, Papa.'

Faro looked at McQuinn who, for once it seemed, proved not insensitive to a delicate situation. Gathering his papers together, he bowed to Rose. 'Morning, miss,' and went towards the door.

'On your way out, McQuinn, be so good as to summon a carriage to take Miss Faro home.'

As the door closed on him, Rose said: 'I'm sorry if you are cross about me going to stay with Grace. I spend most of the day with her anyway. And it also means that I see Vince in the evenings.' She shook her head sadly. 'It isn't working out the way I thought it would. I mean, you are busy, Vince is busy, and I do get very bored staying indoors.'

'I thought you loved Sheridan Place. The number of times you've begged to come and stay with me.' He emphasised the last words.

'So I have, Papa. But in the past I've always had Emily. And I do miss having a companion of my own age. I didn't realise that I'd be staying with Mrs Brook. Not that I object to her, for she is a dear person, but we haven't a great deal in common and she has lots to do with the house to run. I can hardly expect her to chaperone me every time the sun shines and I want to walk in the park or look at some shops!'

As she spoke, Faro for the first time saw himself mirrored in her eyes as a selfish, thoughtless parent. He wanted his daughter when he was available to be with her, not caring that she might have to sit in an empty house waiting for him to come home. With a pang of remorse, he realised that her poor mother, his dear faithful Lizzie, had also spent her life waiting for a husband who was always late for meals and never around when she needed him.

He should have been glad that Rose had made friends, and with Grace Langweil. But he wasn't. The idea of having his daughter stay in a house whose occupants were under the shadow of murder continued to make him uneasy.

A knock on the door and McQuinn said: 'Carriage is here for Miss Rose, sir.'

Taking her by the arm, Faro led her along the corridor and into the street, aware that she looked around smiling, hoping to see McQuinn, and clearly disappointed when he tactfully remained invisible.

Putting her into the waiting carriage, Faro kissed her and said, 'We'll talk about this later, my dear.'

'Promise?'

'Promise.'

McQuinn had returned to the office and was waiting for him. 'Storm in a tea cup, sir?' he grinned.

Faro nodded and said: 'Let's get down to business. We've wasted enough time.'

And he launched into an account of the latest developments of the Langweil case.

McQuinn handed him the list of servants. 'I think that rather settles any ideas we might have that the missing brother is lurking about. There isn't anyone who could remotely be Justin Langweil in disguise. All the middle-aged men are gardeners and malthouse workers. They have been there since they were lads. I'll say it for the Langweils, their staff think well of them. No grumbles from below stairs either. So where do we go next, sir?'

Faro considered the list. 'I want you to find out from everyone at Priorsfield, never mind if they have told you already – ask them to repeat it, every detail they can remember from the moment the visitors left the house the night of Cedric's death until they retired to bed.'

McQuinn whistled. 'That's a tall order, sir. It wasn't yesterday, exactly.'

'I know. But do it.'

McQuinn went to the door and turned. 'I don't get the drift, sir. Do you think Justin Langweil—'

'Never mind what I think, McQuinn. Let's say I'm just not satisfied with the evidence so far. There's something missing. Something that has been overlooked. Someone's not telling the absolute truth and I suspect either concealing by accident or design some vital clue. And we're damned well going to find it, even if it means raising a hornets' nest in the ranks of a loyal and devoted family.' He stood up, gathered his notes together. 'Meanwhile, I'm going to see their lawyer again.'

And see him again Faro did. But not quite as he had expected to. A call at the office revealed that Mr Moulton was seeing a client in East Lothian and was not expected back until later that day.

The weather took a turn for the worse. The mild spring-like days disappeared in rain sheets and a furious gale rattled the windows in Sheridan Place, and sent gusts of smoke billowing down the chimneys.

Even on calm nights, Faro was finding difficulty in sleeping soundly and the sudden unexpected storm did nothing for his composure or his ability to wrestle with the baffling elements of the Langweil murder.

*

Early the following morning, an unforgivably cheerful and healthy-looking McQuinn arrived at Sheridan Place while Faro was breakfasting with Vince and Rose.

'Forgive the interruption, sir.'

Rose was clearly delighted. 'How nice to see you, Sergeant. Have you had breakfast?'

'I have, miss. But thank you kindly—'

'You will surely have some tea with us?'

Before Faro could protest, McQuinn smiled and shook his head. 'Sorry, miss, another time perhaps.' And to Faro: 'I'm on my way to Duddingston, sir. Thought you'd want to come with me. And you, Dr Laurie. You may be needed.'

McQuinn's expression indicated serious police business, not to be discussed in front of young ladies.

His manner was urgent enough for Faro and Vince to jump up from the table and follow him into the hall.

'What has happened?' Faro demanded.

'That lawyer, Moulton, has been found floating in the loch.'

As the police carriage hurtled through Holyrood Park, McQuinn told them that a farmer on his way to market had spotted a wrecked carriage at the bottom of the steep incline they were approaching.

'It had its wheels in the air and the horse was still in its traces but looked as if it were dead. He was curious so he went down for a better look. And there beside it floating in the water was a man's body.'

A small crowd had already gathered at the water's edge. The three men slithered down to join them through the wet grass, for there had been heavy rain during the night. Faro recognised with a sickened sense of disaster the two-wheeler that he had last seen outside Moulton's office.

Vince was bending over the body. After a brief examination he said: 'I should estimate he's been dead for less than twelve hours.'

'That would make it about midnight.' And staring at the front of Priorsfield across the other side of the loch, Faro frowned. 'I wonder what he was doing on the road at that time of night.'

'I can tell you that, sir.'

The speaker was a rough-looking fellow, a stableman by his attire.

'I work at Priorsfield. Mr Moulton was visiting the master and he came round for his carriage about midnight.' Leaning forward confidentially, he shook his head. 'Had quite a bit to drink, by the look of him, though one shouldn't talk ill of the dead and an old 'un like that. Fair staggering he was and in a bit of a paddy. Fair whipped up his horse, too, he did as they trotted off down the drive. Far too old—'

But Faro was no longer listening. 'Tell my sergeant here, will you? What's your name? Jock. Very well, Jock, and while you're here, would you take a look at the wreckage?'

'Oh, I can tell you what caused the accident. The wheel came off. First thing I did when I came down—'

'And how did the wheel come off?'

The man shook his head. 'No idea, sir. The pin was broken. Might have been wear, but I didn't notice any wobble on it as the gentleman left – of course, it could have—'

'Hold a minute, if you please. Look,' Faro interrupted, moving rapidly in McQuinn's direction, 'take this fellow's statement. I don't suppose anyone saw the accident, no one would be on the road in a storm like that.'

'Unlikely, sir. Folks unfortunate enough to be out walking would be keeping their heads well down—'

McQuinn paused as Faro stared at the white-faced house across the loch. 'Do I take it you don't think it was an accident, sir?'

'See what you think when you've had the stableman's story, McQuinn. I'm off to see Mr Langweil.'

By the time the police carriage had reached the house by

circumnavigating two sides of the loch any element of surprise was lost.

Theodore had been walking his dogs and the two Labradors bounded up the front steps to greet Faro. Their master looked genuinely concerned at Faro's arrival.

'Come in, Inspector. I suppose it's about poor old Moulton. One of the servants has just told me. What a tragedy.'

And ushering him into the library, he closed the door, poured himself a drink.

'May I offer you some refreshment, Inspector?'

'Too early in the day for me, sir,' said Faro with a faintly disapproving look at the decanter and wondering if Theodore Langweil normally began imbibing whisky at ten in the morning. Or was it comfort for a very frightened man?

'I understand that Mr Moulton visited you late last night.'

'Yes, he did. Who told you that?' demanded Langweil idly.

'Your stableman. He saw Mr Moulton leave.'

Theodore sighed. 'Then he probably told you that the old man was somewhat the worse of drink.' Without waiting for Faro's comment, he continued: 'I warned him. But he was a headstrong old devil. Never listened to a word of warning from anyone that driving a two-wheeler at a reckless speed at his age – and in a drunken condition—'

'May we go back to the beginning of the evening, sir? May I enquire, what was the reason for his visit?'

Theodore's lip curled. 'Is this an official enquiry, Inspector? I mean, does anyone who visits this house have to have a reason, other than a social occasion?'

When Faro did not answer, Theodore sighed wearily. 'All right. Old – I mean, Mr Moulton, came because I asked him to do so. There were various business matters to discuss, that have been delayed since my brother's death. He no longer conducts his business at any great speed, you understand.'

'At what time did he arrive?'

Theodore thought. 'About seven. He left again around midnight.'

'You must have had a great deal to discuss,' Faro said heavily.

Langweil's face was expressionless. 'We did.'

'And might I presume that the urgency of his visit was somehow connected with the original of the letter from San Francisco which you showed me earlier in the day—'

'Damn your eyes, Faro,' Langweil exploded. 'Of course it wasn't. I – I did—' and then again he sighed, mollified. 'I did mention it to him in passing, of course, just ensuring its safety, and he told me that it was locked in his office safe with the rest of the family documents.'

'So after you had finished discussing urgent matters, you turned to more convivial things.'

'Naturally. Old Mouldy had a rich treasure of wicked tales from behind the scenes in so-called respectable Edinburgh. I always enjoy listening to his stories. Besides, the weather was foul. A sudden storm of rain and hail. We hoped it would settle and when it did not, I invited him to stay the night. But he refused. He insisted on getting home to his own bed.'

Langweil thumped his fists together angrily, as if the full force of the tragedy had suddenly struck a chord of emotion. 'Fool of a man, he would still have been alive if he'd taken my advice – for once.'

'When he left, did you see him off?'

'On a night like that?' Theodore looked amused. 'Why, that is what servants are for, Inspector.'

'Your stableman Jock said Mr Moulton was in a rage. Thought he was very upset about something.'

'Did he indeed? If the stupid fellow had used his head, he would have realised that any old gentleman, known at the best of times for his crusty temper, would have been upset and in a rage at the prospect of driving an open carriage back to

Edinburgh in a hailstorm. You must have heard it in Newington?'

And Theodore stood up indicating that the interview was at an end. As they walked across the hall, he asked: 'Any idea what caused the accident?'

'A broken wheel pin, I gather.'

Theodore nodded. 'I thought it couldn't be just Moulton's reckless driving.'

At the front door, Faro paused. 'Tell me, Mr Langweil, did you have any reason for leaving the house last night?'

'Last night? Of course not, I was entertaining Mr Moulton.'

'Precisely that, sir. I mean during his visit.'

Langweil looked at him as if he had taken leave of his senses. 'I don't understand what you're getting at, Inspector. There was a storm raging outside. I had a guest.'

And bidding him good day Faro rapidly walked towards the police carriage with the satisfaction of seeing Langweil's expression change to one of open-mouthed astonishment as if the significance of the question had just dawned.

Theodore was either an exceedingly accomplished actor or else he was innocent. And if he was innocent there existed a strong possibility that someone else had hastened the old lawyer to his untimely end.

A possibility Faro viewed without any relish, that he might now have a second murder case to solve.

The carriage dropped him outside the consulting rooms Vince shared with Adrian Langweil, where the latter had just heard the news and was very upset. It seemed that of all the brothers he was fondest of the old lawyer, who had always made a great fuss of him.

'He was like a father to me,' he said gloomily, 'I shall miss him.'

Having found Adrian alone and without any appointments

for the next half-hour Faro decided to take full advantage of the situation. The time was long past when he felt obligated to respect Theodore's desire to protect the Langweil family by withholding vital information concerning the missing brother Justin.

Perhaps there was indeed something Adrian was aware of, but had not put into words, which might give Faro the lead he so desperately needed. But at the end of his disclosure about the letter from the San Francisco lawyers, Adrian sighed. 'Poor old Justin. And yet, I'm not really surprised, you know. Good of Theo to try to spare us, but I always had the strangest feeling that Justin had gone for ever, that he would never come back from America.'

'How curious. Had you any reasons for this?'

'None at all. But even when I was quite a little lad I had the feeling that Justin was dead. And that something quite dreadful had happened to – something terrible—'

He paused, biting his lips. 'It was like trying to remember a dream – a nightmare.'

'Could it have been a whispered conversation you overheard about Justin, between your brothers?'

Adrian brightened. 'You might well be right about that. I was a sore trial to them in that I was a bad sleeper, still am, and I used to prowl about Priorsfield in the middle of the night – with a lighted candle – searching for Prince Charlie's lost gold.'

He smiled at Faro. 'You know what children are like, Mr Faro. I got this bee in my bonnet. I was addicted to adventure stories and I got this idea that someday I would find the secret of that lost French gold.'

'I thought the legend was that the French count missed the Prince. That they never met.'

Adrian shrugged. 'I know that. But it didn't satisfy me. I remembered that the rightful heir to the Scottish throne had visited this house constantly when his troops were camped on

Arthur's Seat before the Battle of Prestonpans. It was marvellous ground for a young lad's romancing. And then there was the murdered man – the skeleton they dug up in the grounds—'

Faro smiled. This was a new and surprising aspect of the hard-headed doctor.

'There was – probably still is – a trunk full of dressing-up costumes, old clothes dating way back into the last century,' Adrian continued dreamily. 'In my satin waistcoat and knee breeches I tried to will myself into seeing what Priorsfield was like in those days. It wasn't until my niece Grace was a little girl that I discovered I had a soul mate, someone who shared my feelings that the house was, well, haunted.'

Faro looked at him. 'Yes, Vince said something of the sort.'

'She had better luck than I ever did, although it almost scared her to death. She saw – or claimed she saw, no one believed her but me – the ghost of a man, in the costume of the last century. She saw him more than once—'

Now Faro remembered. 'That was the reason she would never sleep there alone.'

'Oh, how I envied her. I would have given anything to see her ghost. When I think how I used to sit on the stairs and try to escape back into the past.'

A tap on the door interrupted him, announcing the arrival of his next patient.

'How did we get on to all this, Mr Faro? We've come a long way from whatever it was you wanted to know. But I've enjoyed chatting to you.'

Faro went away very thoughtfully. Adrian's story had brought him no nearer to finding the truth about Justin Langweil. This might be an opportune time to visit the old lawyer's office. He had a sudden urgent desire to see the original of that San Francisco letter.

He found Mr Wailes, the lawyer's assistant, in sole occupation of the office. Referred to by Mr Moulton as his 'young clerk', Faro was surprised to see that he was nearer fifty than the twenty years such a description would have merited.

When Faro announced himself as calling in connection with the accident, Mr Wailes regarded him gravely.

He looked very upset, near to tears, hovering over Moulton's possessions returned by the police and spread on the table before him.

'I cannot believe that he has gone, Inspector. He was such a brave, gallant old man—'

Faro listened sympathetically to a eulogy far removed from the irascible crusty old gentleman who left his mark upon the inhabitants of Priorsfield over the years.

Finally he interrupted. 'I wonder if you could help us. I have just been to Priorsfield and Mr Theodore wishes urgently to have confirmation of a document from the family papers.'

It was taking a long shot indeed, Faro realised as both he and Wailes stared at the bunch of keys which had never left Moulton's person until his death.

'Mr Moulton never let them out of his possession for an instant,' said Wailes, doubtfully touching them in the awed manner of a sacred relic. 'In all my years here, I have never opened that safe, nor do I know exactly what it contains.'

He paused, frowning. 'But I suppose now that I am in charge of the office until the terms of Mr Moulton's will have been read and discharged—' Pausing, he sighed.

'There may well be other clients with urgent business,' said Faro, realising that he was taking a mean advantage of the man's distress.

'That is true, sir. Very true. Might as well make a start.' For a moment he hesitated, then picking up the keys he looked at them as if they might burn a hole in his hand:

'Well, sir, at least I have the law present in case anyone should suggest what I did was improper.'

The contents of the shelves were neatly labelled, as Faro might have suspected: the old lawyer had been a very methodical man. The files were all arranged in alphabetical order from which Wailes withdrew that marked 'Langweil'.

'What was it you wished to see, Inspector?'

Faro told him he was looking for a letter from lawyers in San Francisco, marked private and confidential.

'There's only one sealed document here. "To be opened by Adrian Langweil in the event of the death of Theodore and Cedric Langweil." Looks like a will, sir.'

'That can't be it.'

He stared over Wailes' shoulder as the clerk skimmed through the old documents, many of which must have dated back to the original deeds of Priorsfield. But they, though of antiquarian interest, were none of his business.

'You are quite sure of the date?'

Faro did not need to consult his notes to know that the date was right and that if Moulton had exceeded his authority by removing it from its envelope then he would also have filed it in the proper sequence.

Three times Wailes went through the documents. Finally he shook his head. 'I'm sorry, Inspector. There is no such letter in the file. And you have my assurance that if Mr Moulton had it in his possession, it would have been here – right here, sir.'

Pausing, he looked at Faro. 'I can only suggest, sir, that Mr Langweil has made a mistake and that you take up the matter with him again. Twenty years is a long time. Perhaps he reclaimed the document for some purpose and forgot to return it to Mr Moulton. That does happen with clients sometimes.'

Thanking him for his help, Faro walked down the front steps sure of one thing: that the original had never existed except in the fabric of Theodore Langweil's imagination.

*

At the Central Office, McQuinn looked in to see him later that day.

Handing him the statements from the farmer who had found the lawyer's body and the stableman Jock, he said: 'I decided to have another talk to the servants at Priorsfield.

'This will interest you, sir. Mrs Gimmond was grumbling about the hailstorm and the awful weather, especially as she had to give one of the maids a good ticking off. The lass had been in tears, swearing she had polished the front hall floor and that it had been left beautiful.

' "Well," said Mrs G, "it wasn't beautiful when I came downstairs this morning. There were muddy footprints all the way to the library and up the stairs. The master would have had a fit if he'd seen them when he came down to breakfast. A stickler for polished floors he is. Worse than the mistress." '

McQuinn sat back in his chair and regarded Faro triumphantly. 'So what do you think of that, sir?'

'I'd give a lot to know in which direction the muddy footsteps were going.'

McQuinn scratched his chin. 'I think I can give you an answer to that, too. Remember the storm didn't start until ten o'clock. By then Mr Moulton was with Mr Langweil. He was the only guest, the only one to leave the house.'

'Wait a moment, McQuinn.' And Faro remembered having asked Langweil if he had seen his guest off.

'Well, sir, he lied. He or someone else must have been out of the house some time that evening after they ate. And it wouldn't be one of the servants because the footsteps were leading to the library and upstairs. A servant would have gone through the baize door downstairs.'

'You're right. And if Langweil left the house in the storm, he had a purpose.'

McQuinn smiled. 'Like tampering with the wheel of the

lawyer's carriage and then filling him with drink so that he'd be right fuddled on that twisting road by the loch.'

When Faro related the day's events to Vince, he saw by his stepson's expression that he still hoped for a miracle and that Grace's family would somehow be declared innocent of what now looked like two murders.

'I'm particularly interested in Justin Langweil. Especially after what Adrian told you.'

'Oh, I haven't given up hope that we'll unearth him yet.'

'He is certainly the most likely candidate.'

Vince sounded almost hopeful. After all the lad had a bad reputation, better the black sheep than one of the respectable Langweils.

Faro slept little that night. Eventually he got up and brought up to date his notes on the case. Throwing down his pen, he was no further out of the labyrinth.

All the evidence pointed to Theodore being guilty of murdering Cedric and then the old lawyer because he knew too much.

The other idea, ever growing in magnitude, was that the missing eldest brother was very much alive and well in Priorsfield.

There was one other possibility, so obvious that it never even occurred to him to give it a serious thought.

12 Returning home preoccupied with the day's events but determined to set them to one side for Rose's benefit, he was disagreeably surprised to find that he had a visitor.

McQuinn was sitting in the dining room and Rose was talking to him in her usual animated fashion.

Soft-footed as always, they did not immediately observe his arrival on the scene. But seeing them together smiling and happy, he realised with a pang that whereas twelve years might seem a vast difference between a girl of fifteen and a man of twenty-seven, as a couple grew older so did the odds diminish.

And standing there unobserved he remembered that Lizzie had been Rose's age when, a servant in the 'big house', she had been seduced by one of the aristocratic house guests.

Vince had been the result of that tragic ill-fated episode.

A shiver of apprehension went through Faro. That situation must not be allowed to repeat itself in Rose's life. And, blessed or cursed with the ability to put himself in someone else's shoes and walk around in them for a while, he saw for the first time Danny McQuinn through Rose's eyes.

A more than averagely handsome policeman with a more than average dose of Irish charm, easy with women of all classes and all ages. A man an impressionable schoolgirl could very easily fancy that she was in love with—

He stepped forward sharply. McQuinn looked up, once again the dutiful officer, sprang to his feet.

'I was on my way back from Priorsfield, sir. As I was passing the house, I thought you'd better see these.'

Faro said nothing and held out his hand for the list containing the servants' names.

Without looking at his daughter, he said: 'Thank you, Rose. You may leave us now.'

His stern expression cut short any leave-taking between the two and as the door closed McQuinn said: 'These are the only two that need concern you, sir. I've whittled them down to the butler Gimmond, who has been there longest. You've met him. I don't think he could be our man.'

'And the other?'

McQuinn frowned. 'The only possibility would be the stable-man who is also the coachman, Jock.'

'The man we met at the scene of the accident, of course.'

'Except that if he'd been guilty he would hardly have been lingering about the place.'

'He might have wanted to make sure the old man was dead.'

'True enough.'

'What do we know about him?'

'Not a great deal. Came from Colinton way about a year ago. Good references and all that sort of thing.' McQuinn looked at him. 'I know what you're thinking, sir, but he's a bit nondescript to fit the description of the missing heir. I mean, they're a well set-up handsome lot of men, you must admit that. And no one would call Jock prepossessing. He's a shambling sort of cove, what we call shilpit-lookin'.'

Jock the stableman certainly seemed an unlikely candidate, unshaven and distinctly unkempt. Yet that could be a disguise in itself.

'Remember he has been away from home for twenty years –

if he is our man – and a lot of physical changes could have taken place. Again I put to you, McQuinn, that employers only glance at their servants. They have only minimal conversations and from what I've seen even avoid any kind of contact.

'Let's consider opportunity. Tampering with the wheel of Moulton's carriage was easy. And what was to stop him creeping up into the house when everyone was upstairs asleep and administering the fatal dose to the wine bottle? All he had to do was open the door, the men's chairs were at the fire, they had high backs which are meant to protect them from draughts – and the presence of whoever is serving them.'

'You think he intended to poison both of them, sir?'

'I do.'

'But why? What had he to gain?'

'Revenge now seems the most likely motive. I think he intended to get rid of both of them, then disappear. Who would be likely to check a servant who takes off? Then when the noise has all died down he would make a second spectacular reappearance as the heir to Langweils returned from America.'

McQuinn sighed. 'You make it sound very feasible, sir.' He grinned. 'But then you always do. However, there is one more thing. You asked me to get the servants to try to remember anything unusual about the happenings on the night of Mr Cedric's death?

'Well, we may have something,' he continued, excitement creeping into his voice. 'Seems Mrs Gimmond always counts the glasses when they are brought down for washing. They are real crystal and valuable and the master is very particular about them, especially as there are always extra glasses on the side table during a dinner party in case the guests wish to sample other kinds of wine or spirits.

'As I've said, they are carefully counted afterwards and any breakages have to be paid for out of their wages if any go a-missing. Well, on the morning of Mr Cedric's death, Mrs Gimmond was upset and with the house in uproar, she almost forgot about a glass that had been put out without Gimmond noticing that it was badly chipped.

'Mr Theodore had admonished him—'

'What happened to the glass?' demanded Faro.

'Mrs Langweil said she would take care of it.'

'Wait a minute – Mrs Langweil?'

'Yes, sir. Mr Theodore's wife.'

'I thought there were just the two men.'

'Apparently she looked in to say good night when all this was going on.'

McQuinn paused dramatically. 'I'm sure that something of the sort must have occurred to you, sir. That the poisoner could in fact be Mr Theodore's wife. Sure, she had time and opportunity—'

But Faro wanted to close his ears to McQuinn's logical deductions. So Barbara had been present. She could easily have – oh, no. Not Barbara. Not Cedric's murderer.

'The glass, McQuinn,' he gasped. 'What happened to it?'

'I imagine it went out with the rest of the rubbish.'

Faro groaned. The one piece of evidence that pointed to the glasses and not the bottle having been poisoned.

If only Barbara Langweil had not been involved.

His gloomy thoughts were interrupted by McQuinn. 'Shall I check at Colinton village, on what they know about Jock?'

'Yes, do that.'

'What about the lawyer, sir? What are we doing about him?'

Faro had no reason except his own instinct for claiming that the old lawyer's death had been anything but an accident. A broken wheel on an ancient carriage.

He decided, however, that it might be worth looking in at the funeral. If only to have a few words with the clerk Mr Wailes.

He arrived at the cemetery just as the few mourners were leaving. As Moulton had been a bachelor with no family, he learned that

Theodore Langweil had taken care of the arrangements and he wondered if there was any significance in this somewhat hasty committal.

He looked surprised to see Faro.

'Are you here in your official capacity?' he asked.

'I was hoping to have a few words with Wailes.'

'Wailes? Oh, yes. Moulton's clerk. His young clerk,' he added with a laugh. 'Always gave us the impression that he was scarcely out of the nursery, therefore quite irresponsible. Must be fifty, if he's a day.' And looking at his waiting carriage, 'Well, he wasn't here to pay his last respects either.'

At Faro's look of concern, he said: 'Is there something wrong?'

'There could well be, sir. I went to the office after our talk the other night and the accident. I met Mr Wailes and asked to see the original of that letter from San Francisco.'

He cut short Theodore's angry retort. 'We have to check these things, sir, unpleasant though it may be. We cannot take anyone's word for what may be vital evidence.'

'Vital evidence? I don't know what you're talking about.'

Faro regarded him steadily. 'It has never occurred to you then, sir?'

'What are you talking about?'

'The possibility that your brother Justin might still be alive.'

Theodore looked at him as if he had taken leave of his senses. Then suddenly he exploded with laughter. So loud that people turned and stared at him, shocked by such mirth in this place of hushed voices and respectful silences.

'You'll be the death of me, Faro. Really you will.' And seizing him by the sleeve of his cape, he said, 'Justin is dead. Dead. Believe me, if you don't believe letters of proof.'

Pausing, he added: 'Well, did you see it?'

'No, I didn't. Wailes searched the papers and it wasn't there.'

Theodore shrugged. 'I expect he was looking in the wrong place.'

Maybe so, maybe not, thought Faro as they parted company

at the gates. However, he decided to call on Wailes the following morning.

The office was now occupied by two young men who, presuming him to be one of the old lawyer's clients, explained that they were in charge and asked what they could do for him.

'It is Mr Wailes I wish to see.'

'We haven't seen him for several days,' said one.

'Not since he asked us to take over while he went to visit a sick relative,' said his partner.

'If you would care to state your business, we assist Mr Moulton from time to time.'

Faro shook his head. 'Do you have an address for Mr Wailes?'

As they searched in a drawer and eventually produced an address in Fountainbridge, Faro asked the senior of the two, 'And where does this ailing relative live?'

Puzzled looks were exchanged. 'Abroad somewhere, America or Canada.'

'No, Tom,' said his companion. 'That's where she used to live – you've got it all wrong.'

Faro decided to avoid the argument that was imminent. 'He left no address for this person?'

'Didn't seem to think that was necessary with us looking after things here.'

'He didn't talk much to anyone—'

And in a sudden rush of confidence his companion added: 'Certainly not to either of us. Kept himself to himself.'

'Very much so,' was the final pronouncement.

Wailes' address led Faro to a cheap lodging-house, shabby and none too clean. A woman wearing a dirty apron directed him grudgingly to the third floor up, left-hand door.

The stone stair smelt of mingled cats and human vomit.

As he expected, there was no reply and the woman was waiting for him. No, she hadn't seen Mr Wailes for a day or two. 'Hope he hasna' done a flit. Owes me two weeks' rent,' she added anxiously.

'Do you happen to have a key to the room?' The woman nodded uneasily when Faro continued: 'Then perhaps you would be so kind as to produce Mr Wailes' key.' Faro held out his hand. 'Come along, now, I'm a police officer. We need to talk to Mr Wailes.'

'Och well, that's different.' The information seemed to cheer her considerably and leading the way upstairs rattling her clutch of keys she turned and asked excitedly: 'Has he done something, Officer? Never much to say for himself. Seems like such a nice quiet respectable-like mannie. But a body can no' be sure. It's the quiet-like ones is killers, I'm told—'

And throwing open the door she gave a scream of anguish.

Thrusting her aside, Faro rushed into the room, fully expecting to encounter Wailes's dead body lying on the floor.

To his relief the room was empty, but even before the woman flung open the wardrobe and drawers it was evident from her wailing and her frantic manner that Mr Wailes had indeed done a flit, leaving his debts behind him.

Was there some other reason for his sudden disappearance apart from a sick relative? More important, was it connected with some vital aspect of the Langweil case?

Back at the Central Office, Faro put his findings to McQuinn, who asked eagerly: 'Shall we put out a warrant for his arrest, sir?'

13

'We can hardly arrest a man for debt just because he owes a couple of pounds for lodgings.'

'I realise that, sir. But it sounds as if this might be our man.'

'McQuinn, when you've been on this job as long as I have, the first thing you learn is never jump to conclusions, never try to force evidence that isn't there, just because it would conveniently wrap up a case. There's been too much of that already,' he added sternly. 'A history of innocent men hanged because the detective in charge of the case decided they were guilty and turned a blind eye to the evidence that they weren't.'

McQuinn looked surprised but impressed as Faro went on: 'You know my views or you should do by now. I'd rather have a guilty man go free than an innocent man hang.'

McQuinn shrugged. 'Sure, when you put it that way, sir. I expect you're right. So where do we start?'

'A few discreet enquiries at the Law Courts might save us a lot of embarrassment. After all, he might have had some quite legitimate reason for taking off suddenly.'

McQuinn regarded him doubtfully. 'Like what, sir?'

'We can't possibly answer that until we know a little more of his background. Think, McQuinn, there are a hundred different reasons for a man to leave his lodgings without being guilty of his employer's murder.'

McQuinn's expression suggested that he couldn't even think of one good reason.

'There must have been other people in Moulton's office too. Cleaners, messengers, for instance. God dammit, he must have talked to someone.'

McQuinn set off grumpily as Faro drew up the papers awaiting his return. To the known facts in the Langweil case, he added two further names.

The stableman, Jock. Was he known at Colinton? Could he be vouched for by family, etc.?

Moulton's assistant, Wailes. Had he absconded? Could he be vouched for by colleagues and acquaintances at the Sheriff Court?

Faro remembered faces very well. Neither man, he had to confess, had the least resemblance to the Langweil men, who bore a strong family likeness, nor by any stretch of imagination could either be transformed into the missing, presumed dead, brother, Justin.

Yet Jock and Wailes were the most likely – only – possibilities. There was only one thing bothered him about Wailes. In the unlikely event that he was Justin in disguise, then it would have been in his own interests to confirm that the real Justin died in California long ago. But his ignorance seemed quite genuine and Faro remembered how industriously he had searched for the missing document—

Faro shook his head. Perhaps he was on the wrong track altogether and he was making too much of a wild idea that the murderer was a missing brother, killing off members of his family as revenge for his young wife's death twenty years ago.

Before the possibility of Justin's existence, all evidence had pointed to Theodore. Or—

There was one other. His hand trembled as he wrote down

'Barbara Langweil', and he little guessed that within the next twenty-four hours, he was to discover that she had the best motive of all.

The information came his way quite casually, as did so many damning pieces of evidence.

That night the Edinburgh City Police held their Annual Grand Reunion at the Caledonian Hotel. This was a splendid occasion in which serving policemen and retired officers mingled together. The speeches were often long and tedious, but as compensation there was a considerable amount of ale and spirits, by courtesy of Langweil Ales Ltd.

There were for Faro many old and familiar faces and in the bar he was hailed by Peter Lamont who swayed towards him rather unsteadily.

'Good to see you again so soon, Faro,' he said, slapping him on the back. 'Let's take a seat. Have a dram. Your young lad not here with you?'

Faro explained that Vince had been invited but was being kept rather busy at the moment.

Peter chuckled. 'Busy with other matters, eh?' And nudging him, 'That's a right bonny wee lass he's going to marry. Done well for himself, hasn't he?'

Faro agreed.

'I have to apologise for that business at the hotel the other day.'

'What business was that?'

Peter chuckled again. 'My missus put her foot right in it, she did.'

Before Faro could comment, Peter looked over his shoulder and leaned across confidentially. 'That business about Mrs Theodore being mistaken for Grace's stepmother.' He chortled. 'Did you not see me kick her under the table?'

Faro smiled. 'I don't think that would upset Grace. And it was a great compliment to her mother.'

'Her mother!' Peter exploded. 'That's rich.'

'I don't understand what you're getting at,' said Faro wearily.

'Of course you don't, lad. What I'm getting at is that the missus made a perfectly right assumption in the circumstances. You still don't get my drift, do you?' And when Faro shook his head, he said: 'You see when the two couples stayed with us in Perth, well, it was t'other way round. Cedric Langweil's missus was the young 'un. We both realised this when they came to the golf course. Naturally none of them remembered us. Visitors rarely remember the staff who serve them, much less the manager and his wife.'

Faro felt a cold chill steal over him. 'You must be mistaken.'

'Don't be daft, lad. Of course I'm not mistaken. No one could mistake Mrs Cedric for Mrs Theodore.'

Faro knew with a sick feeling of despair that it was true.

'What I'm saying to you, Faro, is that Mrs Theodore spent the night with her brother-in-law.'

'What about the other two?'

'Oh, they shared another bedroom. They weren't going to be left out in the cold, were they now?' added Peter with a grin. 'Way the other half lives, it's all right if you're rich—'

'Are you certain?' Faro interrupted.

'Course I'm certain, the maid saw them in bed together.' Peter dug him gently in the ribs and chuckled again. 'Thought you'd enjoy that wee piece of scandal. Here, your glass is empty. Have another. One for the road?'

'Could your maid swear to this in a court of law?' Faro asked, conscious as he spoke that his lips were suddenly stiff and sore as if the words hurt.

'Of course she could. She's still with us. Happened twice, so she wasn't likely to have made a mistake—'

'Twice, you say?'

'Correct. On the two weekends they stayed with us—'

'Hello, you two – mind if we join you?'

As they made room for McIntosh and his guest, Faro heard little of the ensuing badinage. The party had suddenly gone sour on him, and making his excuses to the Superintendent he left shortly afterwards.

Back in Sheridan Place he did not wait up for Vince. He had no desire to impart to anyone, Vince least of all, the new and damning evidence that had come his way.

It was unlikely that Peter would be mistaken, and if his chambermaid's observations were true then Barbara and Cedric had been lovers on at least two occasions. His righteous indignation did not extend to Theodore and Maud, who had been similarly guilty.

It seemed impossible that those two unlikely people could have been involved in a passionate intrigue.

But Cedric – whom everyone loved. And Barbara. Barbara, his goddess.

As he fought with rising anger, he realised the necessity for calm consideration of this new evidence in the search for Cedric's murderer. At last, coolly, he recognised its significance. That it gave Theodore an excellent reason for murdering his brother.

It also provided a signpost to one of the most popular methods known to the police for a mistress ridding herself of an unwanted lover whose attentions were becoming threatening or embarrassing.

With considerable reluctance he underlined thickly: 'Barbara Langweil', on his list of suspects.

He slept badly that night and next morning he was still unsure how he was going to handle this new aspect of the Langweil murder. The *crime passionnel*: for any policeman who has ever been in love himself and who understands the vagaries of the human condition, it is the crime in which it is the most difficult not to regard with compassion the slighted lover.

At the breakfast table Vince and Rose were chattering happily. Both addressed remarks to him which went unheard and therefore unanswered. They exchanged glances and at last Vince remarked upon his being unusually silent.

Faro tried to show an interest in this talk of weddings; through the murk of his own misery he was aware of Vince's happy mood, more relaxed than he had seemed of late.

He decided against drawing Vince into the further intricacies of this case, knowing that his stepson, strongly influenced by love and loyalty to Grace, had his own most urgent personal reasons for believing with the rest of the Langweils that her father had taken his own life.

'September isn't too far off,' Vince was telling Rose. 'So much to do—'

Unfortunately for the couple's revised wedding plans, on the eve of Barbara's thirtieth birthday party at Priorsfield her husband Theodore and brother-in-law Adrian were poisoned.

Adrian was still alive.

By a miracle, he had taken the merest sip of the **14** Langweil Alba liqueur when a commotion in the hall erupted to reveal Gimmond.

'Sorry to disturb you. But could Dr Adrian come quickly. One of the housemaids – upset a pan of boiling water—'

Before Adrian had finished attending to the crying maid and had dressed her scalded arm, he became aware of feeling distinctly ill. Leaving the kitchen hastily he vomited, retching with stomach pains.

Returning shakily to the scene he had just left, the door was flung open and Barbara rushed in screaming: 'For God's sake, Adrian, come quickly. Theo's lying on the floor. I think he's dying.'

'Get the carriage,' Adrian ordered Gimmond, and followed her upstairs where he took one look at his brother and decided that he had been poisoned. With Gimmond and Jock's assistance, while Barbara surveyed the terrible scene weeping and refusing to be parted from her husband, Theodore was bundled into the carriage.

Ten minutes later they delivered their now deeply unconscious burden to the Royal Infirmary. Jock, given instructions to alert Faro and Vince at Sheridan Place, found Faro alone.

*

The carriage hurtled towards Charlotte Square where Faro expected to find Vince with Grace. As he rushed past the startled maid unannounced, Maud appeared on the upstairs landing.

'Vince? He left about ten minutes ago.'

Faro cursed under his breath.

'Is something wrong?' Maud asked.

Faro considered and then shook his head. No point in alarming Maud at this juncture.

But at his urgent manner and distraught appearance, she said gently: 'Grace has not yet retired. She's in the library. She'll tell you if he was going straight home.'

Conscious that Maud was watching him very curiously, he ran lightly downstairs, and flinging open the library door he found Grace and Stephen Aynsley sitting on a sofa in the lamplight reading what looked like a book of poems.

Their heads were close together. Grace was smiling and Stephen's face, watching her, wore a look of complete and utter adoration.

They were unaware of his intrusion, like two people captured for ever in a romantic painting by the embers of a dying fire.

Faro felt a moment's anguish on Vince's behalf. Did he not realise that Stephen Aynsley, Grace's second, or was it third, cousin, was also madly in love with her?

Then the spell was broken, and they stood up to greet him.

'Vince? He went home, I think,' said Grace. 'What on earth is wrong?'

'Your Uncle Theodore has been poisoned.'

Grace gave a small scream of horror. Her hand flew to her mouth. 'No . . . Oh, no!'

'Adrian got him to the hospital. He wanted Vince to know.'

Maud had followed him downstairs. 'What is wrong?' she demanded. And leaving Grace to tell her, he fled leaving a scene of consternation behind him.

By the time he reached the hospital, Vince was already leaving the ward. 'Thank heaven you got here—'

'Mrs Brook gave me your message—'

'How is he?'

Vince shook his head. 'I think this proves your theories, fantastic as they seemed. It really does look as if the missing Justin must be somewhere around. There is no other logical explanation.'

But there was one, thought Faro grimly. Though, like me, you cannot face up to its grim reality. And at the light step behind them, he turned and looked into the tragic eyes of Barbara Langweil.

His mind was full of deadly accusations, but now, even now, he turned away from them, determined with every doubt fading that he was going to see Barbara as innocent until the evidence proved her undeniably guilty.

There was nothing he could do here and he returned to Sheridan Place for what remained of that night of anguish and uncertainty, of dreams turned hollow, and goddesses who were but human after all.

At eight next morning he made his way to the hospital, but as he was entering the gates the Langweil carriage swept past him. Bearing a trio of weeping women, it told him even before he reached Theodore's bedside that he was already too late.

Theodore's death suggested his innocence in the murder of his brother Cedric and the questionable fatal accident to the lawyer Moulton who knew too much about the Langweil family.

He found Adrian, pale, dazed and sick-looking, staring down

at the sheeted figure on the bed. Faro put his hand on his shoulder. At least he would survive.

Following him into the corridor, Adrian said: 'We did all we could. Dear God, who would do such a thing? When I think if we'd waited and opened it for the party – it might have been Freda. She has a passion for liqueurs.'

Faro looked at him. Had the amateur murderer got the wrong victim once again? Had Adrian's pregnant wife been the intended victim?

'Who would do this? Have you any ideas? For God's sake, Mr Faro, help us.'

Faro shook his head. All his theories – but one – had come to naught. 'Can you tell us exactly what happened before the maid came in and you had the glass in your hand?'

'Maud had left at ten when Barbara retired. We'd finished off the wine, and as it was well past midnight the servants had gone to bed. We were in rather high spirits, however, and Theo went to the cupboard and triumphantly produced Barbara's bottle.

' "She won't mind. Hates the stuff," he said as he broke the seal. "Shall we see if it's at the right temperature for tomorrow's party? Before Freda spots it. Then none of us will get a look-in." '

Adrian groaned. 'It's a family joke, just now; part of Freda's condition is a passion for sweet drinks.'

'Had the bottle come from the cellars in the usual way?' Faro asked.

Adrian looked embarrassed. 'No. According to Theo, it had been a present to Barbara, but liqueurs were far too sweet for her.'

Barbara again.

Faro groaned. 'I'm going to Priorsfield.'

'Do you think he might still be on the premises?'

'I think he might.'

'Then get him, for all our sakes. Get him, Mr Faro. Show no mercy. It must be one of the servants. It cannot be anyone else.'

Calling a carriage, Faro paused at the Central Office to collect McQuinn. Rapidly filling in the details, he waited for his sergeant's reactions.

McQuinn, now with the gift of hindsight, nodded eagerly. 'Always suspected something of the sort, sir. Amazed that you weren't on to it sooner. Are we to make an arrest?'

'The usual procedure, McQuinn.'

As the two men waited in the hall at Priorsfield, Faro gave the final instructions.

'Perhaps we're too late and the bird has flown,' whispered McQuinn anxiously. 'Shouldn't we—'

'No.' And as Gimmond appeared, Faro said: 'See no one leaves the house.'

He doubted he would be received by Mrs Langweil and was almost surprised when Gimmond led him into the library.

'If you will wait a moment, Inspector.'

'Before you go, Gimmond. You have heard about the master?'

Gimmond bowed, his face shadowed. 'Yes, Inspector. The staff are all devastated. He will be a great loss to us. A fine master—'

'You are, I take it, in charge of the cellar?'

'I am. That is solely my responsibility.' Faro's expression warned him of danger and he added hastily: 'There are, however, occasions when the master or the late Mr Cedric might take out bottles without my knowledge. They have their own keys.'

Faro looked thoughtful. 'And on the night of Mr Cedric's death?'

Gimmond frowned. 'I took out the wines required for the meal that evening from the menu prepared by Mrs Langweil and given to my wife.'

'And none of the bottles had been tampered with?'

'If you are implying that the seals had been broken, Inspector, I can tell you it would be more than my job's worth to put such a bottle out for the master's guests.'

'Then have you any idea—'

A faint smile touched Gimmond's lips as he interrupted: 'Is this in the nature of an official questioning, Inspector?'

'No. I thought merely that being in the house at the time, you might have seen something unusual—'

'Or that I might have had a hand in it,' Gimmond concluded the sentence for him.

Faro regarded him with new interest. This was the first time Gimmond had ever referred, even obliquely, to their old association. And Gimmond had without doubt the best opportunity of all to put arsenic in Cedric's glass. Was it possible that the butler and his wife might be implicated in both murders? Could they have been the assassin's accomplices? Had he been too hasty in dismissing Gimmond from his list of suspects?

Watching him closely, Gimmond said softly: 'If you will cast your mind back, Inspector, you will recall that the verdict in my case was "Not proven". Otherwise I would not be in this position of trust, serving the family.' Looking at Faro, he said: 'I am not ungrateful for your silence, Inspector, especially where Sergeant McQuinn's enquiries are concerned. So if there is any way I can help you – you have only to ask.'

'Had Mr Langweil any enemies among the servants?'

'So you think it might be one of us? Now that would save a very nasty scandal, wouldn't it? Find a scapegoat below stairs.' Gimmond laughed mirthlessly. 'Typical police procedure, ain't it. Spare the rich master and blame the poor servant, if you can find one to fit the part.'

He sighed. 'You'll have your work cut out in this house, if that's your game, Inspector Faro. Ask Mrs Gimmond, if you won't take my word for it—'

'About this bottle of liqueur—'

Again Gimmond shook his head. 'None of us ever laid eyes on it. I'm told that Mrs Langweil had been given it as a present. So she said,' he added in mocking tones of disbelief.

Both men jumped when the bell by the fireplace jangled through the room.

'That'll be the mistress. If you will come this way, Inspector.'

In the upstairs parlour, Maud and Freda were consoling their sister-in-law.

Seeing him enter, they looked resentfully in his direction.

'Please, I wish to see Inspector Faro alone,' Barbara whispered. 'Please go, my dears. Of course I shall be all right.'

'Are you sure?' asked Maud. 'Shall I stay? I really would like to stay.'

'No, please go. And take Freda with you.'

Bowing the ladies out, Faro closed the door.

'Sit down, Mr Faro.' She smiled sadly. 'We have rather a lot to say to each other, have we not?'

She had been weeping, and weeping copiously. And Faro marvelled how grief enhanced her loveliness, if that was possible, making her vulnerable and ethereal. More desirable.

An angel in tears. And yet this particular angel might he knew with dawning realisation, be a devil in disguise.

Suddenly his mind was cold and clear. He knew, and had known for a long time, but refused to admit it to himself, why the murders had been committed.

He could no longer cling to the hope, the faint possibility of a missing brother. Or a servant with a grievance.

All that remained was a beautiful woman with the most tawdry secret of all. A lover who was her brother-in-law.

Faro drew in a deep breath. 'Barbara Langweil, it is my duty to inform you that I am here to take you into custody for the murder of your husband Theodore Langweil—'

As he cautioned her he expected her to protest, to soften his heart with womanly tears; he was not kept long in suspense.

Instead she looked at him, dazed, shocked. Then she nodded. 'Yes, Mr Faro, I am guilty. I did it. I poisoned my husband.'

Faro said nothing. There wasn't anything he could say, hoping for a miracle, a denial of guilt with some totally unexpected revelation of damning evidence pointing to the real murderer.

But Barbara shook her head and sighed. 'It is not quite as you are imagining. It so happens that I loved Theodore, I shall always love him.'

And again she began to sob, while Faro stood by helplessly wondering, what then, if she loved him, was the motive.

'Cedric was my lover.'

That his suspicions aroused by Peter Lamont were true after all, gave him no sense of triumph. He felt faintly sick.

'It's a long story, Inspector. You must bear with me a little. I will try not to give way like this, but I will be honest with you.'

And so saying she straightened her slim shoulders and regarded him sadly. 'This whole sorry business began for me when Theodore married me, brought me to live at Priorsfield. Cedric and Maud were living here at that time and I soon realised, for he made no secret of the fact, that Cedric wanted me. He claimed that he was wildly in love and I, fool that I was, even flirted with him a little at the beginning. Naturally I was flattered that both brothers should love me.

'Theodore tolerated it with good humour at first. Then it began to irritate him and he suggested that Cedric and Maud make the move to Charlotte Square. There he thought Cedric's feelings would soon disappear when we met more rarely. But over the years what he regarded as a passing infatuation grew stronger. It became an obsession.'

Her face darkened as she continued slowly as if reliving the scene before her. 'While Theo and I mourned that we had no child as the years passed, Cedric was delighted. He said to me once, "If you had a child by Theo I would want to kill him. Yes, I would, my own brother. I could not bear the thought that he had given you something that I could not. That you could be possessed by him in a way that I could never possess you. Completely, utterly." '

Pausing, she glanced at Faro apologetically. 'I really believed until then that Cedric did not think that Theo and I – well, lived as man and wife. Once he said to me, "I would go mad if I let my mind dwell on Theo kissing you, holding you in his arms at night." '

'What about Maud? What were her feelings?'

'Oh, Maud knew. Cedric actually confided in her.' Barbara shuddered. 'But bless her good kind heart, she never took it seriously. She knew that I was utterly faithful to Theo and that I would never betray her. She had nothing to fear from me.

'And then late last year Cedric seemed unwell. He looked strange, odd. Then one day Theo told me that Cedric had seen a consultant. He was incurably ill. He was under sentence of death, as Theo put it, and had been given only a few months to live.

'As you might imagine, we were all shattered by this news. While Theo was the solemn, dependable head of the family, Cedric was so vibrant, the wit and humorist. They had always been close until I came along.'

She paused, frowning, and then added with a wan smile, 'I did love Cedric, you know. As I loved Adrian, for they were like the brothers I had never had. Then for a while, Theo seemed very preoccupied. I thought it was anxiety about Cedric which we all shared. I asked him about it and he said Cedric had asked him to grant a dying man's request.'

She was silent, staring into the fire so long that Faro whispered: 'Go on.'

She started as if she had forgotten his presence. 'It was – that Cedric had asked that he might share my bed for one night before – before the end. I was horrified. I thought Theo was joking. Then I knew he wasn't. He was almost in tears, my strong unemotional husband. "Do this for me, my darling." '

'I need not trouble you with my reactions to this monstrous suggestion or my tearful reproaches. How could Theo, my husband, even bear to mention such an idea to me. Did he not love me? And what of Maud? But Maud, it appeared, had been consulted and had given her consent.

'Reluctantly, after many sleepless nights, I gave mine. For Theo assured me that it would never change his love for me. He would love me more than ever for making this sacrifice for our beloved brother.

'Arrangements were made. We would stay at a small hotel in Perth where no one knew us. Theo had booked two double rooms under an assumed name. Cedric and I shared one, while in the other Maud had the bed and Theo slept on the sofa.

'On the journey there Cedric was so bright and excited, all trace of illness had vanished, he was literally like a young bridegroom. I could hardly bear to look at him. I felt physically sick at what lay ahead.'

Again she paused. 'I do not know that I can find words—'

Faro reached out, touched her hand. 'My dear Mrs Langweil, there is no need to tell me anything that does not relate to your husband's death – please do not distress yourself unnecessarily—'

'Distress myself!' she repeated, her face bewildered, dazed. 'That night with Cedric was like being with a madman. I did all he wished of me and yet it was not enough. It seemed that he could never be satisfied with what I gave him. He was like a raging animal. I was terrified of him, so different from my gentle, considerate Theo.

'At last dawn came. It was over. And we returned to Edinburgh. Theo never spoke to me about it and soon our normal life with all its social occasions and visits took over so that I would look across the table at Cedric and wonder if it had happened at all or if it was merely a very nasty embarrassing nightmare.

'And then Cedric became ill again. This time he was vomiting, terribly sick. He began complaining about bouts of indigestion but assured Theo that the consultant had said he would have these – towards the end. That this was part of the pattern, that his body was breaking up, its final decay.

'We were prepared for the worst. But even I was not quite prepared for what happened next. Theo came to me and said Cedric wanted one more night with me. This would be the very last, we all knew this. We could see that time was running out for him. But again I rebelled. I could not go through all that again. Never, never. But Theo took me in his arms and said: "This time, my darling, do it for me."

'And so, again, I agreed. Cedric wanted to go to a grander place, but Theo wisely dissuaded him. So we went to the same hotel, a quiet unassuming place where we were unlikely to be recognised, or even remembered, especially when the chambermaid came in and saw us in bed together.'

And Faro remembered Peter's piece of gossip and had not the heart to tell her that indeed no one is safe anywhere from the hand of coincidence.

She had closed her eyes tightly, seemed to have difficulty finding words. 'It was as awful as before, perhaps even more so. And it must have been terrible for Theo and Maud too, although none of us has ever spoken of it. As for me, I told myself, it would never happen again. I had already decided that I would rather kill Cedric – or myself – first.

'But I was safe from Cedric. Three weeks later he was dead.' She looked at Faro. 'You will already have deduced that I had an excellent motive, the very best, for poisoning my poor infatuated brother-in-law. But I didn't, I swear it, although I might have been driven to it, had he not taken his own life.'

'Or was poisoned,' he reminded her.

'Poisoned?' Barbara's laughter declared such an idea incredible, absurd. 'Who on earth would want to poison Cedric? Except me. I was the only one who, God forgive me, hated him that much towards the end.'

She shook her head. 'But I didn't do it. That I do swear. Although I expect they will blame me, since I did poison my dearest Theo, and all because of some silly family scandal that Cedric was holding over him.'

She was silent and Faro asked gently: 'What kind of scandal could have been that important?'

'What indeed? I don't know the details. Only that Theo said: "If you don't do as Cedric asks, he has promised to leave with old Moulton something that will destroy me. That will finish this family for good." Those were his very words.'

'You have no idea what this was?'

She shrugged. 'I got the impression it was some kind of document relating to Priorsfield. But when I asked him to tell me, he just shook his head. "It's better you never know, my dear. This house was built on blood and now it's taking its revenge on us all. Cedric is dying. He has nothing to lose. But I have everything – everything." '

She looked at Faro. 'I haven't anything more to tell you, Inspector. Are you going to arrest me? Am I to come with you now – right away? If so, may I gather some of my things—' And sadly, 'I don't suppose I will ever be coming back here, will I?'

As she stood up to leave, Faro took her arm. 'One moment. Tell me first, why? Why did you poison Theo? And most of all, why did you also attempt to poison Adrian, Adrian who has never harmed you?'

She laughed, shook her head. 'You still don't understand, do you? It was an accident. The poison wasn't intended for either of them.'

Pausing a moment, she added: 'Cedric left that bottle of liqueur with Theo the week before he died. "For Barbara on her birthday." Theo told me it was from a special batch but would need to be brought to room temperature if it was to be drinkable at the party.

'I opened the card in the sealed envelope. It said: "This is for you, my darling, in case I cannot be with you tonight. This will bring us together for always." Theo said it was a typical sentimental gesture by Cedric. But he seemed quite put out. We both were. It brought back memories we wanted to forget, blot out for ever.'

'Have you the note?'

'No. I burnt it.'

'Did anyone else see it?'

'Maud I think – I can't remember.'

'But you remembered the words.'

'I feel that I shall never forget them to my dying day. I see now what Cedric intended. On that last terrible night we shared together, he said: "If only I could take you with me when I go. I swear I will never rest in my grave until you lie at my side." '

At Faro's horrified expression she nodded slowly. 'Yes, Inspector. The poisoned bottle was meant for me.'

15 'Are we not taking her in?' asked McQuinn as Faro came downstairs alone.

Faro shook his head. 'I think not. The evidence is incomplete at present. Points to accidental poisoning.'

McQuinn whistled. 'You mean, she wasn't sleeping with her brother-in-law?'

'What makes you say that?' Faro demanded sharply.

McQuinn grinned. 'Plain as the nose on your face, Inspector. Surprised you weren't on to that straight away. Perfect reason for poisoning a persistent lover. When the murder enquiry looks like revealing all, she has to get rid of jealous husband who threatens to cut her out of the will. So he goes too.'

'You make it sound very simple.'

'You know and I know, sir, that most murders are.'

'What about Moulton, then?' Faro asked as McQuinn followed him out of the library and into the hall. 'Was that an accident?'

'We have no real evidence of murder.' As McQuinn spoke the front door opened and Theodore's two Labradors rushed in, closely followed by Barbara's maid. Calling them to heel, she hurried upstairs, leaving a trail of muddy footprints across the polished floor.

Faro watched her go.

'What is it, sir?'

Faro shrugged. 'Perhaps you're right, McQuinn.' He pointed to the trail of muddy footprints across the floor.

'On the night of Moulton's death, we were very preoccupied by the seeming evidence that someone went out and that someone could have tampered with the wheelpin. Of course, someone was outside – probably Theodore himself – and let the dogs out in the rain. As he did every night before retiring, an event so normal that he never considered it worth mentioning – if he even remembered it.'

As they walked down the front steps, McQuinn looked up at the windows. 'Are you sure we shouldn't be leaving a constable to keep an eye on things?'

'Very well. One of the lads in the carriage. Get him to stay.' As McQuinn opened the door for him, 'No, you take it. I'm walking back to Newington. Have some papers to collect from the house.'

'Sure, sir?'

'Yes. I need some fresh air.'

Considering that it was raining steadily, McQuinn's amazement was understandable.

In Sheridan Place, Faro went to his study, sat at his desk and stared at the Langweil papers. He wished the outcome had surprised him instead of merely confirming his worst fears.

There were still a few gaps but perhaps his meeting with Maud Langweil might throw some sense into his lost logic.

'Maud will confirm what I have told you,' had been Barbara's last words to him. Their painful interview over, he remembered how Maud had emerged from the adjoining room and had taken Barbara into her arms.

Looking across at Faro, she said quietly: 'We must talk. If you would care to call on me this evening . . .' Her frowning glance, a finger to her lips, indicated that Barbara was not to be further distressed.

Perhaps he was a fool, as his sergeant obviously thought,

leaving a self-confessed murderess at large. Not only a fool, but a besotted one, putting all his faith into Maud Langweil's revelations, hoping they might bring about the miracle that would free her sister-in-law from guilt.

Faro presented himself at Charlotte Square at six o'clock, in time to see Stephen Aynsley and Grace leaving the house. Stephen still wore that dazed expression of bemused love. As for Grace, she looked even more scared and bewildered than ever. It seemed that without Stephen's strong arm about her she might have collapsed. With a whisper of comfort, he helped her into the carriage, tucking the rug about her.

'I presume you are not needing us, sir,' he said to Faro.

'Not on this occasion,' said Faro with a hard look in Grace's direction.

She smiled at him wistfully. 'Tell Vince we expect him later this evening.'

Thoughtfully Faro watched the carriage depart. Of course, Grace loved Vince, his worries were nonsense. Possibly this was a situation she was used to dealing with, a bonny young lass who must attract many suitors.

And at that moment he had more pressing concerns.

Maud received him in the drawing room, her brisk manner indicating she was not to waste time on any preliminaries.

'You have my word that Barbara is innocent of Theo's – death. I read my late husband's note before she burnt it. What she told you is the honest truth. Do I surprise you, Mr Faro, that knowing about my husband and Barbara, I did not hate her? Nor him?'

She sighed. 'Barbara knew how much I loved him. And love him still.

'You may find that hard to understand. That a wife can remain in love with a husband who betrays her. You see, I realised that Barbara was only an obsession with him. I could forgive him that. As some men want power, Cedric worshipped beauty. He wanted Barbara for that alone. Not as a wife, not as a life partner.

He wanted a goddess. Perhaps you understand that as a man.'

And Faro, who had taken a hearty dislike to Cedric Langweil since Barbara's revelations, was now guiltily aware that they had much in common.

Maud spread her hands wide. 'Compare the two of us. Any man who wanted to possess beauty would have chosen my sister-in-law.'

About to protest sternly that there were more important facets of womanhood than mere beauty, Faro saw himself in the rôle of hypocrite. Offered a straight choice between the women he would have been less than Cedric, for he would not have given Maud a second glance.

'Cedric thought he loved Barbara,' Maud continued, 'and she destroyed him. Oh, she did not administer the fatal dose, if that is what you are thinking. She was innocent of that. It is as we in the family who knew have always told you, Mr Faro: Cedric died by his own hand, the victim of his lust for her.'

'Have you proof of this?'

'Oh indeed, I have,' she said sadly.

From her reticule, she took a small packet and handed it to Faro. It contained white powder.

'This was Cedric's so-called indigestion powder. Take it, have it analysed. I have already done so. Adrian will tell you it is arsenic.'

'Surely you are mistaken. Adrian gave Cedric a prescription for indigestion.'

'Which he did not need and did not take.' She smiled and shook her head. 'An elaborate farce, Mr Faro, to create the illusion in case any of us had suspicions. But allow me to take you back to the beginning. Last summer there were hints that Barbara and Theo were at last going to be parents. We were all jubilant, all except Cedric. I shall never forget his reactions. He was like a madman, mad with rage. If Barbara had been his wife who had betrayed him with another man, he could not have been angrier.

'I knew then that his feelings for Barbara, which we had all accepted and teased him about all those years, were no longer innocent adoration and admiration of a young and lovely sister-in-law.

'Alas for all, the baby came to naught. We were all devastated. Except Cedric. He was jubilant, he almost crowed with delight. When I said to him reproachfully that having once conceived, it was possible another time – he gave me the oddest look: "Don't set your hopes on it. It won't happen again. I shall see to that."

' "What can you do about it?" I said. "After all, Barbara is your brother's wife." And I am afraid I lost my temper and added for good measure some reproachful words about it being time he put aside this silly infatuation that had gone on long enough.

' "Infatuation is it?" he said. "Perhaps you are right. Yes, it has gone on long enough. I see that."

'I was pleased, for it seemed that the first time I had been brave enough to speak up and show my anger had made him see sense. I wished now I had done so earlier, but I was always afraid that by doing so I might lose him.'

She sighed. 'I was never in any doubt about why he had married me. The Langweils needed my fortune at that time. But I loved him. He was all I had. And I told myself after Grace was born and the years passed happily enough, without too many enquiries on my part, that he did love me a little.'

She smiled and added sadly, 'In the same way as he loved his pet dog or the cat. After my outburst, I was congratulating myself that our visits to Priorsfield were less frequent and when we were there he seemed less obsessed with Barbara. He treated her in an altogether more casual manner – oh, there were many small incidents that made me certain he had got over Barbara.

'And then he began suffering from stomach pains. He said it

was indigestion at first. He was so ill that I panicked, called Adrian, who was very consoling, and said it must have been something he had eaten for lunch at the club.

'A little while afterwards he began to complain of increasing attacks of indigestion, and one night, when we were in bed, I saw him get up and remove something from the top shelf of the wardrobe.

' "What is that you are taking, dear?" I said. He looked round at me, so startled: "I thought you were asleep. This? For my indigestion, Adrian gave it to me. I am supposed to take a pinch every night in a glass of warm milk."

'I said, why didn't he keep it in a more accessible place, such as his dressing room. He got quite upset and said it was to stay up there out of reach of Grace, or me.

'I was amused by all these precautions and said we could always reach it by standing on a stool. He got frantic then and sat on the bed, said I was to promise, my solemn word, that neither of us would take any of Adrian's powder unless we spoke to him first. When I asked why, what was in it, he said it had been specially prepared for his condition and might do us harm, might make us very ill.

'As neither Grace nor I suffered from indigestion, I thought that very unlikely. I dismissed the whole incident from my mind for I soon had more important things to worry about.'

She sighed. 'It was about that time – one evening at Priorsfield – he told us that he had been attending a consultant and had learned that he was dying of a brain tumour.'

She paused, her eyes suddenly tear-filled. 'You know the rest, Mr Faro, for it is as Barbara told you.' Then in sudden embarrassment, 'You know, the weekends when he was allowed access to her.'

'What about the powder?'

'After Cedric died, I found it locked in a desk drawer in his study.'

'Wait a minute, Mrs Langweil, are you telling me that all the while he was supposed to be ill, he was in fact slowly poisoning himself?' asked Faro.

'That is correct. It wasn't until after he died that we – the family – guessed the dreadful truth. That he was never ill, never went to see a doctor. And we realised that he had been taking just enough arsenic to simulate grave illness. He knew about such things, for Adrian once told us it was rumoured that Napoleon took a pinch of arsenic every day to avoid being poisoned. And heaven knows, there is always a plentiful supply in Priorsfield to keep the rats under control.

'Unfortunately, what my poor husband did not realise is that it was possible to take an overdose, for arsenic apparently accumulates in the system.'

And Faro, who thought he knew all about poisons from Vince, realised that had he not been led astray by this bizarre motive he too would have guessed the probable cause of Cedric's death.

'I had not the least idea what really happened. Like the rest of the family, I accepted his story that the side effects of his illness were these stomach upsets, which might worsen but could be held in check by Adrian's prescription.'

Again she paused. 'There was one incident that I see clearly now, but at the time I made nothing of its significance. One night he had been drinking rather heavily at dinner and had fallen asleep without finishing his glass of milk. I had toothache and as it was very late and I did not want to disturb the maids – they are up at six each morning – I went down to the kitchen to make myself a cup of tea and find some tincture of cloves. I'm a tidy person so I took Cedric's glass of milk downstairs and left it in the kitchen sink.

'Next day, Grace came to me in floods of tears. The maids had found her new kitten dead in its basket. I went downstairs to see what it was all about.

' "Something it ate," said Mrs Bates. "You know what cats are like. It gets nothing but good food here," she told me, "and milk too. When I came down this morning I gave it that half glass Mr Cedric had left. I don't like wasting food."

'I didn't want to distress Grace further by telling her that I had inadvertently poisoned her pet. And I had an uneasy feeling then there must be something very strong in Adrian's indigestion mixture to kill the poor creature, but when I asked him, he laughed. "Pure bicarbonate of soda, mostly." So I told myself that the kitten's death had been coincidence, something it had picked up in the garden.'

Faro felt he had to tell someone, and called in at Vince's surgery in the hope that he might still be there. He found him newly returned from a confinement and about to return home.

As they walked towards Sheridan Place, Faro related the new developments: Barbara's story and Maud's evidence.

'Cedric wanted Barbara so desperately, he pretended to be dying as a last resort to sleep with her. He simulated illness by taking small doses of arsenic—'

'And he overdid it, of course,' Vince interrupted. 'He wasn't to know that it accumulates in one's system.'

'He killed himself and tried to take Barbara with him by poisoning the liqueur. And when his plan misfired, he almost succeeded in killing off his entire family. The Borgias couldn't have done better,' Faro added grimly.

Vince nodded. 'We should have believed them when they insisted that Cedric took his own life. They knew so much more about it than we did. He must have been quite mad, you know. Poor Grace,' he continued with a sigh. 'I don't know how she will take this.'

'I imagine the family will let her continue to accept that he believed he was dying.'

'That would be the best way. Certainly it will be my secret. She shall never hear the truth from me.'

But Grace was fated to hear far worse than that before the case that both men thought was closed had reached its final horrific disclosure.

Murders in the Langweil family were not yet over.

Guiltily aware that he had hardly seen Rose for the past two days, Faro decided to go home to Sheridan Place. He found Rose in the dining room. **16**

'You have just missed Danny.'

For a moment he wondered who she was talking about. McQuinn, of course. 'He looked in about five minutes ago. Wanted to see you.'

'Was it urgent?'

'He didn't say. I was to tell you he was on his way to the Royal Infirmary. I tried to get him to wait and have tea.'

Smiling she poured out a cup for her father. 'Your Danny is almost as stubborn as you are. Did you know that?'

'No, I didn't.' Trying not to sound cross, he buttered a scone and said idly: 'So it's Danny now, is it?'

She nodded eagerly. 'Of course. I can hardly call him Sergeant or Mr McQuinn. He's a friend, after all.'

'And how long has my sergeant been a friend?' His tone light, Faro tried to sound amused while inside him anger stormed and roared and threatened to engulf that peaceful tea-table.

Rose looked away, still smiling. 'Since I was a little girl, lost in Edinburgh. You remember. He came to my rescue. I never forgot him.'

And Faro realised what he had never suspected. That ten-year-old girls make heroes out of mortal men. Had she thought of the young policeman all these years, seeing him not as her father did as an irritating necessity of his life at Edinburgh City Police but as a brave handsome Irishman? The thought was terrible, for he realised that never in all their years together had McQuinn been a person in his eyes.

'You don't like him, do you, Papa?' She sounded disappointed, sad.

'Of course I do,' Faro lied. 'He's a splendid fellow.'

Rose's look told him that his voice was too hearty and she didn't believe a word of it.

'I've known him for years and years,' he added defensively.

But Rose was too shrewd not to see through that. 'You mean, you've worked with him, but tell me,' she said, leaning her elbows on the table and regarding him solemnly, 'what do you really know about him?'

'As much as any senior detective inspector needs to know about a junior officer.'

'Such as? Go on, tell me.'

'That he's reliable. A good man to have around in a fight,' he added generously.

Her face told him that wasn't enough. Not nearly enough. That she regarded this as a rather indifferent testimonial of her friend's virtues.

'What do you know of his background, Papa? His early life in Ireland?'

'Not a great deal. As a matter of fact, he doesn't talk much about that.'

'You mean you know nothing? That you've never asked him?'

'Not really my business, is it?'

'As a policeman, perhaps not. As one human being to another, very much your business.' She paused triumphantly and then went on. 'Did you know that both his parents, two sisters and a younger brother died in infancy in the dreadful potato famine? And that the local priest had a sister who was a nun in the convent here in Edinburgh? They took him into their orphanage, educated him. You must know it, Papa. The Sisters of St Anthony, it's just down the road.'

Faro still went out of his way to avoid its gates.

Rose did not observe her father's shudder from the memory of what the sensational press referred to as the 'Gruesome Convent Murders'. One of his most successful cases, it was still unbearably painful to think at what cost to himself he had solved the murderer's identity. And he had reason to be grateful to McQuinn, who had saved his stepson's life.

He said, 'I thought he had kin in Ireland that he visited from time to time.'

'Cousins only. But he still regards Ireland as his home. He still yearns to go back there. It sounds a lovely country, Papa. I'd love to go there someday.'

Faro put down his empty tea cup, and kissing her lightly said: 'Who knows where your travels will take you, my dear. Well, I must be off again. I'll see you later.'

She followed him to the door and he turned: 'What now? You're looking very serious.'

'I'll tell you later, when you have more time.'

'More about McQuinn?' he asked smiling.

'No. Nothing more about him.'

At the Royal Infirmary, McQuinn was waiting for him. 'Piers Strong, sir. He's been attacked by keelies. Wants to see you urgently.'

As they hurried towards the ward, McQuinn filled in some of the details. 'He's not seriously hurt, just a bit bruised and knocked about. Fortunately he's got a good thick skull. Put up a good fight and one of our lads passing by came in the nick of time. One of Big Jem's gang. We've got the lad in the cells.'

Piers Strong, his head bandaged, greeted them wanly.

As Faro commiserated, saying they'd got the culprit, Strong shook his head. 'I think there was more to it than keelies, sir. I have good reason to think this was an organised attempt on my life.'

McQuinn and Faro exchanged glances. Those were the sort of odds where Big Jem was concerned. Those who hired him and his thugs paid handsomely for the risks run.

'Are you sure? What sort of enemies do you have?'

'I didn't think I had any. Now I'm not so sure. I understand that Theodore Langweil is dead. Is that true?'

When Faro said it was, Piers sighed. 'I can tell you this then, sir. He came into the office last week and said he wanted no further work done on Priorsfield and he wanted no archaeological revelations made public. Was that understood, he said. I wasn't sure what he was talking about and I said I didn't think there was anything of archaeological interest, more than that the house had been added to during the years.

' "That's what I mean," says he. "I want your word that you'll keep any observations to yourself. We don't want to be bothered with investigations so I'll make it worth your while to be discreet." And he put down a purse containing one hundred guineas on my desk. I was taken aback, for I would have respected a client's silence without being paid for it.

'So I thrust it back at him. Said I had principles and all that sort of thing. And that if I thought something should be made public then all his damned money couldn't keep me quiet.

'He was furious. And so was I. And somehow that visit set me thinking. But it wasn't until I was hit on the head that it all made sense. He was so anxious that the wall in the small drawing room shouldn't be removed or altered to make way for a bathroom next to the master bedroom.

'And he lied and so did Cedric when they said nothing had been changed in their lifetime. You were there that night, sir. I was and am absolutely sure there was a door that had been covered in. The wallpaper gave the game away.'

'The wallpaper. Now I remember,' said Faro triumphantly. 'Of course you're right. It's too modern.'

When Piers looked puzzled Faro explained. 'I realise I was looking at it in a hotel Vince and I were visiting. The manager's wife said that it used to be fashionable twenty years ago.'

'That's right. I knew then the story about it not being decorated in this generation couldn't be true.'

Faro left very thoughtfully. McQuinn had called on Big Jem in his warren in Causewayside, and by dint of various threats for that gentleman's future which sounded feasible had got him the admission that he had meant no harm, he had been hired to give the wee mannie a fright.

'He was very disgruntled, however. Because Big Jem likes to keep tabs on his hirers. Does a nice little line in blackmail as we know already. Earns himself a few pounds. But this time, he was furious that the balance of payment on the job successfully accomplished would not now be forthcoming: "Hear that the mannie who got me to do the job is deid now."

'And he might as well have put Langweil's name and address into my hands, especially as we thought there might be some connection with Moulton's death too. Although Jem's better with his fists than pulling wheel pins out of carriages.'

When Faro drew his attention to the significance of those muddy footprints they had both seen in Priorsfield, McQuinn seemed disappointed.

'What do you make of it now, sir?'

'I'll tell you better when I've checked on a couple of facts.'

In Sheridan Place, Rose was awaiting her father's return.

'I have something to tell you, Papa.'

Faro was tired. 'Is it important? Can it not wait until tomorrow, my dear?'

She sighed. 'I've tried to tell you several times, but you didn't seem to be listening to me. I'm going back to Orkney, Papa.'

'What about your new school?'

'There is no point in my staying here until term begins, now that Vince's wedding isn't to be at Easter. I've had a letter from Emily. She and Grandmama miss me so much. And I miss them too. Anyway, I'm not at all sure that I want to go to the Academy after all,' she added bleakly.

'I thought you wanted to learn languages.'

She shook her head. 'I'm not sure about that any more. I'm not sure that it's a good idea of Vince's, that I should follow him into Langweil society when he marries Grace in order to find a suitable husband. From the few friends of Grace's I've met, I hardly think I'd find the kind of man I would want to marry in their ranks.'

'But you'll soon make friends at the new school.'

'I don't want friends, Papa. You don't understand, it's my own family I want. And you haven't time for me, really. Even less than when Emily and I come on holiday. If I stay here, we will get cross with each other. And I would hate that.'

'Aren't you exaggerating a little, my dear?'

'I don't think so. You won't – don't approve of people I like.' She looked at him. 'Like Danny, your sergeant. He's the only friend I'd want to have, apart from Grace. And I can see that Danny would become a subject of anger between us.'

'Danny McQuinn, is that it?' Faro exploded angrily. 'Of course I'd object to your friendship – even if it were possible for a man nearly thirty to be friends with a girl of fifteen. I couldn't allow that and you know it. Especially as he is one of my junior officers.'

Rose smiled. 'Yes, it would be rather undignified for you, I can see that.' And leaning over, she touched his cheek and said softly, 'Poor Papa, you do see, don't you, that it is better if I go back home – to Kirkwall? Perhaps when I'm older, when you realise I'm not a little girl any longer, things will be different – easier for us. You will be able to treat me like an equal and accept the friends I want to make in Edinburgh.'

She was silent for a moment and he could think of nothing to say. Denial would be futile. 'If I stay here, I will only get fonder and fonder of Danny and you'll hate that.'

'Fonder and fonder! My dear, Danny is the first good-looking young man you have met. A pleasant change, no doubt, from the rough schoolboys you normally encounter, but do recognise it for what it is. That he has all the excitement of being different, of living in a world that seems dangerous and strange to you.'

He took her hands and held them tightly. 'We all go through this phase in our lives when we are young—'

And not so young, his conscience whispered, remembering Barbara Langweil.

'It's called hero-worship.'

She sighed. 'Some call it love, Papa. And for some it lasts for ever,' she said sadly. 'Sometimes I have a feeling we never grow out of it, as you suggest.'

He could think of no answer that would not give her pain, and asked instead: 'When do you go?'

'Tomorrow.'

'So soon?'

'It's either now or the next boat – next week.'

He remembered there were only two sailings a week.

'But what about Vince – Grace?'

'I've said my goodbyes to Grace. She and Vince have known that I wanted to go home—'

And Vince had never breathed a word to him. 'A well-kept secret, eh?' he said bitterly.

'I wanted to tell you myself. Besides we thought you had enough problems at the moment. And incidentally, they think I'm doing the right thing.'

And coming round the table she flung herself into his arms. 'Oh, Papa, Papa, don't look like that. I'll be back very soon, I promise, even if I don't go to the Academy, Emily and I will come for our summer holidays as usual and for Vince's wedding.'

He slept little that night. To his other failures he added those as a father. He had wanted so much to have Rose by his side, but her ill-timed arrival had shown them both how dreams are better to stay where they are. When they can be taken down and dusted from time to time and replaced, safe and secure, intact, without ever encountering the rougher stuff of reality.

The frantic activities of the next weeks left little time for brooding over his failures. The inquest on Theodore Langweil, his wife cleared of suspicion in his poisoning on the evidence of Adrian and Maud. Cedric had accidentally taken his own life but had attempted to murder Barbara Langweil.

A sensational case indeed where a dead man was guilty of the murder of his brother and the attempted murder of his mistress. Respectable Edinburgh was rocked to its very foundations.

Vince's main concern was for Grace. And for Adrian's future, which might now be blighted. The thought of that so-called indigestion powder which had figured so largely in Maud's evidence might give patients pause for second thoughts.

'Poor Adrian. Guilty by association,' said Vince. 'In a family like the Langweils, it just takes one scandal and the whole lot topple. I hope he's right about leaving Edinburgh and setting up practice on the Borders, possibly using Freda's family name.'

'What will happen to Priorsfield?'

'Hardly a suitable venue for a general practitioner of medicine, is it? Besides it is Barbara's home for her lifetime as long as she remains unmarried, then it passes to Adrian and his family. Neither she nor Maud will be poorly off and I gather there are plenty of eager buyers for Langweil Ales—'

'And for Priorsfield,' said Adrian later that week as the three men dined together, 'if I feel inclined to sell. Barbara is staying at Charlotte Square just now.'

'Maud is trying to persuade her that it would be a good idea for the two widows to share one house,' said Vince.

'I had a visit from Piers Strong. If I do decide to sell, then there are quite a few things needing attention first. The whole place is getting rather dilapidated.' Adrian smiled. 'He has some extraordinary modern ideas. I'd like to find out if there is a secret room. That could answer a lot of things, besides my childhood dream,' he added wistfully.

A bottle of wine later, Adrian twirled his empty glass. 'You know I think it would be a good idea if we visited Priorsfield and had a closer look at that upstairs parlour. Especially with your revelations about the wallpaper,' he said excitedly to Faro.

Vince was full of enthusiasm for the idea. 'A pity we can't go right away, but it's too dark now. The servants would have a fit.'

'Tomorrow, then. Are we agreed?' said Adrian. And as they parted, 'Maybe Prince Charlie's French gold is still there, after all who knows what we will find?'

But Faro found himself oddly detached from the prevailing mood of excitement, unable to dispel an ominous feeling of doom.

17 A pity that the secret room at Priorsfield could not have remained where it belonged, in the bitter past, Faro thought afterwards, regretting that he had added his enthusiasm to what had begun like a boy's adventure story search for buried treasure.

He began to have his first qualms, the first tingling feelings of disaster as he watched the wallpaper, that too-modern wallpaper, being stripped and the padding removed from underneath.

There were cries of triumph, excited laughter, when it was realised that this was not the broom cupboard Theodore had suggested. Instead it was the entrance to a lost room in the house of Priorsfield.

And at the last moment Adrian held the lantern high and Grace shouted: 'Come on. What are we waiting for? This is marvellous.'

Afraid of what they might find, Faro wished that Vince had not been allowed to bring Grace along. Unfortunately when Vince had made the arrangement to meet Adrian and Faro, he had entirely forgotten that he was taking his fiancée to dine at the Café Royal that same evening.

What more natural when he confessed the nature of this other so-important engagement to save himself from Grace's sulks, than for her to insist on accompanying him?

As for Faro, all he felt at that moment was an ominous

dread at Grace's excitement and the suppressed high spirits of
Adrian and Vince as all three men threw their weight against the
door.

'Don't say after all this that it's locked. We'll never find the
key,' wailed Grace. 'It'll have vanished hundreds of years ago.'

'They don't usually lock broom cupboards,' said Vince con-
solingly.

'Nevertheless, there is a keyhole in this one,' said Faro.

For a moment, they stared at each other, frustrated, baffled.
Then Adrian turned the handle.

'It moved,' said Vince. 'I think it's just jammed. All this padding—'

Adrian produced a knife, which was then run round the door's
edge. Again they put their shoulders to it. This time it yielded.

'Great! Great! It isn't locked.'

The door opened slowly, reluctantly, creaking against the dust
and cobwebs that draped like a curtain or a shroud before them
concealing its dark interior.

Adrian went in first, held the lantern high. They were in a
tiny dark panelled room, windowless. All light had once filtered
through a small skylight, now similarly encrusted with the insect
debris and cobwebs of ages.

Vince, with Grace holding his hand tightly, came behind Faro,
who was carrying a candelabra.

Blinking until at last their eyes grew accustomed to the gloom,
Adrian's lantern revealed other things. That this room had been
inhabited. There was a table with a plate on it, a chair. Even a
small fireplace in one corner.

'Open the door as wide as you can,' said Adrian, gasping,
seized by a fit of coughing.

'You can hardly breathe in here,' said Vince.

'Light,' said Adrian. 'We need more light.'

'I expect it was a priest's hole,' said Grace. 'I can't imagine
anyone else living in such a wretched room.'

That was true, for everything was mouldered over with dust and insects, and the ancient odours of decay.

'Smells like an old crypt, doesn't it?'

Grace gave a little scream for there was another sound now. Rats. Rats scuttling, secret-moving, disturbed by this human invasion of what had long been their undisputed territory.

'And what have we here?' Against one wall was a chest. Adrian wiped the top with his sleeve. Once the dust settled and the cobwebs faltered, it was revealed as a very large and ancient oak chest, about six feet long, carved with symbols from another age.

The four stared doubtfully at this elaborate addition to the shabby rickety furnishings of the room.

'Open it,' said Grace. 'Go on.'

'Let's hope it contains the Frenchman's treasure,' said Adrian.

'Oh, wouldn't that be wonderful?'

At first the lid would not yield. Again came the question of it being locked. In the lantern, the candle was burning low.

'No, I think the hinges are rusty—'

The three men, with some considerable difficulty, succeeded in raising the heavy lid.

The lantern was set on the floor and Grace, who had been given the candelabra to hold, held it high. Then her screams rang out as she almost dropped it, the hot wax hissing on to the floor.

There was no treasure.

Only a decomposed body.

For a moment, Faro hoped that this was the legendary Frenchman who had disappeared in mysterious circumstances after a rendezvous he had failed to keep with Prince Charles Edward Stuart.

But the sweet smell of decay belonged to a later age and the mummified atmosphere of the casket had kept most of the dead man's clothes intact. Modern clothes they were, and there was enough hair remaining on the skull, enough withered flesh to be still recognisable as the Langweil strain.

The mystery of Justin Langweil's disappearance was solved at last.

The grim discovery pointed again to murder. But this time there were no suspects, for the answer was all too obvious.

Theodore Langweil had lied. There had never been a letter from San Francisco telling him that his brother had been killed by renegade Indians. For Theodore had undoubtedly murdered his elder brother, with or without the help of Cedric.

And Faro found himself remembering that fatal evening when Cedric was poisoned, how he had overheard a conversation between the two brothers. Theodore adamant against Piers Strong's plans for a bathroom, and the atmosphere of menace he interrupted.

He never quite remembered how they quitted the room, Vince clutching the sobbing, frightened Grace. Or how they raced downstairs as if the murdered man might rise from the tomb and point a withered finger— But at whom?

They ran like frightened fugitives into the night where in the darkness of the drive the carriage waited to carry them back to safe surroundings, to normal life where such things as they had just witnessed belonged in the realms of fantasy, in the nightmares of Edgar Allan Poe.

Faro had not yet retired when Vince, having seen Grace and Adrian home, arrived back at Sheridan Place.

'It did happen – tonight, I mean, Stepfather. All the way back I've wondered if I dreamed it. Of all the awful things that have happened to the Langweil family, this is undoubtedly the worst. My poor Grace. She knows, must know, that her father was involved in her Uncle Justin's murder.'

'With both men dead, we may never know the whole truth,'

said Faro. 'However, I've been thinking about that, realising that Barbara gave us the answer. Don't you remember what I told you? She said that Cedric had promised to betray a family secret that could destroy them all, if Theodore couldn't persuade her—'

'I'm glad they are beyond the reach of the law, Stepfather, and that the family can be spared this additional horror. I presume it does not need to be made public,' Vince added anxiously.

'The skeleton of an unknown man was found behind a blocked-up door in Priorsfield,' said Faro. 'Is that what you have in mind?'

Vince sighed. 'It doesn't sound very convincing, but surely you agree that the family have suffered enough?'

Faro's comment was: 'We know only that a murder was committed, twenty years ago, by person or persons unknown. Information to be filed away as another of Edinburgh's unsolved crimes.'

'Personally, I am more than happy for it to remain so,' said Vince. 'I think this is one time when we might let the past bury its dead in decorous silence.'

And so it might have done, had not Wailes, the lawyer Moulton's clerk, returned to Edinburgh after a prolonged absence. A mercy call on a sick elderly aunt in Yorkshire had extended into weeks instead of days. He had just returned to his lodgings to have an irate landlady report that besides owing her rent, the police were investigating his 'disappearance'.

Settling his debts with some alacrity, he presented himself in Faro's office, very anxious not to be regarded as a criminal. Distressed to hear of Theodore Langweil's death he announced that there were various family documents for Adrian as next of kin.

'Surely his widow is next of kin.'

Wailes shook his head. 'The document I have in mind predates his second marriage. Since there have been certain, er, difficulties I gather, perhaps you would care to be present—'

They met in the doctors' consulting rooms, where Wailes handed over a large envelope that Faro had seen before.

'To be opened by Adrian Langweil in the event of the death of his brothers, Theodore and Cedric.' It held their two signatures and the date 1855.

Adrian had also requested Faro's presence, for he was even more eager than Vince to keep quiet any further family scandal.

The letter began:

This is to confirm that Justin Langweil, our eldest brother, died by our hand on the 26th day of February, 1855.

There was a horrified gasp from Vince and Wailes. Adrian paused before continuing.

Mr Moulton will confirm that Justin was unstable and suffered from moods of extreme violence which necessitated keeping him under restraint—

'A pity that Mr Moulton isn't here any longer,' Wailes interrupted briefly.

We had long suspected that he was insane and getting steadily worse. We were at our wits' end what to do, not caring to face the publicity and scandal of having a madman as head of our long-respected family. The effect on our thriving business would have been disastrous. When he was sane he was genial and helpful, but these lucid bouts were becoming rarer. So we put it about that he was an invalid, which meant that his occasional withdrawals from society (locked in an upstairs room) could be accounted for. Although on such occasions we were careful not to entertain or have any other than family visitors who knew and understood our problem.

Then during one of his better periods he escaped our vigilance and disappeared – we later learned to Glasgow. He had often stated that he wished to leave Scotland and go to America, certain that the climate of California would improve his health.

When several months passed by, we imagined that he had left the country. Imagine our surprise when one day he walked in, with a wife. A pretty young servant lass from Hamilton who he had met during his wanderings in the Highlands.

We rejoiced to see him looking so fit and well. Obviously marriage was the answer to his problems, we told each other. But not for long. Suddenly the violent attacks were renewed. This time they were directed against his helpless wife. In one of these rages, for he was very strong, he struck her and she fell from the balcony on to the terrace.

She could never have survived such a fall. She was dead and he had murdered her. But he was without remorse. With some considerable difficulty we locked him in the small room, once the withdrawing room of the master bedroom. With its skylight roof, we felt he was safe and could do himself no harm.

And there we proceeded to look after him, keeping his presence secret from the outside world. Sarah's death was dismissed as suicide, and we maintained Justin was too grief-stricken and dangerously ill himself to appear at the family funeral. When it was over we were faced with the terrible decision, whether or not to have him committed to an asylum. Obviously we could not minister to his needs indefinitely or keep the servants in ignorance of what was going on.

Once we went in and found him semiconscious. He had been beating his head against the stone wall. We do not know to this day which of us spoke the words which had been growing in our minds, the monstrous decision that had to be made.

He had murdered his young wife. He was guilty and for the sake of the family and the continuance of our good name, we must be his executioners.

The sentence once pronounced, we realised it must be carried out quickly before we could suffer any change of mind. So that night when he was abed we took in a pillow and both of us smothered him while he slept. Then we put his body in the chest where you will find it behind the door in the wall of the upstairs parlour.

Afterwards we blocked up the door and hired a firm from Arbroath to repaper the walls.

We did this woeful deed to protect you, our youngest brother and the survivors of this family who now read this document.

Using the considerable influence of the Langweil name and the discretion of the Edinburgh City Police the murder of Justin Langweil was kept out of the newspapers.

It seemed that there was nothing more that could happen. There remained only the domestic details brought about by the earlier bereavements. Barbara and Maud, the two widows. Would Maud persuade Barbara to remain with her at Charlotte Square once Grace and Vince married?

Grace and Vince.

But here again, was the unexpected for which Faro was quite unprepared.

18 Some two weeks after Justin Langweil's remains had been placed with those of his ancestors in the family vault, after a short service of committal conducted by the Reverend Stephen Aynsley, Faro arrived home one evening to find Grace awaiting Vince's arrival.

Before Faro could exchange more than a dozen words with Grace, Vince appeared, and, leaving the young couple together, he went upstairs to his study.

There was a letter from Rose. He was reading it eagerly when a tap on the door announced Grace.

'Will you please come down, sir? I have something to tell Vince and I would like you to be there.'

Vince was leaning against the mantelpiece, smiling but quizzical, delighted to humour her. 'What is this great secret you are about to impart, my dear?'

Grace winced visibly. 'It is no great secret, and I thought perhaps it was one you might have guessed already.'

Walking over to Vince she took both his hands and held them tightly. 'My dear, I am sorry, but I cannot marry you. I am asking you to release me from our engagement.'

Vince's laugh of astonishment was a little hoarse. 'You are teasing us again, aren't you? Say you are, silly girl. Of course I won't release you. What nonsense is this?'

'It's not nonsense. I only wish it were. I have thought

of nothing else for the past weeks, ever since – that night at Priorsfield.'

'What difference can that make? Justin's dead and buried,' said Vince angrily, and looking at her stony face, he added: 'It's a bit thick, you know, concealing all this from me. I thought you were merely preoccupied with the wedding arrangements.'

'Please, please, Vince. Don't make it any more difficult for me. I cannot marry you. I now know that I can never marry you.'

And turning to Faro, she said: 'Surely you understand the reasons why and can convince him that in view of the recent disclosures about my family, I cannot marry him. Indeed, I am not fit to marry anyone,' she added sadly.

'I don't see—' Vince began.

'Then you should,' she said hardly. 'You are a medical man. Don't you understand I am the daughter of a murderer, the niece of a murderer as well as a madman? For pity's sake, Vince, I am not only ruined by my blood but by marrying you, I would ruin you too.'

'Rubbish,' Vince protested.

She shook her head. 'It is not rubbish. I only wish it were. Adrian has told me how we pass things on to our children, not only blue eyes and golden hair but traits of character. Good things, talents, and bad things too. Adrian is older than you, my dear, more experienced in such matters and I trust his judgement.'

'I thought he liked me—'

She seized his hands again. 'Of course he does. And that is the very reason why he believes my decision to be right. He believes that you have a great future before you.'

'A future that means nothing without you.'

'All right. If you won't think of yourself. And me. Think of our unborn children. What if we had a son and he took after my Uncle Justin, my Uncle Theodore, or even his own grandfather? Or a daughter? Lovely but mad. What then, how long then would love last? How long before we were not blaming each other for having begot such monsters? Oh, Vince, Vince, for pity's sake—'

As she fell into a chair, her slim shoulders racked with sobs, neither man moved to comfort her, both stared down at her and then at each other.

Faro knew that she spoke the truth, as Vince would. Some day, but not now. That knowingly endangering a future generation with family madness was the one unforgivable sin. For madness was like ripples in a still pool. It was not only those nearest it affected but all in its orbit.

And Faro remembered Sarah the gentle wife who had been struck down and killed by her husband in his temporary madness.

At last Grace looked up, wiped her eyes. Rose to her feet and regarding them sadly, removed Vince's ring from her finger.

'Keep it,' he said harshly.

'No—'

'Keep it. To remember me by.'

'I need no ring for that,' she said, her eyes welling with tears. 'I shall never forget you, never. I shall always love you, Vince.'

Vince rushed forward. 'Then forget all this. Marry me. And to hell with the future. We needn't have children. Then all your arguments are futile.'

'No. We both love children. Marriage for us would be a farce without them. And if I were your wife I would want your child.' And pulling away from him, she said: 'I have made my decision.'

'What will you do?'

'I am going to Africa.'

'Africa! For God's sake—'

'Yes. With Stephen.'

'Stephen? Your cousin?'

'I am not going to marry him. Believe me when I tell you that I am not to marry him or anyone. He is not your rival, so don't look like that, Vince. But by going away from Scotland I can serve some useful purpose in the world. I can sort out my feelings—'

'Promise me something then—'

'Of course.'

'Promise me that if you ever change your mind you will come back to me.'

Grace smiled. 'There is no other man I would come back to. You have my word on that.'

'Then give it a year, two years. And if by the end of that time you still want to be my wife, I will be waiting. I promise—'

Faro went out and slowly closed the door. He could no longer bear to witness the sufferings of the young couple whose happiness was dear to his heart.

Instead of fulfilment and joy, what he had dreaded had happened. The evils of the Langweil past had caught up with them and Grace was right too. For not only caught up but overwhelmed, the guilty and the innocent alike. And he thought of that unborn baby, the child of Adrian and Freda who would carry on the Langweil strain. At least Adrian and Grace were guiltless of bloodshed, but who could tell what repercussions lay in store for future generations, if as Adrian suspected evil as well as good could be inherited.

The Langweil case was almost closed. There were no more revelations to destroy them. He had one last call to make.

He was going to Priorsfield, where Barbara Langweil was waiting for him.

'Adrian will have told you that I am leaving Priorsfield.'

Barbara smiled sadly. 'This is a house of sad memories. I still cannot believe that I lived here for twelve years with a man I loved so deeply, and never knew or suspected the terrible crime he and Cedric had committed.'

She paused. 'Do you think it is possible to love that much, and yet never know a secret like that? And yet if he were to walk in the door this moment, I would do the same again. I would do more, I would lie and cheat to save him from the gallows. That is the kind of woman you see before you, Mr Faro. With few moral principles, alas, beyond the workings of her own heart.'

'When are you leaving?' he asked.

Gesturing towards the already shrouded furniture, she said: 'As soon as I have made the final arrangements.'

'You do not care to stay with Maud then?'

'Without Theo my final link with Edinburgh – and this country – is broken. Although I might live here in Priorsfield in comfort for the rest of my life, what kind of life would that be, I ask you, Mr Faro?'

He could think of no reply.

'I am thirty. I still have, with good health and barring accidents, half of my life before me.'

Looking round the room, she stood up, gathered her shawl from the chair. 'This room depresses me. Too many memories. I still see Theo everywhere. Let us go into the garden. The roses are blooming. They are such cheerful flowers, I find it impossible to be sad among roses.'

Faro walked at her side, conscious of that lovely presence, but aware that he knew her not one whit more than when he had fallen in love with her on his first visit with Vince and Grace.

He had imagined that grief might have changed the perfection of that countenance, might have made his goddess into an earth-bound creature—

She walked swiftly for a woman with long-legged, easy strides. 'I am going back to America,' she was saying. 'I have a little money of my own that Theo left me, and with it I shall start afresh, a new life. Somewhere, I'm not sure where yet.'

'What will you do? Have you any plans?'

'I haven't decided yet, but something will come along, I'm

sure. I have friends – humble but good – who will help me make the right decision. I have no one here. No one I care for.'

And her words blotted out the sun from his world, and what he had been going to ask her. To be his wife. The very reason for his coming to Priorsfield died on his lips. As if ice had been carried on the light summer breeze that stirred the perfume of the roses around them.

Trying not to sound wounded he said: 'You must not feel uncared for. You have people here who care and who will miss you.'

She looked at him in amazement as if such an idea had never occurred to her. Taking a moment to answer, she said slowly: 'I dare say you are right. Yes, of course, you are. And you are a very kind man, Mr Faro, a very nice person in spite of being a detective.'

Was that how she thought of him? And Faro, who never cried, felt the prickle of tears behind his eyes. All that love and suffering on her behalf. All his dreams about her and she was totally unaware that he was more than 'a nice person'.

Such fools we are, such fools, he thought.

Suddenly, he stopped, and turning her to face him, he took her roughly in his arms. Held her, savouring the sweetness of the moment, of that slim firm outline of her body so close.

Prepared for resistance, there was none.

Acquiescence then? His heart hammered hopefully.

Did that mean—?

He looked into her face. She was smiling, politely, enigmatically. It was as if he had taken into his arms, in a surge of passion, one of the white marble statues that surrounded the paths and wore the same curiously bloodless expressions.

Embarrassed now, he released her. There seemed nothing more to say and both hastened their steps towards the iron gates at the end of the drive.

As they parted there for the last time, she held out her hand

and then, as if she changed her mind suddenly, she stood on tiptoe, took his face in her cool slender hands and kissed him lightly on the mouth.

'Goodbye, dear kind Inspector Faro. And thank you.'

He touched his lips in wonder. But when he turned round, she had gone. Vanished. Only the roses nodded and the garden was empty.

Walking back along the road past Duddingston he remembered Rose's letter, that she sounded happy, content to be back in Kirkwall with his mother and Emily, surrounded by all that was familiar to her, by loves that were not touched by uncertainty.

And he remembered her words to him as they waited on the dock at Leith for the Orkney boat to leave.

'You were very lucky never to have loved anyone but Mama, so that you can be happy enough with those memories not to need to search for anyone else to replace her.'

He had looked at his daughter. Yes, he would let her believe that, although it wasn't true, and some day, when she was older and happily married with a string of bairns clutching at her petticoat, he might tell her the truth.

About Barbara. And all the others he had loved and lost. Or who had loved him and he had hurt by turning away.

'Do you mind Barbara Langweil?' he'd begin. And he'd see her eyes widen in surprise as he told her of this day, and his last visit to Priorsfield.

And how for some men, it's a lifetime of loving, for some only a butterfly kiss from a goddess in a summer rose garden.

The Langweil case was over, the players in its drama had departed, its stage was empty for all but the few innocents bruised by its impact.

And heading towards the Central Office, as he had done for so many years, and the next case that was waiting for him, he remembered one indisputable lesson life had taught him. Broken hearts are seldom fatal. That given time and patience they invariably heal.

He mustn't abandon hope. Without hope life was indeed a derelict wasteland.

Hope for a daughter that the pangs of first love would heal. Hope for Vince that his beloved Grace would return to him one day and together they would mend their broken lives that had been the Langweil legacy. Hope for himself, for that hazy unknown future and a final confrontation and outwitting of a master criminal.

'The evil that men do lives after them.' So Shakespeare had said. A truth that still remained unalterable and would continue to remain so until man and time itself were no more.

Note to Readers

For those interested in Inspector Faro's earlier cases, the one referred to on page 435 is *Bloodline*; and on page 529 *Enter Second Murderer*, both published by Macmillan.

All Pan Books are available at your local bookshop or newsagent, or can be ordered direct from the publisher. Indicate the number of copies required and fill in the form below.

Send to: Macmillan General Books C.S.
                Book Service By Post
                PO Box 29, Douglas I-O-M
                IM99 1BQ

or phone: 01624 675137, quoting title, author and credit card number.

or fax: 01624 670923, quoting title, author, and credit card number.

or Internet: http://www.bookpost.co.uk

Please enclose a remittance* to the value of the cover price plus 75 pence per book for post and packing. Overseas customers please allow £1.00 per copy for post and packing.

*Payment may be made in sterling by UK personal cheque, Eurocheque, postal order, sterling draft or international money order, made payable to Book Service By Post.

Alternatively by Access/Visa/MasterCard

Card No.

Expiry Date

Signature

Applicable only in the UK and BFPO addresses.

While every effort is made to keep prices low, it is sometimes necessary to increase prices at short notice. Pan Books reserve the right to show on covers and charge new retail prices which may differ from those advertised in the text or elsewhere.

NAME AND ADDRESS IN BLOCK CAPITAL LETTERS PLEASE

Name

Address

8/95

Please allow 28 days for delivery.
Please tick box if you do not wish to receive any additional information. ☐